CARVED

THE ROAD TO HELL SERIES, BOOK 2

BRENDA K DAVIES

BRENDA K. DAVIES

ALSO FROM THE AUTHOR

**Books written under the pen name
Brenda K. Davies**

The Alliance Series

Eternally Bound (Book 1)

Hell on Earth Series

Hell on Earth (Book 1)

Coming August 2017

The Road to Hell Series

Good Intentions (Book 1)

Carved (Book 2)

The Road (Book 3)

Into Hell (Book 4)

The Vampire Awakenings Series

Awakened (Book 1)

Destined (Book 2)

Untamed (Book 3)

Enraptured (Book 4)

Undone (Book 5)

Fractured (Book 6)

The Ravening Series

Ravenous (Book 1)

Taken Over (Book 2)

Reclamation (Book 3)

The Survivor Chronicles

Book 1: The Upheaval

Book 2: The Divide

Book 3: The Forsaken

Book 4: The Risen

To all the kids of Sherman and Leonard streets, you know who you are. Thank you for the many days of playing in the field, running up town, setting off the railroad tracks, jumping in leaf piles, tree climbing, riding bikes, football, baseball, ghosts in the graveyard, and switching Halloween costumes. You made every day an adventure.

GLOSSARY OF TERMS

Adhene demon <Ad-heen> - Mischievous elf-like demon.
Akalia Vine <Ah-kal-ya> - Purple black flowers, orange berries. Draws in victims & drains their blood slowly. Red leaves. Sharp, needle-like suckers under leaves.
Canagh demon <Kan-agh> - Male Incubus, Female Succubus. Power thrives on sex but feed on souls on a less regular basis than the other demons. Their kiss enslaves another.
Carrou Vines <Kar-oo>- Thick black vines. 6-inch-long thorns. Grow around Canagh demon nests.
Craetons <Cray-tons> - Lucifer's followers.
The Gates - Varcolac demon has always been the ruler of the guardians of the gates that were used to travel to earth before Lucifer entered Hell.
Gargoyle - Claws contain a paralyzing agent they use on their prey. When victim is paralyzed, they peel away their skin one strip at a time and eat it.
Ghosts - Souls can balk against entering Heaven, they have no choice when it comes to Hell.
Hellhounds - The first pair of Hellhounds also born of the Fires

of Creation, with the first varcolac who rose. They share a kindred spirit and are controlled by the varcolac.

Lanavour demon <Lan-oh-vor> -The 3rd seal.

Madagan <Mad-a-ghan>- A beast from Hell. Resembles a boar with a giant tusk in the center of forehead. Mottled red and black skin, plumes of smoke from a blowhole in top of head. Extended, round skulls, cloven hooves.

Palitons <Pal-ah-tons> - Kobal's followers.

Revenirs <Rev-eh-ners> - Mummy-like skeletons. Debilitating cry. Suck life from victims with "kiss".

Skelleins <Skel-eens> - Guardians of the Gates.

The Wall - Blocks off all of Washington, Oregon, California, Arizona, New Mexico, Texas, Louisiana, Mississippi, Alabama, Georgia, Florida, South Carolina, North Carolina, Virginia, Maryland, Delaware, New Jersey, Connecticut, Rhode Island, Massachusetts, Vermont, New Hampshire, and Maine. Blocks parts of Nevada, New York, Pennsylvania, and Arkansas. Similar wall blocks off parts of Europe.

Wraith - A twisted and malevolent spirit that the demons feed from. On earth they only come out at night.

Varcolac demon <Var-ko-lack>- Born from the fires of Hell. Only one can exist at a time. When that one dies another rises from the Fires of Creation. Fastest and most brutal of all the demons. They are the only kind that can create and open natural gateways within Hell as well as close them. They control the hellhounds.

Demon Words

Mah Kush-la 'mɑ: <kush-la> - My Heart.
Mjéod <myod> - Mead or a demon drink.

Glossary Of Symbols

Humans took some of them and turned them into what became
known as the Elder Futhark, also known as runes.

Eiaz <E-az> - (Tilted Z) - Speed, heightened senses, and
protection.
Risaz <Ree-saz> - (Straight line with a triangle attached to the
middle) - Force of destruction.
Sowa <Sow-ah> - (Backwards E with sword piercing the center) -
Blade of fire.
Zenak <Zen-ach> - (Three wavy lines) - Eternal fire and life.
Ziwa <Zee-wah> - (Two V's with a line connecting the top, like
fangs) - Guardian of the hellhounds. Mark is considered gift of
strength, endurance, and virility. Considered a blessing and a
curse as well as marks bearer as having a piece of the hellhound's
soul within them.

CHAPTER ONE

RIVER

"River, River wake up."

I stretched leisurely, a small sigh escaping me as I instinctively turned toward the strong fingers caressing my cheek. My eyes fluttered open, and my heart leapt as I took in Kobal looking back at me. It was hard to believe I'd ever found his obsidian eyes, without their whites, a little disturbing. Now, they warmed me and made my toes curl as heat pooled between my thighs.

My gaze searched his chiseled face, noting the angles of his strong jaw, pointed chin, aquiline nose, and high, broad cheekbones. The deep brown strands in his dark hair were highlighted by the dim glow of the lantern on the bedside table. His hair was longer than when I'd first met him; it now fell in waves next to his eyes. Somehow, the longer hair made him look more enticing and dangerous, if that were possible.

My gaze lingered on his full mouth as I recalled the scorch of his kiss. Recalled the way his tongue tangled with mine in such a way that it was impossible to think when tasting him. He made it impossible to do anything other than lose myself to the overwhelming sensations and emotions he so effortlessly evoked within me.

My heart swelled with love. *Mine.*

And I was his. He'd claimed me as his Chosen. In response to his nearness, his bites on my skin tingled. Bites meant to mark me for all humans to see, and for every demon to know to whom I belonged, even if the marks faded away.

I had marked him also. My eyes slid to his neck and the faint hint of my teeth marring his bronzed skin. One of my bites was just above the tips of the intricate flames marking his body. I'd made those bites without fully understanding at the time what had driven me to do so, but since then, I'd come to realize it had been the demon part of me seeking to stake my claim on my Chosen also.

I didn't like how faded my marks had become; I needed to remedy that right now.

His breath froze and his fingers on my cheek stilled when I smiled at him. I went to open my arms to him when I suddenly recalled what had happened last week. A startled cry escaped me. Gripping the blanket, I pulled it against my chest and scrambled up in his bed.

I may be sleeping in his bed, but he hadn't shared it with me since he'd ripped the head off the woman who had been trying to kill me and I'd told him to get out. I knew he'd done it to protect me, that when he'd seen Eileen attacking me he'd lost control, and when Kobal lost control, his demon instincts rose to the forefront.

Yes, Eileen had been trying to kill me, but no one deserved to die the way she had. Her death had been brutal, and Kobal hadn't shown any remorse about it. He didn't understand why I was upset about what he'd done to her.

We were too different from each other to ever possibly work out. A pang stabbed my heart at the thought. *You can say those things to him, but don't lie to yourself, River.*

And it was a lie. I hadn't distanced myself from him because of what he'd done, or how different we were, I'd done it because I was petrified. I'd done it because I had connected with my ancestor, Lucifer, in a dream.

In that dream, Lucifer had promised to use me as a weapon to destroy Kobal. The memory of it caused my blood to run cold; I could still feel the evil emanating from him and beating against my skin. Lucifer had prophesied that I would become evil like him. Kobal believed I could never become like Lucifer, but I wasn't so sure. Whereas I considered Lucifer a distant ancestor, all of the demons, including Kobal and Lucifer himself, considered him to be my father. Some people had black sheep in their family; I shared DNA with the Devil himself, and the knowledge terrified me.

I wasn't so foolish or so deep in denial that I couldn't admit my fear over Lucifer's words was a *big* part of the reason I'd taken a step back from Kobal. I couldn't be the catalyst for his destruction when I loved him so much, and when he'd been the only one of his kind to survive Lucifer for any length of time.

Kobal had never claimed to love me; I knew he cared for me and I was bound to him for as long as my mortal life would allow us to be together, but it was best if we kept our distance from each other. At least that was what I'd told myself a thousand times a day since we'd stopped sleeping together, and for the most part, stopped speaking to each other.

So now, I tore myself to shreds to keep my distance from him. At one time, I'd connected with Kobal through his dreams. There, I'd seen his fantasies of me, fantasies that had eventually come to life, but since I'd pulled Lucifer into my dream, I had somehow shut down my ability to connect with Kobal, or anyone else while dreaming.

Before Lucifer, I never would have thought that I could control my ability in such a way. However, I had a feeling the subconscious part of me that had originally reached out to Kobal and Lucifer, was trying to keep my heart and mind protected by making sure I didn't connect with them now. Or maybe there was nothing subconscious about any of it and my ability to control what I did in my dreams was growing as my powers grew.

Some nights I contemplated trying to connect with Kobal's dreams again, but what I might see there worried me. Would he be dreaming of other women? Would he be dreaming of *me* still? I didn't think I could continue to keep my distance from him if I saw his body moving over and within mine again, not when I craved his touch every second of the day. If he dreamed of someone else, my already battered heart would never be able to take it.

My eyes were drawn to the hellhounds on his left arm when he shifted his weight. They were so realistic looking with their razor-like fangs and curved claws that I could almost feel their breath on my face. Flames twisted around them as they looked ready to leap from his arm.

On his other arm, more flames swirled over his flesh. Within the flames were intricate markings he'd once explained were from his ancient language. The black markings on both of his arms started on the back of his hands and traveled up to his shoulders. The tips of the flames licked the base of his neck before traveling down to his chest.

I couldn't see them now, but I knew each of his pectoral muscles had a circular pattern of flames around them, as was the same with his shoulder blades on his back. The rest of his finely honed body was bare of any markings.

I knew his body almost as well as my own. I knew what it felt like to have him buried deep within me, knew every dip and hollow of his etched muscles, and I clearly recalled the taste of his skin. I'd spent hours locked in his arms.

I shivered at the memory of those moments and pulled the blanket closer against me; he lifted his eyebrow before rising to his full height. A foot taller than my five foot nine frame, he was the most massive man I'd ever seen with his broad chest, thighs the size of logs, and arms the size of large branches. And I had let him go.

You're an idiot. Yep, wasn't going to argue with that, but I would do everything I could to try to protect him, even if it meant hurting us both.

"What are you doing here?" I inquired, proud my voice came out stable when all I wanted was to trace the markings running over his skin as I molded my body against his, holding him and blocking the world out for just a few hours.

"I came to get you," he replied dryly. His detached coldness rattled me as he surveyed me; I despised it even while knowing I'd caused it. "Get dressed."

"We're leaving already?" I blurted, my eyes darting to the wind-up clock on the stand beside the lantern.

We were supposed to start the mission today, heading into the center of the decimated country and toward Hell itself. I'd been told we were leaving at sunrise, but plans must have changed, as the clock now read midnight.

"No. Get dressed and come with me," he ordered.

"Why?"

"Do you have to question everything I say?"

"Yes."

A muscle throbbed in his temple. I didn't know why I was arguing with him. I simply knew this was the most we'd spoken in days and I didn't care what I had to do to make it last longer.

"It's important. Get dressed, River."

He turned on his heel and stalked out of the tent. The only sign he'd been there was the rippling of the flap as it fell back into place behind him. I sat for a minute before tossing aside the covers and swinging my legs over the side of the bed. I tugged on the flaxen brown pants and brown shirt, that had become the mainstay of my wardrobe since arriving on this side of the wall.

Brown was the color the volunteers wore until they completed training. The only color on their uniforms was a single band used to mark their groups. My band had been yellow, but once I'd started training with the soldiers who would be making this journey with us, I'd stopped wearing the band.

I would be going on this mission with soldiers who wore forest green uniforms, but I hadn't asked for different clothes so I could match the others. I'd stood out from everyone since I'd been brought here; there was nothing that would help me blend in with them more now.

Besides, Corson, one of Kobal's seconds-in-command, had informed us during part of our orientation for this journey that the Craeton demons, those on Lucifer's side of this war, would tear us to shreds and bathe in our blood no matter the color of our outfit. The muted colors we wore were to help us blend in with our environment a little better.

Some of Corson's other encouraging words during his spiel were to expect anything and everything. Most of it would be hideously worse and more lethal than anything we could ever imagine. The fact he had sparkly, red, beaded earrings dangling from the pointy tips of his elf-like ears had done nothing to ease the fear his words created.

I knew this journey was going to be awful, and many probably wouldn't survive it, but I tried not to dwell on it. Dwelling on the unknown was a guaranteed way to shred the already thin line holding my composure together.

I'd been on an emotional roller coaster ride since being forced to leave my family behind and come here. Being informed I was part demon and angel and the only living descendent of Lucifer hadn't helped. To cap it all off, I'd fallen for a bossy, domineering, short-tempered demon, who had completely stolen my heart before I'd ended the relationship. I couldn't deal with worrying about what was to come on top of it all.

I ran a brush through my raven-colored hair before setting the brush on the bedside table. Ducking through the flap, I entered the main part of the tent with the table and sideboard inside of it. I tried not to look at the cot Kobal had been sleeping on since our fight, but my eyes completely disobeyed the commands of my brain.

My heart plummeted when I saw his bed was undisturbed,

again. Where had he been staying? Had he returned to the bonfire and the humans and demons who went there to have sex? He had killed one of the humans, but the women in town still desired him. I hated the way they watched him, practically drooling whenever he walked by. Despite his lethal, foreboding air, he still oozed sexuality, and women were attracted to it like bees to honey.

You ended it with him.

For the life of me, I couldn't remember why when I stepped out of the tent and spotted him standing beside the flap with his arms folded over his chest. The warm July breeze ruffled his hair as his eyes raked over me. The moonlight caressed his body, making him appear as if he were a part of the night—which, I guess in many ways, he was.

Looking at him, I couldn't help but recall the flex and bunch of his muscles when my hands ran over his unrelenting flesh, the salty taste of his skin beneath my mouth, and the pulse of his shaft within my body. The sounds of ecstasy and possession he'd released while inside of me echoed in my head.

I fisted my hands and looked away from him as memories threatened to drown me within their depths. He'd ripped the head off a woman. He may care for me, but he may not ever be able to love me in the way a human loved another human. In the way I loved him.

He could love you more, *in his demon, Chosen way. Besides, you know there's something more than human about the bond between you.*

I felt my defenses slipping when his eyes met mine and his head tilted to the side. *Lucifer vowed you would become like him. He flat out told you he would use you as a weapon against Kobal.*

Lucifer lies. He's Satan; he knows the Chosen bond will only make you both stronger.

Kobal said you were acting hysterically. Okay, the fact he'd said that to me during our fight still rankled. Maybe I had been a little hysterical while I'd still been covered in the blood of the woman he'd killed, but he could have kept his thoughts about it to himself. Although Kobal had never been one to keep his thoughts to himself, and tact was not something he considered, ever. His honesty was one of the things I liked most about him, even when it hurt to hear. However, now, I could admit I'd been over-whelmed by his actions that day and not entirely thinking clearly.

He hadn't been sleeping in the tent with me recently; Bale had been staying with me instead. He was most likely passing his nights in between someone else's legs now, I reminded myself. I managed to gather my pride again and tilt my chin up at him. He'd proven to be just like every other man who had passed in and out of my mother's life over the years. I tried to latch onto that idea, but inside, I knew it wasn't true.

If I hadn't pushed him away, he never would have turned to another.

CHAPTER TWO

River

"Come with me," he said and stepped away from the tent.

I frowned at his broad back, but followed him down the hill toward the town. The moonlight lit the way well enough that a lantern wasn't required to see. The red lights on top of the wall cast shadows over the ground as they blinked on and off repeatedly. I'd grown accustomed to the lights over the two months I'd been here and rarely noticed them anymore, but now their red glow seemed almost ominous.

"What's going on, Kobal?" I asked when we were halfway down the hill.

"Afraid I'll hurt you?"

I didn't blame him for being surly, but I could feel my pride pricking as I glared at his back. "I never have been before. I'm not going to start now."

He glanced over his shoulder at me, his eyes narrowing when he found me giving him the death stare. "Because you can take care of yourself?"

My teeth might fracture from the amount of pressure I put on them while trying to remain somewhat pleasant in my response. "I can."

That wasn't a lie; I could take care of myself. I may not be able to tear off someone's head or have waves of fire erupt from my hands like him, but I'd gotten a lot better at harvesting power from the life I felt pulsating in the earth around me. I could also shoot enough flames to set his ass on fire.

The flames he knew about, but I'd kept my growing ability to wield the power of life to myself with the intention of surprising him with it. We'd stopped talking before I could show him how much better at it I was getting, and we hadn't trained together since. I also kept my growing ability hidden from Bale and Corson, the two demons who had taken over my training when things between Kobal and me had ended. It wasn't that I didn't trust them, I did, but Kobal had once warned me to keep the extent of what I could do a secret, and I was still taking that advice.

"It's a good thing I trained you so well then," he said and turned away from me.

Well, that officially ended any softening I'd been feeling toward him. I was tempted to throw a ball of life-filled energy at him to show him how well I'd also trained myself lately, but though I wanted to choke him half the time, I'd never do anything to hurt him, physically.

My nails dug into my palms, and I glowered at his back until we reached the school where the people ate their meals every day. Curiosity tugged at me as I followed him into the building, but I didn't ask him what was going on again.

Our feet slapped against the tile as we walked. The fluorescent lights above us reflected on the floor, causing it to be almost blinding. Whatever was going on had to be important as all the lights in the building were always turned off at night. Electricity was precious and most of it went to maintaining the wall now separating the destroyed states from the still-intact, outlying areas.

I'd resided in one of those outlying areas and been happily

oblivious to the war humans and demons waged against Lucifer and his followers, until my mother turned me in for being different. The soldiers had taken me away from my brothers and brought me here afterward.

We rounded a corner and my step faltered. Standing in the hall were the rest of the men and women I was supposed to be leaving with today. They all glanced at me before hastily looking away and finding something else to focus on. Ever since I'd flame-broiled an ugly, boar-like creature known as a madagan, they'd been uneasy around me. They'd *really* avoided me since my ex popped the head off one of them like she'd been nothing more than a Barbie doll.

Gathered with the humans were the five demons who were closest to Kobal. Corson leaned against the wall, chewing on some gum while he smiled flirtatiously at a pretty, redheaded woman. Yellow birds dangled from the tips of his pointed ears. Kobal hated that Corson wore the earrings the women he slept with gave to him; I found it funny and it made him stand out as the only demon with a sense of humor.

Kobal had once told me Corson was an adhene demon, a mischievous elf-like demon, and it was entirely fitting for him with his ears, personality, and lithe build. His black hair was so dark in color it looked almost blue in the lights shining down on him. It stood out in spikes around his narrow face.

His citrine-colored eyes locked on me; he popped a bubble with his gum as he gazed between Kobal and me. I could feel the tension radiating from both of us as we stood rigidly in the hall and resolutely refused to look at each other.

"Is someone cranky when they're woken up or are we having another lovers' quarrel?" Corson inquired of me.

I suddenly understood why Kobal had said he often had the impulse to rip the earrings from Corson's ears. Kobal spun toward him. Corson straightened away from the wall and tugged the earrings out. He grinned at me when Kobal turned away; I scowled back at him, which only caused him to chuckle.

Corson and Bale had become the two I'd spent the most time with recently. Bale was always reserved when she was around me; Corson was slowly becoming my only friend in this place. As much as he annoyed me at times, I enjoyed his company.

He may be my only friend here, but I knew he would always choose Kobal over me. Kobal was his king, and they'd been together for centuries as they fought and battled together to fix what Lucifer had torn apart when he'd entered Hell. I was simply the woman fate had saddled Kobal with, and fate had one twisted sense of humor when it came to the two of us. The king of Hell's Chosen was the descendent of his worst enemy and a mortal to boot. Oh yeah, someone was getting a good laugh somewhere over this one.

"What's going on?" I whispered to Corson when Kobal moved on to speak with Bale and Morax.

"You'll find out," he replied and slipped the earrings back in.

"Corson—"

"It's a good thing," he assured me.

I glanced at him questioningly, but he conveniently turned to speak with Verin. Stunning, was the only word I could think of for Verin. If she'd been glimpsed from our dimension by humans who could see beyond the veil, as some things from the demon world had been, Verin would have been the origin for the legends about sirens or succubae.

Her hair and eyes were the color of the sun. The ends of her hair brushed against the curve of her tiny waist. Most of the men, and some of the women, would stop to watch her when she walked past, but she was Morax's Chosen, and no one was going to mess with him.

Morax appeared formidable and strange to any human he encountered and probably more than a few demons too. His green skin had the appearance of scales due to the deeper shades of green swirling across his flesh. Add in his six foot two height, long powerful tail, razor-sharp teeth, two sets of simultaneously blinking eyelids, orange snake eyes, and most people were ready to run before they ever saw the six-inch horns growing out of his bald head and curving toward each other.

No one was going to hit on Verin with Morax in a mile vicinity. I had no doubt he would make the death of anyone who tried as unpleasant as possible. My gaze landed on the bites on both of their necks, marking them as each other's Chosen.

Even before I'd known what those marks on them meant, they'd fascinated me in a strange way. Now I knew it was because the demon part of me had instinctively recognized what they were.

Kobal's marks on me were fading. The ones I'd left on him were nearly gone, and I wanted them *back* so badly I could almost taste Kobal's flesh yielding beneath me as I sank my teeth into him. I shook with a racking need and closed my eyes against the pull trying to draw me toward Kobal. A pull I would never be free of no matter how much distance I attempted to put between us. Our bond would never be broken.

Feeling a little more in control of myself again, I opened my eyes as Shax approached Verin and Corson. Most of the women's eyes turned to follow Shax as he moved. At six foot one, he was the most human looking, and the most handsome of the demons. His blond hair hung in waves about his chiseled face, a face probably better suited to an angel than a demon. His sunflower-yellow eyes glimmered warmly and the clothes he wore fit his body like a glove.

"They're filling the last truck full of food now," Shax said to them.

"Good," Verin replied.

Movement at the front of the row of people drew my attention as Colonel Ulrich MacIntyre, or Mac as most called him, poked his head out from the cafeteria. He said something to Bale and Kobal who nodded in return.

Bale's fire-red hair flashed in the light when she turned to face the people standing behind her. Her red-hued skin made her look as if she were made entirely of fire. She flashed a feral smile at the guy closest to her, who had made the mistake of getting caught staring at her ample cleavage. Eyes the color of limes raked over the man as he became riveted on his boots.

Kobal spun and walked down the row of people to stand beside me. My skin pricked at his nearness. His fiery scent filled my nostrils as I deeply inhaled it into me. I resisted the urge to hug myself in a vain attempt to hold myself together when he turned to face the others.

"Once you step through that door, you will all be closely monitored. Everything you say will be overheard, so keep that in mind. If even *one* of you reveals anything about what is on this side of the wall, *every* person within that room will be forced to stay here," Kobal said. "There will be no turning back for them either."

Murmurs slid down the line as people tried to figure out what he was talking about. I stared up at the straight line of his jaw as I puzzled over his words.

"Nothing is to be revealed about what we do here, absolutely *nothing*, or you and your families will *all* be made to pay the consequences of your actions," Kobal continued.

My eyes went to the door as the murmurs in the crowd died instantly. It couldn't be; *no* one who hadn't volunteered was allowed to come to the wall. I'd been one of the exceptions, taken unwillingly when they'd still been trying to find Lucifer's descendent. They'd finally hit the jackpot with me.

Mac held the door open further. People glanced at each other before starting to move forward into the connecting room. When the first people disappeared and cries of joy could be heard, the line moved faster and faster through the doors. I stood, frozen, as I tried to process what was going on and my heart hammered in my chest.

Were my brothers in there? Were they waiting for me? I was too frightened to find out the answer, too scared my mother had somehow managed to mess this up and I would go through the door only to find no one waiting there for me. As the last person filtered through the door, sobs and laughter drifted down the hall toward me. Mac pushed the door open a little further and looked at me expectantly.

"River?" Mac inquired.

Kobal's obsidian eyes were unreadable when they met mine. He'd told me he'd try to arrange it so I could see my brothers again before we left on our mission, but that was before I'd told him to get out of my life. Had my refusal of him changed his mind about me having a chance to see my brothers again?

No, he wouldn't do that. He may have little regard for human life, but he wasn't cruel. He wouldn't have brought the families of the others here and not my brothers, but I still found myself unable to move.

Something in his expression changed; there was an easing to him I hadn't seen in days. "Go on," he encouraged, his tone far kinder than it had been earlier.

It took everything I had to make the first step. Once I did, I didn't think my feet hit the floor again until I was on the other side of the door. The cafeteria was a teeming mass of people, crying and laughing as they embraced and spoke eagerly. Rising onto my toes, I frantically searched over the crowd for Gage and Bailey.

"Pittah!"

I spun to my right, tears filling my eyes when I spotted Gage running toward me with Bailey in his arms. It had been months since I'd heard him call me by his nickname for me and seen their beloved faces.

A strangled cry escaped me as I took a stumbling step forward before running toward them. Bailey lifted his head from where it laid on Gage's chest when he caught sight of me. He removed his thumb from his mouth and cried out my name, "River!"

I flung my arms around them and hugged them close.

CHAPTER THREE

River

"What is going on here, River?" Gage asked when we'd settled into a corner behind a table in the far back of the room. We had ignored the table and settled onto the floor. While all the other families had a couple of older military men and women like Mac hovering around them and monitoring their conversations, I'd been assigned the only demon in the room, the only one who could pass entirely as human, Shax.

"I can't talk about it," I told him as I took Bailey from his arms and settled him into my lap.

I brushed back strands of Bailey's fine, blond hair from his chubby face. He curled up against my chest and nestled into my neck. I'd almost forgotten how warm and soft he was. Almost forgotten the scent of his baby powder and the milk he drank. He'd grown so much in these past two months and I had missed it. I may miss all the rest of his days too.

I'd tried not to let thoughts of my brothers and the hole that being torn away from them had created in my chest consume me while I was here. Now all the sorrow and loneliness being away from them had caused flooded me with emotion.

Bailey pulled his thumb from his mouth as he stared at me. "Don't cry, River."

I bit back a sob and bent over to kiss his forehead. "I can't help it. I'm so happy to see you."

He closed his eyes and nuzzled closer against my chest, his tiny hand fisting in my shirt. I hugged him closer before focusing on Gage. "How have you been?"

He pushed back a strand of his sandy blond hair. It had grown longer since the last time I'd seen him. His brown eyes were troubled as they searched mine; the freckles across his cheeks and nose more visible from his tan.

"We've been fine," he replied.

"Are Lisa and Asante treating you well?"

"Yes, we're fine, really. We miss you."

I rested my hand on his cheek. "I miss you too, so much. Are you being fed well?"

He leaned back and held open his arms. "Do I look like I'm going hungry?"

"You look like you've gained some weight," I admitted.

"Ten pounds," he said proudly. "Between Asante's work as a peace keeper and the food we were promised when they took you, we have too much and often give it to those more in need."

"That's great," I managed to say around the lump in my throat. At least something good had come of me being taken away from them. I kissed Bailey's head when he released a small snore. "What about *her*?"

"She has to go out more now that we're not there to take care of her, so I've seen her in town a few times, but I won't speak to her. Few will." Gage knew immediately who *"her"* was. Our mother, the one who had turned me in with the hopes of getting more for herself. Fortunately, she ended up without her children and with nowhere near what she expected she'd be given.

"She never really talked to people anyway," I said.

"And now she's an outcast for turning in her own child."

Gage's voice had an edge of steel to it, and for the first time, I noticed how much he'd matured. He'd become a man while I'd been gone. His voice had changed and become deeper and a dusting of blond hair lined his upper lip.

"I'm proud of you," I whispered.

He leaned away from me. "For what?"

"For being you, for taking care of Bailey, for being my rock."

"If I was anything worth being proud of, I'd have been able to stop them from taking you in the first place. Are you the one they were looking for?"

I glanced at Shax as he gave a subtle shake of his head no. "I can't talk about that," I murmured.

Gage's eyes shot to the demon behind me, and he leaned closer. "What about you, are they treating *you* well here?"

"I'm fine."

His gaze raked over me. "You've lost weight."

"We do a lot of training. Believe me, there is plenty of food for all of us."

I refrained from slapping my hands over my neck when his gaze honed in on the fading marks there; it would only make him more curious if I did. "Are those... *bites*?"

My head spun as I tried to come up with some kind of believable response. "Ah, no... they're shots. It's the way they inoculate us here."

I couldn't tell if he bought it or not as his eyes remained locked on my neck. "River—"

"Really, I'm fine." I took hold of his hand and squeezed it. "I'm learning new things every day and we have plenty of food and warm shelter. I'd prefer to be home with you two, but that isn't my reality."

"Why did they let us come here?"

"I don't know."

"What is up with the wall? What's on *this* side that they don't want us to see or know about on the other side?"

It didn't surprise me that he'd struck right to the heart of the matter; he'd always been smart. "I can't talk about anything like that, Gage. Please don't ask me anymore."

His jaw jutted out, and his mouth pursed in frustration. "We don't have much time together."

"No, we don't."

"Will you ever be able to come back to us?"

"I'm going to do everything I can to make that happen," I vowed. "No matter what it takes."

I didn't look at Shax as I made this promise. I was afraid he'd be shaking his head no at me again, but if I somehow survived this journey to Hell, then I planned to reunite with my brothers no matter what it took.

"Tell me what has been going on in town, how everyone is doing. Is there any new gossip?" I asked. "What have you been doing?"

He settled in beside me with his shoulder against mine. He revealed the goings on around town and how he'd started to see more of this girl named Cherry. I'd noticed her interest in him before I'd been taken away. His head fell against my shoulder as he spoke and he stifled a yawn. I wrapped my arm around him, holding him close as his voice became more muffled.

I'd been thinking how grown he'd become, yet he snuggled against me much like he used to do when he was a baby. While the war was raging, I would lay awake at night, holding him and praying we would survive to see the morning. After the war, Gage had been plagued by nightmares. He'd often wake in the middle of the night and come to my room. He'd known better than to turn to our mother.

When he'd turned eight, I'd sometimes wake to hear him crying out in the night, but he had decided he was too old to crawl into bed with me. For all I knew, he still had nightmares, but he'd stopped talking about them after Bailey was born and he'd started keeping his bedroom door closed. He was determined to be the strong, big brother for Bailey.

I lifted my head to stare at the ceiling, fighting against the tears filling my eyes as I felt their warm breaths on my skin and inhaled their familiar, loved scents. Kobal had done this, and though he'd brought all the families of those who would be leaving tomorrow here, I knew he'd done this for me. I'd never be able to thank him enough.

Bowing my head, I pressed my cheek against Gage's head. I tried not to fall asleep, what little time we had left together would go by too fast if I did, but sleep dragged me into its depths anyway.

～

KOBAL

Standing in one of the hallways branching off the cafeteria, I watched as River ran and embraced her brothers. The youngest one stuck his arms out to her, eagerly going to her when she took hold of him. The older one beamed as he hugged her. The corners of my mouth twitched at the radiant smile on her face and the joy in her eyes.

So rare her smile, so fleeting. I felt like it had been months instead of days since I'd last seen it. She didn't smile at me anymore, and she seldom had a reason to smile when she was around the humans. They barely spoke to her and most of the time they didn't bother to acknowledge her existence.

It had to be lonely for her here. I'd never considered that until I saw the tears brimming in her eyes at the sight of her brothers. The faint freckles on her nose were more visible in the harsh light, as was the scar at the corner of her right eye. A scar she'd received as a child from an incident involving a fishing hook. The polished, seashell necklace she always wore shone in the lights overhead.

The pure violet of her eyes twinkled, causing them to stand out vibrantly against her sun-kissed skin and pitch-black hair. My greedy gaze ran over her round face and proud chin as I memorized this look of sheer joy on her face. Many wouldn't consider her beautiful, but more pretty. To me, she was the most beautiful woman in the world. I would give anything to give her this happiness every day for the rest of her life. Instead, I was going to be tearing her away from this happiness to drag her into an endless nightmare that she may not survive.

It was the only way to save us all, and she was far stronger than even she believed. She'd survived against madagans and revenirs already; she'd withstood the distrust and seclusion she'd endured in this camp. She'd also taken everything I'd thrown at her in training and then again in my bed.

I'd been so determined to go easy with her while I was within her. She was mortal, I didn't want to harm her, but she'd never allowed me to keep myself restrained and had taken my marking of her flesh, my claiming of her, and my insatiable appetite for her body with an eagerness that more than matched mine. I'd never believed I would find my Chosen, and certainly hadn't expected for my Chosen to be the mortal daughter of Lucifer, my greatest enemy, but she'd been more than I ever could have imagined from my Chosen, and by her own choice, she was no longer mine.

I should walk away from her and give her the freedom she'd requested from me, but I couldn't. I had no choice in the matter; she had to stay with me. I was the only one who could keep her safe from the looming threat ahead of us, and she may be the only one capable of putting a stop to Lucifer's reign of terror.

Lucifer had already managed to break one of the seals of Hell. If he succeeded in breaking more while the gateway was still open, no wall would be able to keep the horrors living within Hell away from the human race.

I couldn't let River go back to her old life. Her old life wouldn't be there for much longer if I did let her return to it and the gateway remained open.

Besides, she was mine. She was angry with me now, and I knew I'd handled the situation with the woman who tried to kill her poorly, but when I witnessed her lunging at River with a knife, I reacted as I should have and slaughtered her. The appalled expression on River's blood-splattered face when she'd gazed at me as if she didn't know who I was afterward was forever emblazoned in my mind. I'd hated that look and that I was the one to cause it.

If I could change things, I still would have killed the woman, but I would have done it in a much more private setting, far away from River and human eyes. As much as I didn't like it, we were a part of the human world now, and I had to consider them. *None* of them had taken the woman's death well.

They'd all been exceptionally distrustful of the demons afterward, but especially me. That was why I'd had Mac gather all of the families here instead of just River's. The original plan was to bring only River's family to the wall, but we decided to bring them all here as a gesture of goodwill and to remind the soldiers what they were fighting for. I resented having to do anything to coddle the inferior, overly sensitive human species, but I'd do it all over again to see the radiant look on River's face.

I'd get her back, but I wouldn't apologize for killing that woman. It had been necessary. River would come around eventually; she had to. Hopefully, sooner rather than later as I didn't think I could take much more of this separation from her.

Every night I lay awake, listening to her sleeping, inhaling the scent of her. I tormented myself with memories of what it had been like to be inside of her and to hold her close against my chest while she slept. I couldn't take it anymore, and for the past two nights, I'd slept on the ground a little distance away from the tent. Outside, I couldn't hear her sighs as she tossed about in her restless sleep.

I'd half expected her to walk back into my dreams, but the real her had yet to return to them, while I held the dream version of her in my sleep. I didn't know if that was because she had completely shut me out, or if it was because she had shut everything out after she'd connected with Lucifer.

Resting my hands on the sides of the metal door leading to the cafeteria, my claws extended to dig into the concrete wall as I watched her sit in a corner with her family. Their heads bent close together while they eagerly spoke with one another. Her brothers' coloring was opposite of hers, but I could see some similarity in all of their features. The way they tilted their heads or waved their hands in the air was especially alike as they interacted with each other. The smallest one, Bailey, I remembered her saying, gripped her shirt with his tiny fists and closed his eyes.

This is how she would look holding our children; she'd shower them with the same affection and glow with love for them like she did for her brothers. I wanted it so badly I shuddered with the need for it before recalling she'd told me to get out of her life. My claws tore holes into the wall; the broken bits of concrete clattered against the tile when they fell around my feet. I slammed my hands against the wall and turned away.

I struggled to regain my composure as I walked down the hall to where Mac stood with Bale and Corson. He'd put those fucking earrings in his ears again. I resisted the impulse to tear them out.

"How is it going in there?" Mac inquired.

"They all seem happy." In truth, I'd only paid attention to River. "Thank you for arranging this."

"You were right. It will help them to trust you more and you're going to need that for what you're about to face."

"How will the humans in camp react when they learn what went on here tonight?" Corson asked Mac.

"There will no doubt be some resentment," Mac said, "but I think they've all learned they can't always get what they want. If things go well tonight, I'll arrange to have more families brought in for brief, monitored visits. Future visits will be on the other side of the wall, and in smaller groups, but it will help build morale if they're occasionally able to see their families again."

"If we're successful, there may not be a reason for the wall anymore," Bale said.

"True," Mac agreed.

"Is everything ready to go?" I inquired.

"It is," Mac said briskly.

"Good." I leaned against the wall to wait until morning, but after a half an hour, I found myself wandering away again. Shax was inside watching over River, but I couldn't resist seeing her smile again. Stepping before the door, longing speared through my gut when my eyes landed on her once more.

CHAPTER FOUR

RIVER

"River." I lifted my head to blink against the dim rays of sun filtering through the windows of the cafeteria. The warmth against my chest made my heart swell when I looked down at Bailey and Gage nestled within my arms. "It's time for us to go."

Shax's words drew my attention to him. I tried not to cry while I hugged my brothers closer. Gage stirred, but Bailey's breath warmed my skin as he kept his mouth against my neck. I'd just gotten them back and now I had to leave them again. Maybe for good this time.

I will not cry.

"I have to go," I said when Gage lifted his head from my shoulder.

Tears filled his eyes. He blinked them back and bit into his quivering lower lip. "We'll be okay. I'll take care of him," he promised.

"I know you will." I squeezed his hand and rested my forehead briefly against his. "I'm going to do everything I can to see you again."

I went to pull Bailey away, but his arms tightened around my neck. His lashes tickled my skin when they fluttered open. "No!" he cried as I tried to pull him away again.

"Stink Bug, you must go," I choked out. "I'll see you again soon."

I kissed and hugged him before Gage lifted him away from me.

"No, no, no, no!" Bailey shouted.

His screams hurt far more than any revenirs shriek ever had as they stabbed through my heart. My throat clogged; I was finding it increasingly difficult to breathe. Bailey waved his hands in the air and tried to squirm free of Gage's hold. Shax stepped away from us, moving a few feet toward the table to stare at one of the side doors.

Straightening my shoulders, I leaned forward and kissed Bailey's head. "It will be okay, Bailey. I love you forever and a day."

Bailey burst into tears when I embraced them both. "They told me I have to let you go, but I don't wanna!" he sobbed.

I brushed his hair back from his forehead as I bent to kiss his flushed cheeks. "I know, B, but I have to go. I promise to do everything I can to see you again as soon as possible. I love you."

Bailey inhaled hitching sobs, but he didn't cry out again or try to grab for me.

"I love you," Gage said. "Be careful and take care of yourself."

"I love you too, and you make sure to do the same."

I turned away and strode toward the main door before I started screaming *no, no, no* in the middle of the cafeteria too.

You're doing this for them. They must be kept safe and this may be the only way to ensure they have any kind of life.

I joined the other soldiers filing through the door. I could smell the scent of their tears as they left their loved ones behind again, but I sensed a resoluteness in the set of their shoulders. Muffled sobs from those we were leaving behind followed us out the door.

Looking back, I gave a final wave and smile to my brothers before stepping into the hall and heading out on a journey where I would most likely meet my death. Tears slid down my face, not for the possible loss of my life, but for the loss of them. They'd been my entire world since they were born, and if dying meant saving their lives, I would do it.

I wiped the tears away and stopped by where Kobal stood at the door to the outside. He stared across the grass toward the tents on the top of the hill before turning his head to look at me. I had no idea what he was thinking when his eyes met mine, but a muscle twitched in his jaw.

"Thank you for this," I said.

His full lips remained compressed for a minute more before he finally spoke. "It was necessary to rebuild the trust with the humans."

I stared at him, uncertain of how to take that. "I'm sure it worked."

"Did it?" he inquired.

I *really* didn't know how to take that. Was this his way of apologizing? If it was, I had to admit I didn't think he needed to apologize. His nature caused him to act the way he did when he killed Eileen, and my humanity caused me to be a bit disturbed by it. He shouldn't have to apologize for who he is. His actions hadn't been right to me, but they had been right to him. For him to apologize for that would be like expecting a shark to apologize to a fish after eating it.

He continued to stare at me expectantly, but I was still trying to figure out what he meant when he turned on his heel and walked away. "You will be riding with me." The words were thrown at me over his shoulder. "And if you think about arguing or doing something different, I'll have you strapped into the vehicle in front of everyone."

I should be mad over his high-handed command, but he'd given me back my brothers, if only for a little bit, and I found I didn't have any anger in me right now. I was certain that feeling wouldn't last long.

~

KOBAL

I couldn't look back at her as I strode across the grass passed where the vehicles that would take us from here had been parked. The tears in her eyes tore at my insides, and the cries of her youngest brother resonated in my ears. I'd never before felt any sympathy for a human until River walked into my life. I never would have gone out of my way to make one of them happy, because their happiness meant nothing to me.

Now all I wanted was her happiness, more so than finally claiming my throne—a throne I'd worked my entire fifteen hundred sixty-two years to claim. The gateway had to be closed, Lucifer had to be stopped, but right then, I would have walked away from it all, given Bailey back to her, and taken her far from here.

The seals would eventually break open, Lucifer would one day feel his growing army was strong enough to walk the earth and take on the obstacles he would face here, and the wall would fall, but River would be happy until then.

And then she would die.

My claws tore into my palms when I fisted my hands. I would do what must be done, like I had from the second of my creation, but instead of doing it for my throne, I would do this for her. I would kill that bastard once and for all to give her the life she deserved, even if she never allowed me into her life again.

Finally feeling stable enough to look at her, I glanced over at her bent head. Her gaze was on her boots as she followed me across the grounds to the tents. Pulling the flap of my tent aside, I waited for her to enter before following her inside.

"Gather your things," I said, far more brusquely than I'd intended.

My eyes fastened on her mouth when she tilted her head back to look at me. I recalled the sweet taste of her lips as the fresh rain and earthy scent of her filled my nose. My cock swelled as my desire for her increased.

The fading marks on her flesh almost caused an involuntary snarl to tear from me. My hands fisted, my claws lengthened as I resisted the impulse to grab hold of her and claim her again. Demons would still recognize her as my Chosen without my marks on her. They would scent me on her, but I wanted the humans to know too. She was *mine*.

"What are you doing?" she cried when drops of blood spilled from my palms to fall on the earth. "Kobal, stop it!"

I snatched my hand away from her when she went to take it. Her touch was too much right now; I couldn't handle it. "Don't!" I hissed from between my teeth. "Don't touch me right now, not unless you're going to welcome me inside of you again."

The color drained from her face as she glanced between my hands and my face. She radiated distress, yet the scent of her increased with her growing hunger for me. She may have told me to get out of her life, but she would never be able to deny her attraction and need for me.

"Kobal—"

"I am on the verge of taking you right now, River, so either say yes and I'll have you naked faster than you can blink, or get your stuff and let's go."

Her body swayed instinctively toward mine before she took an abrupt step back. Disappointment crashed through me. All of my demon instincts screamed at me to take her, to claim her, to mark her once more. Beneath my skin, the hounds rippled as they howled their discontent.

I didn't know how, but somehow I managed to keep myself restrained from dragging her against me and crushing my mouth to hers. Unable to deny the desires of her body and her demon instincts, she would yield to me, but then I'd only have moments of release before her human side came back into play. Her anger with me would return, and she'd hate me more for it.

I wanted her back, but she would be in my bed again because she chose to be there, and not because we both lost control of ourselves.

"This isn't what I wanted it to be like between us," she whispered.

"Isn't it?" I grated.

She recoiled from me. "No, never."

"Go, River."

She hesitated before spinning on her heel and fleeing for the other tent. She looked back at me from the flap and opened her mouth to say something but stopped herself then ducked out of view. My breath exploded from me.

This was going to be an excruciating journey if I didn't get her back soon.

CHAPTER FIVE

RIVER

When I finished packing and left his room, I discovered Kobal was no longer inside the tent. Walking outside, I found him waiting for me a few feet away and looking more in control of himself as blood no longer dripped from his palms. The sun beating down on him brought out the lighter strands of brown in his dark hair and emphasized the muscles in his arms and shoulders.

Love and desire swelled forth within me, but I quickly tamped them both down. I'd seen the ravenous gleam in his amber-colored eyes as he'd watched me just minutes ago. More so than his bloody palms, those amber eyes gave away his lack of control. I knew they only turned that color when he was highly aroused or ready to kill. Since I knew he would never hurt me, it could have only meant one thing.

The amount of restraint he'd shown only made me love him more, but I couldn't give into the needs of my body and heart. It felt as if my heart had been carved from my chest and stomped into the ground when I'd turned away from him in the tent, but it was the best for us both, wasn't it?

My gaze went to his neck. My heart sank and something inside of me screamed when I saw the bites I'd left on his neck had completely healed and faded away. Any demon would know I was his without his marks on me, but would they know he was mine without my marks on him?

It shouldn't matter, but it did.

He never looked back at me as he led me toward the twenty vehicles waiting to make the trip. Most of them were pickups, but a few cars were going too. The decision had been made to leave the heavy-duty military vehicles behind in case we failed in our mission.

They would need the vehicles here to defend the wall and to recruit new volunteers if we died. Plus, it would be easier to carry enough gas with us for the smaller vehicles, and if one or more of them broke down along the way, we'd have backups. All of the vehicles were loaded with food, water, and gasoline. I felt like we would be riding in ticking bombs, but it was better than walking the whole trip.

We'd been told all of the radiation from the nukes our government had released on the center of the country had been absorbed into Hell, where it had no effect upon the demons and creatures within.

I didn't know who the human guinea pigs were that tested that theory, but we'd been assured their skin hadn't fallen off and they hadn't sprouted tails. They'd also taken radiation samples and found nothing in the air. There had been some radiation detected in the ground still, but not enough to be a health risk or to warrant biohazard suits, though I still would have preferred one. I was strange enough without growing a third eye or an extra hand.

What effect the radiation had on the life in and around the surrounding area before being absorbed by Hell had been minimal. Again, this is what we'd been informed, but I still couldn't rid myself of the certainty we'd come across skyscraper-sized spiders and mosquitos, or people who had turned to cannibalism and now resided in the mountains.

I shuddered at the possibility. They had said we would encounter many horrors during our journey, and after the madagans and revenirs, I knew they would be bad. I really hoped they were all demonic horrors and not man-made ones too.

How much my view of the world had changed in two months was not lost on me. One day, I'd been hoping to catch a fish. Now I was hoping not to encounter mutated creatures but only things from Hell on our way to Hell.

"We'll be riding in this one," Kobal said to me and slapped the bed of a white pickup truck before walking away with his shoulders set rigidly.

With a sigh, I tossed my bags into the bed of the truck before walking around to the passenger side and the man standing by the door. I recognized him from the group of human soldiers I'd been training with for the past week, but we'd never spoken to each other and I didn't know his name.

He'd always stood out to me more than the others because he'd been the one to defend me to Eileen before she tried to kill me. He was also one of the men to have had the unfortunate experience of holding one of Eileen's arms while Kobal ripped off her head.

His indigo gaze ran over me as I neared. His dark brown hair had been shaved down to stubble. With his shoulders thrust back, he looked like a proud military man; the opposite of me. Extremely handsome with a square jaw and chiseled features, he had to be at least six feet two inches of solid muscle, but for some reason he appeared small and boring in appearance to me.

A shadow fell over us, drawing my gaze to Kobal as he stepped next to the driver's side door of the truck. *He* was why everyone looked so much smaller and less attractive to me now. His gaze raked over both of us before he tugged the door open.

"Get in," he commanded gruffly.

"You first," I said to the man and gestured at the door.

I refused to be stuck in the middle of the two of them and so close to Kobal. I didn't trust myself around him, especially not after what had just transpired in the tent. He was too much of a temptation, one whose lap I might climb into and tear the clothes from in order to get at the flesh underneath.

The man looked like I'd told him to climb into an occupied coffin, but he opened the door and slid into the middle. Thankfully, the truck didn't have a hump in the middle of the floor; otherwise, I would have felt bad for making him sit there. I slipped off the katana on my back and placed it in the bed of the truck before adjusting the holster and guns at my side. Taking a deep breath, I slid into the truck and closed the door once more on life as I'd known it.

The man hunched his shoulders up in an attempt not to touch Kobal or me. I didn't feel insulted by it, everyone did that around me now, but I was beginning to rethink asking him to sit in the middle. The poor guy wasn't going to be able to move after today if he sat like that the whole time.

I ignored the hard stare Kobal gave me as I rolled down my window and draped my arm out to rest it on the hot metal of the door. I questioned Kobal's ability to drive a vehicle until he turned it on and shifted the handle on the steering column into drive. Not like it would have mattered if he couldn't drive, I didn't know how to do it, and I wasn't so sure Hunchy beside me did either. When Kobal wrapped his hands around the wheel, I was relieved to see his three-inch-long claws had retracted and his black fingernails were now back to normal.

Kobal led the way out of town. He drove onto the broken roadway I'd often seen winding into the vast nothing of our country from the practice field where we'd spent hours training since I'd arrived. I now realized it was literally the highway to Hell.

Looking in the mirror, I spotted the large group of volunteers, soldiers, and demons who had been left behind to protect the wall gathered to watch us go. There were so many counting on us not to fail. Closing my eyes, I took a deep breath to steady myself. This had to work. *I* had to succeed, somehow.

We'd barely made it a mile before the charred remnants of homes began to mar the landscape around us. Red and gray brick chimneys rose into the day from a few of the remains. Some homes had porches untouched before their crumpled walls, and others had half a house still standing testament to the lives that had once filled them.

A lump formed in my throat when we passed a playground. Green grass had grown up to brush against the bottom of the swings as an unseen breeze blew them gently back and forth. The metal of the swing set sagged in the middle, bending beneath the weight of the rust eating away at it. The castle made of tires and wood had buckled and nearly touched the ground.

Even falling apart, Bailey would have loved to play on the castle, and I could almost hear the echoing laughter of the children who had once run through here.

I turned away from the playground and focused on the rutted and broken road before the reminder of Bailey made me cry again. Kobal slowed the truck to only ten miles an hour to navigate the road. We'd been told that if everything went well, we'd make it to our destination in a week.

I highly doubted everything would go well, but I kept my pessimism to myself. I was already on the blacklist, adding a gloom and doom personality on top of everything else would only make things worse.

My teeth clacked together, and my knee hit the glove box when we bounced over a large rut. Beside me, Hunchy hissed in a breath when the jarring impact almost caused him to touch me. I wondered if the humans would be so wary of me if they knew I was part angel as well as demon, but I'd been told to keep the knowledge of what I was a secret from them.

To the humans, I was some sort of freaky human who could set things on fire and had been sleeping with the head-ripping demon.

I wouldn't have talked to me either.

CHAPTER SIX

RIVER

A good hour passed with Hunchy trying to stay as still as a statue and Kobal glaring at the road like it was the enemy. The tense silence was starting to grate on my nerves when I finally decided I should stop calling him Hunchy. "What's your name?" I asked the man beside me.

He flinched at my voice. After all this time, I should have been prepared for others' reactions to me, but I wasn't as his flinch caused me to recoil. Turning toward the window, I fully expected him to pretend he hadn't heard me as I tried to shake off the lingering pain his reaction had caused. They hated me so much that they even hated the sound of my voice.

I lifted my hand to rub at my temples while trying to ignore the man at my side.

"I'm First Sergeant Sue Hawkson," he said from beside me.

My eyebrows shot into my hairline when he spoke to *me*. "Sue?" I asked in disbelief, certain I'd heard him wrong.

He flinched again, but I realized it wasn't my voice causing his discomfort. It was my question. Turning toward me, his indigo eyes relentlessly held mine. "Yes."

I closed my mouth and blinked at him a couple of times. He had the weirdest name I'd ever heard for a guy, but who was I to judge? I was the descendent of '*Don't call me Lucifer*' Satan.

"And I thought my mom made an odd choice with River."

His full mouth actually quirked into a smile. "My mom was worse."

"What's so wrong with Sue?" Kobal took a break from glaring at the road to glare at us.

Sue's shoulders shot up to his ears as he leaned away from Kobal. I bit back a laugh at the motion clearly meant to protect his head and neck. Kobal must have recognized the same thing as he scowled at Sue before turning to focus on the road once more.

"Sue is usually more of a girl's name," I explained.

"Let's not sugarcoat it. Sue *is* a girl's name," Sue replied.

"Why would your mother name you after a woman?" Kobal demanded, ever the one for tact.

Sue relaxed enough to let his shoulders down in a shrug. "She was a big fan of Johnny Cash."

Now he'd lost me. I stared at him questioningly, hoping he would explain further, but unwilling to push him in case he stopped talking.

Sue ran a hand over the stubble on his head before speaking again. "One of his songs was, *A Boy Named Sue*."

"Oh," I said. "I'm not sure I know that one."

"The father leaves, but before going, he gives his son the name Sue to make him tougher," Sue explained. "My father was killed in a plane crash before I was born."

"I'm sorry."

He waved a hand dismissively. "Years ago."

"I do remember that song a little." I smiled at him, happy to have a human talking to me again. "So your mom believed the name Sue would make you tougher?"

"She did, and like I said, she loved Johnny Cash."

"Why didn't she name you Johnny then?"

He released a snort of laughter. "I've asked myself that same fucking question many times over the course of my life."

"I guess I can see her reasoning on it if she believed the name would make you stronger."

"Can you?" he inquired. "Because I can't. Most people call me Hawk, because of my last name, but having the name Sue was a lot of fun in grade school."

I bit on my lip to keep from laughing and leaned against the door of the truck. My gaze fell on Kobal's white knuckled grip on the steering wheel as he stared between the two of us. He looked almost comical, crammed inside the vehicle. His head was bent to avoid hitting the roof, and if he'd had horns, they probably would have dented the roof if not pierced through it. His knees brushed against the bottom of the steering wheel.

"Where are you from?" I asked Sue.

"Falmouth."

"Really?" I perked up when he said the name of the town next to the one I'd grown up in. Not only was he talking to me, but he would also remember our home and the ocean. My fingers slid over the shells on my necklace as memories of the briny scent of the ocean water teased me. "I'm from Bourne."

He broke into a wide smile. "Neighbors. We used to kill you guys at baseball in middle school."

"Before my time," I said. "After the bombings, I took care of my family, so I didn't get a chance to go to school again for long, much less play sports."

"That's the whole reason I volunteered when I could, so my mom and little sisters would be taken care of. My stepfather died of cancer when I was fourteen. How old are you?"

"Twenty-two, you?"

"Twenty-five."

We fell into a conversation about home and what we missed the most. We talked of what things were like before the war and how awful those months after had been when uncertainty and chaos ruled. I couldn't believe how good it felt to talk to someone who understood what it was like to leave home, to be here.

Kobal didn't speak or look at either of us, but I knew he listened to every word as his body became more rigid and his grip tightened on the wheel.

∼

KOBAL

Sue had been unmoving, barely blinking or breathing since River's head fell onto his shoulder an hour ago. He looked like he might try and burst through the windshield to get out of here as he struggled to decide what to do with her and me.

I would have found his dilemma and the expression on his face almost amusing, if the idea of her touching him didn't have me so on edge. Instead of laughing, I was trying not to shove him through the back window so I could have her head on *my* shoulder.

He seemed to understand the jeopardy he was in. I could hear his heart jackhammering in his chest, sweat beaded his forehead, and the pungent aroma of fear wafted from him. He hadn't moved an inch the entire time she slept propped against him, too afraid to touch her in order to push her away.

I could clearly recall how it felt when she'd rested her head against me in the past. The warmth and suppleness of her body, the smell of lemons and fresh rain that drifted from her silken skin had all become a part of me. Scents had always been something I was acutely attuned to, and in all my years, I'd never smelled or experienced anything as magnificent as River. Her body moving beneath and over the top of mine had been the most exquisite sensation I'd ever felt in my fifteen hundred and sixty-two years of existence.

Having her hand over my heart and her lying beside me trustingly had been humbling. She was the only woman I'd ever slept beside for the night, the only woman I ever would. Being inside of her and claiming her had changed something within me, and then I'd lost her.

Fuck!

I jerked the wheel into a clearing at the top of a hill and put the truck into park. I'd planned to stop here for the night anyway, but now I needed out of this vehicle. River lifted her head from Sue's shoulder. She blinked at him before jerking away. Her face flushed as she wiped at her mouth.

"Sorry," she muttered.

Sue gave a brisk nod as his gaze went longingly toward the door. I thrust my door open and climbed out of the cramped vehicle. I'd rather lift it up and heave it onto its side than get into it again, but unfortunately we needed it.

"What are we doing here?" River asked when she climbed out the other side of the truck.

As her eyes searched the horizon, a tremor ran through her and she circled her arms around her waist. I glanced over the burned out city below us. It was a half a mile down the hill, but close enough to see that it sat in ruins. From our vantage point, we'd be able to see anything that might come at us.

I'd seen the city before, but seeing it through her eyes, I realized it would be frightening and sad. The nukes may not have been dropped in this area, but there had still been bombs, fires, and battles waged throughout it. The few buildings still standing were crumpling beneath the years of neglect and weather they'd endured.

What remained of the buildings was gray or black with soot and fire damage, but in and around the roadways and debris, grass had bloomed, trees had taken root again, and life was returning. Deer moved amid the rubble, munching on the grass as they went. I knew other, more treacherous animals lurked amongst the buildings too, but for now, the deer were safe to venture out.

"Time to call it a day," I told her.

"Will the revenirs be in that city?" she inquired.

I pulled my attention away from the fading sunlight glinting off some of the smoke-stained windows to look at her. "They could be, but I doubt it."

"Why is that?" Sue inquired.

"The animals are still alive. The revenirs would have fed from them without humans present. Without a life force to feed from, even revenirs die."

"So does that mean there could be a bunch of rotting, mummified animals out there looking for a life force too if the revenirs fed on them?" River asked in a choked voice.

"No, only demons reanimated before and now humans. The animals of Hell, such as the madagans, simply died after the revenirs fed on them. They were not strong enough to reanimate."

"Good news," Sue muttered.

"Are we going through there tomorrow?" River asked and waved a hand at the city.

"We are," I confirmed. I'd traveled this way the last time I'd returned to the unnatural gateway years ago. This trip wouldn't be easy, and I knew there would be more than a few detours, but this was the most direct route to the gateway right now.

Walking to the back of the truck, I pulled out a sleeping bag for River. "Follow me," I said to her.

I could see her stubborn streak rising with her chin. She didn't argue, but instead turned toward her new friend. "I'll see you later, Sue."

"Call me Hawk, please, everyone else does."

My teeth ground together when she smiled at him, but I remained unmoving as she walked toward me. "I can find my own place to sleep for the night," she told me.

"I prefer you away from the humans."

Hurt flickered through her eyes, but she walked beside me toward the trees. "I'm human."

"You know that's not completely true." I didn't know how I managed to keep making her madder, but the look she shot me said she would have gladly driven my nuts into my throat.

Good thing she hasn't completely mastered wielding the flow of life yet.

"I know I'm more human than not. I care, I have compassion, and I love," she replied.

"Demons love too."

"I don't think it's in the same way."

"No," I growled, "it's deeper, more intense, and a bond created for eternity. Is that how humans love?"

"I'd like to think so, if they didn't die or…"

I stopped walking to face her when her words trailed off. "Or what?"

"Some leave or are forced to leave. Some… change and become something completely different."

There it was, what I believed to be the root of this rift between us. Lucifer had gotten into her head when she'd dreamed of him and turned her fears against her. I could not *wait* to kill that prick.

"I can assure you, I'm never going to leave you," I told her. "Or change."

Her brow furrowed. "I didn't say you were."

"But you will leave or change?"

"Time will tell," she murmured. She tore her eyes away from me and looked around the place where we stood. "Is this where I'm supposed to sleep tonight?"

Frustration warred within me. I wanted to shake her, to demand she talk to me. At the same time, I wanted to draw her close and hold her. However, she'd purposely changed the conversation, and pushing it would only cause her to withdraw from me further. I ran a hand through my hair as I turned away from her, deciding to let it go, for now.

"No." I started walking again, leading her toward a copse of trees that would keep her more sheltered than the humans settling into the clearing.

"Being segregated from them isn't going to help them trust me," she said.

"But it will keep you safe."

"They're not a threat to me. Eileen was a fluke. She was obsessed with you and saw me as an obstacle to being with you."

The reminder caused my fangs to lengthen. It had been my past with the human that had nearly gotten River killed, but I'd never promised the woman anything, or ever offered to further our relationship to anything beyond our one sexual encounter.

"Her sense of reasoning was flawed," I told her.

"Maybe *your* sense of reasoning is flawed," she retorted.

"Sex was the only thing between us." I hated her involuntary wince from my words, but there was no denying what had happened between Eileen and me.

"She disagreed."

"She was an idiot, and if she hadn't tried to kill you, she would still be alive."

"We're so different," she murmured.

"We are," I confirmed. "Your compassion for a woman who would have gladly seen you dead confounds me. I will never understand it, but I accept it." Her head tilted to the side as she studied me. "You have to accept that anyone who is a threat to you will meet a violent death by my hand, no matter if you welcome me into your bed again or not."

Her eyes darkened at the reminder of what we had once shared. She instinctively swayed toward me. When I pressed closer to her, her breath caught and she bit on her bottom lip as her head tilted back to watch me. The scent of her arousal caused my cock to swell.

"He'll use me against you," she whispered.

"No one will get the chance to do that."

"I could become like him."

"That's a *lie*. Don't you ever believe it."

Her hands lifted toward me before falling back to her sides. She shook her head and took a step back.

"River—"

"Kobal!" The shout drew her attention away from me and toward Bale as she strode across the grass toward us. I opened my mouth to tell Bale to leave us, but her next words stopped me. "Something has been spotted on the horizon!"

I gripped River's arm, pulling her protectively against my side as I walked with her out of the trees and back toward the hill where the demons and some humans had gathered. I stepped in between Bale and Corson as I searched where Bale pointed into the city. An icy chill ran down my back when I recognized the creatures on the horizon.

"What are those?" River breathed.

"Lanavours," I grated from between my teeth. "The third seal has fallen."

"Nightmares now walk the earth," Verin said. "Which means the second seal has also been set free."

"Shit," Corson muttered. "Not good, this is *not* good."

No, it most certainly was not good, considering what had been locked behind the second seal. I glanced at the hellhounds on my arm. I still felt no severing in the connection between myself and any of the hounds, but I had to get to them soon and find out what was going on. Find out how something was getting by them to break the seals I'd left the hounds behind to protect. If River could close the gateway, I'd return to Hell after to seek out the answers eluding me now.

"Are we in danger here?" River asked.

"No, not if we stay out of sight," I replied. "Go join the humans and get some food. I must establish a guard. Shax, go with her."

"You know," she said quietly, "ordering me about is not sexy and it's certainly *not* endearing. I also don't need a bodyguard."

With that, she turned on her heel and walked away. I bit back a groan. Every step I took forward with her seemed to result in two steps back. Shax hesitated as he looked between the two of us.

"Go," I commanded, knowing she would resent it but unwilling to leave her unprotected.

He nodded before following after her. River strode over to

where the humans had gathered to watch the lanavours moving through the fading light illuminating the city. Shax shadowed her.

Turning away, I scowled at Bale and Corson when I found them snickering as they tried to hide their laughter.

"Tact," Corson said to me.

"Fuck tact."

"Yes, but tact would probably get you laid again."

Corson backed up, his grin vanishing when I stepped closer to him. I was more infuriated that he'd talked about River in such a way than his flippant attitude.

"Easy," Morax counseled as he stepped in between us and rested his hand on my chest. "He doesn't understand the bond, Kobal. With luck, he will one day."

Corson glared at him before his eyes darted toward me. Morax nudged Corson back with his shoulder. "This isn't something you screw with, Corson," I heard Morax whisper to him. "I don't know how he's keeping it together now."

I had no other choice but to keep it together.

I focused on the city again and the creatures moving along the far edge of it. We'd have to do everything we could to keep the humans far from them. I'd seen what these things could do to a demon. What they would do to a human was something I couldn't think about, not with River so near.

"Should we go another way?" Corson inquired.

"They'll probably move on before morning," Bale said.

"I think they're moving on now," Verin replied. "There are less of them already."

"There are," I agreed.

I'd kill them all if they came this way, but the lanavours could inflict a lot of damage before I was able to destroy them.

CHAPTER SEVEN

RIVER

My eyes fluttered open. I lay completely still as I stared at the night, trying to recall where I was and what had woken me. The trees swaying in the slight July breeze, the sleeping bag around me, and the fresh scent of the summer air reminded me that we'd left the wall behind and I was camped out in the woods.

Then, I heard a noise. My eyes shot to the woods. Heat burned across my cheeks when I recognized the muffled moans of sex coming from the trees to my right. I couldn't see beyond the foliage blocking my view to who was out there. It sounded as if they were fifty feet or so away, but the forest distorted and reflected sounds so I couldn't be sure.

Please don't be Kobal. I didn't think I could take it if I had to listen to him having sex with another woman.

The idea of it made my stomach turn as I was bombarded with the urge to scream or cry. Together or not, I may kill him if he were out there right now with someone else. I didn't think he would be so cruel as to have sex with someone else so close to me, but when it came to our relationship, I barely knew up from down anymore.

A man grunted and a woman emitted a muffled cry. It didn't sound like Kobal, but perhaps his idea of being kind was to try to cover his voice. Flopping onto my back, I went to tug the pillow against my ears to block the sounds when I found a pair of entirely black eyes staring at me from where he lay on a sleeping bag a few feet away.

The moon's rays caressed his bare chest, illuminating the flames on him and the chiseled ridges of his abs. The term washboard didn't begin to describe those abs. Every powerful muscle of his body was carved perfection. My hands clenched against the compulsion to run my fingers over his jaw and feel the smoothness of his hairless skin beneath my touch. My heartbeat picked up as the impulse left me breathless.

"They woke you," he said, his voice gruffer than normal.

"I thought it might be you." I realized my brain was still sleep addled when those words blurted out of me.

His gaze ran over my face as he propped his head on his hand. "Not unless I was with you in those woods. If you'd let me, I'd be inside of you again tonight."

My mouth went dry at his words and the memories they evoked. I could clearly recall the sensation of his body moving over and within me. The taste and smell of him beneath my mouth and fingers. The rigid length of his erection as he pumped his hips in rhythm with mine. I felt half drugged by those memories and he was simply staring at me in that unwavering way of his.

"You returned to the fire," I managed to get out.

It was the biggest defense I had against him right now as I completely forgot every other reason I'd been using to keep myself from him. He'd told me I was his Chosen, that he'd claimed me, but when I'd turned him away from my bed, he'd happily returned to the orgy-like sex taking place nightly at the large bonfire the demons held at the wall.

He frowned at me. "No, I didn't."

"Then where were you?" My voice came out more accusing than I'd intended, but the sharp knife of jealousy twisted in my heart. "You left Bale watching over me and didn't come back to the tent."

His teeth grated together so forcefully I could hear them. "You believed I was having sex with another?"

Obviously. "Weren't you?"

"No. I realize you are part human, you were raised as one of them, have their emotions, and you don't fully comprehend demons or the way we are, but you are my Chosen. You may not understand what that means to a demon, to *me*, but understand this, there is *no* one else for me. I have no desire for another woman and no one else will ever satisfy me again. I had to get out of the tent to keep from crawling into bed with you. I slept on the ground outside where I couldn't hear you at night, but I could still keep you safe."

Words failed me as what he'd said made my entire body tremble and my heart soar. However, there were still so *many* reasons why being with him was a bad idea. I merely had to remember them all, and right now, my body didn't care what my brain stuttered out.

"I'm mortal," I whispered.

I didn't know why I'd said it other than it was the one thing neither of us had ever acknowledged about our relationship. I would age and die and he would still be here, looking the same and living for another millennia or hundreds of millennia more.

His nostrils flared, and his nails lengthened into claws briefly before retracting again. "I know."

"You'll be left alone when I die."

"I'll never be alone while I have your memory."

"Corson told me about his parents. He told me his mother couldn't handle the loss of his father and threw herself into the fires after."

A muscle in his jaw twitched. "And you fear the same for me?"

"More than you know."

"Do not."

"That's easier said than done. In my dream, Lucifer—"

"He lied, River," he bit out from between his teeth. "Demons are stronger when they find their Chosen, he knows that. Your powers are growing and will continue to do so, he knows that too. He will do or say anything to stop you, to stop me. *You* could never become like him, ever."

The crickets chirruped around us as clouds rolled in to block some of the moonlight spilling over us. "You believe him to be my father, and he believes I will become evil. My mother always told me I was the spawn of Satan, tainted and corrupted. What if they're all right and you're not willing to see it because I am your Chosen?"

His lips skimmed back to reveal his lengthening fangs. "The woman lying before me, the one who held her brothers so close and with such love could never become those things. You are far from corrupt or evil. Your mother and Lucifer sought to break you, but they didn't. You are everything you humans would consider good, River."

"What if he uses me against you?" I whispered around the lump in my throat his words had created. I didn't stop him when he reached out to brush his thumb across my cheek. "I'm the only weapon he has against you that he never had before."

"He doesn't have you, and he never will. You're also a *strength* I never had before, and he knows that."

His fingers slid over my face and he stared at me with a reverence that robbed me of my breath. He made me feel like the most beautiful woman in the world when he looked at me like that.

"I can't condone what you did to Eileen," I said.

The faint, fiery scent of his skin drifted to me as he moved closer to me. He smelled better than the ocean, I decided, and he was such an opposite force from the sea that had been such an integral part of my life before him. Fire and water had become everything to me.

"I know I handle things with you badly sometimes, but it's only because I *have* to keep you with me for as long as I'm allowed to have you. When I saw that woman trying to kill you and I couldn't get to you…"

He broke off, and for the first time ever, I saw a vulnerability in him I'd never imagined could exist. The molten-gold color his eyes became robbed me of my breath. I loved those obsidian pools, but these amber eyes, so much more human with their whites around his cornea, were more feral and wolf-like. They were more *him*.

"I snapped. I'm not saying it won't happen again. It will if your life is at stake," he said. "And I will not hesitate to do it again. Not for you. But I will not do it with such haste again, and I will not kill a human unless it is necessary."

I remained unmoving, unsure of what to say or do. He was overbearing, bossy, impatient, and vicious, but he *did* care for me. And I had lost my heart to him before I'd even realized it. I was bound to him in some way I could never explain and couldn't deny.

"What if Lucifer somehow gets a hold of me, and don't say it will never happen. It could. What then?"

"Then I will do everything I can to get you back."

"He must be stopped."

"I know."

I seized his hand, drawing his eyes away from my lips and back to me. "No matter what it takes, he must be stopped."

His hand squeezed mine. "I will do whatever is necessary to put back to right what Lucifer and the humans have destroyed."

"Including sacrificing me."

I could feel the fury vibrating through him as his muscles bulged before me. "I will do what must be done. There are thousands of demons depending on me, fighting for me. They have been for over fifteen hundred years. I won't let them down."

I rested my palm against his cheek, relishing in his flesh beneath my hand. My body reacted as if it had been starved and was finally being sated as it jerked toward him and golden-white sparks of life danced over my fingers.

"I will defend your life with my own, River," he grated.

"I'm scared of what I could become."

"I know, but I'm not."

I didn't argue with him further. I couldn't. He believed in me and I believed in him.

My hand pressed more firmly against his cheek as he held my gaze. A wetness spread between my legs as my starved body prepared itself for what it had been lacking. *Him.*

Growling low in his throat, his hands settled on my waist and he dragged me against him, sleeping bag and all. His teeth bashed against mine when his mouth claimed my lips in a brutal assault. I eagerly welcomed him as our lips ground together and my mouth opened to the demanding probing of his tongue. He swept past my lips and into my mouth to taste me in deep, penetrating thrusts that had me nearly going out of my mind with need.

Too long. Denied for far too long.

I needed him and the rush of life and power he brought to me. Needed him inside of me, claiming and marking me again. The sensuous dance of his tongue entwining with mine had me tugging at his hair and grinding against his erection like a wild woman.

Yes, we'd both been starved, and I didn't care how brutal it was. I wanted him inside of me so badly I found myself pawing at his back and chest. Grabbing hold of my sleeping bag, he jerked it back. I didn't know if the zipper came undone or if he simply tore it apart, and I didn't care. The night air brushing over my skin did nothing to cool the ardor growing within me.

A mewl escaped me when he pulled back, his lips brushing against mine as he spoke. "No going back, no denying me. If we do this tonight, River, I will never let you go again. *Ever.*"

His amber eyes searched mine as savagery radiated from him. I couldn't catch my breath, couldn't think. I knew he meant those words, knew if I tried to escape him again, he would never let me walk away. If I tried to, I may become the thing that destroyed the man he was now and turned him into something far more savage and uncaring, like Lucifer.

But could I throw myself into this? Could I push aside all doubts and worries and give myself over completely? Then I recalled Corson's words to me right after I'd separated myself from Kobal. *"Will you survive without him?"*

The answer now had been the same as it was then, no.

This powerful bond between us, our uncertain future, and Lucifer's words all frightened me, but I couldn't continue on without him. He was a piece of me.

His eyes became distant, and his hold on me eased as he started to draw away from me while I tried to put everything together. "I won't ever tell you to go again," I whispered.

His body thrummed with tension before something within him seemed to unravel completely. The harsh sound he released reminded me of an animal defending its mate. My fingers curled into the thick muscles of his broad back when he leaned over me, dragging me against his chest.

His hands were curling in my shirt. Seconds before he tore the front of my shirt open, exposing my flesh to his hands, I recalled I'd started to strip before going to him to save my clothing. I'd slept with my bra on in case we had to move fast from here. He didn't bother with trying to find the clasp before slicing the front open with one of his claws.

I sucked in a breath, arching toward him when he pulled his mouth away from mine to greedily lick and knead at my exposed flesh. I squirmed beneath him, my body begging for more, seeking release from the overwhelming sensations crashing through me. I considered myself mostly human, it was what I knew best after all, but in his arms, I was something completely *in*human. Something uninhibited and primitive.

My nails raked down his back. He lifted my hips into the air and thrust his erection against my center in a way that had my breath coming in rapid pants and my body bucking uncontrollably beneath his.

His tongue laved my nipple, swirling around it before sucking it eagerly into his mouth. He pulled on it as he nipped it with his teeth.

"Kobal!"

I had to be put out of my misery, but I never wanted this wondrous torment to stop. As he released my nipple, I felt the scrape of his four fangs against the sensitive flesh of my breast before he bit. A shriek of bliss caught in my throat as waves of pleasure battered my body. My hands scrunched in his hair, holding him closer as he marked me as his again. I didn't realize how badly I'd missed this claiming until my entire body cried out in relief and bliss.

He released my breast before biting down on my shoulder and then my neck. My nails raked over his back again, causing him to moan. Turning my face into his shoulder, I didn't resist the impulse to bite down. I clamped onto his flesh to once again mark him for everyone to see. I was going to orgasm just from the taste and feel of him as the tension within my body coiled higher and he ground against me.

His hands tore at my pants, ripping the button and zipper away as he shredded the cloth from me. "Harder," he snarled in my ear. My teeth clamped down on his shoulder more as he pulled aside my ruined clothes to bare me to him. "*Harder*, River."

I felt his hands tugging at the button on his pants and then heard more cloth being torn away. I bit deeper into his flesh, spilling his blood. The hot influx of it filled me, seeping into my body.

CHAPTER EIGHT

KOBAL

I couldn't control myself as her luscious breasts molded against my chest and her small teeth punctured my flesh. I could never forget how amazing it was to have her in my arms, but the sights and sounds of her overwhelmed me. The *scent* of her had me on the verge of coming as I slipped my hand between her thighs.

The black curls shielding her sex were already wet with her wanting for me as my fingers slid over the delicious heat of her. "So wet," I breathed against her ear. "For *me*."

Her bite on me eased, causing my hands to entangle in her hair as I held her closer. "Only for you," she panted against my neck.

I pulled her head back to expose the delicate column of her throat. Striking, unable to control myself, I sank my fangs into her at the same time I thrust a finger into her tight, hot recesses. A cry escaped her as she ground more demandingly against my finger. Stretching her further, I slipped another finger inside her to better prepare her for me.

Her hands slid between us, her fist wrapping around my rigid dick as she stroked upward, causing my hips to surge forward within her grasp. I wanted to draw this out, to make it last for hours, but if she kept doing that, I was going to spill all over her lithe body.

Sparks of life danced across her fingertips, lighting the night as they burst over my skin. I withdrew my fangs from her neck to watch her as the sparks illuminated her pretty features and the exquisiteness of her amethyst eyes staring dazedly back at me. I'd encountered many beautiful women in my extensive life, but all of them paled in comparison to River with those sparks playing over her face and bathing her in an ethereal light.

She was mine. She was where I belonged and always would. I thrust forward again, driving my fingers deeper within her. Bending my head, I swirled my tongue over one of her taut, dusky nipples, relishing in the gasp she emitted.

"Kobal!"

My name on her lips caused me to shudder. Her thumb rubbed over the tip of my dick, spreading the bead of moisture forming there across the sensitive surface. My cock jerked in her grip, aching for release. I could explore her body for hours again later. Right now, I had to be inside of her before I lost complete control of myself.

RIVER

"I have to be inside you."

His words barely registered in my dazed mind before his fingers were slipping away and he was pulling his shaft from my grasp. His hands curled into my skin as he lifted my hips. I felt the head of him against my entrance before he thrust his hard, thick erection into me and his body took possession of mine.

Home. I was home again.

I couldn't breathe, couldn't think beyond my need for him and the ecstasy rocking through me. Why had I ever denied us both this? Why had I ever wasted one second not being with him?

I couldn't recall now as my heart swelled with love and my muscles grasped greedily around the heavy length filling me until I couldn't tell where he stopped and I began. He was a part of me, and I was a part of him. Reacting on instinct, I sank my teeth into his shoulder again and licked over the saltiness of his skin.

My hands grasped at his firm ass as he pulled back before driving into me again. I let go of my hold on him, inhaling greedy gulps of air as I became caught up in the tempest of our reunion. I was so close to finding the release I'd been denying myself, so close to the edge.

A mewl of disappointment escaped me when he abruptly pulled out of me. Lifting me up, he turned me over so I was on my hands and knees before him. My fingers dug into the cool earth as he knelt behind me and nudged my knees apart. Taking hold of his shaft, he guided it to my entrance once more and thrust into me again.

The flow of life beneath my hands and the feel of him within me, caused more sparks to fire over my fingers and hands. Their glow spread to my wrists as he encircled one arm around my waist to keep me up when my arms almost gave out.

I couldn't breathe. I was too consumed by the sensations rioting through my body to think of anything beyond how right this felt. He took me with a savagery I'd never experienced before, and I loved it. I craved his ownership of my body right then more than I wanted my next breath.

Fisting my long hair in his hand, he leaned back, pulling me off the ground so that my back was against his chest as he continued to drive into me. His other hand wrapped around my throat, holding it loosely in his grasp while he pinned me against him. My fingers dug into his arm as his next bite caused fresh waves of pleasure to radiate through my body.

Releasing his bite on my neck, his breath rasped against my ear when he rested his lips there. "Are you ready to come for me,

River?" His fingers tightened on my throat. His other hand slid between my legs to brush teasingly against my clit. My hips surged toward his fingers as he relentlessly pumped in and out of me. "Are you?"

"Yes!" I panted, out of my mind with the need for release.

His fingers stroked over me as he continued to thrust into me. I fractured, my body coming completely apart as waves of ecstasy crashed through me and my limbs went weak from my orgasm. Behind me, he again sank his fangs into my shoulder before abruptly pulling out of me. Against my back, I felt the hot brand of his semen lashing my skin.

His breathing was ragged when he released his bite on me, buried his face in my neck and inhaled. I wanted his release inside of me, to feel him filling me, but no matter how badly I wanted it, I knew it was a bad idea. He hadn't spilled inside of me since our first time when we'd both agreed getting pregnant right now would prove disastrous.

A shiver went through me when he sat back and the night air brushed over my flushed skin. Grabbing a ruined piece of clothing, he tenderly cleaned my back off before dragging me down to the ground and enveloping my body with his. He tugged the sleeping bag around us both and rolled over to cushion me against his chest.

"I was too rough with you. Did I hurt you?" he inquired.

"No you weren't. I… that was amazing," I breathed.

His fingers trailed up my arm before resting on one of his bites on my neck. "I meant what I said, I won't let you leave me again." His voice was ragged and hoarse against my ear, and his arms tightened around me as he pulled me closer.

I ran my hand over his sweat-slickened flesh. "I know. I won't try to leave you again, but that doesn't mean I won't fight you on some things."

His breath tickled my neck when he chuckled. "I'd never expect you to stop standing up for what you believe in."

"Good."

"We're just getting started tonight, Mah Kush-la."

Hearing his endearment for me, meaning my heart in his own language, caused warmth to pool through me. It had been far too long since I'd heard him say it. "I certainly hope so."

I felt him lengthen against my thigh before he slipped into me again.

CHAPTER NINE

KOBAL

"You really have to stop ruining my clothes."

I glanced over at River as she held her shredded shirt and torn bra before her. "I'd prefer it if you didn't wear anything," I admitted with a smile.

Her head tilted to the side as she placed her hands on her bare hips. "You'd prefer it if I walked around naked in front of everyone?"

My smile vanished at the idea of anyone other than me seeing her body. My admiring gaze ran over her full breasts and flat, faintly muscular stomach. Her rounded hips were enticing, but not nearly as enticing as those black curls shielding her sex from me. And those thighs, I grew hard simply thinking about spreading those thighs and dipping my head between them to taste her. She was toned from all of her training, but still curvy and her stamina nearly matched my own.

"No one else will see you," I told her.

"Well, that is what's going to happen if you keep ruining what little clothing I brought for this journey."

"Good point."

"I'm going to need some clothes from the truck."

"I'll get them." I walked over to kiss her forehead. My eyes closed as I inhaled her delicious scent and pulled her against me. I hated this vulnerable, unfamiliar feeling within me. I was leading her toward her possible death and all I wanted was to protect her from any harm.

She was mortal, but she didn't have the same frailties as most humans. She had more lethal power within her than many of the demons I'd encountered over my extensive life, but she could still be killed with a single blow. I could end her mortality, take away her biggest vulnerability, but at what cost? What would she become if I turned her? Would she even survive it? Would she even want to try to become an immortal once she learned the risks?

They were questions I wanted the answers to, but I wasn't willing to put her in the position of answering them now. When this was over, I would discuss it with her.

"Kobal, I'm naked."

"I know." My hands slid over her hips toward her thighs.

"We have to get moving."

"We will."

She laughed and took a step back. "Now." I went to take hold of her again but she danced beyond my reach. "They're going to come looking for us soon if we don't get moving."

I groaned in frustration, but she was right. Searching the surrounding forest, I scented for any hint of a threat, but all I detected was the wildlife creeping through the underbrush and the birds flitting through the trees. Satisfied it would be safe to leave her here, I lifted her sleeping bag and draped it around her shoulders before kissing her nose. "I'll be right back."

It took only a few minutes to gather her clothes and some breakfast for her before returning to her. I watched her dress then handed her the food. She eagerly ate the apple and beef jerky before rising to slide her holster and guns around her waist and buckling it there.

Almost everyone else was gathered around the vehicles when we exited the woods. I kept my hand on her elbow as I led her toward where Sue stood by the passenger door of the truck.

All of the humans' eyes followed us, but none of them spoke or whispered like they had when I'd first claimed her as mine. And there was no denying I'd claimed her again. We both bore the marks on our necks for them to see.

"I'm going to have you drive, Sue," I said when we reached him and I handed out the keys.

"Hawk," he said and took the keys from me.

I didn't acknowledge his correction before turning to River. "Ride with him." A muscle in her jaw twitched when her teeth clamped together. I forced myself to add, "Please."

She relaxed a little. "What about you?" she inquired.

"I'm going to walk through the city with the others. There are too many places for something to hide amongst those buildings. We'll be ready in case of an attack."

"I'll walk with you."

"I'd prefer it if you didn't."

"I'm stronger than you think," she insisted.

"I know."

"Then let me walk with you."

My eyes fell to the marks on her neck, the four sets of imprints from where my upper and lower fangs had sunk into her repeatedly. *Mine.* My initial impulse was to tell her no and order her into the truck, but that would only earn me her lethal stare and the cold shoulder. She'd just returned to me; I didn't want to risk losing her again, but giving in to her went against every instinct I had to protect her.

Pick your battles.

I didn't pick my battles. I was the rightful king of Hell. I spoke and others obeyed. She was the only one who challenged my decisions. The only one who had the courage to do so.

"I'll agree to it if you agree to do what I tell you if something happens," I said.

A smile lit her face. Apparently, compromising *was* the better way to go as she fairly bounced on her toes while she squeezed my hand. "I will."

I lifted my head to find Corson biting on his lip, trying not to laugh. My glower caused him to turn away, but his shoulders shook with laughter as he walked. The new, dangling blue feathers hanging from his ears were begging to be torn free. River hurried to the back of the truck and pulled out the katana she'd stashed there. She slid it over her shoulder and adjusted it before looking toward me expectantly.

"Let's go!" I barked.

River fell into step beside me as the vehicles began their descent toward the remains of the destroyed city below. Her arm brushed against mine as we walked next to the pickup and into the city. Her right hand rested on one of the handguns strapped to her side.

She'd become extremely adept at using the weapons over the past couple of months, but it was the life energy she could draw on and wield that would be her most lethal weapon. If she learned how to use it better. Bale and Corson had both said she'd made some improvement with it, but her ability was nowhere near as developed as I would have liked it to be. I had faith her powers would grow the more she used them, and I didn't doubt she would have to use them a few times before we arrived at the unnatural gateway.

We couldn't have delayed our timeline for leaving the wall. The longer we waited, the more seals Lucifer could break open and the more disastrous life would become on earth. It had taken him thirteen years to figure out how to break the first seal, but now they were falling quickly, and there was no way of knowing if more than the first three seals had already been broken.

The humans had weapons that were effective against us, but

they wouldn't be able to stop the creatures spilling out of Hell if all those seals fell. Nothing could. The balance between Heaven, Earth, and Hell had kept the humans safe and held steady for hundreds of thousands of years. Then, Lucifer had been cast from Heaven six thousand years ago, and instead of dying as the angels had intended, he'd somehow figured out a way to enter Hell.

His desire to take over the underworld had led to numerous battles and wars that my ancestors had led and died in. I was the first varcolac to have fought him numerous times and survived. Thirteen years ago, our battles within Hell had been thrust into the human realm when the humans had torn open an unnatural gateway into Hell. It had been the first gateway that I couldn't close on my own, and it had effectively ended the division between our two worlds.

When the gateway had first been torn open and demons had spilled into their realm, the humans had panicked and tried to destroy us. They soon realized that their guns could slow us, and their bombs could kill us, sometimes. Other times they just pissed us off more.

Mac had been wise enough not to try to bomb me when I'd first encountered him and his small struggling army a year after the humans had ripped Hell open. We were the best help the humans would ever get against fighting Lucifer and keeping him from walking this land again.

Tilting my head back, I studied the clear sky and the midmorning sun already baking the landscape around us. The heat of the sun was nothing compared to the fires of Hell. I had barely broken a sweat, but many of the humans around me were trying desperately to hide in what little shade they could find. River was sweating more than I was, but I'd noticed the heat had less of an effect on her than it did her fellow humans.

Another demon trait. Another sign she might be able to withstand Hell enough to enter it if she's unable to close the gate and we are unable to draw Lucifer out.

It was bad enough I was taking her this close to Lucifer and the pit of Hell, but I still held out hope that she'd never have to know what it was like to walk in there. It was my home. It's where I had been forged from the Fires of Creation themselves, and it was no place for her. If I succeeded in claiming my throne, I would spend a lot of my time on Earth with her afterward.

Beside me, the truck creaked as it bounced over the pitted road. Green grass had taken over the base of the buildings surrounding us. Ivy climbed high to consume their dilapidated façades.

Despite the new growth, signs of war and devastation were still visible throughout. I knew River spotted the skeletal remains near the base of a fountain when she took a step closer to me. Everywhere I looked, more piles of bones could be seen laying in and among the new vegetation.

"So many lives lost," River whispered.

When we passed another building, crows bellowed caws of annoyance as their wings beat against the air. More birds soared into the sky from a crumbling building with a red maple tree growing up through its empty center. Beneath the rubble, I spotted more remains of the dead, trapped and forgotten forever in the destruction.

"Did anyone survive what happened out here in these states?" she asked.

"Some did. Mac did."

"He did?" she squeaked.

"Yes. Mac was in Chicago when the boundaries between our dimensions were ripped apart. He was part of the military there and was ordered to pull out almost immediately. Your government tried to evacuate as many people as possible when the gateway was opened, but when the horde spilled out from Hell, they panicked. So did the countries on the other side of the world. They all bombed in the hopes of stopping the flow and saving the rest of their people."

"But it didn't stop the demons?"

"It killed some of them if they took a direct hit. It helped to stem the flow by making them warier of humans. Radiation has no effect on us, but dropping a bomb on us can kill us. The human leaders were smart enough to realize they couldn't continuously try to destroy us though."

"And why is that?"

"Because I would have slaughtered them all before I allowed such a thing to continue. Lucifer's followers, the Craetons, have to be stopped, but I would not stand by and watch the humans destroy my entire species because they screwed up. Badly."

"And you think you could have gotten to our president and all the leaders around the world in order to kill them?"

"I know I could have. It wouldn't have been difficult for me to do so."

Her gaze ran appraisingly over me. "No, I suppose it wouldn't have. Not for you."

"Besides, they didn't know that Hell would absorb most of the nuclear fallout. In the beginning, the only reason they stopped bombing was because they believed if they continued to do so, they would kill all of humanity with radiation exposure. By the time they realized they could drop more bombs, we'd already joined forces with them. We agreed to work together to build the wall, train the volunteers, and take down the Craetons. Then, after Bale's vision, we worked together to search for you."

She frowned as she studied a sagging building before turning back to me. "It's so weird to think you were looking for me for four years before we met."

"I've been looking for you since the moment I first rose from the Fires of Creation." I hadn't realized it until meeting her, but now I knew it to be true.

My heart clenched as she gazed at me in what could only be called wonder. This woman, with her demon and angel lineage was far more fragile than me with her mortality, yet she made me feel as weak as a human when she gazed at me like that. If something ever happened to her…

Nothing would, I would not allow it.

"I bet you never expected your Chosen to be a human, much less a descendent of Lucifer," she said.

I'd come to realize she refused to see herself as Lucifer's daughter, but she was. I believed it was her way of distancing herself from the bastard who had created her. "You're also part demon," I reminded her.

A smile tugged at the corners of her lips. "And part angel. Bet you didn't see that one coming either."

I leaned closer to her and pressed my mouth against her ear. "But you fuck like a demon."

She turned red so fast I could feel the heat coming off her flesh. The look she shot me would have made most men cover their balls, but I also heard the increased beat of her heart and the hitch in her breath.

Brushing back a loose strand of her hair that had slipped from the knot on her head, my fingers lingered on her cheek before I stepped away. She was still staring at me as if she couldn't decide if she wanted to punch me or jump me, when the pure amethyst of her eyes faded to a lighter violet color. She stopped abruptly, and her head tilted back to study the surface of the building behind me. I realized in that second she was having a vision.

I'd learned there was no rousing her when a vision took her over; I despised how vulnerable she became during them. Gripping her arm, I focused on her in the hopes she would drag me into her vision as she had before, so I could see what she was seeing. It didn't work; her eyes were already returning to their normal hue as she came around seconds later.

"There is something up there," she breathed. "Hideous, awful." She pulled her guns from their holsters. "And they're coming."

"Stop," I commanded, slapping my hand on the side of the pickup.

Hawk hit the brakes so forcefully the truck lurched and the tires squeaked. I turned to search the burnt-out building River was focused on as the other vehicles halted on the road. There was no movement from inside the twisted steel beams and piles of broken glass, but I didn't doubt River's visions. If she'd seen it, it was coming.

"Get out of the trucks and get your weapons ready!" I called to the others. Hawk pushed the door of the pickup open an inch before I shoved it closed again. "Not you. You have to be ready to get her out of here if I need you to," I told him. River shot me a look. "You agreed to do what I told you," I reminded her.

Her jaw clenched, but she gave me a brief nod. My attention returned to the building as I scanned the floors looming high above us. Doors closed around me as the humans exited their trucks and moved in closer. In the stillness following, I heard something flapping in the breeze and spotted the tattered remains of a curtain hitting the side of the building as it blew out of one of the windows.

Corson and Bale moved to flank River. The seconds turned into a full minute before a single ticking sound drew my attention to a broken window higher up. A single, gray claw had appeared to curve around the edge of the steel frame of the window. My gaze fixated on it as the claw tapped against the frame. It was impossible to tell exactly what kind of demon or Hell creature we were facing without seeing its whole body.

Then a head poked over the top of the window. My lips skimmed back, and my fangs lengthened as flames erupted from my fingers and licked toward my shoulders.

"Gargoyles," Corson growled.

"Are you serious?" a human blurted.

"Yes," Corson replied.

I watched the creature crawl out from over the top of the broken window. It's scaled, slate-colored skin cracked and flaked off as it leisurely climbed down the building on all fours. The sticky, glue-like substance on its palms gave it traction as it moved. Its three-foot-long tail flicked back and forth like a bored cat on the hunt, and there was no doubt this monstrosity was on the hunt.

There were few things in life I found truly ugly, gargoyles were one of them. They had pushed in snouts, mustard-colored eyes, and razor-sharp teeth that clacked together when they closed in on their prey. That clacking sound increased in intensity as it continued its descent and its tail twitched faster.

Gray wings unfurled from its back and flapped once. They crashed against a remaining pane of glass, causing jagged fissures across the surface. Startled cries escaped a few of the humans. They had to keep it together, or they would all be slaughtered, and we couldn't afford to lose them so early in the journey. I needed their extra protection for River.

"Guns ready!" I commanded. "And whatever you do, don't let them scratch you with their claws!"

"Them?" a soldier asked.

As if on cue, at least fifteen more gargoyles emerged from inside to perch on the broken edges of the building. They sat as still as their stone counterparts in the human realm. Humans had come so close to recreating things they'd glimpsed through the veil that had once separated our worlds; gargoyles may have been one of the closest.

The gargoyle's stillness and their ability to remain unmoving for years on end was well known by the demon world. They often entered a hibernation state when they were unable to kill and feed. Kept separate from all demons in Hell, behind the second seal, gargoyles were often reserved to punish demons who tried to launch an uprising and failed, or for the worst souls who entered Hell. Their claws contained a paralyzing agent they used on their prey. When their victim was paralyzed, the gargoyles would peel the skin from their victims, one strip at a time, and leisurely eat it in front of them.

Once there was nothing but muscle and bone left, the creatures would wait until the skin regenerated before starting the whole process all over again. I'd witnessed it once, and though I'd appreciated the brutality and torment of the act, I'd never gone back to watch it again.

They all fluttered their three-foot-wide wings at once, causing a breeze to blow down the building and over all those gathered below. A wailing cry escaped them before they launched simultaneously into flight. Gunfire exploded in the air as they swooped down on us.

CHAPTER TEN

RIVER

The flames licking over Kobal's skin warmed my body as the grotesque gargoyles launched themselves into the sky. Their wings whistled as they cut through the air and dove toward us. The flying monkeys in *The Wizard of Oz* had frightened me as a child. These monsters made them look cute.

Gunfire erupted around us. I lifted my Glock and took aim at the one honing in on Kobal. What was inside of me was far more lethal than any bullet, and I'd been getting better at using my abilities, but there was no guarantee I'd be able to control them. I couldn't take the chance that I might mess up somehow and take out one of the buildings, or worse, one of the demons or humans.

I fired, hitting the gargoyle in one of its gnarled wings. All that succeeded in doing was causing black goo to shoot into the air and pissing it off. Its roar vibrated the earth beneath my feet as it continued to swoop toward us.

Kobal released a stream of fire from his hand that knocked it off its course. He wrapped his arm around my waist, jerking me against him and spinning toward the side as one I hadn't seen dove at us. It folded its wings against its back as it came at us with the speed and accuracy of a missile.

Kobal dragged me beneath him, pressing me into the ground and rolling with me. His body covered mine, keeping it completely shielded as another gargoyle swept by us. Somehow, he managed to turn over and release another wave of fire. The flames smashed into the creature and licked over its skin. The gargoyle screeched as it flew backward, its body a spiraling ball of fire tumbling through the air before crashing against a stone fountain.

Gunfire continued to erupt around us, but the hideous creatures dove in and out, dodging the bullets with preternatural grace. Those that were hit showed no sign of slowing down as they continued their attack.

The flames licking over Kobal increased until his entire upper body was consumed by the fire. I didn't know why they didn't sear my skin from my body, but I could feel their growing heat.

Surrounded by screams of terror and panic, I focused on bringing the fire within me to life. Fear was the biggest motivator for my fire, and right now, my heart felt like it was going to explode out of my chest. I had enough adrenaline coursing through me to fuel the fire for a day.

Flames spread over my fingers and up to my wrist. Leaping to his feet, Kobal spun as gunshots burst through the air and more people screamed. Lifting my flaming hand in front of me, I slid under the truck and rolled to the other side, keeping it away from my clothes.

Kobal could protect the people on that side, but there were others over here who needed help. I stuck my hands and head out on the other side just as piranha-like fangs snapped in my face. The motion blew my hair straight back and covered me in a blanket of hot, rancid breath.

I ducked back beneath the vehicle, trying not to vomit as the strips of flesh caught between the creature's teeth waved back and forth. The gargoyle shoved its snout beneath the truck. Its talons clicked over the broken asphalt as it hunted beneath the truck for me.

I glanced at the gas tank behind me then the fire encircling my hand as one of those claws came within a centimeter of my arm. It was only a matter of time before it got me. I could go back, retreat to Kobal's side, but I wasn't ready to give into this monster, not yet.

Timing its snapping jaws, I waited until its mouth was closed before grasping its snout. Bits of flaky skin broke off beneath my hand, and scales abraded my palms from its sandpaper-like flesh. Before it could open its mouth again, fire flared hotter from my hand and seared across its snout.

The creature released a howl before recoiling from beneath the truck. A breeze drifted over my cheeks when its wings fanned the air. It launched itself backward into the sky and out of view. My gaze lifted to the undercarriage above me; thankfully, it wasn't on fire.

I remained still for a minute, trying to get control of my galloping heart before rolling out from beneath the truck. Fire crackled over my palms as I released a blast into the air. It was nowhere near the inferno of flames Kobal could emit, but it caught one gargoyle in the belly and sent it screeching backward.

Leaping to my feet, I braced my legs apart as the fire swirled up to my elbows. Another gargoyle turned and dove toward me as more of them flew out of the building across the way. They were everywhere at once, filling the air with their compact bodies. Shadows danced over the asphalt from the creatures circling above before diving at us again. The screams from the people surrounding me grew as the gargoyles continued to attack them.

Hawk leaned out the passenger side window beside me and fired his gun at one of the ones diving toward me. Black goo burst from its wings, but it kept coming with its lethal talons extended.

I waited until the creature was only five feet away from me before releasing a fresh blast of fire. The creature howled but continued its forward momentum. Ducking down, I threw my hands over my head and rolled out of the way as it flew over the top of me. Its scaly, solid wings scraped against my shoulder before it hit the bed of the truck with a twisting wrench of metal. Two of the truck's wheels lifted off the ground before the vehicle crashed to the earth again. I hadn't realized there were a few people in the back of the truck until the force of the gargoyle's impact knocked them over.

Panic shot through me at the possibility of it going after them, but its yellowish eyes focused on me. It opened its mouth to reveal all of its flesh-eating teeth and the blackness beyond before launching itself off the truck. The gargoyle flew overhead before turning back once again to swoop low across the ground toward me.

Hawk pulled out another gun and opened fire as flames danced across my fingers once more. The gargoyle's wings flapped loudly as it sliced through the air before it closed them against its back to hone in on me. I didn't think there was anything that could throw off its deadly trajectory.

Another thud of metal sounded behind me and then Kobal leapt down from the back of the truck to land in front of me. Instead of throwing fire, he ran toward the creature and darted to the side at the last second. Grabbing hold of the tip of one of its wings, he snatched the gargoyle back. The pavement dented and cracked when he drove it into the asphalt hard enough to rattle the ground beneath my feet.

Lifting his foot, he smashed it into the gargoyle's back, breaking its spine. The creature screeched as Kobal twisted its wing over its back until the wing flapped brokenly in the air. Kobal seized its head and yanking backward, he tore it from the gargoyle's shoulders. The creature's non-broken wing beat lazily against the ground before going still.

Kobal tossed the head aside and jumped over its body. He raced toward me, grasped my arm, and threw his hand in front of Hawk's gun. "Stop shooting!" he shouted at Hawk a second after Hawk fired another shot.

"No!" I screamed when a bullet pierced through his palm and blood welled forth, but Kobal never missed a step as he propelled me toward the truck. His amber eyes were bright, his body thrummed with barely contained ferocity. "Kobal—"

"I'm fine," he interrupted tersely.

Hawk was pale as we approached. His gaze focused on the bullet wound in Kobal's hand. He had to be thinking Kobal was about to kill him, and though I knew it had been an accident, a part of me wanted to kill him for it.

"Move over!" Kobal barked at him.

Hawk scrambled away from the door when Kobal opened it and thrust me inside. "What are you doing?" I demanded.

"Get her out of here!" he commanded Hawk.

"Kobal... no... I can't—I won't leave you," I stuttered in protest.

"You promised, *whatever* I said," he reminded me before focusing on Hawk. "Get her out of here and don't look back. Protect her life with yours. If something happens to her, or if she gets away from you, I'll kill you myself."

"Kobal!" I lurched for his arm before he could close the door on me. "No! I'm supposed to help with things like this!"

"No, you're supposed to be protected from things like this until we reach the gateway."

I opened my mouth to shout more protests at him, but I knew he wouldn't be swayed. I had promised, and more people were dying while we sat here fighting. "How will we find you?"

"I'll be right behind you." He cupped my cheeks in his large palms and kissed my forehead before pulling away. "Go!" he ordered Hawk. "And don't look back."

Kobal slammed the door on me before I could leap out of it, and Hawk stomped on the gas. "Hold on!" Hawk yelled out the driver's side window.

The tires spun on the pavement, squealing as they tried to gain purchase on the battered road. My hands fumbled for the handle above my head when the truck caught on the asphalt and leapt forward. A scream from the back caused me to whip around as I realized who Hawk had been shouting out the window at.

A man standing in the back tumbled over the side of the truck and bounced across the pavement. I hadn't realized there were still people in the back of the truck, and Hawk seemed not to care about their safety as he didn't ease on the gas.

The woman and man still in the truck fell back, bouncing over the supplies before crashing into the tailgate. The man flipped over the back of the truck, but somehow managed to grasp hold of the tailgate at the last second. Only his knuckles and fingers gripping over the edge were visible. I feared his legs and feet bounced over the ground behind us.

The woman lurched toward him and grabbed his wrist. I heaved a breath of relief when his head popped up over the back of the truck. Then a leg swung over the tailgate and the woman managed to help pull him back into the truck bed.

"Don't do it!" Hawk snapped when my hand fell on the door handle.

"They need our help against those things!"

"I don't know what you are, but I do know you shoot fire, came from where humans reside, not demons, and this mission wasn't organized until *you* arrived. It's been made clear to us throughout our training for this journey that your life is the most vital part of this mission, and I will do whatever it takes to fulfill my duty."

Gone was the hunched-over man who'd spent most of yesterday trying to avoid touching the two of us. In his place was a soldier. He glanced at me, his indigo eyes remorseless. "He'll kill me if you get out of this truck, and personally, I like my head where it is. It's a pretty good-looking head."

My hand fell off the handle. I couldn't argue with his statement, and I couldn't live with myself if Kobal killed him because of me. I spun in my seat to take in the carnage behind us. I bit back the bile rising in my throat when I saw the arms and legs scattered across the road. Intestines and blood splattered the earth, torn from the bellies of humans and gargoyles alike. The blood was almost technicolor against the burnt-out gray and black city.

As I watched, more fire erupted into the air, lighting the creatures diving toward Kobal and the others who had grouped together to present a united front against their attackers. I had no idea how many humans were still alive, but I didn't hear gunshots peppering the air with the same frequency they had in the beginning.

From the corner of my eye, I spotted something coming down the road. My eyes widened on Corson, with his head bent and his arms and legs pumping as he raced toward us far faster than I'd ever considered possible. He easily closed the distance between us to run beside the truck. Over his shoulder, I spotted two gargoyles breaking away from the others in pursuit of the truck.

"Don't slow down!" Corson shouted when Hawk eased on the gas.

Hawk pushed back down on the accelerator as Corson ran beside us for a good fifteen feet before grabbing the side of the truck and vaulting into the back. I fumbled with the window in the middle of the glass behind me as the two gargoyles dove for Corson. The demon with the blue feathers dangling from his ears let out a roar of fury. I gawked at the claws that burst from the backs of his hands. Over a foot long, white talons shone as Corson ducked low and slashed upward at a gargoyle soaring above him.

I shoved the window open just as black goo and intestines splashed over Corson and into my face. Recoiling, I frantically wiped at the warm splatters coating my lips and lashes. The gutted gargoyle crashed into the road before us. It bounced over the pavement before coming to a stop ten feet directly in front of us.

Hawk swerved the truck to avoid hitting the easily hundred-pound creature, which was the size of a German Shepherd. Unprepared for the motion, I fell against his side as the tires squealed in protest on the pavement. The three in the back cried out when they were thrust against the side. The woman almost toppled out, but Corson grasped her wrist and jerked her back. Somehow, he managed to avoid slicing her flesh open with his lethal claws. Corson shoved her against the cab of the truck before turning to face the remaining gargoyle coming at us.

I pushed myself off of Hawk and turned back to the window as the city vanished from view. The sides of the road narrowed in on us; boulders crowded against the sides of the vehicle as we steadily climbed higher.

"What are you doing?" Hawk demanded when my fingers curled around the edge of the sliding window.

"Helping," I replied.

I shoved myself through the window, kicking my feet as I squirmed to pull myself into the bed of the truck. I fell into the back, landing on a pack of bottled water that bit into my ribs. The woman ducked and came up firing her gun when the gargoyle dove at her, not making the mistake of going at Corson as the other one had.

Shoving myself up, I held onto the window to brace myself before rising to my feet. Corson glanced over at me as the gargoyle turned and came back at us. The creature opened its awful black pit of a mouth and shrieked. Fire slid across my fingertips. It wasn't as powerful as it had been before, and I realized my demon ability to throw fire tired out far faster than my angelic ability to harvest and wield life did, but flames still danced over my flesh.

Corson stepped to the side as the gargoyle dove at us. It meant to take out the truck, I realized when it shifted course and aimed for the back tires. It would flip us completely if it succeeded in hitting us.

The flames blazed across my flesh as I raised my hands and let the fire have its way. It erupted from me in a short burst, but it was enough to hit the creature and knock it off course. The gargoyle screamed as fire licked over its body and it plowed into the rock walls lining the sides of the road. The rock walls exploded from the impact. I threw my arms over my head to shield myself as bits of debris pelted the truck and us. Shards of broken rock sliced across my arms, spilling my blood.

I dared to chance a glance when a sound like thunder erupted through the air. Even with our growing distance from where the gargoyle had hit, I could feel the earth quaking beneath the truck as the gargoyle's impact caused some of the surrounding rocks and boulders to break free of the mountain. It appeared as though they slid toward the earth in slow motion at first, before tumbling faster and crashing against each other in an immense cloud of rolling dust.

I could only stand and gawk at the rockslide as more and more fell. My heart sank when some of the dust cleared to reveal the pile of boulders blocking the roadway behind us. "No!" I shouted.

Lifting my head to the sky, my knees wobbled when I spotted the flames and smoke rising high on the horizon from the city we'd left behind. "Kobal," I whispered.

"He'll be fine. They'll find a way around the rocks," Corson said. Kneeling down, he leaned through the window to speak with Hawk. "Keep driving and don't stop for anything."

CHAPTER ELEVEN

KOBAL

Bending, I gripped the undercarriage of a pickup truck and heaved it upward, flinging it away from me. Metal bent and twisted, and glass shattered as the roof of the truck folded in on itself when it rolled side over side. It tumbled toward the building, crushing four gargoyles beneath its punishing weight. Supplies spilled out all over the street. Water bottles, clothes, and food scattered everywhere as humans scrambled to get out of the way of the flying debris.

Another gargoyle landed to the right of me, running forward on its back legs before falling to all fours and bounding across the roadway like a dog. Bale raced forward, grabbed it by its tail, and whipped it around. She bashed it off the roadway, breaking its bones and pulverizing its head before spinning in a rapid circle and releasing the limp body. The gargoyle soared through the air and crashed through the glass of another building with a resonating bang.

More gunfire erupted, cutting down two more gargoyles and splattering them over the road. I glanced over the blood and death surrounding us before focusing on the two remaining gargoyles.

They leapt between the buildings, bounding back and forth as they avoided the bullets the humans fired at them.

I flexed my hands, my skin pulling across where Hawk had shot me, but the wound was almost healed already. A strengthening due to my bond with River, I realized. I'd always healed faster than the other demons, but not this fast.

"Hold your fire!" I shouted as the gargoyles perched in a crouched position at the top of one of the buildings.

Their mustard-colored eyes watched us; their fangs were bared as their tails twitched in the air behind them. We couldn't leave without destroying them; they would only pursue us and draw unnecessary attention to us if we did. We had to kill them and do it quickly.

I'd sent River out of here to keep her safe, but I'd be damned if I remained separated from her for long. Right now, there were far too many dangers out there for her to be without me.

No matter how much I would have preferred to go with her, I couldn't. These things had to be destroyed and as many human lives preserved as possible. I was the biggest weapon we had against the gargoyles, and turning my back on the humans now would almost ensure a mutiny.

Corson would keep her safe. Usually, he was easygoing and fun for the humans to be around, but when pushed, he could be almost as lethal and ruthless as me. It was why I'd sent him with her over any of the others.

Fire continued to lick around my wrists as I watched the gargoyles. They didn't speak, but I could sense them communicating with each other, plotting their next move. Turning the hounds lose would do no good. They were ruthless, but they couldn't fly or scale the remains of a skyscraper, and I didn't want the humans to know I was capable of releasing the hounds yet either.

"What are we going to do?" Bale asked.

"Tear them to shreds," I replied, "but I don't think they're going to volunteer to come down here and let us have at them."

Morax stepped forward and craned his head back to gaze at the gargoyles. "No, they're going to wait us out and follow us afterward."

"I'll burn them down," I said. "Be ready for them when I do."

Shax cracked his knuckles. "We will."

Stepping over the broken glass, body parts, and gargoyle remains littering the street, I kept my eyes on the two creatures perched on the windowsill a good seventy feet above me. Saliva dripped down their chins to plop onto the ground in goopy splatters. My upper lip curled in disgust as I walked into the building and moved around the pieces of jagged metal littering the floor.

The clicking of the gargoyles' claws on the steel beams above drew my attention to their shadows moving toward what remained of the top of the building. The rusted metal that had collapsed into the center of the building stood in odd angles around the floor now covered in moss. Creatures, most likely mice and rats, scampered away from me to hide beneath the rubble.

Turning, I tilted my head back to look for the gargoyles who had moved another ten feet higher. They sniffed at the air before one of them crept cautiously over the side and halfway down an intact pane of glass. It didn't come any closer, afraid of the fire around my hands and wrists.

The other one perched on top of the steel, its claws curving around as it scraped back and forth to create a loud screeching noise. From outside, I heard a few humans cry out from the sound. My teeth ground together as I willed them to come closer to me so I could put an end to this and get back to River.

Normally, they may have sat up there until the end of time, willing to wait all of us out until we died. However, my flesh was the one they'd love to tear into the most, and I was counting on that to lure them both into coming closer. While I may not have been the original varcolac demon to lock the gargoyles behind their seal, I had made sure they stayed locked away.

I waited until the other one took another step toward me before shooting a wall of fire up the inside of the building toward them. The remaining glass from the windows blasted outward before falling to the ground in a crescendo that drowned out the startled cries of the humans. The first gargoyle leapt back before the fire could reach it and jumped to the safety of the higher levels with its partner.

"Son of a bitch," I snarled, keeping my flames focused on the bracings holding the remains of the building up.

Beneath the wall of fire, the steel glowed an orange-yellow color as it heated. The bracings holding the war-torn building together sagged as the metal bent downward. The gargoyles leapt back when the wall sagged beneath their feet.

They scrambled out the window and bolted down the front of the building when it began to give way beneath the punishing heat of the flames. Their sticky palms allowed them to stay ahead of the flow of debris as the building rolled over itself while collapsing toward the street. The rumbling sound of it grew until it reverberated in my ears and echoed throughout the city.

I reined the flames back in when gunfire erupted outside again. Rushing forward, I leapt over the rubble lining the floor as the building gave way faster beneath the weight of the collapsing steel beams. I ducked, throwing myself forward when the wall rushed toward the doorway, threatening to block the exit.

Raising my arms, flames shot upward to knock aside the debris looking to bury me beneath its crushing weight. I rolled through the doorway as the building fell with a thunderous crash that shook the earth.

Leaping to my feet, I jumped over a pickup as one of the gargoyles dove at Verin, knocking her over the fountain. Morax bellowed with rage, rushing forward and leaping onto the gargoyle's back when it landed beside her. Pulling his hand back, Morax drove his fist through the back of the creature's head and jerked his arm back, ripping the tongue out the back of the gargoyle's skull.

Around me, the remaining humans stumbled back, revolted by the thrashing creature. Morax seized its head and twisted its neck with a violent jerk. It fell forward, collapsing into the fountain as Verin shoved herself to her feet. Morax grabbed hold of her and drew her against his chest to hold her close.

Turning, I found Bale and a human stepping away from the remains of the last gargoyle. I recognized the man as Captain Timothy Tresden, the soldier Mac had assigned to lead the human troops. At five foot eight, he wasn't tall, but he was solidly built with a thick neck and broad shoulders. His deep-brown skin was splattered with the black blood of the Gargoyle he'd helped Bale slaughter. Wiping the blood away, he flung it to the ground with a flick of his fingers. His sable eyes briefly met mine before fluttering away to take in the massacre that had taken place around us.

I looked over the human bodies littering the ground before focusing on the survivors. We'd started out with fifty people. Now there were only a couple dozen left. I'd known the humans would sustain heavy casualties, but I hadn't expected it to be in the first full day outside of the camp.

"Shit!" I hissed.

"Weeding out the weak," Shax muttered.

"How many more seals do you think have fallen?" Morax demanded.

My teeth ground together. I felt the hounds stirring within me, seeking out answers as to what had happened to their brethren, answers I wanted as badly as they did. The hounds were an intricate part of me. I wore the mark of Ziwa, the guardian of the hellhounds. I bore the hellhounds on my body and within me when no other varcolac had before me. They gave me strength, and they protected me, but they also made me far more volatile than the varcolacs who had come before me.

I welcomed the blessing and the curse that came with sharing my soul with them, and now something was happening to them and I would not tolerate it. The hounds weren't dead. I would feel it through the bond connecting us if they were, but something had happened to incapacitate them while guarding those seals. I had to find out what and I had to do it soon.

The opening of the seals must be stopped. There were many other abominations kept behind those barriers. Abominations that should never have seen the fires of Hell, never mind the light of the human world. It had taken my ancestors thousands of years to lock them all away; it would be impossible to reseal them all at once.

I could open a gateway now and return to check on the hounds, but I couldn't leave River out here for the amount of time it would take to return. Once I found her, I could take her back to the wall and go, but that would only delay our journey to the unnatural gateway, which was something Lucifer was probably hoping for. I had no choice but to push on and hope the hounds could keep the rest of the seals from falling.

"What were those... *things*?" a woman demanded, her voice breaking and taking on a hysterical note.

"Gargoyles," Shax said flatly. "They've been taken care of now."

"Taken care of!" she screeched shrilly. "Look around you! I don't see any of your body parts littering the ground! Why are we here? We can't do anything against these things!"

"Enough," Captain Tresden said in a calming tone.

"Were we brought here to use as decoys for *her*?" The woman's voice grew louder on each word. Her brown eyes rolled in her head as she gazed at the blood and body parts splattering the street.

I had no tolerance for humans when they were becoming hysterical, but I had to be careful not to break the tenuous trust I'd regained by reuniting them with their families. Walking away from her now would do little to help with that. "No, you weren't brought here as decoys," I replied.

"No? They just *slaughtered* us!" The woman wrung her hands before her and shifted her feet.

"We will be better prepared for what comes next," Shax said

and bestowed the charismatic smile on her that had always made him the most popular with the females in Hell and on Earth. "Gargoyles have roosted together for thousands upon thousands of years. They most likely wouldn't have separated once they were free of Hell."

"What does that mean?" another human demanded.

"Most likely, we just killed them all, and if we didn't, then there are only a few more out there. They never had large numbers."

"We weren't prepared for this," the woman whimpered.

"Yes, you were," I replied. "You were told what you might be able to expect. You were told this was a mission many of you wouldn't survive, but you volunteered anyway. You have the training to protect yourselves. Even after witnessing what you already have of the creatures from Hell, you still believed you would easily defeat the things out here; you can't. We had hoped that more seals hadn't fallen after the revenirs, but they have, and more will most likely fall too. You can either toughen up or die. Those are your choices."

Done with her, I turned and walked away to survey the damage done to the vehicles and supplies. Out of the twenty vehicles, only ten trucks remained. We had to salvage what we could of the provisions before we were able to leave. The eyes of the demons bored into my back, but they all wisely chose not to mention the word tact right now.

"Gather what you can of the scattered supplies," I commanded. "We're leaving in five minutes."

The woman began to cry; the others looked pale and dazed as they stared at the shredded remains of their troop. We had chosen the best of the best from the soldiers guarding the wall, but the gargoyle attack had rattled many of them.

There were simply some things the human mind couldn't wrap itself around. No matter how well we'd trained them, there would be some who fell apart when faced with the creatures we would encounter on our way. And there would be more creatures, maybe not as lethal as the gargoyles, but there were others out there just as horrifying as those we fought today. We already knew the lanavours were free, and they made the gargoyles look like kittens in comparison.

My gaze went back to the road Hawk had taken to get River out of the city. I'd sent her away for her own safety. Now I had to get her back.

"Get to work!" I barked to those still standing around.

The humans immediately scattered to try to salvage what they could from the destroyed vehicles and human remains.

CHAPTER TWELVE

RIVER

"What do we do now?" I demanded of Corson. I grasped my hair whipping free of where I'd tied it back and held it down as the pickup bounced over the ruts and holes in the road.

"We go to where we're supposed to meet Kobal," he replied.

My knees went weak with relief; at least they'd arranged a meeting place before Corson left to come with us. I slid down against the truck to sit with my back against the cab. "Where?" I asked.

"There's a town about fifteen miles away. It's not as badly ruined as the others we've been through."

"Some of the towns survived somewhat intact?" the woman asked.

"Yes," Corson replied. "Not many, but some."

"The rockslide will slow them down," the man said.

"It will," Corson agreed before glancing at me. "But he *will* make it."

The man and woman moved aside some bags of supplies before settling in. Black goo coated some of the canvas bags, but hopefully the supplies within were still good. Corson remained standing, his claws retracted and one of his arms hooked through the open window in the back of the truck to hold on. Gargoyle gunk splattered his face and clothes, but he didn't pay it any attention as his eyes scanned the horizon with a ruthlessness I'd never seen in him before.

Kobal sent him with me for a reason, I realized.

I turned toward the other two. I'd been training with them before we'd left the wall behind, but there was something more about these two that teased at my mind.

Then, I recalled the woman with the almond-shaped, ocean blue eyes, and black hair had been the one to successfully chop off a demon's hand during a training exercise when Kobal and Mac had still been trying to determine who would be coming with us on this journey. I'd been watching them at the time the woman successfully managed to strike the blow against the demon, when many failed.

After cutting off the demon's hand, she'd been separated from the group of hopefuls and led over to stand with the man sitting beside her now. A man who had earlier succeeded in slicing the ear from a demon. At the time, I'd envied them their easy camaraderie as they'd exchanged smiles and high fives.

I extended my hand, fully expecting them to spurn it but unable to resist seeking out some of that camaraderie for myself. "I'm River Dawson."

"First Sergeant Erin Choi," the striking woman replied and took hold of my hand in a firm handshake. The use of her rank to introduce herself was a sharp reminder that the rest of the humans with me were far more military than I was, though things had relaxed somewhat since we'd left the wall, or at least I hadn't noticed as many people saluting each other out here as I had back there.

Erin's sleek black hair, cut into a bob below her ears, shone in the sun. She had dainty features, unblemished skin bearing the hint of a tan, a slender nose, and full lips. She was about five inches shorter than me with a delicate build that made her appear fragile, but I sensed a wealth of strength in the hand holding mine.

"Nice to meet you." I turned toward the man at her side and held my hand out to him.

He took hold of it and shook it briskly. "Sergeant Anselmo Vargas, most people call me Vargas."

The gold cross he wore around his neck caught and reflected a beam of light when he leaned toward me. Vargas's black hair was cropped close to his head in a buzz cut. Sweat beaded across his deep olive skin and broad cheekbones. His eyes were so rich a brown they were nearly black, but they held flecks of golden brown within them. He was about five ten and lean with rigid callouses on the hand gripping mine.

"Nice to meet you," I said.

"You also," he replied.

I released his hand and sat back against the truck as I tried not to smile over the realization neither of them had cringed or hesitated before shaking my hand. Maybe not having Kobal hovering over me was making them a little braver, or maybe it was because I had flame-thrown a gargoyle into a wall to save us. Either way, I felt almost human again, as I finally got a taste of the normalcy I'd been missing so much.

Why? I pondered as I drummed my fingers against my shins. *What was so great about normal?*

Nothing, I realized, at least not for me. For me, attempting to be normal had meant years of trying to hide the things I could do from others, years of stressing over being found out and labeled a freak. It had meant four long years of fearing being discovered once the military started circulating fliers looking for people with special abilities.

Maybe I didn't care so much about feeling normal again, but more about feeling accepted by someone other than my brothers and Kobal. I'd come to actually enjoy the things I could do. I may not be great at all of it yet, but I was learning and improving every day. Drawing on life gave me a rush and made me feel connected to the world in a way I'd never felt before my powers had grown. Throwing flames was a good way to stay alive.

However, I still missed people. Lisa had been my closest friend at home, but I'd had many others in my small town and I'd known almost everyone. The people there had respected me and cared for me even when my own mother wouldn't.

I thrived on all the life interconnected and weaving around me in tangible waves no one else on this planet felt, or at least that's what Kobal said. I didn't like feeling disconnected to any of that life, even the humans who would like nothing to do with me.

Draping my arm over my legs, I stared at the odd combination of burnt buildings and thriving, green life reclaiming the earth surrounding us as Hawk drove. Every once in a while, I would glimpse wildlife moving through the small, slender trees sprouting up beside the road. Amid some of the younger trees were a few older, larger ones that had somehow managed to survive the destruction of the bombs and the Hell unleashed upon the earth.

I wanted Kobal back, but it could be hours, possibly days before they were able to get around the blockage in the road. I glanced toward the sky, half expecting to see one of those monstrous things swooping toward us again, but it remained blessedly clear.

"Where am I going?" Hawk asked as he eased off the gas.

"Go straight for now," Corson replied.

Turning, I knelt in the back of the truck to peer over the top of it as we entered a new town. My eyebrows rose at the sight of all of the houses lining the road. A few of them had blackened roofs and soot-stained walls, but most of them remained untouched. They were empty reminders of a better place and time.

For some reason, these still standing remnants were lonelier to me than the burned-out and broken structures we'd passed before. I could almost see the people and families who had lived here, hear the laughter of the children who had run through the streets, and the voices of the neighbors as they shared gossip over their white picket fences. There had been barbecues and sparklers, tears and drinks within these homes. There had been love before the war and the opening of the gateway had brought death.

Birds chirped and sang as they fluttered through trees. Squirrels and other animals turned and scurried into the sparse woods when they heard the truck approaching.

"It's so strange," Erin murmured.

Vargas rose to his feet and braced his legs apart. He surveyed the area as he spoke, "It's been strange for years now."

"There had to be survivors from here," I said to Corson.

"I'm sure there were," Corson replied.

"Where *are* they?" I asked.

"The ones who were old enough, and who volunteered for it, were absorbed into the troops along the wall. The others were all moved to an encampment near the Canadian border. They were never allowed to rejoin the citizens of your country. The same was done with those who survived the gateway opening on the other side of Earth. They were taken to an encampment near the border of Italy. All remaining governments never intend for the truth to get out about the cause of all this destruction," Corson replied. "The survivors were kept segregated and under constant guard until the wall was completed."

"So they became prisoners," Erin whispered.

"Better than the alternative," Corson replied with a shrug that caused the blue feathers hanging from his ears to twirl.

"Which was?" I prodded.

Corson's unwavering gaze held mine. "Death."

Vargas kissed the cross hanging around his neck before turning to stare at the houses surrounding us.

"They wouldn't have…" Erin said, her voice trailing off.

"Wouldn't they?" Corson inquired. "If any of this got out, it could cause a major uprising against the governments who created this mess in the first place. Not to mention, it would most likely result in open season on demons by the freaked out humans."

"They would come to accept you," Erin said.

"How much precious time would it take for them to do that? How many lives would be lost first, and how many more seals would fall as Lucifer continued to prepare for his return to Earth?"

I dropped down from my kneeling position and sat in the back of the truck. Lowering my chin onto my knee, I watched the buildings slipping by us. The people who had lived here now led a life on this side of the wall, not one they'd volunteered for, but one thrust upon them by events beyond their control, like me. They had *survived* though, not everyone had been destroyed by the destruction the human government had unwittingly unleashed by opening the gateway.

"One thing I've always wondered," Vargas said. "Why didn't the demons following Lucifer spread out across the land before the wall was assembled?"

"The Craetons who follow Lucifer stayed with him in Hell. The Palitons who follow Kobal, stayed close to him or obeyed his orders to spread out once here. Many of the other Hell creatures, for example the madagans, aren't exactly the smartest in the world. They're like our animals, wild and lethal, but their thought processes don't involve taking over the world. Confused and disoriented by being set loose, many of them didn't travel far in the beginning. By the time they started to spread out more, the beginnings of a wall in many areas had been started, and we'd already come to an uneasy treaty with the humans."

"Uneasy?" Erin inquired.

"We weren't exactly welcomed with open arms in the beginning. Humans tend not to handle change or the unknown well. I'd say we're a good combination of both."

"You are," I agreed.

"En masse, we might make your intolerant heads explode." I shot him a look in response to his statement; he grinned back at me. "They didn't exactly take kindly to *you*."

"They don't know what to make of me. They can at least see you're different and now accept you for what you are. They may not know everything you're capable of, but they know you're trying to help them."

"And they think you're what...?" His voice trailed off as he stared pointedly at Erin, Vargas, and Hawk.

"First," Vargas said as he sat back down, "I think you have a point that it would be disturbing for them to learn what is on this side of the wall, and that our government had a hand in helping to unleash it, but I think people would adapt to the truth over time. If given the chance."

"The chaos that could result before people adapted to the truth may be the undoing of what is left of your civilization," Corson reasoned. "And no one is willing to take that chance."

Drawing his knee against his chest, Vargas tapped his fingers on it as he pondered Corson's words. "Perhaps you're right, but it doesn't sound as if we'll ever get the chance to know how they would handle it."

"Most likely not," Corson agreed.

Vargas focused on me. "Second, you're right, we know what they are and part of what they're capable of, but *you* look just like us. You came from a human town, yet you have abilities like them. We have no idea what you are, or what you're capable of."

"I'm human," I replied. "Mostly," I added honestly.

"She's possibly our only hope for ending this," Corson said.

"No pressure though," I snorted.

His eyes were unblinking when he turned to look at me. "None at all."

I didn't know if he didn't get sarcasm or if he truly meant it. Kobal had said the same thing, no pressure, but I knew they all expected me to at least be able to do *something*. The only problem was I might have already discovered all the things I could do, and I didn't think any of them had anything to do with closing an unnatural gateway into Hell or killing Lucifer.

"What *else* are you then?" Vargas pressed.

"That's not really your concern," Corson told him.

"I don't understand why they can't know," I said.

"Because it's not time for them to know."

I sighed in aggravation and turned to look at Vargas and Erin who were staring at me curiously. "I lived most of my life believing I was human. I *am* mostly human. I'm more like one of you than I am anything else."

Corson's eyes burned into me when I finished speaking, I held his gaze unwaveringly with my chin raised high. They were part of this mission. They had been told to keep me alive, and would do everything they could to fulfill that duty, yet they had no idea why. They deserved to know some of why they were putting their lives on the line for me.

"That's all you need to know," Corson grated.

"It is reassuring to know, even if that's all you can tell us," Erin said.

I gave her a small smile, grateful to hear someone say that. She smiled back at me before focusing on the town once more. Bending down, Corson rested his fist on the truck bed as he leaned closer to me. I glanced at the back of his hands. His talons had retracted; I tried to find some evidence they had once been there, but his flesh looked perfectly smooth and normal now.

"Are you sure you're more human than anything else?" he inquired in a voice so low that it didn't carry beyond us.

Before I could respond, he turned away to speak to Hawk through the truck window again. "You're going to make a right at this intersection. There's a high school with a large field in the back. We'll wait for the others there."

I was still trying to puzzle out Corson's question when Hawk made the turn. Of course I was more human than not, wasn't I? I was mortal like a human, and my body parts wouldn't regenerate after being lopped off. At least I didn't think they would. I wasn't going to leap at the chance to test the idea.

I loved Kobal and most times Corson was fun-loving and easygoing, but the demons were all emotionally aloof. Unless that emotion was anger or passion and then it was a free-for-all. I was far from aloof or distant with my feelings; I put more value on sex than the demons did. Until me, Kobal had viewed sex as the easing of a need with no attachments involved.

Was my more emotional behavior because I was more human than angel or demon, or was it simply because I'd only ever been a human, living with other humans?

I was still mortal, but did being mortal make me more human or was it simply a consequence of having been born on Earth? My ability to summon fire came from being part demon and the ability to draw on life from being part angel. My visions and prophetic ability could be from either part, or even from my human part, as some humans did have extrasensory abilities too.

Ugh, I rubbed at my temples with my fingers. It was all too confusing, and in the end, what did it really matter if I was more one thing than another? I was still simply me, the biggest hope for humanity and demons alike. Go me.

My stomach rumbled as the July sun reached its apex in the sky. Its rays beat against my skin, but its warmth didn't bother me like it did the others. Erin waved a hand at her flushed face and Vargas wiped the sweat from his brow; sweat stains marred their clothes and caused them to stick to their bodies like a second skin.

Did the ability to tolerate heat better mean I was more demon? *Cut it out! You'll drive yourself nuts with this one!*

I lifted my head to glare at Corson for implanting this train of thought in my head, but he wasn't paying attention, and if he had been, he probably would have been amused. Tearing my attention away from him, I glanced at the supplies when my stomach rumbled again. Between the happenings of last night and today, all I wanted was some food, a chance to clean up, somewhere to sleep and Kobal. I had a good chance of achieving the first two, but I'd never be able to sleep while Kobal was still out there with those things.

Hawk drove into the parking lot of the high school and around to the back before stopping the pickup next to the back of the building. Climbing out of the truck, we made quick work of finding food and drinks in the bags of supplies we pulled from the back. We settled in the shadow of the building to eat and drink in silence.

"There's got to be somewhere we can clean ourselves up," I said when everyone was finished eating and we had packed up and returned the supplies to the truck. "I'm sure the school has locker rooms and showers."

Corson looked at the building, rubbing his smooth chin as he studied the brick façade. "We don't know what could be in there, and it's a lot of space to search in order to make sure we're alone. It could take hours."

"Probably a fair amount of rats and other animals inside," Erin said.

"Maybe we could use one of the houses that are still in good shape," I suggested.

I held my breath as I waited for Corson's response. I was desperate to clean off the gargoyle ooze still sticking to my skin, but if he believed it was better for us to stay here, I wouldn't argue with him. I wasn't willing to take any chance of possibly missing Kobal.

Corson continued to stare at the building before dropping his hand down and glancing at his goo-stained shirt. "Yeah, we can try one of the houses."

I barely managed to stop myself from throwing my arms around his neck and kissing his cheek. He grinned when he realized what I'd almost done. My hands fell to my sides again and I took a hasty step back. "It's okay. I know I'm irresistible," he said with a wink.

I laughed as I jumped into the bed of the truck. "Unfortunately, I don't wear earrings."

"That is a deal breaker. I do so love my jewelry."

Vargas rolled his eyes while Erin chuckled and Hawk gazed at him as if he'd sprouted another head. "Fucking demons," Hawk muttered as he walked away.

"You know you wish you had as many earrings as I do," Corson called after him. Hawk flipped him the bird over his shoulder. Corson climbed in to stand beside me in the bed of the truck. "We'll keep this conversation from Kobal, right?" he asked me.

I chuckled as Hawk pulled out of the parking lot. "We will," I promised.

CHAPTER THIRTEEN

RIVER

We drove through the town, searching for somewhere to stop. After a few minutes, Hawk parked in front of a handful of homes still in relatively decent condition. The four of us approached the best looking house with the least amount of vines and vegetation trying to take it over. I didn't know what our odds were of finding running water inside, but I was willing to have my hopes crushed rather than just sitting around in gargoyle blood all day.

Stepping onto the sagging porch, I spotted the remains of chipped red paint peeling away from the house. As I walked across the porch, one of the boards cracked under my foot and gave way an inch before catching.

When I was sure it wouldn't collapse, I lifted my head to study the street. I held my breath as my gaze darted over the hushed roadway. The cracking sound probably hadn't been that loud, but it still echoed in my ears and I was certain that if anything or anyone was lurking nearby, they'd heard the sound.

"It's fine," Hawk said. "It wasn't that loud."

I tore my attention away from the roadway as Corson turned the doorknob. He pushed against the door, but the swollen wood held firm in its frame. Resting his hand on the door, he leaned his shoulder into it and shoved harder against the wood. It gave way beneath his weight with a crack of wood and a squeak of rusted hinges.

He swept inside in a crouched position with his talons fully extended. The rest of us had our guns in hand, but I didn't think we'd get a chance to fire them before Corson eviscerated any threat coming at us. The tips of his claws scraped across the wood floor, gouging its surface and kicking up dust as he moved.

Stepping into the house, I froze and sucked in a breath as I looked around. It was like opening a time capsule; it appeared as if nothing within had been touched since the day the bombs had fallen. The layer of dust covering everything was so thick that if I'd had allergies, I'd be in the middle of an attack so bad right now, I'd sneeze all the dust out of the room. The scent of mildewed, old, rotten wood hit me, causing me to wrinkle my nose at the oppressive smell.

Behind me, Erin sneezed and my nose tickled so badly my eyes watered. I walked into the living room behind Corson, my eyes going to the dust-coated pictures on the mantle and the single, small sunflower sprouting in the center of the chimney.

I had no idea how the flower had gotten there, perhaps dropped down the chimney by a bird or dragged in by some animal, but the cheery yellow flower was the only spot of color amongst the gray enshrouding the home. Its head tilted back to absorb the small stream of light filtering down the chimney. My eyes were riveted on it as I was torn between being awed by the sign of life and beauty continuing on here, or crying from the emptiness and loss encompassing this place.

This had once been someone's home, and now it was nothing but a rotting structure. I tore my eyes away from the flower and back to the rest of the house. Pictures still lined the wall, but there was so much dust on the glass I couldn't see what was held within their frames. Knitting needles and a basket of thread sat next to the rocking chair beside the fireplace.

I rubbed my hands over the goose bumps popping out on my arms. I'd been so focused on everything in here that I hadn't noticed the others had already moved on. I found them in the kitchen, standing by the sink. Erin was turning the faucet on and off but no water came out.

"Probably tree roots in the pipes," Hawk said.

"Could be a well and, with no electricity, the pump won't work," Vargas said.

"Possibly," Hawk agreed. "Either way, it doesn't do us any good."

Corson jerked his head toward the back door. "We'll try the next house."

I followed them outside and across the backyard to the house next door. My eyes scanned over the growing trees and woods creeping in. Before, I'd heard the laughter of those who had once resided here; now their tears and screams of terror resonated within me as they'd fled from the war baring down on them.

I felt hollow inside, empty and cold despite the nearly hundred-degree temperature of the day. Death hung heavily on my soul when we arrived at the back porch of the next house.

The door was already partially open. Either it had never been closed by the people fleeing, or it had been reopened by an unseen hand. Corson led the way inside again. The dust coating in this house wasn't as thick as it was in the other one, but rotting leaves, dirt, and assorted debris littered the once tiled floor.

The others walked over to the kitchen faucet while I made my way into the living room and stood staring at the thick, green vines growing through the floor. The vines had twisted their way up the front of the gray stone fireplace to allow only peeks of the old splendor to show through the vegetation.

Something about the fireplace drew me toward it. Unable to resist, I walked across the floor and stepped carefully around the rotting floorboards to stand before the fireplace. The thick vines scraped against my skin when I shoved my hand through their drooping green leaves. The granite mantle of the fireplace was cool against my skin as I felt blindly over it.

My hand enclosed around a picture frame and I pulled it forward. I wiped away the dust covering the glass to reveal the fading picture within. The edges of the photo had curled in, but I could make out the family portrait. A man and woman smiled proudly as they stood behind two little boys and one younger girl. All of the children smiled broadly, each of them showing off at least one missing tooth.

I held the photo before me, unable to tear my gaze away from the family that didn't exist anymore. I don't know how I knew it; I just knew the family in this picture had no longer been the same before the war had even erupted.

"There's no water here, either," Corson said.

My eyes remained on the photo, my fingers resting on the face of the little girl as she stared at me from beyond the glass. Stared at me from a world beyond this one, a world I couldn't touch, or perhaps I somehow could.

Where had that idea come from? I shook my head to try to clear my mind of the strange notion that I could somehow reach out and communicate with the girl, wherever she was.

Not here, not anymore. Gone beyond this plane. Taken from her family before the war.

"River."

My hands tightened around the frame as I struggled to tear my attention away from the photo.

"Did you hear me?" Corson asked.

"No water here," I said in a hoarse voice.

"We're going to move on."

"Wait."

"For what?"

I didn't have an answer for him, but I knew there was something in this house I was meant to see, something more than what was in this room. Moving away from him, I walked toward the stairs. I peered into the dark shadows obscuring the top half of them before jogging up them with no concern about what might lie ahead, or that they might give way beneath my weight.

"River!" Corson hissed from behind me.

Arriving at the top of the stairs, I stood in the hall for a couple of seconds. Dim light filtered in from around the dingy curtains at the end of the hall. Dust motes danced in the air as I strode forward to stand before the first door on my right. Years ago, I'd stopped questioning any weird instinct guiding me forward or my visions. I'd never had answers for any of my questions until I'd met Kobal.

He'd finally explained what I was, what made me so different from all the other seemingly normal people around me. Though I may not have liked the answers he gave me, I didn't deny they were the right ones. Now, I didn't question the things I experienced or saw in a vision, because I knew they would reveal something to me that *had* to be seen.

I gripped the knob on the door and twisted it. The door remained closed, the wood swollen from the elements and years of neglect. Pressing my shoulder against the wood, I pushed on it a couple of times before putting my entire body behind it and shoving hard.

"*River!*" Corson bit out in exasperation as he reached the top stair and turned toward me in the hallway.

The door finally gave way beneath my weight and flung open. I stumbled forward a step before catching myself. The door crashed against the wall and bounced back toward me, but my hand shot out to stop it from closing again. I took a startled step back as I gazed in disbelief at the room before me.

It was the little girl's room, or at least I assumed it was because of the canopy bed and the cotton-candy-colored walls. The fabric of the canopy had faded over the years and the dust on top of it made it difficult to discern the color, but there were still some bright pink patches showing through the dirt and age.

My gaze roamed over the room, my heart leaping and crashing in such a strange way I wondered if I was having some kind of heart attack. Everywhere I looked, the faces of angels stared back at me. There weren't merely one or two of them, not even a dozen or so, but hundreds, perhaps thousands of them lining the floor-to-ceiling shelves of the room.

All of the angels' little cherubic faces were dusty, but I could still make out their different expressions and poses. Most of them were in prayer, some had their wings stretched outward, and others were playing with each other with clouds beneath their feet. Some were porcelain dolls, others were miniatures, and more than a few had been hand-carved and painted.

I'd never seen anything like it. They were beautifully strange, yet something about them made my skin crawl. There were *so* many.

Beside me, Corson's mouth hung open. His eyes surveyed the room as if the angels were going to come to life and fly at him. After everything I'd seen since leaving my *normal* life behind, I wouldn't be surprised if they did come alive, but I didn't think it was going to happen. At least, I *really* hoped it didn't. I didn't believe that whatever had drawn me here was bad, but I couldn't think of anything more terrifying than these figurines coming to life right now.

My gaze fell on a sign hanging by the window. The floor creaked beneath my feet as I walked over to pull the sign from the wall. I wiped away the dust to reveal the name, *Angela,* painted on it in pink.

I traced my fingers over her name as images unfurled within my mind; images of laughter and happiness before all the anguish and loss. The days of a young girl playing with her brothers on the playground, then later lying in her bed with her stuffed animals crowded around her while her body wasted away.

Never before had I been able to see into another's life like this before. I didn't know if it would ever happen again, or if I was only meant to see Angela's short life, but this new development didn't frighten me.

"They called her their angelic Angela," I murmured. "Cancer took her too young."

"Why would you say that?" Hawk asked from behind me.

I glanced over at where he stood just inside the doorway with an expression nearly identical to Corson's as he surveyed the room. They both looked prepared to defend themselves against an impossible angel uprising. Vargas appeared behind him, his eyes widened as he surveyed the room, and his fingers brushed over his cross before his hand fell back to his side. Beside him, Erin took one step into the room before quickly stepping back.

"Sometimes I just know things," I answered and returned the sign to where it hung on the wall.

Tilting my head back, I lifted my hand to the mobile over my head. My fingers slid over the cherubs hanging from it and dancing in the air beneath my touch. I turned away from the mobile and moved closer to the window to stare out at the hushed street.

I bit my lip, suppressing a gasp as the shimmering image of a young girl standing on the sidewalk materialized before me. Her wheat blonde hair hung in ringlets around her shoulders, her kelly-green eyes were vivid in the sun spilling around and through her transparent body. She looked the same as Angela, the girl in the picture downstairs, and she wore the same red and white checkered sundress from the picture.

I knew it wasn't real, that the little girl didn't exist, but I couldn't look away from her. There had been a lot of strange occurrences in my life, some I'd written off and forgot, others had stuck with me, but *nothing* like this had ever happened before. I closed my eyes and rubbed them with my fingertips. When I opened them again, she was still standing there, a see-through vision who held my gaze.

"Do you see her?" I inquired when Corson walked over to stand next to me.

"Who?"

I wasn't surprised by his answer, but I'd still hoped that

someone else could see her too. "No one. I thought I saw someone, but I was wrong."

The little girl continued to stare at me, her pretty features sparkling with the rays of the sun filtering through her body. Angelic would have been the best way to describe her. I flattened my fingers against the glass as the girl wavered and vanished before blinking back into form further across the road. She turned and lifted her hand to point at the horizon. I followed her finger until I spotted something standing along the tree line on a distant hillside.

"What are those?" I inquired and pointed toward the shapes moving swiftly across the ground. I didn't know if it was the distance, a trick of the light, or if they were really doing it, but they seemed to be floating across the earth.

Corson's eyes narrowed as he studied where I'd indicated. "Lanavours," he grated. I recalled the name from last night and the creatures roaming the city. "We have to get out of this town."

"What about Kobal?" I demanded.

"He'll find you, but not if they find us first. We don't have enough weapons or people to deal with them, and believe me, you do *not* want to deal with them. The gargoyles were more fun."

Those words made my blood run cold. Anything worse than a gargoyle was something I preferred not to mess with. Turning away from the window, I snatched one of the angels from the shelf. I had no idea what possessed me to do such a thing, but it felt right in my hand as I rushed out the door after the others.

CHAPTER FOURTEEN

KOBAL

I stared at the boulders blocking the road, my fury mounting when I spotted the crumpled remains of a gargoyle wing poking out from the rubble. We could climb over the boulders, but that would mean leaving behind all the supplies and vehicles. It would mean continuing on foot from here, something that would take far too much time considering the mortals.

"Shit!" I exploded.

Grabbing a boulder the size of a small car, I lifted up and heaved it out of the way. The boulder smashed off the rock face across from me, disintegrating into smaller pieces that crumpled onto the top of the giant pile in our way. Humans scampered to get away from me and the broken bits of rock bouncing across the surface of the asphalt.

I looked toward the next rock with the intent of throwing it out of the way, but there were hundreds of them separating River from me. It would take hours to work our way through them enough to be able to pass. I hadn't set it free, but fire licked over my hands and up toward my elbows as I stared at the obstacle before me. My flames would be of no use against stone. The force would push the rocks back, but with the mountains blocking both sides of the road, there was nowhere for the rocks to be pushed to. Turning, I studied the road behind us. It branched off a few miles back, most likely making its way around to the town where Corson and River had gone, or at least it would go close to it.

"We're going to have to double back," Morax said.

"I know," I murmured. "Let's go!"

Around me, what remained of the human contingent returned to their vehicles. They went in reverse until they found a place to turn around. I climbed behind the wheel of another pickup and Bale slid into the passenger side. Backing down the road, I spun it around and drove forward to take the lead when the other vehicles stopped to wait.

I found the other road and drove down it rapidly. I didn't care about the creaking, thudding sounds of the pickup or the tires as I pressed the gas pedal to the floor. I had to get to River, had to see her, had to know she was safe.

It took far more time than I would have liked, but we finally pulled into the town where I'd told Corson to wait for us. The sun had set an hour ago; the moon hung over the tops of the trees to illuminate the roadway almost as well as the headlights did.

I caught a lingering hint of River's fresh rain scent, a scent that radiated from her soul and was an integral part of her. It was far too faint for her to still be in this town. My hands curled around the wheel as I fought against ripping it from the truck.

Fear wasn't something I was familiar with, but now it incessantly crept through me. They had been here; they never would have left if something hadn't driven them away.

What if something had taken her?

Bowing my head, my nostrils flared and my muscles bulged as I grappled to maintain my self-control.

"What is it?" Bale inquired, and I heard a hitch in her voice I'd never heard before.

"They're not here," I growled.

"How do you know that?"

"I *know*."

She held her hands up and leaned against the door to put more distance between us. I shoved my foot down on the gas and drove toward the school where I'd told Corson to wait. As I drove, I detected traces of River's scent at different places throughout the town. I'd check those locations for some sign of where they'd gone after the school.

At the intersection, I began to turn toward the school, but Bale grasped my arm and pointed at a sign on the other side of the road. I'd been so focused on getting to the school that I hadn't noticed the white sheet draped over the sign and tied around the post. *Lanavours in the area. Had to leave. Go straight. Will leave signs, R.*

The R barely fit onto the bottom of the note scrawled in what looked like blood. As we drew closer to the sheet, I caught a waxy, unfamiliar scent through the open windows of the truck. I didn't know what they'd used to write the note, but it wasn't blood.

"Lanavours," I grated.

"They couldn't have stayed here," Bale said. "They had no choice but to leave."

I nodded, but my teeth were beginning to throb from clenching them so tightly.

Bale squeezed my arm, drawing my attention to her. "Corson and the others will follow the same route we intended to, for as long as they can. We're not that far behind them, but you have to let the humans rest. They can't keep the same pace we can."

"They can sleep in shifts and we'll keep driving until we find them."

"Kobal—"

"We can't be more than a few hours behind. The humans can rest when we catch up. We can't stop here in case the lanavours are still around anyway." Bale released my arm and sat back. I didn't look at her again as I drove down the road. "Keep your eye out for another sign."

"I will."

~

RIVER

I took over driving for Hawk when the sun rose. It was the first time I'd ever been behind the wheel of a vehicle in my life. My hands shook in the beginning, my heart knocked louder than a poltergeist on the walls, but taking hold of the wheel made me feel powerful. Now, I just had to keep the truck in the center of the road and stop trying to use both feet on the pedals.

When a squirrel ran out in front of me, I accidentally hit both the brake and the gas at the same time, one with each foot. The truck jerked forward with a squeal. Corson, Erin, and Vargas were thrown up against the cab of the truck by the sudden start then stop. Groans sounded behind me as their bodies bounced off the metal with multiple heavy thuds.

"Sorry!" I called back to them.

"One foot for both pedals," Hawk said for the umpteenth time, his eyes red-rimmed from exhaustion as he gazed at me from the passenger seat.

"Okay," I muttered and forced my left foot away from the brake pedal.

After a while, I got the hang of it and the others drifted off to sleep, except for Corson. His back was against the window behind Hawk, his eyes half-open as he watched the passing scenery. For all I knew, he could be sleeping. Kobal slept with his eyes closed, but they were all different kinds of demons, each with their own traits.

"We should leave another sign," he said after a half an hour, confirming my doubts as to whether or not he was awake.

I pulled to the side of the road and jumped out of the truck without putting it into park. My left foot hung out the door, running over the ground as I scrambled with my right foot to find the brake. The truck lurched to a stop and, thankfully, no one was slammed against the cab again.

"You have to put it in park first," Hawk muttered without opening his eyes.

"Thanks for the info."

"Anytime."

I shifted the stick on the steering wheel into park and cautiously took my foot off the brake. I held my breath as I waited to see what would happen, but the truck didn't move. Grinning and fighting the urge to pat myself on the back, I hopped out. Corson's earrings swung back and forth as he glanced between me and the truck with a look that clearly said he believed the truck was smarter than me.

"I've never driven before," I said defensively.

"You've seen it done before though, right?"

"Until recently, it had been years since I'd last seen it done. I doubt you came out of Hell with the knowledge of all things human."

"We came out knowing a lot of things," he said as we walked toward a red stop sign on the side of the road. Tucked under his arm was one of the sheets we'd taken from Angela's house. "I watched humans more than a lot of the others did."

"How come?" I asked.

He draped the sheet over the sign before tying it securely to the post. "I don't know. It was something to do. You're a self-destructive, crazy species, but you're entertaining to watch."

"Kind of like a soap opera for demons."

"A what?"

"They were these TV shows my mother used to watch back in the day."

"I didn't see much of your TV."

"Interesting. So what am I writing?"

I pulled out the tube of red lipstick we'd found in Angela's home. It was the only thing we could find to write with; everything else had dried out over the years.

"Write: *staying on the original route*."

"Should we stop and wait for them here?"

"No, I know a place that will probably be safer for us to stop and wait," he replied. "Until we get there, we have to get as far from the lanavours as we can."

"How bad are those things?"

"Bad."

The word didn't make me shiver, but the haunted look in his eyes did. If the demons didn't want to face them, I definitely didn't. "Should I tell them where we're heading?"

"No, nothing and no one else can know where we're going. Kobal will figure it out."

My stomach turned at the possibility of something else out there, possibly stalking us right now. I lifted the lipstick to the sheet and began to write. *Staying on the original route, R.* I twisted the lipstick down and replaced the cap.

"How many humans do you think survived the gargoyle attack?" I inquired.

"I don't know."

My head bent as the memory of those broken bodies and screams drifted back across my mind. "I don't want anyone to die because of me."

"They're not dying *because* of you. They're dying to *protect* you."

"Is there a difference?"

"Yes. There is a possibility you could save their entire species. That is a worthy cause, one they are willing to fight and sacrifice for. They're dying because some of your species royally *fucked* up."

"And what if there is nothing I can do about closing the gateway or Lucifer?" I asked.

"Then we come up with a new plan."

"A new plan," I murmured as I gazed at the distant horizon.

"Kobal won't stop until he's caught up with us," Corson said.

"I know."

I ached for him; I wanted him beside me right now. I had to know he was okay and that the gargoyles hadn't hurt him. Deep inside, I believed I'd know if he'd been injured or killed, and not because of my ability to know and see things, but because my soul would recognize the loss of his. We were inextricably bound together.

My hand instinctively lifted to touch the marks on my neck. My heart raced at the realization they were already healing. Something primitive stirred within me, and I immediately recognized it as a demon instinct, too strong and volatile to be human, too sexual and possessive to be angel. I had to have him back soon.

"Back at Angela's house, when you were looking out the window, what did you see on the street?" Corson asked in a low voice when we started back toward the truck.

I stopped walking, my gaze went to the tiny, kneeling porcelain angel figurine I'd stolen from the house and set on the dashboard of the truck. Once I'd cleaned it up, I could clearly see its cherubic cheeks, green eyes, and wheat-blonde hair. Its head was tilted back, its wings unfurled behind it as it stared at the sky with a look of peace.

I'd unknowingly snatched an angel closely resembling Angela. I didn't believe in coincidence in this world. At least not where I was concerned.

I'd also never been one for lucky charms. I'd always believed that what would be would be and no amount of rabbit's feet, clovers, idols, or even prayer could change that, but I couldn't bring myself to part with the angel right now.

"I thought I saw someone, but I was wrong." For some reason, I felt I had to keep Angela to myself, for now.

"I see," he murmured.

I didn't know if he completely believed me, but he didn't press me any further. "How far are we from this place you think we'll probably be safe at?"

"We should make it there tonight."

"Good." I walked back to the truck. "Would you like me to keep driving?"

"You might as well learn how, or at least I hope you can learn."

That was confidence boosting, but I slid behind the wheel and turned the key in the ignition to start it. I remembered to shift into drive before hitting the gas pedal, something I hadn't done the first time I tried driving this thing. A step in the right direction, I thought and pulled onto the road.

CHAPTER FIFTEEN

KOBAL

"I think I know where Corson is taking them," Bale said as the edge of the sun dipped beneath the horizon.

I had a pretty good idea where Corson was going too as I stared at the newest message left behind for us. It was a genius idea, but I didn't know how River was going to react to what she would discover when they made it to their destination.

"Pearl's," I said.

"Yes. We must stop, Kobal, at least for a little bit. The humans haven't had anything to eat or a bathroom break in hours."

Resentment slithered through me. I felt completely unstable, but then I'd been unstable ever since I'd put River in that truck and told Hawk to drive away. Now I was leaning toward an escalating rage as I felt the hounds' hostility building within me. River was my Chosen and they were as eager to get her back as I was.

I wasn't used to this vulnerability clawing its way through my insides. I'd led River out here, I'd sworn to keep her safe, and now she was out there with countless enemies hunting for her. Lucifer had seen her, he knew what she looked like now and so would his followers.

I wanted to continue onward, I wouldn't be able to take another easy breath until River was by my side again, but Bale was right. The humans needed a break. It would do all of us little good if they were too exhausted to continue.

River will have the same needs, I reminded myself. They wouldn't be pushing themselves as relentlessly as I was pushing these humans. We were gaining on them, and Corson was most likely heading for Pearl's. They might be able to find safety there for a little bit, or at least long enough for us to catch up.

Demons steadfastly avoided Pearl's, and I doubted any humans would go anywhere near it, if there were any still alive in the area. Corson was probably dreading every second they got closer to the place, but he would do what he had to in order to keep River safe.

I stared at the red writing on the sign for a minute before thrusting the door of the truck open and stepping out. I strode toward where Captain Tresden sat in the pickup behind me. "We'll stop for a half an hour," I said briskly.

He nodded and climbed out of the truck before barking the order to the rest of the troops. Verin, Morax, and Shax strolled over to join Bale and me by our pickup. "You think Corson's going for Pearl's?" Shax asked.

"Yes," I replied as I rested my arms on the bed of the truck. My foot tapped against the ground while the humans hurried into the woods and gathered food from the supplies. Most of them went to the woods to relieve themselves first, willing to eat on the drive if they had to.

"I hate that place," Morax muttered.

"Which is why Corson would go there," Bale said. "*Everyone* hates it."

"True." Morax shifted to watch the trees as people reemerged from their shadowy depths.

Turning away, I searched the horizon before shoving myself away from the truck. I walked down the road, passed the sign River had written, and over to a small hill in the road. Peering over the top of the hill, I stared down the road, searching the woods for any hint of something lurking amid the trees in the descending twilight.

The lanavours were still out there somewhere. Unlike the gargoyles, they would separate as they moved over the earth. They liked to attack in packs, but they would form smaller packs and spread out.

Movement drew my eye to the tree line as some of the branches and leaves rustled and creaked. I didn't breathe as I waited for whatever was down there to reveal itself. Red flashed through the leaves before disappearing. Taking a step forward, I watched as the trees parted to reveal two humans, a man and a woman, moving amid the foliage.

All of the humans were supposed to have been cleared from this area years ago, but I'd always suspected some of them had escaped the evacuation. Given all the things the people on this side of the wall had to deal with, it was amazing any of them had survived on their own. What these people had endured, witnessed, and done in order to survive in the wilds would make them tough sons of a bitches, or complete lunatics.

Either way, I didn't want them drawn to the soldiers we had with us. There was no telling the kind of people they would be at this point.

The couple made their way through the tree line, eventually fading from view. I remained where I was, unwilling to turn and walk away. I didn't trust that the couple wouldn't try to double back to get at our supplies if they knew we were here, and I believed they did. They hadn't survived this long without learning their environment and having killer instincts.

I felt Bale near my side before she spoke. "It's been half an hour."

"Get the humans together and tell them to prepare for an attack; we're going down there to make sure it's safe before proceeding," I replied.

"What did you see?"

"Two people, but there might be more and they could be setting a trap."

"Just what we need," she muttered and turned away.

I remained where I was until she returned with the other demons who spread out alongside of me. I caught a glimpse of something shiny in the foliage, most likely a rifle or scope. Yes, they definitely knew we were here, and they were waiting.

CHAPTER SIXTEEN

KOBAL

"They want the supplies," Bale said.

"Yes," I agreed.

Captain Tresden walked over and stood at the top of the hill beside us. "What is it?" he inquired.

"Humans with guns. They've set an ambush for us in the woods," I replied brusquely.

"I'll talk to them," he offered.

"They're not going to listen. These humans have survived out here for thirteen years. I can guarantee they care little about what you have to say," I told him.

His mouth pursed as his eyes narrowed. The small movement of a branch about a hundred feet away and on my right caught my eye. The humans were daring enough to move in closer. I didn't see any more glints from scopes or any movement, but the acrid scent of body odor wafted to me from the woods.

"They're moving closer," I said before facing Tresden. "Tell the soldiers to hold their fire unless it becomes absolutely necessary to kill these people. We're going after these humans before they can get any closer."

"I will," he replied before walking away to prepare the soldiers.

"I'd prefer not to kill them if we don't have to," I said to the demons gathered around me.

They all exchanged startled glances. "Seriously?" Verin inquired.

I glanced at the soldiers behind us as they gathered their weapons and got into a defensive position. When I turned back to Verin, I responded to her using our native tongue. "Yes. Would you prefer to destroy them?"

"No," Verin replied and tossed her sun-colored hair over her shoulder. "I just never thought I'd hear you sympathize with the plight of a human."

I turned away from her. Maybe I wouldn't have before River, and most of the time, I had little sympathy for humans in general, but these were different from the many I'd encountered over the years. These humans had managed to survive out here in the wilds all this time.

"They're probably more demon in nature now than human," I commented.

"Most likely," Bale agreed.

"So how are we going to handle this?" Morax asked, his tail thumping on the ground as he cracked his knuckles.

"We'll slip in behind them, take them by surprise. If some of them die in the process, so be it, but keep as many of them alive as possible," I said. Turning, I strode over to Tresden and the soldiers. "We're going to attempt to subdue them without a fight." I switched back to the English language as I spoke. "If one of them slips by us and makes it up here, shoot to kill."

"We will," Tresden said.

"Should some of us go with you?" a young woman asked.

"No, stay here to defend the supplies in case something goes wrong."

I doubted anything would go wrong. They may be more savage than many of the humans we were used to dealing with, but they were still only human. Walking away, I jerked my head and gestured for the demons to follow me into the woods as night descended. Slipping into the shadows of the forest, a small thrill of excitement went through me as I began to hunt.

RIVER

I stepped out of the truck to gawk at the massive building before me. There were actually lights on inside the building, lots of them. There had been electricity at some of the gas stations on the other side of the wall, but I'd never seen one as lit up as this one was. I had no idea how this place had so much electricity fueling it, but the entire outside of the building was awash in a harsh glow that made me wish for sunglasses even though the sky was pitch black.

Clouds had obscured the moon and stars hours ago, making our headlights the only thing lighting the road. About a quarter of a mile back though, this place could be seen lighting up the night like a lighthouse beacon.

The large, metal awnings outside of the building covered at least twenty gas pumps. Some of them had hoses hanging down from the silver ceiling toward the smooth, paved parking lot. This parking lot was one of the few I'd seen where the asphalt hadn't been destroyed by the weather or the war.

The nearly pristine surface was more disturbing than reassuring. *Why is this place so untouched?*

To my left, a flickering neon sign reading *Pearl's* stood beside the building. The light of the sign and the glow from the building blazed through the fog creeping low over the land.

"What is this place?" I asked.

"I believe they used to be called truck stops," Corson replied.

That was when I saw the darkened words beneath *Pearl's* reading *Truck Stop*. The bulbs used to illuminate *Truck Stop* must have gone out over the years.

"Is this what we've been heading for?" I asked Corson.

"Yes," he replied at the same time something moved behind one of the slated blinds covering the floor-to-ceiling windows making up the entire front of the building.

"What was that?" Vargas lifted his rifle before him and settled the butt firmly against his shoulder.

My hands rested against the guns holstered at my side as I caught a flash of motion behind one of the windows again. The reassuring weight of the katana rested against my back, but I reminded myself that my greatest weapons lay within my own hands.

The lights outside and the dazzling lights spilling out from between the cracks in the blinds made this place entirely too attention grabbing for my liking. How could we possibly hide out in this place until Kobal and the others arrived? There was no way anyone within a quarter-mile radius would be able to miss it.

Why did Corson bring us here of all places?

I strained to see past the blinds, but I couldn't make out what was moving beyond them.

"Your guns won't work on what's inside." All of our heads shot toward Corson as he uttered these words.

"Why does that not sound reassuring?" Erin asked.

"It's not meant to be," Corson replied.

"What are we walking into?" I demanded.

"Nothing deadly. It won't be pleasant inside, but there most likely won't be any humans or demons in there."

I didn't think any part of this journey was supposed to be pleasant, but if Corson found this unpleasant, we were probably going to hate every second of it. At least whatever was in there wouldn't kill us, always a bonus.

I followed Corson toward the door with Hawk beside me. Erin and Vargas kept watch at our backs. Our footsteps slapped over the asphalt as we moved toward the building; they were the only sound in the muggy night.

Despite all the light out here, to my right were the shadowed recesses of an alley next to the building. Not much of the light spilling out of the windows and beaming on us from the awnings overhead pierced the darkness beside the building. The grills of a few Mac trucks parked in the alley sparkled in what little light fell over them. If their flat tires and rusting bodies were any indication, they hadn't moved in years. From what I could see, none of them had trailers attached to them.

Reaching the door of the building, Corson grabbed the metal handle on the door and pushed it open. A bell rang on the other side. The crisp, clear sound of it was extremely loud in the hush surrounding us. The jarring bell wasn't what startled me most about the door opening, it was the way Corson strolled in as if he owned the place.

The rest of us exchanged baffled looks while we remained standing outside the doorway. We were nowhere near as nonchalant about entering as Corson had been. I pulled out my gun as Hawk put his foot against the bottom of the closing glass door and gently pushed it back open with the toe of his boot. The bell didn't ring again but rather made a tinkling sound this time. I edged past Hawk, swinging my gun from side to side as I did a brisk search of the interior while the others entered behind me.

Corson stood before me, a smirk curving his lips when my mouth dropped open at the spectacle that greeted me. Sitting in the booths of the diner we'd stepped into, some of the occupants turned sideways to see us, others swiveled away from the counter, and still more stopped in the act of moving down the black and white tile covering the floor.

There were at least fifty individuals within, maybe more, and all of their expressions mirrored the same shock I knew was on my face. I almost took a step back, but Hawk's breath warmed my neck as he blocked my retreat. Vargas kissed his cross, and Erin looked as if she would rather be facing a gargoyle again.

"You don't belong here!" a woman shouted at us and rested her hand on her plump hip. Everything about her was gray, from her coloring to her gingham dress to the apron over it. Her gaze swept disdainfully over all of us. "*None* of you belong here."

No shit.

"Only resting for a bit," Corson told her with a dismissive wave of his hand.

"This isn't your place!" the woman insisted.

Corson waved us toward the stools at the counter. "Have a seat."

The occupants of those stools shot him nasty looks and folded their arms over their chests. They weren't going to vacate their seats, and I wasn't about to try to make them. We didn't move. I didn't think any of us dared to as the woman approached us with a thunderous expression on her face.

"You're *not* welcome here!" she yelled.

"You have two choices," Corson bit out at her. "You let us sit and wait peacefully, or she," he thrust his thumb over his shoulder at me, "burns this place to the ground. Pick your poison."

"Corson!" I hissed, unwilling to piss off anything in this building. I had no idea what they might be capable of doing if they were pushed.

He shot me a silencing look over his shoulder. The woman stopped advancing on us and swung her faded gray eyes toward me. Her other hand went back to her hip as she glared at us. If she started stomping her feet like a bull, I would be out of here before she could charge us.

"She isn't capable of that!" the woman declared and thrust a finger at me.

"Believe what you like, but I would suggest not pushing your luck. Go back to your business and leave us be," Corson said. "We're just waiting for some friends, and then we'll be gone."

The woman didn't look at all pleased by this notion. My stomach churned with acid as everyone in the building focused on me. The hair on my nape rose, and my hand on my useless gun became so sweaty I had to slip the gun back into the holster before I dropped it. I hated that Corson had used me as a threat, but she didn't come any closer to us.

The woman continued to study me like a dissected frog before her brow cleared and her hand fell away from her waist. "I know who she is," the woman murmured.

Around us a ripple went through the crowd, some moved closer to me. Their interest beat against my skin as they scrutinized me. "It is her," another one whispered. "The demons have found her."

I could feel Vargas, Erin, and Hawk's gazes burning into me. "How do you know who I am?" I inquired.

"Word gets around. The afterlife is smaller than people think, especially on this side of the barrier between our worlds," the plump woman replied.

So, there was an afterlife gossip vine. That was a strangely un-freaking-believable realization.

Corson stepped aside and gestured toward the counter once more. This time, the stool's occupants hurried to get out of the way as Corson walked toward the vinyl-covered seats. The four of us remained where we were for a full minute before cautiously following him as he settled on one of the stools.

I turned sideways to avoid brushing against someone. I had no idea what would happen if I did, and I didn't want to find out. I was almost to a stool when my arm passed straight through a man who rose to let us pass. Goose bumps broke out on my chilled flesh and full realization finally sank in.

We were standing in a truck stop diner full of ghosts.

CHAPTER SEVENTEEN

RIVER

I sat hunched over on my stool, unwilling to move as ghosts hovered near my elbows. And hover they did. Their feet never touched the ground as their heads turned curiously back and forth while they inspected me. I tried not to gawk at their gray, transparent forms, but the longer I sat there, the more they gathered around me.

"Are you really what they say you are?" a man with sideburns and a pompadour asked me. He wore a pair of bellbottoms and an older-looking, button-down shirt left partially open to reveal the upper part of his chest. His shoes were flat with rounded fronts and only a couple of shoelaces on them.

"I don't know what they say I am," I murmured, leaning away from the one with a pompadour when he floated closer.

"The key to it all. The answer we've all been seeking to put to right the world again."

No pressure though.

I resisted waving my arm at him to get him to move away, but I didn't want to touch one of them again. "Not so sure about that," I said instead.

"Do you really think it's her?" another one of them whispered to some of the others.

"The demon said she could burn this place down with her bare hands, but she's not a demon. She must be the one everyone has been talking about," a young man wearing the shredded remains of a gray uniform said. He'd been a Civil War soldier judging by his clothing and wide-brimmed hat.

Apparently, I was the hottest topic on the afterlife gossip vine. Even after everything I'd seen over my lifetime and these last couple of months, this was one thing I'd truly *never* seen coming. I dimly recalled my mom sitting around watching talk shows when I was a child. Right now, I felt like one of the people sitting on the stage as the audience judged them. All I needed was for someone to stand up and yell at me, *Lucifer is her creator!*

I shivered at the notion and tried to move away from an old man who floated by with round glasses perched on the tip of his bulbous nose. He inspected me as if *I* were the freak show. Oh, who was I kidding, I was a freak, but they were freaking *ghosts* for crying out loud. They could cut me a break.

"Don't yell at her, Ethel," another one said and floated over to the woman who had first spoken with us. "She could help us."

My eyebrows shot up at that statement. I looked to Corson who leaned over the counter and waved at the ghost with the pompadour. The image of his hand moving back and forth through the man was about as comforting as sleeping on a bed of glass.

"Shoo!" Corson said to him.

The man pouted, but he floated away to stand by one of the tables. "What is this place?" Vargas inquired in a low breath.

"They can hear you," Corson replied. "No reason to whisper. Ghosts may have the form of mist, but they can hear a gate opening from a mile away, isn't that right, folks?"

There were many disconcerted comments from the ghosts such as, *dick* and *asshole*, following his statement, which only confused me more. Corson swiveled on the stool so his back was to the counter; he leaned against it casually with his elbows propped on the smooth surface behind him. He actually smiled as he surveyed the disgruntled forms staring back at him.

"It's the truth," he said to them. "It's why you're all here."

"I don't understand," Erin said.

"A few of them are here because they were scared and didn't pass on to Heaven when they were supposed to. Souls can balk against entering Heaven. They have no such choice when it comes to Hell."

"Why not?" I asked.

"Heaven is a place where the good get to reap their rewards. If they chose not to, then that is their choice. However, *no* one avoids the punishment of Hell if they rightly deserve it. Those souls who chose not to move on become trapped on Earth until they're granted another chance to go to Heaven. However, *most* of these ghosts are here because they didn't quite have what it took to make it into Heaven or Hell. So they're stuck here because they didn't have the balls to be bad enough for Hell, and they didn't have the decency to be good enough for Heaven," Corson explained.

Who knew ghosts could scowl? I did now, and all of those scowls were focused on Corson. If they had been flesh and bone, I had no doubt they'd be trying to kick his ass right now.

"Corson, be nice to them," I whispered.

"Why? Most of them weren't good people. It's why they're here. They're paying their penance until their time has been served."

"Wait." Vargas rested his fingers against his temple. "Are you telling me Earth is Purgatory?"

"Are you really surprised?" Corson inquired.

I frowned over his question, unsure how to respond. We were sitting in a diner full of ghosts, could anything surprise any of us anymore?

"If you really think about it, it makes perfect sense. They're trapped here, watching the world continue on, watching their loved ones die and travel on to a place where they can't go. They have to watch all of you live your lives, while constantly wondering when their time will finally come so they can pass on too," Corson continued.

"Sounds awful," I said and glanced at the figures pressing closer to us. "So why are you all gathering here?"

"One of the gates is here," Pompadour said.

"Gates to what?"

"To Heaven," he replied as if I were about as bright as tar, which right now, I felt like my mind was as covered in goo as the rest of me.

"It's not a gateway," Corson said with a roll of his eyes. "Ghosts are *always* exaggerating."

"Then what is it?" I asked.

"When a person dies, there is a portal for the soul to pass through that some consider a gateway. Whether it is or not, I don't really know. The area we're in now experienced a high concentration of death in the past. In areas where there is a lot of death, the passing of the many souls who *deserved* to pass on to Heaven or Hell, and did so, leaves an imprint on the land."

I bit my lip to keep from laughing when Pompadour gave Corson the finger.

Corson smiled back at him sweetly before continuing. "Areas with large imprints on them tend to be a draw for ghosts looking to escape Purgatory. They hang around in the hopes that one of the many portals that have already opened here, will open again."

He threw his arm out to indicate all the occupants of the diner. "You can't skip the line," he told them. "You have to serve your time. Hanging around here is getting you nowhere. Nothing is going to open for you until you've been deemed worthy of passing on."

The pretty ghost wearing a poodle skirt put her fingers under her chin before flicking them at Corson. Her skirt didn't move when she spun away from him. A man wearing what I thought had once been a uniform shirt and no pants turned and floated through the wall. I swallowed heavily at the disconcerting sight of something so human looking passing through something solid.

"Sometimes the portals open," Ethel protested.

"Because the spirit passing through has served its time, not because they've found the key to skipping ahead," Corson retorted. "Fools."

"Holy shit!" Hawk blurted, drawing everyone's attention to him. "It really is a truck stop instead of Saint Peter's!"

Vargas, Erin, and I looked at him as if he'd lost his mind, and right now, I wouldn't blame him if he did. "What?" I asked.

The color had drained from his face; he looked nearly as ashen as the specters floating around us. "It's a song called, "Man on the Moon," he murmured. "I used to love it as a kid, but I never would have dreamed it was based in reality."

The title of the song seemed oddly fitting considering I felt like I was on another planet as another ghost floated by me.

"Humans glimpse more than they know between the dimensions sometimes," Corson said. "The writer of your song may have seen something at some point."

"So was this place built for the ghosts to come here?" I inquired.

"No, humans built this place because it was good business. The ghosts came here because of its location and because they could," Corson replied.

Was this why I had seen Angela on the side of the road? Was she a ghost? Then again, Corson and the others hadn't seen her, and they could clearly see the ghosts in here. She'd also appeared in vivid color while these ghosts were all gray and faded.

I turned to Corson. "So the ghosts interacted with the people who used to come here?"

"No, humans can't see ghosts, or at least they couldn't," Corson replied. "Of course, some spirits are stronger than others. If one of those stronger spirits had an ability while human, they were able to retain that power, and those rare spirits were able to make their presence known to a human. You mostly called them ghosts, though some were known as poltergeists. There were also a few humans who would catch glimpses of ghosts beyond the veil keeping them blocked, but for the most part, ghosts hover in the background, watching and waiting for their turn to pass on."

"I... uh... I beg to differ. I can see him perfectly fine," Erin stammered. She leaned away from a man in his twenties with round glasses and hair down to his shoulders. His tie-dyed shirt had a grayish hue to it like the rest of him. He was trying to peer down Erin's shirt as he rose higher into the air above her. "Pervert," she accused.

The man grinned at her, flashed the peace sign, and floated away. "Totally worth it," he said to another one.

"Jesus," I muttered and pressed my shirt closer to my chest when a few of the other male ghosts clustered closer to us.

"Can Jesus help us?" Pompadour asked excitedly.

I gaped at him before shaking my head. "I... I don't know."

"No. He *cannot* help you. Fucking ghosts. *Serve. Your. Time*," Corson enunciated, earning him more fingers and rude gestures from the dead and see-through crowd.

I leaned away from one rising over the top of me and angling his head to try to see around my hand at my throat. "Back off, buddy. You may not be corporeal, but I'll figure out a way to kick your ass."

"She might be able to do it," another one said and nudged him with an elbow.

They both drifted away before turning their attention to Erin. "And I'll kick your asses for her too!" I snapped at them.

I was beginning to understand Corson's obvious dislike of ghosts.

"Thank you," Erin said to me. She kept the top of her shirt pinned against her chest.

I wasn't ready to release mine yet either. Some of the women ghosts moved around Hawk and Vargas with an admiring gleam in their eyes; the soldiers paid them no attention. "How come we can see them now?" I asked Corson.

"Because when Hell was ripped open, all the intricately woven tapestries keeping the worlds separate and hidden from each other were torn apart. Ghosts are no longer hidden behind their veil and are now visible to humans."

"Why haven't we seen them until now then?" I asked. "It's been thirteen years."

"Because we much prefer not to watch life continuing on," Gray Uniform replied. "It has become much more peaceful and pleasant for us out here."

"Plus, all that screaming." Pompadour shook his head. "It gets tiring after a while, so most of us stay where the humans aren't."

"Are these some of the souls the demons feed from?" I asked Corson.

The ghosts closest to us swiftly moved back, a few of them went straight through the wall and vanished. "No. They may be annoying little pissants, but they're serving their punishment. We have nothing to do with them."

"Oh," I said as I watched some of the ghosts move closer again. They smiled as they bobbed in the air. "Where exactly are we?"

"Gettysburg, Pennsylvania."

That much of my history lessons I did remember. A chill ran up my spine as I stared at the man in the gray uniform before looking at where the other man in a uniform had departed out the side of the building.

"Oh," Erin breathed.

"Makes sense," Hawk murmured.

"So humans don't come to this place because it's inside the disaster area and because now they'd be confronted with dozens of ghosts floating around yelling at them to get out," I said. "But why don't demons come here?"

"Because, with so many ghosts gathered in one place, there's a good chance there will be an opening for one of them at some point and they will be accepted into Heaven. The opening isn't going to take a demon, or anyone else who doesn't belong in it, with them, and no angel is going to come out, but being so close to something leading into Heaven isn't our idea of a fun time. Plus, ghosts are annoying."

I couldn't argue with that.

"So are demons," Pompadour said and floated closer. "And ugly."

"I do better with the ladies than you do, spectral boy," Corson replied.

"Don't taunt the ghosts," was never a sentence I'd ever imagined saying, but I did.

I rubbed at my temples as the ghosts huddled closer to us once more.

"Can *you* help us?" a young woman asked me. Her hair was tucked beneath a bonnet and an apron covered her dress. "I gave up my chance to pass on because I wanted to see that my child and husband were well after my death, but they left the earth years ago and so did their offspring, yet I've remained."

The beseeching look in what I thought were eyes that had once been brown tugged at my heart. "I can't help you," I whispered around the lump in my throat.

The woman crowded closer to me until her icy form brushed against my arm. "But you could speak with the angels for us."

"My God," Vargas muttered.

I scowled at him when he gawked at me and crossed himself. "I can't speak to angels," I told him. Spinning on the stool, I faced her again. "I *can't*. It's not something I'm capable of. I'm sorry."

She went to grasp my hands, but her fog-like flesh passed directly through mine. The cool breeze and chill permeating my skin were the only indication she'd managed to touch me in some small way. Yet, I felt her anguish as if it were my own. My head bowed as I inhaled a jerky breath. I hadn't had this type of response to the other ghost who had brushed against me. I didn't know why I reacted so strongly to her, but I had to help her, although I had absolutely no idea how to do that.

"Ignore them," Corson said. "They'll follow us to the gateway of Hell if they think you can do anything for them."

"She needs help," I whispered.

"Too bad," he replied and rose from the stool.

The ghosts fluttered away from him as he strode forward. They filled in behind him after he walked by. They were all see-through, but looking at Corson through the thick crowd of ghosts gave him a wavy, slightly distorted appearance. Corson made his way around the back of the counter to explore the contents there. More ghosts glided closer to me, floating around to twist their heads in order to peer up at me.

"Have you ever tried talking to the angels?" Ethel inquired.

"No," I replied, wishing they would leave me alone. "I shouldn't be here."

Maybe most of them were being punished, and probably deserved it, but I couldn't help pitying them. It must have been unbearable to be trapped in the middle like they were, unable to communicate with the ones they loved. All the while knowing that if they were able to communicate with them, their loved ones would run screaming. Even more horrible would be staying behind for loved ones who ultimately passed onto another place while they remained stuck in the in-between.

"It's the best place for us right now." Corson never looked up at me from his search of the other side of the counter.

"No, you shouldn't be here," Ethel agreed. "You might bring one of those who search for you here, but maybe you could help us before they come for you."

I blinked at her and Corson snorted, "See, this is why I hate ghosts. You're all always looking to escape your punishment and serve yourselves. Did you ever stop to think that maybe the reason you're still here is because of your selfishness?"

"You try floating around being nothing of substance for years on end!" Ethel retorted. "Then tell me if you can think about anything other than freedom!"

"At least you have an afterlife," Corson replied. "I bite it and that's it, no more. Poof, dust in the wind."

"Really?" Erin asked.

"Yes," he replied and shoved a box of dust-covered silverware he'd pulled out from behind the counter back under it. "Immortality comes with a price, nothing afterwards. It's the same for the angels if they perish. However, Heaven is a lot more stable for them since they threw their garbage out and we got stuck with it."

I didn't miss the bitterness in his voice; I'd heard it often enough when Kobal spoke of the angels too. The demons may not have been the mortal enemies humanity had always believed them to be, but when the angels had thrown Lucifer out of Heaven and he'd figured out a way to enter Hell, the angels had earned the wrath of many demons.

"Interesting," Hawk murmured.

"Boo hoo," Ethel replied and planted her hands on her hips again. "You get to live forever, but if, by chance, you do die, you're done. Poor you. Just don't die."

Corson looked up from the dusty stack of faded menus in his hand. He placed them on the counter and leaned toward her. Judging by the look on his face, if she'd been real, her guts would be spilling across the counter right then.

"Poor you, Eth," he said. "You're getting exactly what you deserve. Try being a decent human next time around, or even an honorable ghost for once." He turned his back on her and walked away.

"Get out!" Ethel commanded in a thunderous tone that made the hair on my arms stand up.

"Corson!" I grated through my teeth.

He kept walking toward the swinging silver kitchen doors as if he didn't have a ghost staring daggers into his back.

"I think he pissed her off," Hawk muttered when the light over Corson's head flickered before blazing to life once more.

CHAPTER EIGHTEEN

KOBAL

I moved noiselessly through the forest as I scented the air and searched for the humans. In the distance, an owl screeched, but I couldn't see it through the canopy of branches stretching over my head. The moonlight filtering through the trees caused shadows to dance across the pine needles and leaves lining the forest floor.

Following the potent aroma of body odor, I came up behind a human lying on his stomach on the ground. Branches stuck out from his hat, and dirt streaked his face and clothes as he stared at the road with a rifle against his shoulder. Halting, I gestured for Morax to go around to the man's right while I went to his left.

Gliding through the trees across from me, I spotted Morax moving with his tail curled over his head and a lethal expression on his face. He broke away from the trees and slipped up behind the human as I emerged from the other side. When the man's eyes shot to me, he gasped and spun to aim his rifle at my chest.

Morax swung his fist down, driving it into the human's temple before the man ever knew he was there. The man's eyes rolled back in his head and he slumped to the ground. Morax ripped the rifle from his limp hands. He glanced between the man and the rifle, his muscles flexing as he looked about to bash it into the man's temple. My command from earlier held though. He lowered the rifle and rested the end of it on the ground at his side.

"Leave his weapon," I ordered. Morax tossed the gun a few feet away at the base of a small oak tree. "Let's go."

I slipped deeper into the woods, moving through the forest with ease. After centuries of maneuvering the treacherous pathways of Hell, Earth and any of her many obstacles were easy to get through.

The coolness of the shade within the woods brushed over my skin. The decaying odor of the leaves and pine needles littering the forest floor filled my nose, but I could still pick out the aroma of human sweat. It drew me onward to where the other humans were hiding.

Behind me, the demons moved soundlessly through the brush. This dimension was not our home, but over the last thirteen years, we'd become accustomed to it. We'd adapted in ways I'd never believed possible when we first arrived here, and now Earth had become as much a part of us as Hell was.

Climbing onto a small boulder, I perched at the top and knelt to survey the forest. All I'd ever wanted since arriving on this plane was to destroy Lucifer, return home, and claim my throne. After meeting River, I still wanted all of that plus her by my side. The more I contemplated our future though, the more I realized I'd prefer to keep her out of Hell as much as possible and away from everything that went on there.

I had never envisioned staying on Earth, but as I looked over the surrounding wilderness, I realized I wouldn't be leaving it behind after Lucifer was defeated. Not for good anyway. This was River's world, and I would make my home here with her.

The humans had unintentionally set us free, but I realized now there would be no more locking ourselves away in the bowels of Hell again. Maybe it hadn't been meant for demons to walk freely in the human realm, but many things had happened in the six thousand years since the angels threw Lucifer out that were never meant to be.

The angels had started the chaos, the humans had accelerated it when they'd torn open the gateway, and we were the ones cleaning up both of their messes. We would reap the benefits of staying on this plane if we so chose, and we didn't have to live among the humans. There was plenty of land for us to occupy in the areas that had been ravished during the war.

Glancing back, I looked at the others perched on the boulder behind me. How many of them would choose to stay here if we succeeded in closing the unnatural gateway? We would have to return to Hell occasionally in order to maintain our immortality and to feed, but would these demons choose to live their life here instead of there?

All those who decided to remain here would have to stay close to me in order to cross back and forth. I would still be able to maintain control of my kingdom by controlling the only gateway again, as I always should have. Life here might be unsettled in the beginning if the humans were against it, but they would have no choice in the matter. They would have to accept it as we would not be giving this world up.

Turning away from them, my fingers rested on the cool stone as I draped my arm over my knee and scented the air once more. If we didn't uncover all the humans soon, I'd torch these woods in order to flush them out. I may prefer not to kill them right now, but every second I wasted searching for them was another one River was out there without me.

"Do you smell them?" Bale whispered.

"Yes. This way."

I climbed off the rock and followed the scent of the humans through the woods. Crouching low, I paused when I spotted a red shirtsleeve poking out from around the corner of an oak tree. Without having to speak, Shax slipped past me and strode forward. Having all fought together for centuries, communication wasn't necessary to know what was expected of each other.

Shax was a few feet away from the shirt when he stopped and frowned at it. Stepping forward, he grabbed the clothing and pulled it toward him.

"Shit!" I hissed when I realized he was holding a shirt but there was no human wearing it.

The crack of a twig jerked my head around as three people slipped out of the hollow logs where they'd been hiding. Mud and dirt streaked their faces, and they were covered in leaves and branches. They were just a few feet away from us, but I could barely detect their scent as they'd covered themselves with as much of the aroma of the woods as they could.

Yes, they had definitely learned a lot from their time in the wilds.

They raised their guns and fired as one. I snarled when one of the bullets took me high in the shoulder and another tore into my gut. Pain seared hotly through my body as the humans continued to fire their weapons.

CHAPTER NINETEEN

RIVER

I rose from my seat as Corson headed for the swinging doors with Ethel close on his heels. He tilted his head back to look at the flickering light before continuing through the doors. The other ghosts separated around me to let me pass as I walked forward.

"Could you try talking to the angels for us?" the pervy guy in the tie-dyed shirt asked me.

"Believe me, the angels don't want to hear from me, and if they could hear me, they'd probably laugh at me," I answered him. "I'm far from a saint, and I don't think they'd be overly appreciative of my existence to begin with."

They had kicked Lucifer out of Heaven in the first place. I doubted they wanted much to do with his last descendent.

"That can't be true," Pervy insisted.

"I'm sorry, but I have zero contact with the angel crowd."

They're getting what they deserve, I reminded myself. I still hated the way his face fell at my words. *Most of them are anyway.*

My hands left a streak on the dusty surface of the metal swinging doors when I pushed them open. They creaked but moved with relative ease as they swung inward. The stainless steel appliances within the kitchen were too covered in dust to sparkle in the overhead lights, but I could see the silver metal peeking through the grime. Corson was inspecting the fridge and appliances on the other side of the room with Ethel floating close behind him. She watched him as if she were convinced he would steal something.

I tilted my head back to look at the lights above his head as he walked. "How are the lights on?" I asked.

"Ghosts can't do much, but they can produce a small light," Corson replied, trailing his fingers over the corner of a cabinet. "Before the veil fell, humans sometimes caught sight of that light at night, or in your pictures. When enough ghosts are grouped together, they can produce more of that light and focus it into lightbulbs and such. Since they're afraid of the dark, they often like things brightly lit."

"Ghosts are afraid of the dark?" I demanded.

"They are. I guess it reminds them of those minutes or hours, or however much time it was, between when they died and their spirits rose. Is that it, Eth?"

She completely ignored his question.

"I think I've heard it all now," Hawk said from behind me.

I glanced at him over my shoulder. I hadn't heard him enter the kitchen, but he stood in the doorway with a disbelieving look on his face that likely mirrored my own.

"You don't know what it's like to be stuck in the in-between," Pompadour said as he floated around Hawk. "The darkness there is absolute, unending. You wake up not knowing what is going on with you, but knowing that you *died*. Then, finally, you see light again and realize you are a ghost stuck in between. You wouldn't like the dark either if you'd ever gone through it."

I imagined the feeling of panic they experienced would be like waking up in a casket, six feet under the ground. Chilled by the thought, I rubbed at my arms as I turned away from him.

"Before everything changed for us, many ghosts would go from place to place to stay in the light without anyone ever knowing they were there. Now, we can no longer do that without being seen, and there isn't enough electricity to always be able to stay in the light. Besides, those of us who have been here longer usually overcome our fear of the dark," Ethel said defensively.

"That must be why you're at this amazingly bright truck stop then," Corson replied.

Ethel flew at him with a screech, stopping just inches short of where he stood. Corson lifted an eyebrow at her before turning away.

"It's true!" she snapped before turning to me. "We overcome our fear after a while, or at least some of us do, but where else would we go, if not here?"

I had no answer for her. Helplessly, I lifted my hands and shrugged. I would have stayed around other ghosts too, rather than wandering off on my own. Misery loves company after all.

Pompadour hovered by my shoulder, as I moved around the kitchen. I turned to find his hazy eyes focused on me. "I can't help you," I said in exasperation.

"You've been marked," he replied.

Corson stopped walking and turned to face us. "I told you to leave her alone."

His gaze shot to Corson. "Not by you."

Pompadour moved so close to me that, if he'd been human, he'd be on top of me. I took a step away only to have him crowd me once more. Yep, I disliked ghosts, or at least the pushy, annoying one staring at my neck.

"An angel marked by a demon," Pompadour murmured.

"I'm not an angel!" I retorted.

"You look like one with your eyes."

"How do you even know what an angel looks like?" I demanded.

"We may not be allowed to enter Heaven or Hell, but sometimes we can see through the veil, and all of the angels have your eyes."

So I'd been told. "Leave me alone."

"Hey, back off, man," Hawk said. He stepped forward and tried to push Pompadour away. His arm only went straight through him, causing Hawk to shiver.

Pompadour danced away and started back toward me, but Corson came at us. His claws extended, his eyes burning with citrine fire. Corson may not be able to touch them, but Pompadour floated back a few feet from me anyway.

"I said back off of her!" Corson spat.

"You can talk to the angels, even if you've allowed yourself to be tainted by a demon, they'll still answer you," Pompadour pressed.

"I'm not tainted!" I snapped. "And the only things I talk to are in *our* dimension."

I turned away from him, but he moved to float in front of me. I was pissed and tempted to punch him, but I'd look ridiculous swinging away at mist.

Before I could say anything, Corson lifted his hand, stretching his palm out. I saw only a hint of something white in his palm before he blew it at Pompadour. The ghost shot back and kept on going as Corson approached.

"Back off," Corson growled at him.

Pompadour turned and fled back into the dining area.

"What was that?" Erin asked from the doorway. I hadn't realized she and Vargas had walked over to stand there with the doors open. "He's sulking over in the corner right now."

"Salt," Corson replied and placed a blue container on the counter. "They don't like that either, do you, Eth?"

She scowled at him before fleeing into the other room.

"What does it do to them?" Vargas asked.

"Stings their foggy asses. They'll leave us be for a while, but I have a feeling they'll be pestering you again," he said to me. "I didn't realize they would figure out who you are."

"It makes sense they would know," I muttered and glanced back toward the main room.

"Why is that?" Corson asked.

"Because, like me, they don't fit in anywhere anymore either."

Vargas, Hawk, and Erin exchanged confused looks. Corson rested his hand on the counter, his claws retracting while he watched me. "We should return to the front," he said.

I started for the swinging doors but stopped when the world around me faded away and I found myself standing in the center of the parking lot staring at three demons who were watching the building.

In the glow of the building, the eyes of two of them shone red and their teeth gleamed when they pulled their lips back to reveal their mouths full of pointed, razor-sharp teeth. The third had pure black eyes, but unlike Kobal's, his were more like a human's eyes with the white surrounding the black iris.

The demons couldn't see me, but I felt as if I were standing right in front of them, inspecting them closely. The two with the red eyes had pig snouts and lobster-looking claws instead of hands. Kobal had once told me that if I ever had the misfortune of encountering a lower-level demon, I would instantly know the difference between their animalistic appearance and that of the upper-level demons who had horns and tails. Staring at these two, I knew he'd been right and that these two hideous creatures were lower-level demons. Which meant they were as physically strong as a demon, but they didn't possess abilities like many demons did.

However, the other one with them with the black eyes was breathtakingly stunning. His silvery blond hair framed features so sculpted I found myself unable to stop staring at him. Handsome and lethal, perfect and soulless. I knew it instinctively, felt it in the marrow of my bones. He would smile beautifully and laugh while he plucked limbs from bodies and absently tossed them aside.

"Ghosts," one of the pig noses snorted.

"According to that ghost we just saw, the one we've been searching for is in there," Handsome replied. "Perhaps the specters serve a purpose after all. Come."

The vision ended with an abrupt jerk back into my body. My foot, frozen in mid-air when the vision took over, hit the ground. I tried to clear my head of the lingering images and the sense of betrayal creeping through me. The ghosts had no reason to be loyal to anyone of us, but to betray us outright to these monsters cut like a knife. I hoped whoever it was that had betrayed us spent an eternity trapped in-between.

"We have company," I said to the others. "And one of those free-floating bastards out there told them we were in here."

"What kind of company?" Corson demanded.

"Demons, three of them. Two lower-levels with pig snouts for noses and one who is... well, he's stunning."

"If I ever figure out how to exorcise a ghost, I'm coming back here for all of you!" Corson shouted toward the front.

"It's not possible to exorcise them?" Erin asked.

"Not that I know of," he replied briskly. "They simply move somewhere else. Follow me."

He hurried through the kitchen, stopping by a counter and bending down to pull out more containers of salt from underneath. It hit me then that this was why he'd been exploring all the shelves. He grabbed two more containers of salt and stood up. The young girl with the bonnet came flying into the kitchen.

"There's something coming," she whispered frantically as she stopped to float before me. Her troubled eyes darted around as she rang her hands before her. "You must run."

"I don't run," Corson grated before he glanced at me. "Normally," he amended.

"The ghosts will give us away if they follow us," Vargas said.

"I told you not to taunt them," I said to Corson who shot me a look that clearly said he'd choke me if he could.

The others all took a step away from him, but I held my ground. The girl drifted closer to me. "No, they won't follow you. They don't like him." She flicked a pointed glance at Corson. "They don't like any of his kind. They like *you*. They believe in you and think you're the key," she said with eyes that looked as though they were watering.

Was there anything on this planet that didn't have its hopes pinned on me?

"Ronald never liked any of us," she continued. "I think that's why he went to the demons. He didn't care about any of us."

"Ronald?" I asked.

"The Union soldier who left."

I recalled the pant-less soldier who had left through the wall earlier. "And you are?" I asked the woman hovering before me.

"Daisy."

"It's good to meet you, Daisy." I actually meant that. I wasn't so fond of her ghostly companions, but if I ever did talk to an angel, and that was a pretty *big* if, I'd definitely put in a good word for Daisy.

"You also, World Walker."

"Excuse me?" I blurted while the others exchanged startled glances.

Daisy opened her rosebud mouth to reply, but the ringing of the bell on the front door stifled what she would have said. We all froze, our gazes locked on the swinging doors leading to the dining room as Ethel shouted at the demons that they weren't welcome here. At least it was her universal greeting and we hadn't been singled out.

"Where are they?" Someone demanded from up front, and I immediately recognized it as the voice of the handsome demon.

Daisy jerked her head at us and fled toward the swinging doors at the back of the kitchen. She disappeared through the doors without causing them to move a centimeter. Corson's hands clamped around the salt, but he nudged me to go before him.

I snatched a container of salt from the counter and followed Daisy toward the back of the kitchen. She said the ghosts wouldn't follow us, but I wasn't going to continue on without the only sort of deterrent we had against them.

Taking a deep breath, I braced myself as I rested my hand

against the cool metal door. I didn't know if the doors were going to squeak or not, but it wouldn't matter if they did, we had no choice but to move deeper into the building. Pressing against the door, I slowly pushed it open as I waited for some noise that would give us away.

Thankfully, the door didn't make a sound and I went through it with the others close on my heels. Once on the other side, I stopped to shove the container of salt into the waistline of my pants, tucking it securely against my hip.

Tugging my shirt over it, I pulled one of my guns from the holster and held it pointing down in front of me. My hands may be my most lethal weapons, but I didn't want to give anything away too soon. No, it would be a complete shock to them when I lit their asses on fire or shot a ball of life harnessed from the earth into them.

We moved down a small hallway before stepping into a cavernous room. I looked up to search for Daisy and froze. My heart plummeted at the sight of the thousands of transparent faces that turned to look at us when we entered the warehouse filled with boxes of supplies stacked from floor to ceiling against the walls.

All those eyes stared at us as some of the ghosts floated forward. Most of their heads tilted in curiosity. Some of them looked completely bored, while others bounced up and down with the energy of a five-year-old who'd just eaten their entire birthday cake in one sitting.

The salt tucked against my side felt woefully inadequate as they drew closer and closer.

CHAPTER TWENTY

KOBAL

Two more bullets slammed into my shoulder, causing me to stagger back a step. I spun, leaning back and toward the side when the whistle of a bullet sliced through the air toward me. A small breeze tickled my cheek as it went by. It would have hit me dead between the eyes.

"Fuck!" I snarled.

Bale cried out when blood pooled across her thigh to soak her pants. Morax leapt on top of Verin and pulled her down beneath him. His body jerked as it was pummeled by bullets. Intending to draw the human's attention away from them, I dodged to the side as another round of gunfire pierced the air.

Racing through the forest, bark exploded around me as the bullets smacked into the trees near my head. My claws extended, and my fangs pricked and lengthened. I should end this now, but still I hesitated to kill them. These humans had survived this long; I actually admired the cunning and strength it had taken them to do so, and I had promised River I would restrain myself from killing unless it was absolutely necessary.

However, if this didn't end soon, I was going to torch these assholes and call it a day. The bullets in my body burned as they worked their way out while I raced through the woods, circling around them.

The woman kept her gun trained on me as she followed my movement through the forest. Moving too fast for her, no more of the bullets she fired at me pierced my flesh. Resting my hands on a boulder, I vaulted over it. Bullets smacked off of its solid surface and shards of rock shot into the air. I ran behind the boulder and burst out the other side, jumping over a log before turning and charging at the woman.

Her bullets sliced over my skin but none of them directly hit me. I was almost on her when a man stepped in front of her and lifted his gun to aim at me. I grabbed the end of his rifle as he fired. The bullet tore a hole into my palm and out the back of my hand as I yanked the gun away from him.

His mouth fell open before I drove the butt of the rifle into his forehead with a loud crack. Blood exploded from his skin, his head jerked back and he crumpled to the ground.

"No!" the woman cried.

Spinning the rifle around, I pointed the gun at her. Warm blood oozed from the hole in my hand and dripped onto the forest floor as the woman stared defiantly back at me with her gun aimed at my chest. "Drop it!" I barked.

The other man with her stepped closer against her side and protectively in front of the one I'd just knocked out. The man raised his rifle and aimed it at Shax.

"You're only going to kill us anyway," she replied.

"If I wanted you dead, you would be already." To emphasize my point, flames rose around my wrists. "Now, put it down!"

Her hand wavered, and her blue eyes widened on my flames before she lowered the weapon. Stepping forward, I ripped the rifle from her hand and tossed it aside as Shax and Bale approached the man. They both looked mad enough to kill. Shax jerked the rifle out of the man's grasp and threw it into the woods.

"Morax, you okay?" I demanded.

He shook his head as he sat back. A bullet was making the way out of the back of his skull, and more holes riddled his shoulders and back. "Fine," he grunted as the bullet in the back of his skull finally fell out.

Verin sat up before him, her hand resting against his cheek. She leaned forward to kiss him before leveling the human woman with a lethal stare. The woman stared back at her as I lowered the rifle and set it butt first onto the ground.

"What's your name?" I asked of her.

"What does that matter?" she retorted.

I shrugged and threw the rifle into the trees. "It doesn't."

"Why aren't you going to kill us?" the man inquired.

"I never said *I* wasn't going to," Verin muttered as she wiped away some of the blood on Morax's cheek.

Across from me, the woman lifted a blonde eyebrow and wiped her forearm across her dirt-streaked forehead. Her pale blonde hair hung over her shoulder in a braid. Leaves and twigs were interwoven through the braid causing it to blend in with the forest around her.

"Bale, go back and let the others know they can proceed, and bring us some rope," I requested.

She nodded then turned and disappeared into the forest without a sound.

"I'd rather be dead than be a prisoner," the woman grated through her teeth.

I chuckled as I folded my arms over my chest. "We don't do prisoners. You're going to be staying right here."

Her eyes widened as realization dawned on her. "Tying us up here is as good as killing us. You have no idea the things that are in this forest."

"I have a very good idea what is in this forest. You had better hope your friends regain consciousness in time to untie you two, but I'm not leaving you free after you tried to ambush us."

"No one ambushed you. You came into *our* territory."

"Wren—"

"Shh," she hissed at the man beside her when he started to speak.

Verin helped Morax to his feet; they spoke in a low whisper before she broke away. She continued to glare at the two humans as she stalked over to stand beside me. "What would you call it then?" Verin demanded. "You were setting yourselves up to attack us when we came down the hill."

"I'd call it protecting what is ours," Wren replied flippantly.

"Those supplies and trucks are ours, Wren," I said, drawing her infuriated gaze back to me.

Her lip curled up in a sneer. "Not if they're in *our* territory. Besides, we always have to defend ourselves against demons such as you."

The woman irritated me, but something about her reminded me of River. Most likely, it was her unwillingness to back down. They were both stubborn and defiant, but this woman had a savage air about her that River didn't possess. This woman would cut off someone's head as easily as shake their hand.

"You have no idea what kind of a demon I am," I told her as the rumble of the trucks neared. "Or the things I am capable of. Consider yourself lucky to still have your feet attached to your body and your tongue in your throat."

For the first time since the altercation began, the woman showed some hint of alarm as the color drained from her dirt-streaked face. Beneath the layers of grime and her abrasive demeanor, she may have been pretty, but it was difficult to tell.

"If it wasn't for us, your entire species would be dead already!" Verin said. "And believe me when I say you're walking the edge of death right now."

Wren shot her a look, her mouth clamped together but hostility radiated from her.

"Easy," Morax said and walked over to rest his hand on Verin's shoulder. "I'm fine."

Verin took a deep breath before relaxing her shoulders. She

brushed her fingers over the dried blood still sticking to the fading bullet hole in his cheek. "Yes, you are," she murmured.

Wren's eyes shot back and forth between them before her gaze landed on me. I stared back at her, keeping my expression blank as I felt the sting of the rest of the bullets working their way out of my body. A door closed, and a minute later, Bale returned with rope in her hand.

"You can't tie us up and leave us here," the man said. "Just kill us. It would be kinder in the end."

"Tempting, but I promised someone I would try not to kill humans anymore. Maybe leaving you here is a death sentence, but maybe it's not. Not my problem either way," I replied. "Hands out."

Wren tilted her chin up further but didn't move her arms.

"Either do it willingly, or I'll knock you out and tie you up. I think you have a better shot of surviving if you're not unconscious," I told her.

She hesitated before thrusting her hands out before her. Taking hold of her wrists, I tied them together before wrapping the other end of the rope around a tree and binding her there while Shax and Bale worked to tie the man up. Retrieving the rifle, I propped it against a tree.

"We are not all monsters," I said to her.

She jerked on the rope and lifted her hands into the air. "Are you sure about that?"

A cruel smile twisted my mouth as I leaned toward her. "You have no idea what monsters truly are, but if we fail, you will. If that happens, you will look back on this moment and *know* I was right."

"Fail at what?" she demanded.

"I see you again, I *will* kill you," I told her, ignoring her question. She glowered at me but didn't say a word. "Let's go," I said to the others. "We've already wasted too much time."

A sense of urgency drove me as I ran through the woods to the waiting trucks. I had to get to River before it was too late.

CHAPTER TWENTY-ONE

RIVER

"Shit," Corson muttered as he stared at the ghosts floating above and swooping toward us.

"Please don't piss them off," Erin whispered.

"This way," Daisy said as she hovered before us.

I tried to take them all in, but there were so many various ages, eras, and races of ghosts, that I couldn't quite process what I was seeing. They clustered against us, causing the air to grow colder from their nearness, as Daisy led the way across the concrete floor of the vast warehouse.

None of the ghosts touched me, but the hair on my arms stood on end. The temperature couldn't be more than twenty degrees at the most, something for which my thin, brown shirt was completely inadequate. I understood why this place had been so bright now though; there were enough apparitions in here to light the entire barrier wall.

"Is this her?" one of them asked as he floated by my face, peering at me far too intently for my liking after what I'd put up with from Pervy and freaky Pompadour.

"Shh," Daisy murmured. "They're being hunted. We must get them to safety."

"Is it her?" he asked again.

I realized as we continued forward that ghosts really had no concept of manners, life or death urgency, or being discreet. Daisy disappeared through another set of swinging doors and I hurried behind her, eager to escape from the thousands of ghosts staring at us.

One of the doors squeaked when I pushed it open, but not loud enough to carry far. I assumed we'd be outside once we left the warehouse; instead, we entered another room full of more ghosts. There was absolutely nothing else in what I assumed was another storage room except for the ghosts and us. We were never going to escape them, I realized. Even if we could lose the demons, we would never be free of all the freaking ghosts.

"Is it you?" my new persistent stalker demanded of me.

"I am me," I replied, wishing I could hide in a vat of salt right now.

He zipped around so he was floating less than a foot in front of me, causing me to stop abruptly. He didn't look much older than I did and the military fatigues he wore resembled the cut and design of this time period.

"I can't talk to angels," I said in exasperation before he could ask.

He hovered in front of me before darting away to join the mass of others forming a circle no more than five feet away. It was like being enclosed in a blurry, gray bubble as they zipped back and forth all around us. I couldn't tell if they were agitated or excited, but I wanted out of here and away from them.

"Maybe you should tell them you *can* talk to angels," Vargas murmured.

"I'm not going to lie to them," I said.

"They'd follow us all the way into the pits of Hell if she told them that," Corson said. "They may not like to move around at night, but they can cover a lot of distance during the day."

"Can you close the unnatural gateway into Hell?" another asked as she floated up beside me.

I took an involuntary step away from her. "I don't know."

"I think you can do it."

I had the backing of the ghost population, good to know.

"Looks a little too skinny and weak to me," another said.

Okay, I didn't have the backing of all of them.

"She does," some of the others murmured.

There really was nothing like being insulted by a bunch of ghosts to help build my confidence.

"Looks can be deceiving," some of the others murmured.

"I think she looks strong."

"Maybe she is."

"I wonder what she can do."

My head bounced back and forth as I tried to follow their conversation.

"She's a World Walker, of *course* she's strong."

There were those words again. My forehead furrowed when that statement caused them all to become more agitated and their whispers grew louder.

"What does that mean? What's a World Walker?" I inquired, but none of them heard me, or at least they didn't respond as they continued to swirl and talk excitedly amongst themselves.

"Shh," Daisy said. "They've come for her. If you don't quiet down, they'll find her and then we'll have no hope."

The ghosts' murmurs died down and they stopped zipping around. Daisy waved us forward and passed straight through yet another set of swinging doors. I hesitated outside the doors, wanting to question the ghosts more, but Erin nudged me forward. "Later, let's get out of here first."

I relented to her prodding as the ghosts hovered closer to me once more. Vargas and Corson were the first ones to push open one of the next doors. I followed behind them and stopped abruptly when we entered into a garage bay.

A Mac truck was parked on one side of the bay. The passenger side door was open to reveal the black interior and a pair of fuzzy dice hanging from the mirror. I spotted dusty and faded pictures sticking out from around the flipped up sun visors.

The lack of ghosts in the room caused me to stop abruptly on the other side of the door. After encountering so many of them along the way here, the bay seemed barren. The only light came from a bare bulb hanging from a ceiling cord next to the truck's driver side window.

"Why are there no ghosts in here?" I asked Daisy when we caught up to her at the back of the garage.

"It smells funny," she replied.

I exchanged a look with the others. It smelled of motor oil, rubber, diesel fuel, and grease, but nothing so outstanding I would find it repelling.

"What is it you don't like about the smell?" Hawk asked.

"I don't know," she replied absently. "It just smells off."

Something more than salt repelled ghosts. I'd have to find out what that was in case I started to develop a following of spectral beings who believed I had a direct line to the angels. I'd bottle it and use it as a perfume if I had to.

"What do the ghosts think I can do for them, besides talk to the angels?" I asked her when she stopped beside a single, metal door.

She glanced over her shoulder at me. "You might be able to close the gateway."

"What good will that do for ghosts?"

"We want to be invisible again. At one time we believed nothing could be worse than being invisible and unable to communicate with the living. We were wrong. We now know there is nothing worse than being a constant source of fear to most humans. There are those rare humans who accept us, but we have become outcasts, trapped out here in the middle of nowhere."

"And if I can close the gateway, you'll go back to obscurity?" I inquired.

"We hope so," she whispered.

I didn't say there was a good possibility I couldn't do what so many hoped I could. I tried not to think about it myself. If I failed, I failed all humankind and demon-kind. And now, apparently ghost-kind too. If I thought about all of that too much, I'd climb into the black pit where the mechanics once worked underneath the truck, hug my knees to my chest, and never come out again.

I was twenty-two years old and they'd plopped an entire destiny I'd never known about into my lap. I took a deep breath to steady myself as the weight of the world settled onto my shoulders. Now I knew what Atlas had felt like, but he'd been a titan and I was a mere mortal. I may not be completely human, but I was still susceptible to death and dismemberment.

Now thousands, probably millions of ghosts around the world, either believed or doubted I might be able to pull off something I didn't pretend to comprehend.

If you can't do it, it doesn't mean you failed. It simply means all of them were wrong.

I told myself this, but if I failed, it would haunt me for the rest of my days, and I would blame myself.

"Are you okay?" Erin asked from beside me.

I forced myself to speak through the lump in my throat. "Yes."

"This door goes outside," Daisy said.

In the room behind us, shouts erupted. "Get out!" someone screamed.

"Not welcome! Not welcome!" Became a chanting mantra that blocked out any other noise.

"We have to get out of here," Corson said.

Daisy vanished through the door. Corson grabbed the handle and twisted it hard enough to break it off as he pushed it open. No light illuminated the alley when we stepped into the hushed night. I froze when I discovered Daisy flattened against the side of the building, somehow looking paler than she had before.

"Daisy, are you okay?" I inquired.

"Hate the dark," she murmured.

"Unbelievable," Vargas muttered.

"Go back inside," I said to her. "Thank you for your help."

"We'll keep them distracted for as long as we can. Good luck to you. I have faith in you," she gushed before fleeing back inside the building.

CHAPTER TWENTY-TWO

KOBAL

"Have you ever considered staying on Earth if we close this gateway?" I asked Bale as I drove the truck.

I barely paid attention to the ruts and holes in the roadway as my teeth clacked against each other and my head bounced off the ceiling numerous times. Most of the bullets had worked their way out of me and my flesh was repairing itself, but the jarring of the truck caused some of the wounds to tear and spill fresh blood over my clothes.

"I think we all have," she replied. "But that is your choice to make. It would be your decision to allow us to remain."

I glanced over at her before swerving out of the way of a hole in the earth. The tires spun in the grass and dirt lining the side of the road, pinging the undercarriage with debris before I corrected the truck back onto the road.

"Are you thinking about it?" she asked.

"I'm considering it."

"Because of River?"

"She would be part of it," I admitted.

"And the other part?"

"We've been screwed over by angels and humans for thousands of years. I see no reason to be locked away in Hell again if we don't have to be. Before it was necessary to keep our existence secret because that was the way our world coincided with the human world, but that isn't necessary anymore. We no longer have to live in secret. Granted, a good chunk of the human population still doesn't know we exist, but I see no reason why these desolate areas can't become ours when this is over."

"You'll have demons around you all the time, looking to pass back and forth in order to feed and retain their immortality. You won't be able to keep your gate open to allow us to survive on Earth. There are still things living within Hell that should never be allowed to roam free here," she said.

Hunger seared through my veins and made my gut clench at the mention of feeding. I couldn't recall the last time I'd fed. It had been longer than my customary week, but I couldn't stop now, even if it would only take a few minutes to find some wraiths to feed from.

"There will be a lot to work out in the beginning, but I see no reason why we should be denied a world of light when we're the ones helping to keep it that way," I said. "Most will probably prefer to return to Hell, but some would probably stay."

"Most will probably stay here," she said quietly.

I glanced questioningly at her.

With a sigh, she rose up from where she'd been leaning against the door to sit straight in the seat. "Many of us prefer it here. It smells better. The humans can be annoying, but a few of them are enjoyable, and you have to admit, Earth is just an overall nicer place to be. We're the monsters here, and I'm okay with that. Lucifer has to be stopped, the gateway has to be closed, but afterward, many would stay if they could."

"Why didn't you express this opinion before?"

"I never believed you would ever consider it. You were always so adamant about defeating Lucifer and returning to Hell. It is your throne."

"It will be my throne here too."

"What if the humans object?" she inquired.

"They won't have any choice as far as I'm concerned."

Bale's mouth quirked in a smile. "No, they wouldn't. We all would return to Hell with you if that was what you decided, but I'd prefer to stay. Hell was the only home we'd ever known for centuries, but I actually like this planet. Our queen is also here, and she's one of the few humans I actually respect and admire, as do the others."

A muscle twitched in my jaw as we bounced over another rut in the road. "If I could, I would take her mortality from her now, but I can't try to do it until this is over. I can't take the risk she won't survive it while the gateway is still open."

"I know."

I focused on the road again as the headlights bounced over the broken asphalt before us. "We're getting close to Pearl's."

But would it be in time?

~

RIVER

"Come on," Corson said.

He kept his back against the building as we made our way toward the trailer-less Mac trucks I'd seen parked beside the building when we first arrived. Slipping past the front tires of one, we knelt by the bumper of a large blue truck to survey the parking lot while Erin, Vargas, and Hawk kept an eye on the building behind us.

I could see our white pickup parked about a hundred and fifty feet away. It was so close yet so unbelievably far away. "Are we going to make a run for it?" Vargas inquired.

"They were right behind us inside the building. We might be able to make it," I said.

"And if they split up before entering the building, or after they entered, and one of them is out front now?" Corson inquired.

"Bullets hurt us, but they don't stop demons, and your abilities are too sporadic to rely on right now."

"They've gotten better," I reminded him.

"They have, but are you willing to run out there and expose all of us to someone who may be waiting? These aren't the same as the creatures we've seen so far. These are Lucifer's followers, and if one of them isn't a lower-level demon, then he has abilities."

I shuddered at the implication of his words and the calculation our trackers were probably using. One of them would be waiting for us up front somewhere, and I had a feeling I knew who it would be. I felt trapped, pinned to the spot, as I glanced at the door behind us before turning back to look at our pickup again. Why couldn't I have a vision when I *really* wanted to have one?

"Do you hear or see anything back there?" I asked.

"No one has come out yet," Erin replied.

"They won't be much longer," Hawk said.

Vargas crept closer to the rest of us. "We can't continue to sit here."

"We wait to see who comes out the back," Corson replied.

"And if they have split up and pin us in between them?" I asked.

"They've already pinned us if that's the case."

"What if we went around to the back of the building and out the other side of it? We'd have to leave the truck, but it sounds like we may have already been forced to abandon it." As soon as I said this, my fingers curled with the compulsion to wrap them around the angel I'd left on the dashboard of the truck.

No such thing as a good luck charm.

Maybe not, but I wanted it back.

"We won't have enough time to get by the door before they come out," Corson said.

"We could get in one of these trucks and wait for them to come by," Hawk suggested.

Corson's head tipped back as he studied the doors above our heads. "Do it. You two, get in that one," he pointed to Hawk and

Erin before pointing at the blue truck to our left. "You get in that one," he said to Vargas and pointed to the red one on our right. Finally, he turned to me. "You, come with me."

The three of them rose and cautiously pulled open the doors of the trucks. Hawk waited for Erin to climb in before following behind her. Vargas didn't bother with the door, but climbed up the side of the wheel well and in through the open passenger window. I followed Corson around the front of the red truck and over to a black one. Rising up, Corson slid his hand under the handle and cautiously pulled open the passenger side door before stepping aside and waving his hand for me to enter.

I scrambled inside. He climbed in behind me and noiselessly closed the door. "Stay down."

He gestured for me to sit back so he could move in front of me on the bench seat to the driver's side. Lying down, he tilted his head so he could watch the driver's side mirror. I pushed my back against the seat and turned so I'd be able to see out the passenger mirror.

From my angle in the mirror, I saw more of the other trucks in the alley than anything else. I couldn't see the door into the garage bay, but I could see enough of the alley that I would spot the demons when they were twenty feet away from the truck.

My heart pounded against my ribs, and sweat trickled down my forehead and temple. I steadied the tremor in my hand when I held my gun against my chest. I felt like I'd turned into a piece of stone as all of my muscles froze, and I barely breathed while time seemed to stretch on endlessly.

The interior of the truck reeked of mildew and something feral, probably mice or some other wild creature that had made this truck its home. Cracks lined the seat beneath me and springs jabbed me in my back and ass. Tufts of yellow cushion poked through the pieces of vinyl seating, which had been chewed off completely in some places. Light from the front of the building dimly illuminated the dashboard.

Something squeaked beneath the truck, causing Corson's head

to snap around and adrenaline to rush through me. When another squeal sounded, Corson relaxed and my shoulders sagged at the realization it was some animal making its way through the night. I lifted my head a little over the top of the dashboard, but I saw no shadows or movement on the brightly lit pavement in front of me.

Corson grasped my arm and jerked me down. He pointed at his ear before laying further down in his seat once more. My attention returned to the mirror as the first boot and pant leg stepped into view. I tensed and gritted my teeth together.

Another leg materialized and then a third and fourth, only two demons. I glanced at Corson, reading the truth in his eyes. The other one, and I *knew* it was Handsome, was at the front of the building, waiting for us.

The demons didn't speak as they moved past my line of vision in the mirror, but stone crunched beneath their boots when they stopped beside the truck. I could almost feel them through the metal separating us, standing there, searching the night.

My lungs burned, but I refused to so much as breathe while I waited to see what they would do.

Then I heard the stone crunch again as their steps continued on. I didn't kid myself into believing they would leave or think we'd somehow managed to escape them. No, they would be coming back and there was only one place for them to look when they did.

CHAPTER TWENTY-THREE

KOBAL

I stepped out of the truck to survey the wreckage blocking the middle of the road. Four vehicles had tumbled across the roadway and crashed into each other between the rock wall and the guardrail lining the other side of the road.

"They would have come this way," I said as I stepped away from the driver's side door. "Pearl's is five miles straight ahead."

"They may have doubled back," Bale suggested, but I heard the tone of disbelief in her voice.

"This was recent," I said.

"How can you tell?" one of the humans inquired.

"Gas is still dripping from that car." I pointed at the side of the small, overturned, red car and the bead of gas forming at the bottom of the gas tank. "This wasn't an accident. These cars were purposely put here."

"Why would someone do that?" Verin inquired.

A cold chill shot through my heart as my fangs burst free. "They know where River is."

"How could they possibly know that?" Bale asked.

"Ghosts," Shax sneered.

"Lucifer is behind this," I said. "He's sent someone for her."

"How do you know that?" Shax asked.

I switched into our language to answer him. I didn't care if it upset the humans not to know what we were speaking about; I didn't want them to have any information about River that they didn't need to know. "She connected with Lucifer in that dream she had a while back. He knows she is my Chosen and his progeny. He didn't know where she was living before, but he would have surmised she is American from speaking with her, and her dialect is of the northeast. He must have sent some of his minions in search of her, and now they know where she is."

"Shit," Morax said.

Desperate to get to her, I stormed over to one of the overturned cars. My muscles bulged and sweat beaded my brow as I grasped the roof of the car. With a low growl, I lifted it from the ground and flipped it away. The screeching sound of metal twisting filled the air as the vehicle bounced over the road.

Springs and glass scattered across the road before the car slammed into the guardrail and teetered precariously on its side against the rail. Beneath the weight of the car, the guardrail bowed outward before giving way. The car slid over the side of the embankment.

Turning away, I gripped the front bumper of the other car and bent down to lift it up. My shirt tore across my back as I threw the vehicle aside. More metal screeched and sparked across the asphalt, but I barely noticed it before I turned my attention to removing the truck and finally the SUV from the road.

When I'd cleared the truck out of the way, the broken road lay beyond, stretching endlessly into the night. River was only five miles away, but it felt like hundreds of miles separated us. Running back to the vehicle, I didn't wait for Bale to get completely inside before stomping on the gas. She cursed loudly and grabbed the door to close it.

"Easy, Kobal, you're going to break one of the tires off," she cautioned.

My teeth ground together as the truck bounced over the ruts so hard that my knees hit the wheel and my head bounced off the roof. I didn't ease off the gas. I couldn't. We were so close, yet I could feel River slipping away.

She was in danger, and whoever was in pursuit of her now would take her to Lucifer, where he would try to twist her and do things to her that would break her. Or he would kill her outright if he felt she couldn't be of use to him.

I'd die before I ever let anyone hurt her in such a way.

An unfamiliar emotion swelled within me. It was more than fear, more than desperation and it took me a minute to pinpoint exactly what it was; terror. I'd never experienced it before, not even when Lucifer had nearly killed me all those years ago, had I felt terror. I'd only known anger then and a determination to survive so that I could destroy him.

River was mine to protect and cherish, but I began to realize there was more to what I felt for her than the Chosen bond forged between us. I cared for her, I respected and admired her, and now it sank in that I was also in love with her.

I'd told her that demons loved too, and I had meant it. However, I never thought I'd be talking about myself when I said those words to her. I'd seen the love between Morax and Verin, as well as other demons with their Chosen. I'd witnessed the love of demon parents for their offspring, but I'd never had parents and I'd never been in love, before.

Being bonded to her as my Chosen was one thing, this was something else entirely, something deeper. I didn't know why I hadn't seen it sooner, why I hadn't told her, but I saw it now. Love for her swelled within my chest, clutched at my heart and drove me to push down harder on the gas pedal.

The truck groaned when it left the road and crashed down with enough force to crack something beneath it. "Kobal!" Bale hissed when her head hit the ceiling.

"Hold on!"

I jerked the wheel in order to avoid a hole that would have

broken off a tire if we'd been doing ten instead of pushing sixty. None of the other vehicles kept up with our pace, except for the one Shax drove, and he was a good fifty feet behind us. Bale clutched the handle over her head, but she still slammed into the passenger side window so hard the glass fractured beneath the impact of her elbow. She rubbed at her injury while she glowered at me.

We were only two miles from the truck stop when another rut in the road sent us into the air again. Crashing back to the earth, whatever had cracked beneath before, now gave way with a reverberating bang. The entire truck wobbled before the passenger side tire spun away from the vehicle. The truck tilted to the right, the bumper leaning toward the road before plowing into the asphalt.

Sparks flew up against the windshield as the vehicle continued its skid across the pavement. It tore up the roadway and sent chunks of asphalt flying by us before it dug in entirely and the ass end of the truck lifted behind us. I pressed my hands against the roof, bracing myself when I realized the truck was going to flip.

A creaking sound filled the cab as the back wheels rose directly above us so the vehicle stood on its front bumper. The truck hesitated there for a second before going over with a loud squeal. My teeth jarred together from the impact as the truck rolled over. Going over the guardrail, the truck flipped end over end as it plunged down the hillside.

The world became a blur as supplies tumbled out and smashed into the window behind me. The window finally gave way. Glass crashed and bounced around us as it filled the cab. Metal crumpled and broke in a rising cacophony of sound. Packs of food, water, and clothing slipped in from the cab to bash against my side and face as the truck rolled one more time before coming to a stop on the passenger side against a grouping of trees.

The roof all around me was dented in, but my hands had kept the roof directly above me from caving in. My side and jaw throbbed from where debris had pummeled against me. Taking stock of the rest of my body, I realized everything else remained intact.

"Bale?" I asked.

"I'm fine," she muttered, and I spotted her as she pushed herself up from the floor. Blood trickled down her cheek as she glared at me, but I saw no other injuries on her. "Fantastic driving."

I ignored her as I tore the steering wheel from the column and tossed it aside. Lifting my feet, I drove them into the windshield that had somehow managed to stay intact. The splintered glass shattered beneath my boots. Grasping what remained of the roof, I pulled myself from the wreckage. Once I perched on the dented and torn remains of the hood, I turned to take hold of Bale's arm to help her out of the demolished vehicle.

She perched beside me, her hair a tangled mess around her as she surveyed the hill we'd crashed down.

"I have to go." I leapt away from Bale, my feet hitting the soft ground with a thud.

I didn't look back as I raced up the side of the embankment toward the road. Rage swirled within me as my heart raced. Anyone who dared to touch one hair on River's head, I'd tear them to shreds and bathe in their blood.

Bale cursed loudly, but I heard her footsteps as she followed me up the hill. Lights from Shax's vehicle lit the roadway when it came to a stop at the top of the hill just as I burst free of the broken trees the truck had destroyed on its tumble down the hill.

"Stay with the humans!" I barked at him. "Wait for them to catch up!"

Turning, I fled down the road, forcing myself to run faster than I ever had before.

CHAPTER TWENTY-FOUR

River

"What do we do?" I whispered to Corson.

"You don't do anything but stay in this truck if they come back. Kobal will have my ass if something happens to you."

I knew he could feel me staring daggers into his back, but he didn't bother to look at me again. I refrained from saying I could take care of myself. It would be pointless; he wouldn't change his mind.

Corson's hand stretched out for the handle as Daisy's upper body materialized through the floor of the truck to her waist. Corson and I recoiled from her. Blood burst into my mouth when I bit my tongue to keep from shrieking. Daisy lowered her lashes, fluttering them in what I took to be an abashed expression, but I thought she was also fighting a giggle.

"Don't do that!" Corson spat.

"Sorry, I came to warn you they were at the front of the building," she apologized.

"We know."

"Thank you, Daisy," I said and glared at Corson.

He scowled back at me before turning to watch the mirror

again. Daisy's head and torso remained floating half in and half out of the truck. The disconcerting sight gave me the creeps; I wanted to tell her to make it stop and either get in or out, but I couldn't bring myself to hurt her feelings. We wouldn't have made it this far without her help, and she had braved the dark to come help us further.

"Can I do something else to help?" she asked.

"You've done more than enough," I assured her.

"Stay in here so they don't see you leaving," Corson told her and rested his hand on the handle.

"You can't go out there," I said to him.

"Can't stay in here," he replied.

I opened my mouth to protest, but the muffled sound of a click stopped me. He edged the door open enough for him to slide down the side of the truck and land on the ground. "Stay," he said to me before quietly closing the door.

Lifting my head a little, I cautiously peered over the dash as Corson stepped into view in front of the truck. I held my breath as he strode toward the gas pumps and the front of the building with an actual *swagger* in his step.

"When will they be able to see him?" I asked Daisy.

"When he gets around the corner, or at least that's where they were before I came out here."

I turned so my hand rested on the other handle. Corson would kick my ass, but I couldn't leave him out there alone. "Can you go under the truck and let me know if it's safe to get out?"

Daisy bit on her bottom lip and straightened her shoulders. She visibly wavered, or what I took to be a ghost shaking, before vanishing from the floorboard. I braced myself for her reappearance, but my pulse still did a little two-step when her head emerged a foot in front of mine again.

"You can get out," she whispered.

"Thank you. Go back inside, Daisy."

She visibly quaked again before disappearing in a blur I could barely follow with my eyes. I didn't think I'd ever get used to seeing ghosts go through things; it was too weird. I took a deep breath as I rested my hand on the handle before silently opening the door.

I slipped from the truck and scurried around to the back of it before Corson spotted me and lost his mind. I knelt by the back left-hand corner of the truck and poked my head around the rusted bumper as Corson stepped out from around the corner of the building. Lifting his fingers to the side of his head, he gave a brief wave before firing three shots from his gun at something I couldn't see.

"Hey you fuckers!" he shouted. "I'm guessing you're as stupid as you are ugly!"

He just loves to taunt things.

Corson spun back toward the alley. Going to my hands and knees, pebbles bit into my flesh as I rolled under the truck and across the ground to the front tire. Rising, I flattened my back against the cracked rubber of the tire. My lungs burned as my breath remained trapped in my chest.

Corson may like to taunt things he probably shouldn't, but it worked as the two demons with the pig snouts chased him into the alley. Their feet slapped over the dirt and rock as they followed him past the entrance to the garage and around the back of the building.

I remained unmoving, frozen against the tire as I waited for Handsome to show himself. I didn't have to wait long. His black pants and shiny boots stepped into view at the head of the alley. He appeared to have no interest in chasing after Corson. I didn't think Corson had expected him to, but was going for a more divide and conquer plan.

"I know you're here," Handsome called down the alley in a singsong voice nearly as beautiful as he was. "I can *smell* you."

The strange inhaling noise he made after this statement made me cringe. I had no idea who he was, but he would never get his hands on me; I'd die first. Which might be a possibility.

No, I realized, these creatures would do everything they could to take me alive, and that may end up being far worse than death. Kobal had told me that if his marks upon my body faded away, demons would still sense them and know to whom I belonged. Did they scent Kobal on me now, or would they have to see me in order to know who had marked me?

My fingers dug into the dirt beneath me. My biggest fear had been the Craeton demons capturing me and taking me to Lucifer to use as a weapon against Kobal, and now it may come true. Taking a deep breath, I adjusted the katana on my back as I steadied myself. I would not allow that to happen.

And what will become of him if you die? He brushes off your questions about what happens to one Chosen when the other is gone, but Corson's mother killed herself when his father died.

That may be true, but right now, it didn't matter. All that mattered was trying to survive a confrontation with this monster without being taken.

I pressed closer against the rubber, wishing I could somehow melt into it like Daisy. I listened to Handsome's feet crunching as he strolled down the alley; the annoying little tune he whistled set my teeth on edge.

My fingers dug into the tire as I turned to watch him, rotten bits of it broke off beneath my fingers and clung to my flesh. He stopped on the other side of me, so close that if I reached out I could touch the tip of his black boot. I remained motionless, waiting for my opportunity to make a move. I'd only have one chance against him.

Power radiated from him; his life force crackled against my skin. My fingers itched to feel the pulse of his life. He'd be enough to fuel a big ball of 'I'm going to kick your ass' life, but he'd never allow me to hold onto him for enough time to really get the ball to grow. He didn't give off as much life force as Kobal did, but it was more than Corson and the other demons.

"Come now, girl, let's not play this game. It's beneath you." His voice sounded abnormally loud in the unnatural hush surrounding the truck stop, or maybe my senses had kicked into hyper-drive.

He turned away from me, and before I could guess his intentions, the sound of metal ripping apart screeched across my eardrums. I winced at the grating noise seconds before gunfire erupted. The door of a truck fell onto the ground, kicking up dirt and pebbles as it bounced against the tire where I remained hidden.

The gunfire stopped. Vargas grunted, and the man's heels came off the ground as he leaned into the truck. *No!* I wouldn't let anyone else be taken or harmed because of me.

Rolling out from under the truck, I emerged as Handsome pulled Vargas out of the truck by his ankle and dangled him in the air like a child's doll. This creature would pluck Vargas apart one body part at a time.

Snatching up the door Handsome had dropped on the ground, I lifted it up and swung it into the back of the demon's knees. This close, I could see he had some kind of black protection or armor shielding his back to mid-calf. His knees buckled, but somehow he managed to stay upright. Rising to my feet, I lifted the door again and crashed it onto his back. This time, he finally released Vargas, who fell on his head.

Vargas's body slumped to the ground, unmoving. I couldn't tell if he was dead or unconscious, and I didn't have time to look as my attention was focused on his attacker. My hands, jarred and partially numb from the impact of the second hit, lost their grip on the door.

Handsome turned toward me, but he wasn't quite so good looking now as the bullets Vargas had fired had pierced his forehead, taken out a chunk of his cheek, and embedded in the back of his jaw. His tongue wiggled back and forth in his mouth against the place where his cheek had been.

As I watched, his body pushed the bullets out, making them squirm backward like worms rising from the earth during a rain. I had no idea if Kobal or any of the others could do something like this; I'd never seen any of them get shot. He'd said human weapons could hurt them, but it would take a lot to kill them. Apparently, it took more than three bullets to the face, and I had no idea how many others had pierced this guy's body before he'd succeeded in disarming Vargas.

Handsome's black eyes blazed with malice when they latched onto me. A shiver went down my spine, and a sense of déjà vu washed over me as I gazed into those black eyes. Eyes that had once held color and warmth, now held nothing but malice and cruelty within their coal-colored depths.

Azote. I had no idea *how* I knew this, but when his name blazed across my mind, I knew it was right, and with his name came the realization, *Not armor! Not demon!* My breath froze, and my blood turned to ice as I realized he was one of the angels who had fallen from Heaven with Lucifer.

"Shit," I breathed.

His full mouth curved into a smile as his wings rippled behind him but didn't unfurl. Black, like Lucifer's had been in my dream. I knew these wings would be as malformed and lethal as my ancestor's were when stretched out. This close, I could see the deadly, silver tips of the wings resting behind his head. Those tips weren't as long as Lucifer's, but they were a good three-inches of 'poke my eye out' fun. I didn't dare tear my eyes away from him, but I knew without looking there would be two more silver tips at the bottom of those hideous wings.

"That wasn't a very polite way to greet your uncle," he murmured, his voice still pretty and his face nearly repaired. "I was sent as a welcoming gift for you, child, to assure you were taken to where you belong. Your father sends his regards."

My stomach lurched as I realized Azote was the gift Lucifer had promised to send me in my dream. He'd sent this angel, and possibly others to find me, to bring me back to him because they all truly believed Lucifer was my *father*.

I was going to throw up, as soon as this was over.

At least the others hadn't heard what he'd had to say. Vargas was still out of it, if he wasn't dead, and Hawk and Erin were too far away to have heard his words. They may have been warming up to me throughout all of this, but I doubted anyone would want to associate with the descendent of Lucifer.

Spinning, I threw myself to the side when one of those black wings swung at me in an attempt to knock me on my ass. The wind the motion created blew my hair forward as the wing whistled only centimeters above my head. He wanted me alive, but he didn't care if I still walked.

Scrambling forward, I rolled and seized the discarded door again as Vargas's head lifted and his eyes blinked blearily at me. His head swayed on his shoulders, but he managed to lift his gun and hold it before him. I lifted the door, using it as a shield when Azote swiped at me with his wing again.

The wing hitting against the metal knocked me into Vargas. My back pressed against his chest as we were pinned against the tire by my demented, angel "uncle." Azote's wing tip screeched across the metal door like fingernails on a chalkboard. I cringed and resisted the impulse to cover my ears against the sound.

"Get under the truck," I commanded Vargas.

Vargas's breath was heavy in my ear. "I can shoot him again."

"That only pissed him off."

Azote drew his arm back and drove his fist into the door so hard that he dented the middle of it. My eyes crossed as I stared at the perfect imprint of his fist now touching the tip of my nose. The metal creaked when he yanked his hand from it. Taking the opportunity, I drew my feet up against the inside of the door. With a loud shout, I thrust it away from me and straight up at him, knocking him back a step.

I didn't stay to see what happened as I swiftly rolled under the truck behind Vargas and popped up on the other side of it. I leaned my back against the step rail on the passenger's side, while I struggled to get my breathing under control and formulate a plan. If I could draw Azote into the open, I may be able to hit him with some fire, but I had no idea what would happen in these close confines.

I rested my hand against the ground, feeling the spark of life beneath me, but like the fire, I didn't dare unleash it amongst these trucks.

"Come now, child, do you think that's going to stop me?" Azote taunted from the other side of the truck.

I was beginning to think nothing could stop him, but we had to keep moving.

The driver side door on the truck across from us started to open. I leapt forward and pushed it closed again before it could open more than an inch. Erin's head popped up behind the window.

Stay hidden, I mouthed to her.

I kept my hand against the door, ignoring the 'if looks could kill' stare she gave me as I strained to hear what was going on around me. Right now they were safe and off of Azote's radar; I hoped to keep them that way. Vargas stayed against my back, facing in the opposite direction while we waited to see what Azote's next move would be.

A loud groaning noise filled the air. I had no idea what was going on until the truck we'd rolled under tilted toward us. "Roll! Roll! Roll!" Vargas shouted.

I clawed at the dirt and rocks beneath me as I scrambled forward. Throwing myself down, I rolled beneath the truck with Vargas at my heels as the other truck hit the ground behind us with a loud crash. A rush of air blew dirt into my eyes when I turned to look back.

I hastily wiped away the grainy bits of dust sticking to my lashes. My body froze when I found myself staring at the roof of the other truck directly across from us. Beside me, a tremor ran through Vargas's body.

"We have to move," Vargas panted.

"Yes," I whispered.

Rolling out from under the truck, we leapt out on the other

side as Hawk flung his door open and jumped down. Erin followed close on his heels. I didn't try to stop them. If Azote turned this truck over, they'd be trapped inside with only one way out. We stood, listening to Azote's crunching footsteps as he strolled across the lot toward us.

"Come out, come out, wherever you are!" he called in a singsong voice that made me decide to set his balls on fire first.

CHAPTER TWENTY-FIVE

RIVER

"Behind the truck," Hawk commanded and waved a hand toward the back of the vehicle.

It wouldn't do us much good, but it would buy us some more time to prepare for Azote's attack. We made it to the back of the truck as Azote stepped around to where we'd been standing. Hawk gripped my hand and pointed at my guns while Vargas reloaded his.

On the count of three, Hawk mouthed. I nodded and pulled one of my guns free of its holster. It would be better to keep my fire ability hidden for a little longer anyway. The less the fallen angels knew about me, the better off I'd be. Hawk held up one finger, then two, then three...

Stepping out from the shelter of the back of the truck, the four of us opened fire on Azote. The gun felt reassuring in my grip, but I knew it would do little against the angel. His body and shoulders jerked backward in tiny, quick motions as the bullets pummeled him.

Then, a sneer curved his mouth and his wings folded against his back. He rushed forward so fast I barely saw him move before he smashed his hand into Vargas's chest. Vargas went flying backward until his body hit the ground with a loud thump. He kicked up plumes of dirt as he bounced across the dirt and came to a halt near the building.

Hawk swung toward Azote, but the angel snagged hold of the end of his Glock and tore it from his hand as if it were no more than a water gun. I dropped my gun when Azote went for Hawk. Before he could grab him, my hands flew up and a blast of fire burst from my palm. Azote jumped back when the crotch of his pants erupted into flames. Fury twisted his features as he beat out the fire licking over his clothes before they could spread too far.

Hawk gawked at him before spinning away to retrieve his weapon. Erin released three more shots before her gun clicked with the sound of an empty chamber; she slowly stepped further away from Azote. I lifted my hands, harnessing my fear to release another blast of fire. Flames erupted and poured from my hands, but Azote blocked the flow by wrapping his wings around his body protectively. The fire swirled over him, beating against his wings and illuminating them in a red and orange glow. The flames illuminated the veins pumping black blood through his bat-like wings.

Fire proof wings, good to know.

"Run!" I yelled at Erin and Hawk when Azote took a step toward us with his wings still up to protect against my fire.

"Not without you!" Hawk declared.

Hawk grabbed for me, but I dodged his hand then darted around Azote's unfurling wings to drive my fist into his cheek. He staggered back, more surprised by the blow than actually effected by it, as his head barely moved. I didn't give him much time to process what was going on before I lifted my leg and drove my foot into his chest, shoving him back another step.

"River!" Hawk shouted. "*Run!*"

He didn't have to tell me twice. Turning, I fled through the trucks toward the parking lot. My feet pounded over the packed dirt and rocks of the alley as my legs and arms pumped faster than ever before. I didn't look back but kept my gaze focused ahead; I didn't want to see what was behind me. Azote would gladly pluck them to pieces, but it was me he would come after now.

I burst into the light of the gas pumps. I didn't bother to go for our truck. Even if I could make it there, the vehicle would do me little good. Azote could lift a Mac truck; he'd have the pickup rolling end over end faster than I could say boo. Plus, I couldn't leave the others behind. I didn't know where Corson was, but I knew he hadn't abandoned us.

I was halfway to the gas pumps when something hit me in the back and sent me rolling head first across the asphalt. The whoosh of flapping wings caused air to blow against my back, and I realized Azote had dive-bombed me. So much for uncle-y love.

Coming to a stop near the edge of the parking lot, my bruised and battered body protested the motion, but I got my hands beneath me and shoved myself to my knees. I was almost to my feet when a hand in my back shoved me forward. My knees screamed when they cracked off the asphalt; trickles of blood slid down my shins to stick my pants to my flesh.

Rolling onto my back, I looked up to find Azote stalking toward me, all six feet of solid muscles and murderous resolve. He was still at least fifty feet away from me, too far to have been able to push me over the second time. Then what had happened?

I looked around, but didn't see anyone else near me, not even a ghost floated by. My gaze fell to the front windows of the truck stop where countless faces peered out from the windows. Their misty bodies were cut into pieces by the blinds slicing through them.

Rising, I shoved my hands beneath me and pushed myself into a sitting position. I was halfway up when Azote lifted his hands and waved them at me. "Stay down," he commanded.

Helpless to resist the invisible force pushing against me, I was shoved back again. *Telekinesis.* The realization made my stomach turn. Now I knew how he'd managed to flip the truck over. What I didn't know was how the hell I was going to get away from him.

He'd been playing with me this whole time, toying with me until now, and the look on his face made it clear he was tired of his new toy.

His shiny black boots stepped beside me. The tattered remains of his pants revealed he wasn't wearing any underwear, but thankfully, there was enough of his pants left to cover his groin.

"You are something," he murmured. "He's going to be so happy to meet you, child."

I managed to get my elbows under me so I wasn't flat on my back, but I found myself unable to move further.

Kneeling beside me, his finger slid under my chin and lifted my head up. "And look at these hideous marks on your neck." His mouth twisted into a cruel smile. "You definitely are your father's daughter, going after the strongest one of them, binding him to you. Your father couldn't crush their leader, so you screwed him."

"I'm nothing like him!" I spat.

"We shall see. I wonder what else you can do."

"River!" Corson's bellow drew both of our gazes as he charged out from the other corner of the diner. His talons were fully extended, dripping florescent green blood onto the asphalt as he ran. The blood covered his clothes and hair. The other two demons were nowhere in view, and judging by the look of Corson, they wouldn't be coming back either.

Azote rose to tower above me. He raised his hands and flung Corson back, pinning him to the wall of the diner. Bursts of gunshots rang out from the area where I'd left the others. I turned to find the three of them standing at the end of the alley with their guns raised. The monster before me spun, his hand flying up. I watched in dismay as the bullets slicing through the air, froze inches before his face.

"Your friends don't realize I already have you and I don't care if they live or not." With a flick of his wrist, the bullets turned and sped away faster than my mortal eye could see.

"Run!" I screamed at them, but they were already fleeing into the shadows of the trucks.

A pain-filled scream rang out from the darkness. With Azote's attention distracted from me, I jerked to the side and swung my legs out. My feet caught Azote at his ankles and knocked him back. Flames erupted at the ends of my fingers. Lifting my hand, I threw another burst at his back, but he spun around, flinging it away with his wing and sending it spiraling into the night.

"You're lucky he wants you alive!" he spat at me.

I managed to scramble back to my feet and made it two steps before something hit me again. I cried out, my hands hitting the ground and barely keeping me up as more blood trickled from my scraped knees.

Across the way, I caught a glimpse of Corson pulling himself off the building and struggling forward. His steps were sluggish, his body bent forward and his arms out before him as he pushed onward against the invisible barrier trying to hold him back.

I pressed my hand against the asphalt, taking a deep breath as I tried to calm my rioting emotions. Fear fueled the fire, but intense emotion was what I had to draw on to dig into the life force flowing all around me. Unfortunately, fear was at the forefront of my emotions right now.

Taking another deep breath, I closed my eyes as I sought the vast conduit of life flowing through the earth. The thick slab of asphalt beneath me blocked some of its flow, but a spark flared across my fingertips.

Kobal had once said this would be my most powerful weapon, and though I'd gotten better at wielding it, I couldn't get the flow of life to build further in me as terror coursed through my body in jolting bursts.

Azote turned back to me, his gaze landing on the golden-white sparks dancing across the tips of my fingers. The look of longing that filled his face was so raw it stole my breath. He groaned in anguish as a tremor worked through him.

I'd once speculated that Lucifer had become so twisted and ruthless because he'd somehow lost his connection to the innate flow of life all the angels felt. Looking at Azote's face now, I knew I'd been right.

Maybe the fall from Heaven had started the corruption of the angels, but the severing of their link to all living things had completely broken them. Which meant Lucifer may have been telling the truth about me after all. I could become evil; the possibility was within me.

Azote's gaze came back to me. The awe and yearning faded away to be replaced with a look of hatred so deep it rocked my soul.

"It's true!" he hissed.

I swung my other hand up, and with a scream, released another ball of fire. I was tired of these pricks, every last one of them. He raised his hand up to knock the ball away, but it still caught hold of his sleeve and licked toward his face. While he was distracted by the flames, I rolled over and leapt to my feet.

Just keep running.

I didn't look back as I ran; I was almost to the edge of the parking lot when I felt a hand grasp my neck. I didn't have time to blink before I was lifted off my feet.

KOBAL

At the top of the hill, my breath rushed in and out of me as I looked down upon the brightly lit truck stop less than half a mile below me. Moving too fast, I'd left Bale behind, but I knew she was coming. A burst of flame drew my attention to where River lay on the asphalt at the feet of someone I couldn't make out against the fire coming from her hands.

River scrambled to her feet, fleeing across the lot. Corson staggered forward, seemingly released from some invisible barrier that had been holding him back. He raced for the one who had been attacking River, his claws out as he leapt up and drove his hand down. The flames extinguished and whoever it was spun to face him. River's attacker screamed in agony when Corson's talons tore through their side.

Corson swung up again, but without even moving a muscle, River's attacker threw Corson into the air and away from them. Corson hit the pavement and skidded backward on his ass toward the building. Spinning back around, the creature went after River once more.

I almost bellowed her name before biting it back. I'd give anything to let her know I was coming for her, but right now, I couldn't give up the element of surprise.

I was halfway down the hill when I realized her attacker wasn't a demon but the fallen angel, Azote. His black wings briefly fluttered when he turned his back to me and his silver hair shimmered in the light flowing over him. His hand encircled River's neck, lifting her off her feet. Rage caused flames to erupt from my hands and circle my wrists. *No* one would ever treat her in such a way and live to tell about it.

My muscles swelled and heaved as the hounds clamored to get to her. Able to move faster than me, they would reach her before I could. Throwing my left arm out, a surge of power slid over my body and down to my fingertips when I set them free. The female, Phenex, erupted from me first in a ball of fire. Flames encircled her as she hit the earth, even her eyes held fire when she lifted her head to look at me. Crux, her mate, followed closely behind her.

Turning away from me, the hounds became surging balls of fire that vibrated the ground with their heavy leaps and bounds as they ran across the earth toward River. Flames and sparks trailed behind them, growing dimmer as the fire enveloping them began to extinguish itself.

Azote pulled River back and tossed her away from him. She bounced across the asphalt before staggering back to her feet and taking a few sideways steps. Falling to the ground, she crawled forward until she made it to the edge of the parking lot. With his hands clasped behind his back, Azote whistled as he strolled after her, playing with her like a cat with a mouse. Azote hadn't seen the hounds yet as his back remained to them, but when he did this game would end and he would do what he could to take River away from here.

She threw herself forward, her hand falling onto the earth. I saw her body shudder as her head lifted and her eyes widened at the hounds barreling down the hill toward her. I should have shown them to her before. She had no way of knowing they were her protectors, not a new attacker.

Azote took another step toward her as she flipped onto her back. Golden-white sparks of light danced across her hand before she turned her palm toward him and released the flow of life she'd harnessed in a powerful blast the likes of which I'd never seen from her before. The stream of light slammed into Azote's chest, flinging him across the parking lot. His arms flailed in the air before he crashed onto the pavement. He skidded on his back into one of the gas pumps.

My heart soared at River's growing ability to wield her lethal power at the same time it sank. Her ability was effective against the fallen angels.

Which meant it would work against Lucifer; she could face him.

The hounds raced past River with a bellowing howl that rattled the windows of the truck stop and reverberated the ground beneath my feet. Azote rose to his feet just as Phenex reared back on her powerful hind legs and leapt forward.

CHAPTER TWENTY-SIX

RIVER

I lay, gaping at where I'd flung Azote into the gas pumps. Small bursts of sparks continued to arc through my fingers as he started to climb back to his feet. The ground beneath me quaked from the impact of the beasts I'd seen racing toward us.

My heart thundered at the sudden appearance of this new enemy. My body was more bruised and battered than it had ever been before. I'd just had my ass handed to me by an angel, and now I'd have to fight off these new creatures too.

The beasts howled as they rushed past me, rattling my eardrums and causing some of the ghosts inside the truck stop to flit away from the windows. I'd never seen anything so amazing or impressive as the dying flames trailing behind the massive creatures.

Azote regained his feet a second before the first one leapt at him. The creature's mouth was wide open and its six-inch hooked claws were ready to rip into Azote's flesh. The beast pounced on him, sinking its fangs into Azote's forearm. It then began to roll across the pavement like an alligator in a death roll with Azote hanging out of its mouth.

The other creature stopped to watch the action with a tilt of its head before it changed direction and charged toward me. I scrambled backward on my elbows before staggering to my feet. They had been set on attacking Azote when they'd first arrived, but maybe they were as indiscriminate about who they killed as the madagans had been. My hands flew up, ready to blast this thing away from me, but before it reached me, it spun around to stand directly between Azote and me.

I stood gawking at the creature as it roared again, revealing fangs that would make a sabre-tooth tiger cower. Its sleek black coat shone as its hackles rose and the front of its body hunched down a little. The brilliant amber of its eyes reminded me of...

Kobal!

My head shot up, and my eyes scanned the road, but because of the complete darkness out there and the brilliant light before me, I could barely see fifty feet away from me. He was out there somewhere, he had to be, and these were the hounds he'd told me he harbored within him.

Hellhounds. As I stared at the gigantic head before me, I could see exactly why they were called that. It had a head that looked like a wolf's, but a prehistoric wolf, one who could shred a T-Rex. Its head came up to my chin and its broad shoulders were at my chest.

This thing could crush me with one blow, but it stayed in front of me, its claws clicking on the pavement as it prowled back and forth, eager to join the fight. The other one had pinned Azote; its claws curled into his stomach to tear into the sensitive flesh. It had to be excruciating, but Azote didn't make a sound as his hands held open the jaws trying to clamp down on his head.

I didn't see it, but I felt the blast of power Azote released to launch the hound off of him. The creature skidded across the earth and crashed against the side of the building. More ghosts zipped away from the windows before returning to cautiously peer out again.

The hound before me released a hair-raising snarl and

launched forward at the same time something leapt out of the shadows beyond the pumps to land on Azote's back. It took me a second to recognize Kobal as his face was twisted into a mask of pure fury and his eyes burned amber fire. Despite my concern for him, relief and love swelled within me. He was okay; he was *here*. Fire licked up his wrists and across his forearms and shoulders. The tips of his four fangs glistened before he sank them into Azote's throat. Azote screamed; his hands beat over his head in an attempt to dislodge Kobal. Releasing his bite on Azote's neck, Kobal spit out the chunk of flesh he'd torn from him.

His claws tore across Azote's chest, slicing open flesh and spilling more blood onto the ground. The hounds paced anxiously before him, their tails swishing as the scent of Azote's blood permeated the air. Kobal seized Azote's throat, lifted him off the ground, and then smashed him into the asphalt.

Azote released another blast of telekinetic power I could feel from where I stood. Kobal's hold on him was knocked off and he was propelled a few feet back, but he didn't go flying across the parking lot like Corson and the hound had. Either Azote was tiring or his power didn't have the same effect against Kobal.

The hound guarding me pounced on Azote and bit down on Azote's head. Azote howled; his hands beat against the beast in an attempt to dislodge it. Shaking off the stupor clinging to me since I'd thrown Azote across the parking lot, I pulled my katana from its sheath on my back and ran toward them.

Arriving at Azote's side, I gripped the handle tight before lifting the katana and swinging it down with all my might. The sword whistled through the air before burying itself into the side of Azote's neck. I assumed one swing would cleave his head from his body, but it barely sliced more than two inches into him before getting stuck on sinewy muscle.

Azote's fingers scrabbled at the blade, tearing flesh to the bone. Kobal stepped beside me, nudging me out of the way as he wrapped his hand around the handle and yanked the Katana free. Lifting it up, he swung it down with enough force to slice Azote's head from his body. The hound swallowed it down in one gulp that caused my stomach to turn.

The katana clattered to the ground when Kobal released it. He grabbed hold of my arm, dragging me against him. The sickness in my belly eased when he wrapped his arms around me, lifting me into his embrace. My arms slid around his neck, and I flattened myself against him as I clung to him. The hounds roamed around us, rubbing against my legs as they dangled in the air over the beasts.

Despite everything that had transpired, my body instinctively reacted to Kobal's. The overwhelming demand to get closer fell over me like rain. My hands frantically ran over his shoulders and back as I sought to reassure myself he was really here.

"Kobal." The coppery smell of blood and the stench of gasoline filled my nose, along with his natural, fiery aroma when I buried my face in his neck.

He nuzzled my hair as his lips traveled over my cheek, and his fingers took hold of my chin to turn my mouth to his. My heart beat a staccato rhythm in my chest when his golden eyes blazed down into mine.

Need.

Sensing this, his mouth took ruthless possession of mine in a kiss that seared straight into the core of my soul. His tongue slid against my mouth and his fangs scraped over my lips, drawing blood, but I didn't care. My fingers slid into his hair, tugging him closer as I felt the rigid evidence of his arousal rising to press tantalizingly against my aching center.

I forgot all about where we were and all my bumps and bruises, as my world became centered on him. He was all I could taste and feel as our breaths mingled together until they were inseparable. My hands fell on his bare shoulders as he grasped my hair and pulled my head back to deepen the kiss.

"Oh," I sighed against his mouth.

His tongue, heady and demanding, thrust against mine in a powerful dance that left me weak and trembling. I couldn't get enough of him. I'd refused to allow myself to think I may never see him again, but it had been a constant worry in the back of my mind. Now, I never wanted to let him go.

One of the hounds growled, piercing through the haze of desire and bringing me back to the reality of where we were. Kobal's breaths were ragged against my lips when he broke the kiss. He stared at me for a minute before lowering me to the ground.

Clasping my face, he cradled it gently within his hands as his black claws retracted. "Are you okay?" I barely recognized the roughness of his voice, the desperation in his eyes.

"I'm fine. The others…" I recalled the cry of pain I'd heard when Azote had turned those bullets back on them. "The others!"

I pulled away from him and turned to find Hawk, Vargas, and Erin standing by the corner of the building. They were all pale, their shadowy eyes hollow, but their shoulders were thrust back proudly. Vargas had his hand clamped against his upper arm, and blood trickled from between his fingers, but the others appeared unharmed as the three of them walked over to join us.

Corson stepped beside Azote's body and kicked one of the black wings until it flopped onto the ground. "This was a big blow to Lucifer. He just lost one of his higher-up angels."

Though Azote was dead, Kobal positioned himself in between me and the angel. His body was rigid as his chest brushed against my arm and he stared at the mutilated body. "I know."

I'd thought he'd be happier about that development. Instead, he had the look of someone about to attend a wake. He lifted his eyes to meet Corson's gaze. Something traveled between the two of them, but before I could question him on it, Erin spoke.

"That was an angel?" she asked in a choked voice.

"Azote," I murmured. "One of the angels who fell with Lucifer."

Kobal's eyebrows drew together sharply. "How do you know who he was?"

I glanced at him before looking back at the black blood flowing from Azote's neck. "I just knew, somehow."

I decided to wait until we were alone before telling him everything Azote had said and the reaction he'd had to the sparks dancing across my fingers. Sparks which had affected him far more than my fire had. I understood what had Kobal so on edge as I realized I would most likely be able to use my ability against Lucifer too. Kobal and Corson had already arrived at this conclusion.

Did I dare get that close to Lucifer in order to use my ability to wield life against him? I didn't fear him, and I didn't fear death; I didn't want to die, but I would die to save those I loved and countless others if I had to. However, I worried Lucifer may somehow be able to turn me to his way. He must know what had severed the angels' bond to the flow of life. Could he do it to me?

It didn't matter. We still had a lot of distance to travel before we got to that point. I'd worry about it when we were closer to the gateway to Hell. Now, I had to be concerned about making it there. Turning, I surveyed the road, but saw no trucks driving down it. I spotted Bale as she jogged out of the shadows and across the lot toward us.

"Where is everyone else?" I demanded, my voice shriller than I'd expected.

"They'll be here soon," Kobal assured me. "We were simply able to move faster by foot."

"Because you destroyed our ride," Bale muttered.

I glanced at Kobal questioningly.

"Bit of an accident," he said with a negligent shrug.

My gaze ran over his body. Bruises marred his smooth jaw and blood streaked the corner of his right eye. He wore no shirt, but his pants had holes in them with blood crusting around them. On his chest were the faded, puckered marks of what looked like… "Are those *bullet* holes?" I demanded.

"We had a run-in with some humans who have survived in this area for a long time. I left them alive."

"They *shot* you?"

"They did."

My teeth grated together. The idea of anyone hurting him drowned out any happiness I experienced over learning there were more survivors out there. "I'd have killed them."

His mouth quirked into a heart-melting smile that had the tension in my shoulders easing a little. His fingers slipped over my cheek, brushing aside loose tendrils of hair as he stepped closer to me. "I promised you I'd be more tolerant of the humans."

"Not ones who try to kill you!"

His smile only widened. I glared back at him. "I believe I said the same to you at one point."

Crap. I'd walked right into that one, which was something he well knew as his eyes sparkled with amusement.

"The way Eileen was killed was wrong and, well, shocking," I murmured. "But..."

"But?" he prodded when my voice trailed off.

I lifted my eyes to search his much-loved gaze. My heart swelled as my fingers curled around his thick wrists and my body instinctively swayed closer to his. The flow of his life force flooded me, easing some of my exhaustion and pain from battling Azote. "But I better understand why you did it, now. I'm glad you kept the humans who attacked you alive."

He chuckled as I released his wrists. "Are you now?"

"Yes," I said reluctantly. "But if they try something like that again—"

"I already promised them death if I ever saw them again."

"Good."

Bending his head, his lips brushed against my ear as he turned us away from the others. "I do so enjoy when you are fierce, Mah Kush-la."

"I reacted too harshly with Eileen," I whispered. "I was... afraid. Afraid of everything Lucifer had said to me in my dream, afraid of the violence I witnessed from Eileen and then you."

His hand grasped my neck loosely. "I know, but I will protect you with everything I am from Lucifer."

"Can you protect me from myself, or protect yourself from me, if it becomes necessary?"

His muscles rippled against me and he inhaled a shuddering breath. "I will always do whatever is necessary for the world to be put to rights again and to keep you safe."

I rested my forehead on his chest, my eyes closing as his warmth enveloped me. My fingers traced over the chiseled muscles of his abs as I sought to touch more and more of him. The contradiction of his silky skin over the hardness of his muscles was one that always made my mouth water and my pulse quicken as I couldn't get enough of touching him.

"I hurt you when I pushed you away." I shuddered at the words as anger at myself slithered through me. It was the first time I'd ever truly acknowledged that. I may have been trying to protect him in some ways, but I'd also wounded and confused him. "I'm sorry for that."

Kobal stiffened against me, and his hand tightened on my neck. "I understand why you believed what you were doing was right. I also understand that I reacted badly with Eileen. I regret that and apologize her death happened in front of you. We were both neither right nor wrong when it came to her," he said in my ear. "It was a situation that will not be repeated. Nor will the events following it *ever* be allowed again."

"No, they will not," I vowed. His muscles loosened against me. I couldn't help but smile at him when he kissed my forehead and stepped away. My head tilted back to take him in. "Are *you* okay?"

"I'm fine, now. I'm not letting you out of my sight again."

I chuckled as he turned to face the others, but I didn't want to let him out of my sight again either. Corson and Bale studied me intently while the others kept glancing between Azote, Kobal, and me. I noticed they all kept their distance from the hounds prowling in a protective circle around us.

194 BRENDA K DAVIES

Vargas, Erin, and Hawk looked about as confused as they would if someone handed them a ten-thousand-piece puzzle and told them they had an hour to solve it. Bale and Corson actually smiled at me.

"She can draw on and wield life better than I thought," Bale said.

"I've been practicing with it," I admitted.

"Sly, like a demon," Corson said with a wink, and I suddenly understood the admiration in his and Bale's eyes.

"Is that what the golden-white thing you hit him with was, life?" Hawk asked.

CHAPTER TWENTY-SEVEN

RIVER

"Yes," I replied, earning a censuring look from Kobal.

"How did you do that?" Vargas inquired.

"That's not for you to know," Kobal answered before I could.

I frowned at him, but his chin was set and his eyes were stone-cold as he gave a subtle shake of his head. I understood his reasons for keeping my ancestry a secret, but they also deserved some answers. I realized they wouldn't be getting them when Kobal moved me so I couldn't see their gawking, curious expressions.

One of the hounds sat at my feet and released a yawn as it rubbed its head against my arm. Its thick coat was unexpectedly soft given it was a Hell beast who had recently eaten the head of a fallen angel.

I couldn't stop myself from running my fingers over its thick coat, which was something it approved of as its head butted against me. It had been trying to be tender, but it still knocked me back a step.

"Easy, Phenex," Kobal said.

Its tongue was rough when it licked over my flesh, but not unpleasant. "Phenex?" I asked.

"Yes, she is the female, and Crux"—he gestured to the slightly larger one who trotted over to rub at my other arm—"is the male and her mate."

I couldn't help but smile as the beasts prowled around the two of us. "They're beautiful."

"I have to put them back," Kobal said.

I was extremely curious to see how that worked as he walked a few feet away from me. The hounds trotted after him and obediently sat one on each side of him. He rested a palm on each of the hounds' heads. The muscles in his back bulged and flexed; the veins in his arms stood out as the hounds blurred.

Kobal inhaled deeply and threw back his head. He'd never looked more stark or beautiful to me as power emanated from him in waves. A sucking sensation filled the air around us when the beasts began to absorb back into his body.

The marks on his arms and chest rippled as the hounds began to disappear into him as seamlessly as a wave rolling away from the beach. Watching him, I understood better why he stimulated the sparks of life from me more than anything else. I had never before encountered anything that could match his level of power. The flow of life within the earth was immense, but it was also dispersed throughout the world. All of Kobal's power was harnessed solely within him. This was why Lucifer hadn't been able to destroy him like he had many of his ancestors.

There was nothing like him in this world, nothing that could handle this the way he did as he caged the hounds within him once more. My fingers longed to run over his back, to feel the sculpted ridges of his muscles flexing beneath my grasp, to feel his power jumping and flowing beneath me, *within* me.

My breasts ached for him to touch them, to cup them before he bent his head over them…

I shook my head to clear it of those thoughts, but when he turned toward me, I couldn't stop myself from moving closer to him. Taking hold of his outstretched hand, I nestled against him when he pulled me to him. The tremor in his body had nothing to do with the power he'd drawn back into himself and everything to do with his hunger for me.

I assumed he'd pick me up and carry me away to find somewhere private. I wouldn't have fought him on it, but he remained where he was. He turned his face into my neck, his fangs scraping over my flesh. I held my breath while I waited for him to bite down. His body shuddered with restraint as he pulled his mouth away from my neck and rested his lips against my temple.

"Soon," he whispered.

My heart pounded as I turned my cheek to his. "I missed you."

"More than you will ever know."

Headlights cutting through the night at the top of the hill drew my attention to the line of vehicles weaving their way toward us. "They're here," I breathed.

"We have to go," Kobal said.

He didn't release me, but instead lifted me and carried me toward our pickup. "Wait!" I cried before we reached the truck. I squirmed in his arms until he set me down.

"What is it?" he asked.

"I have to thank them."

"Who?"

"The ghosts."

Kobal's eyes slid to the building, and his upper lip curved into a sneer when he spotted the transparent figures at the window. "One of them turned you in."

"*One* of them did. The rest of them helped us." I pulled from his arms, but he grabbed my wrist before I could walk away from him.

"As much as I hate to admit it, they did what they could," Corson said as he walked over to stand beside me.

He tugged the earrings from his ears and tossed them onto the ground when Kobal slid a threatening look toward him.

"I have to talk to them," I insisted.

Kobal squeezed my wrist. "I will come with you."

I strode across the parking lot toward the building with Kobal at my side and the others following close behind. The ghosts flew away from the windows as we neared.

I went to push the door open, but Kobal's arm shot out around me and he shoved the door inward. The ringing of the bell dimmed as Kobal held the door for me to step inside before following me in. A chaotic frenzy of ghosts greeted us. Some of them made for the kitchen, while others flitted around the ceiling of the dining room or huddled in the booths.

Ethel, our not-so-friendly greeter from earlier, didn't yell at us to get out again. She hovered near the kitchen doors with Pompadour beside her. Many of the ghosts' already translucent bodies looked a little paler, if that was possible, than they had the last time I'd seen them.

"They're going to burn us down."

"No outside."

"No dark."

"Ronald did this. He caused it. He brought the demons here for her. We didn't do it." The panicked voices of the ghosts became a noisy buzz as they all spoke over each other.

"I came to say thank you," I yelled, loudly enough for them to hear me over their frantic chatter. "For helping us."

The ghosts overhead slowed, their bodies and features becoming more distinct as they separated out of their group. At the back, a couple dozen heads poked through the wall from the kitchen.

"Fucking ghosts," Kobal muttered from beside me. He stepped closer, his chest brushing protectively against my arm as he surveyed the room with a look that said he would set it on fire if they made one wrong move toward any of our party.

"That's what I've been saying," Corson said from behind me.

Erin, Vargas, and Hawk looked on as the ghosts started to float down from above us. "What did she say?" one of the heads from the kitchen asked.

Daisy floated into the room to hover before me. "She said thank you."

I smiled at the young woman. "Especially you."

Daisy grinned at me before turning her attention to Kobal. Some of the others moved closer to float before him. Their heads twisted and turned as they studied him before looking at me.

"The rightful king of Hell and a World Walker, no one would have ever believed it possible," Ethel said as she floated closer.

I went to ask what a World Walker was again, but the ghost in the poodle skirt distracted me when she glided closer to Kobal. I recognized the lascivious look in her eyes as she surveyed him. If she'd had a body, I would have knocked her on her ass. "He is rather... dangerous," she murmured.

"You mean yummy," another woman said to her; both ghosts exchanged a giggle.

Some of the male ghosts floated closer to Erin and me. I took a step back when one of them started to rise above me, his head craning from side to side as he tried to see down my shirt.

"Back off!" Kobal snarled at him when he realized what the ghost was trying to do.

The ghost pouted as he turned toward him, but his pout vanished and his gray color lightened when he took in Kobal. None of the other males came toward me, and Corson stepped in front of Erin to glare at any who dared approach her.

"They're all pervs," Hawk muttered in disgust.

"Will you talk to the angels for us now that we helped you?" Pompadour asked.

"I already told you I can't. I don't know how," I said, beginning to regret my decision to come back here in order to thank them.

"You can figure it out," he insisted.

"No, I can't."

"Suck it up, non-corporeals, you're gonna be here for a while," Corson sneered at them.

"Stop provoking them!" Erin hissed at him before smiling and waving to the ghosts. "Thanks all!"

Daisy floated closer to me. "Good luck," she said. "You'll be able to do this."

"I hope so." I stopped myself from telling her I would see if there was something I could do to help her leave here. If I made her that promise, we'd have a horde of ghosts following us for the rest of our trip. I couldn't make the promise out loud, but I would do everything I could to help her move on from here.

"Let's go," Kobal said and nudged me toward the door. "Thank you for helping her," he said to the ghosts before closing the door.

Corson's eyes widened and Bale's head shot up at Kobal's expression of gratitude to the ghosts. Admittedly, I was a little amazed too. I wasn't sure I'd ever heard him thank another. He didn't look at his stunned friends as he bent to swing me into his arms. I smiled at him before draping my arms around his neck and resting my head on his shoulder.

When I glanced behind me, the ghosts were back at the windows watching us. Some of the women actually fanned themselves. I turned my attention away from them as Kobal strode across the parking lot toward the truck. He kissed my forehead and opened the passenger side door of the pickup to slide me onto the seat.

"You drive," he said to Bale before climbing inside, lifting me, and settling me onto his lap.

He cradled me against his chest while the others climbed into the back of the truck. Hawk and Corson started going through some of the bags before pulling out bandages and first-aid supplies. They handed them over to Erin as she knelt next to Vargas.

"There will be more room for you in some of the other vehicles," Kobal told them through the open window in the middle of the truck.

Erin lifted her head from where she was working on cleaning Vargas's arm. A bullet had torn away a chunk of skin on his bicep. She gazed at me before focusing on Kobal. "We're staying together," she said.

CHAPTER TWENTY-EIGHT

RIVER

The cool stream of water washing over me felt like heaven after hours of being covered in layers of grime, blood, and black goo. I scrubbed vigorously at my skin with a bar of lemon-scented soap before turning my attention to my hair.

I lathered it with shampoo, digging into my scalp to try to get it clean before ducking beneath the water. I did a second layer of shampoo and then took the straight razor to my legs. Bruises already ran over my side and down my thighs from Azote tossing me around, but I'd become accustomed to bruises since arriving at the training facility. They would eventually fade.

As I cleaned myself, I told Kobal everything Azote had said to me during our fight. He remained on the shore, unmoving as he watched me. His only reaction to my words was the deepening molten-gold color of his eyes.

"He was the gift Lucifer had promised me in my dream. He truly believed himself to be my uncle."

A muscle jumped in Kobal's jaw. "Forged from the same being, angels think of themselves as brothers and sisters, so that makes sense."

"So I inherited a whole cadre of insane, demonic angels who will believe themselves my aunts and uncles, or my sisters and brothers, good to know," I muttered and scrubbed at my arms again with the soap.

"You were not created like they were. They probably won't think of you as a sibling, but they obviously consider you a relative."

"Delightful. Are all angels telepathic like Azote?"

"Not all of them, but some do wield that power. Azote was one of the more powerful angels. Killing him will hurt Lucifer."

"Good. He also said I was definitely my father's daughter, going after the strongest one of the demons, binding you to me. He said Lucifer couldn't crush you, so I screwed you."

Kobal's lips skimmed back to reveal his fangs. "And you believe him?"

I didn't believe him. The only thing that had ever pulled me to Kobal was my uncontrollable craving for him. I knew some of my draw to him was the demon part of me having recognized him as my Chosen and needing to claim him, but most of it was the man himself and the tenderness in him for me alone. However, it frightened me that the fallen angels seemed to believe I would be the key to his downfall.

"When I welcomed you back into my arms, I made my choice. I put my faith in you, and us, and I will happily do so every day for the rest of my life, but you have to understand my fear," I told him.

His fangs retracted when some of the strain eased from his body. "I do, but you know that's not why we are together."

"I do," I agreed. I knew my next words would probably irritate him more, but he had to hear them. "I also saw the look on Azote's face when he spotted the sparks of life on my fingers, before I was able to really give him a good blast. It was so… lost and… hopeful. So broken. I believe I was right. What truly ruined the angels who were thrown from Heaven, what made them so twisted and evil was the loss of their bond to the flow of life. I think I could become like them too, if I lost the connection."

I held my breath as I waited for his explosive denial that I could never become anything like them. He'd always denied Lucifer's words so vehemently before.

Now, he remained unmoving, his eyes hooded as he stared at the water flowing around me instead of at me. My confusion grew as I watched him. I'd expected anger when I'd revealed this to him, not the sadness radiating from him now.

Finally, he lifted his gaze back to mine. "Then we will have to make sure the bond is never broken."

"Yes," I agreed, but the sadness didn't leave his face. "Why does that upset you?"

"Nothing upsets me now that you're here again."

I didn't fully believe his words. Something wasn't quite right with him, but I didn't have the energy or drive to pursue it right now. I finished shaving before ducking beneath the water a final time. Returning to the surface, I pushed my hair back from my face and made my way toward the shore. My exhaustion slipped away when Kobal's eyes raked voraciously over me.

Damp from his own dip in the river, his hair was almost black as it hung around his face and clung to his forehead and cheeks. My body quickened as I drank in the sight of him.

I hadn't expected him to climb out of the water before me, pull on his pants, and stand guard while I continued to bathe. I'd expected him to take me, to mark me as his once more and ease the need growing in me since we'd been separated. Instead, he held a towel open for me and enfolded me within it when I stepped toward him.

He desired me, I could see that in the fire of his eyes and the arousal straining against the front of his pants, but instead of drawing me against him, he rubbed the towel over my arms and body before reluctantly releasing me and stepping away. He handed me my clean clothes, which had been sitting on a large rock on the riverbank.

I hadn't bothered to bring any underwear with me. I tugged on my pants and buttoned them before pulling on my shirt. He didn't say a word as he retrieved the lantern sitting on the shore before taking hold of my hand and leading me toward the makeshift tent he'd built by draping canvas over some branches. He'd carefully laid out blankets on the ground before we'd gone to bathe. I didn't see any of the others or hear anything over the chirrup of the crickets.

Kobal pulled back the canvas and gestured for me to enter ahead of him. Stepping inside, I turned to face him as he tugged the canvas into place.

He placed the lantern down and lifted my hairbrush from where it sat next to my backpack. His hands were gentle on my shoulders when he turned me around. Taking hold of a piece of my hair, he lifted it and, with tender care, worked the brush through the matted tangles in it.

The act was so soothing and intimate I didn't know how to react to it as I watched the light of the lantern dancing across the green canvas surrounding us. It felt as if the world outside these walls ceased to exist while we stood silently together. With unmitigated patience, he spent half an hour working at the knots in my hair until it fell around my shoulders in wet tendrils that dampened my shirt.

He set the brush down, and with his hands on my shoulders, turned me to face him. I tilted my head back, my breath catching at the burning intensity of his eyes. He hungered for me as badly as I did him, yet he'd taken care of my outward needs first. I hadn't believed it possible to love him anymore than I already did, but I was wrong.

His hands slid over my shirt. I almost pushed them back so I could take it off before he tore it from me, but he took hold of the bottom of the hem and leisurely lifted it up my stomach. My arms rose in the air as he tugged it over my head and tossed it aside. His nostrils flared as his gaze roamed over me. He'd just watched me bathe, but it felt as if this were the first time he'd ever seen my breasts bared to him.

Always before, our lovemaking had almost been a savage experience, consuming us both. He had needed me more than he'd needed to breathe.

Now, that desperate urgency shone in his golden eyes, but his touch was delicate and unhurried. The backs of his fingers skimmed over my belly, rubbing against my skin and sending a firestorm of passion through me. I wanted him inside of me so badly I ached for it, but I remained unmoving before him, curious to see what he intended.

As his hand slid up to cup my breast, my nipple rose eagerly to the pad of his thumb brushing over it. My breath sucked in when he bent his head to suckle upon it. My fingers threaded through his damp hair to pull him closer. His knuckles skimmed over my sides again before his hands gripped my ass. He pulled me against him as he nipped and licked at my nipple before giving it a small tug.

"Oh!" I gasped, my hips jerking forward.

He locked me against his body, lifted me up, and carried me over to the pile of blankets set against the wall. Kneeling down, he laid me down before sitting back on his heels to unbutton my pants, slide the zipper down, then pull them off. His fingers slid up my thighs, tracing over my skin in a teasing dance that had me panting for breath and desperate for him to ease the passion he stoked ceaselessly within me.

"I almost lost you," he murmured, his eyes locking on mine. "Azote was so close to taking you from me."

"I'm still here," I whispered.

"Always here, always with me," he rasped.

"Yes."

With his eyes still on mine, he bent and kissed the inside of my knee. His palms spread my thighs further apart as his tongue seared over my skin toward my aching center. My heart raced with excitement, but I tried to close my legs when his tongue dipped lower toward the part of me yearning for him.

His hands were firm against my inner thighs as he held them open. "I'm going to taste you, River. I'm going to savor every inch of you, and you're going to let me."

My breath caught at his words, and I trembled beneath him. I wanted this, wanted the answer to what it would be like to have his mouth on me in such a way. I'd seen him do it to me in the dreams we'd shared, and I'd craved it, but the thought of him doing it now made me as nervous as it did aroused.

Unwilling to deny him anything, I opened my legs wider when he settled himself more firmly between them.

~

KOBAL

My erection throbbed so forcefully against my pants that I had to grit my teeth against the pain. However, I was determined to taste her, to take my time with her, to enjoy her. My fingers slid over her as I inhaled the heady aromas of lemon and her tantalizing fresh-rain scent on her silken skin. The bruises marring her flesh stirred my rage, but touching her in this way, knowing she was safe in my arms again, helped to calm me.

I scraped my fangs against her inner thigh before sinking them into her. She jerked, her head fell back, and a low moan escaped her as her back arched off the blankets.

My marks, *my* Chosen.

I clasped hold of one of her breasts, kneading and massaging it as I slid my thumb over her hardened nipple. I couldn't tear my gaze away from the mesmerizing vision of her full breasts and the look of ecstasy on her face. She was so incredibly beautiful like this that I could deny myself for hours if it meant watching her as she was now.

Such an enticing blend of demon, angel, and human.

Too much angel. So much of it that I now knew I could never

take the risk of breaking her connection with the life all around her by making her immortal.

Not now! Don't think of it now.

Releasing my bite on her flesh, I licked away the blood beading on her skin before running my tongue over her as I moved toward what I sought. The scent of her arousal grew stronger, sharpening my instinct to see her satisfied, to give her the release she needed.

My eyes feasted on her damp curls and wet sex. *Irresistible, like her.*

Sliding my hands under her ass, I lifted her against me as I settled my mouth over her center. Her heat and wetness enveloped me. I moaned as my tongue licked over her. The taste of her liquid heat and the scent of rain seared my senses. Her hips undulated as they rose and fell beneath me, seeking more of my touch.

I couldn't get enough of watching her. Her full breasts swayed with her movements, and her arms fell open at her sides as her hands twisted into the bedding beneath her. Taking hold of her right hand, I lifted it up and placed it against her breast. She froze, and her smoky eyes latched onto mine as I kneaded her hand over her breast, rubbing her thumb across her dusky nipple.

Tearing myself away from her intoxicating taste, I lifted my head. "Let me watch you pleasure yourself."

She bit on her lower lip as if she were unsure, but beneath my palm, her hand moved over her breast, rubbing and kneading as golden-white sparks traced across our skin. She was exquisite; sweet and loving, uninhibited and eager to please. She was everything I ever could have dreamed of from my Chosen, and so much more.

My head dipped between her legs again. I watched her hand sliding over her breast before moving to caress the other one. Parting her further to my exploration of her, I drove my tongue deeper into her. Leisurely, I moved one hand from her ass to stroke her clit with my thumb.

My shaft pulsed with its need to be buried inside her, to spend myself in her body, but I continued fucking her with my tongue as I watched her uninhibited movements and feasted on her molten heat and honeyed taste against my mouth.

"Kobal!" she panted, her head thrashing to the side as her hips rose and fell demandingly against my tongue. Her back arched up and her head fell back when I stroked my thumb over her clit again, pushing her over the edge. I eagerly took in the hot wash of her orgasm, drawing it deeper into me as she cried out.

Unable to restrain myself from taking her any longer, I released her and sat back to yank off my pants. My dick jumped eagerly when River's dazed eyes fell on it and a seductive smile curved her luscious mouth. Settling myself between her legs, I took hold of my cock and guided it into her warm, tight sheath.

I thrust forward, burying myself to the hilt within her body, as I settled myself deep within the only place I truly belonged. Hell, Heaven, Earth, none of it mattered when I was inside of her. I dropped my head to hers as I slid my fingers over the curves of her face.

"Mine," I growled against her mouth.

She clasped hold of my cheeks as her tongue ran over my lips. "And you are mine."

"Yes," I agreed as I withdrew before thrusting forward again.

Her striking amethyst eyes darkened as she held my gaze. "I love you, Kobal, more than I ever believed possible."

It was the first time I'd ever heard those words from anyone before. They seared into my heart, tightening my chest as I gazed at her in wonder.

"I love you too." She was so much more to me than my Chosen. This infuriating, powerful, stubborn, proud, loving woman was *everything* to me, and there was nothing I wouldn't do to protect her. "You truly are my heart, Mah Kush-la."

Tears bloomed in her eyes. Gathering her within my arms, I pinned her against me and sank my fangs into her neck as I lost myself to the fulfillment only she could give to me.

CHAPTER TWENTY-NINE

RIVER

When I woke the next morning, I nestled closer to Kobal's warmth, burying my head in his solid chest. I wasn't ready to get back on the road yet. I wanted to forget this entire mission and lose myself to him and the little cocoon we had created. I had missed him so much, my body had hungered for him every second we'd been apart, and now he was back and the world was going to do everything it could to tear us apart once more.

He dragged me closer against his chest.

"It's daylight," I murmured.

"It is," he agreed, his hand running down to grasp my ass.

"We should get ready."

"I am ready."

I couldn't stifle my laugh as he dragged me onto his chest to rub his rigid arousal against me. I stopped caring about getting ready to go when he slipped inside of me. Lowering my head, I kissed over his neck before biting down on his shoulder to mark his flesh.

An hour later, I reluctantly pulled myself away, gathered my clothes and towel, and waited for Kobal so we could return to the stream to bathe. Most everyone was packed by the time we returned to the camp.

I climbed into the truck, settling in the middle as Hawk slid in beside me. Corson, Vargas, and Erin climbed into the back to sit with Bale who was already waiting there. Standing beside the driver's side, Kobal reached into the truck and wrapped his hand around my angel figurine on the dash.

I lurched forward, grabbing his wrist before he could pull her away. "What are you doing?" I demanded.

He glanced at me then at the figurine in his hand. "I hate these winged pricks."

"I know, but it stays." His eyebrows rose at the frantic note in my voice, and I had to admit it astonished me too, but he *couldn't* take it away from me. "I, uh… I found it and I want to keep it."

My breath rushed out when he settled the angel back on the dashboard. He slid into the truck beside me, his gaze going between me and the angel. "Do you know what that's about?" he asked.

"I really don't," I admitted. I still couldn't explain my need for the figurine to myself, never mind someone else.

"There were probably thousands of them in that creepy-ass room," Hawk said. "She only took that one."

"What room?" Kobal inquired as he started the truck and pulled onto the road.

I explained to him the house and the room we'd discovered, leaving out the part with Angela. I needed some time to try to figure her out on my own still, but I told him the rest. "I only knew I had to have it when I saw it," I finished. "And I'm not ready to let it go."

"I see," he murmured, though I knew he understood it about as much as I did.

"How much longer do you think it will be until we get to the gateway?" I asked as a way to distract all of us from the angel.

Kobal's knuckles were white on the wheel as he stared ahead. "Three, maybe four days."

I turned away before he could see the apprehension his words provoked in me. I didn't know what would happen when we arrived at the gateway, but I was terrified I would lose him.

"I *am* going to keep you safe," he vowed.

"I know. I've gotten stronger, better able to draw on life. I just have a difficult time remaining calm enough to push my fear aside and do it when being attacked."

He stared at the road for a minute before looking at me. "How much better at it?"

I glanced at the others in the back of the truck; they were all leaning toward the open window, but their eyes were deliberately focused elsewhere. I swore Hawk was holding his breath beside me as he kept his gazed fixed out the passenger side window. Kobal glanced at them, a muscle in his jaw twitching. He didn't know if he could trust them, but I did.

We'd all kept each other alive at the truck stop. They'd seen what I could do, and they knew what Azote had been. They still had *no* clue what I was, other than to know I had a giant bull's-eye on my back for demons and fallen angels alike, but they'd still climbed into this pickup truck with me again today. They had to know that even with Kobal and the other demons present, it was still more treacherous to be around me than away from me.

We're staying together, Erin had said, and she'd meant it. I had to fight back the tears threatening to fall at their loyalty and friendship. They deserved to know at least some of what was going on.

"I'm far better than I was. I practiced a lot during the time we weren't speaking and before then. I was hoping to surprise you with it."

Kobal released the steering wheel and grasped my hand. I immediately felt the swell of power from him arching over my fingers. "Later you can show me what you're capable of," he said.

"It's nothing overly impressive."

He smiled at me. "If it's you, it's impressive."

It was so weird to hear and see him this way. This demon who had always been so aloof and callous, except when alone with me, was more open now, more loving. *He loves me.* I thrilled at the reminder, my hands sparking with golden-white light because of it.

I bit on my lip, unable to tear my gaze from his pure obsidian eyes. His fingers slid over mine and across the back of my hand in a way that had my insides turning to mush. Turning away, he focused on the road again, but his hand remained locked around mine.

I glanced at the others in the back of the truck and Hawk, but none of them asked any of the questions I knew had to be churning in their minds. Bale and Corson exchanged looks and shook their heads. The two of them grinned before elbowing each other.

I stifled a laugh over their amusement and turned to watch the scenery go by. We passed through more nearly untouched towns, and others so brutalized there was still little vegetation creeping in to reclaim the land. However, the devastated areas were beginning to crop up more and more often while the untouched ones were growing fewer and farther between.

Animals moved about the remains we encountered, but I saw no people, and I wasn't sure I wanted to after the ones Kobal had encountered. There were a couple of times we had to turn around and find another route as we came across bridges that had collapsed or completely blocked roadways since the last time Kobal had been through here. I held my breath over the few bridges we did cross, convinced we were going to topple into the water or onto the roadways below us, but somehow they held up.

The sun was about to touch the horizon when Kobal pulled into a large field behind a burnt-out building and parked the truck. I wasn't certain where we were, and after this day of constantly turning around, if someone told me we'd only traveled five miles from where we'd started, I would have believed them.

Opening the door, Hawk climbed out and I followed behind him. I stretched my back and cramped muscles before helping

Kobal and the others pull out some of the supplies we would need for the night. After establishing a sleeping area, I sat and ate dinner with Vargas, Erin, and Hawk while the demons and Captain Tresden spoke near a copse of large elm trees.

The first star poked out in the sky when Kobal walked over to join us. Kneeling beside me, he tucked a stray wisp of hair behind my ear and kissed my cheek. He extended his hand to me and I took hold of it. Rising to my feet, I brushed the grass from my ass before following him over to the base of the elm.

"I have to go feed," he said.

"I'll go with you."

"This may be something you'd prefer not to witness, even if you can see the wraiths, which is doubtful."

"I should know more about what happens. I am part demon after all," I said with a smile.

"More angel than anything else."

"I think we both know that's a lie."

He chuckled, but I hadn't missed the hint of sadness in his eyes. "It may look like absolutely nothing to you," he told me.

"I'm prepared for that."

"Don't say I didn't warn you."

"I won't." I wanted to ask him about what was upsetting him, but decided against it. My curiosity to see him feed was stronger than my need to question him, and if I pushed him, he might change his mind.

He kept my hand in his as we turned and slipped into the woods. Throughout the forest, I glimpsed fireflies flitting through the air, tiny pinpricks of light in the dark canopy of trees. One good thing about this trip, so far we hadn't encountered over-grown insects looking to eat us. Bugs didn't bother me, but the idea of man-eating spiders made my stomach turn.

The crickets chirruped loudly as he moved with confidence over the forest floor. His hand rested on the log of a fallen tree before he turned to me, placed his hands on my waist, and easily lifted me over it. I couldn't resist kissing him when he settled me on the other side.

"Don't distract me," he murmured.

"I would never," I replied and playfully bumped his hip.

His hand moved so fast I barely saw it before it was grasping hold of my waist and drawing me flush against his side. His fingers stroked over my flesh as he led me further through the forest. At the edge of the woods, he pulled me to a stop. Leaves dipped down from the trees above as I stared at the hill stretching before us.

The stars blinked to life through the inky canvas of the night. On the horizon, the full moon was a bright orange color when it peeked out from behind the hill. It looked so close, I felt like I could walk to the top of the hill, reach out, and touch it. The spectacular beauty robbed me of my breath as I watched its steady ascent.

Turning my attention from the orange globe, I realized Kobal's eyes weren't on the moon, but on something else within the sky. Something I couldn't see beyond the canopy of trees hanging over us.

"What is it?" I asked.

"Wraiths," he replied.

My eyes narrowed as I searched for whatever it was he saw. "What are wraiths?"

"They are what we call the souls who are sent to Hell," he replied. "They become twisted and warped after years of torture, punishment, and our feeding from them."

I knew he somehow fed off the souls sent to Hell, but I had no idea what it entailed. "Are they dangerous?"

"Some are more powerful than others as some spirits can retain abilities they may have had while human, but they cannot harm humans. Some of the wraiths left Hell when the gateway opened, but many of them still reside within its bowels. Wherever the wraiths are though, they can never escape a demon once we latch onto them."

I tilted my head back to peer at the sky again. "Are they around us all the time and I just can't see them?"

"No. Since we've entered your realm, they only come out at night. Their twisted bodies thrive on shadows and can't handle the sunlight."

"Where do they go during the day?"

"They hide in the earth, but they're unable to stay there once the sun sets."

"Are they out every night?"

"Yes."

"So they're kind of like ghosts?"

"Sort of, but whereas ghosts were already a part of your realm, even if you couldn't see them, wraiths never will belong here and will only be visible to those of us who feed on them. Are you sure you wouldn't prefer to stay here?"

"Yes."

"Come."

Tugging on my hand, he led me to the top of the hill. The orange glow from the moon illuminated the other side of the hill with every step we took, revealing more woodland. This area had somehow survived the war; the healthy trees towered into the sky, more so than any others we'd seen on our journey so far. I hadn't seen so many large trees grouped together like this since leaving my home.

Kobal's head tilted back and a rumble vibrated his chest. The muscles of his arms bunched and flexed. I'd never seen him look like this before; he was a hunter seeking his prey, but then he'd tried to keep the predator side of his nature from me as much as possible.

"When was the last time you fed?" I asked.

"It's been a while."

"Because you were trying to reach me?"

His gaze flickered to me before focusing on the sky again. "I was perfectly capable of waiting."

Still, I hated to have been the cause for the depth of the hunger

I sensed coming from him. My fingers squeezed around his. "I've drawn you into my visions before and entered your dreams, maybe I can see the wraiths through your eyes."

"I'm not sure you want to see this, River."

"I want to see everything that has to do with you. *Every*thing."

He hesitated for a minute; then his hand squeezed mine. Drawing me against his side, he clasped my neck, rubbing his thumb over my flesh as he kissed my forehead. I closed my eyes, taking comfort in him while my senses flooded with the force that was Kobal.

I felt an opening, a drawing like what I experienced when I'd sucked him into my visions those couple of times before, but this was more compelling. Now it felt like a dam broke within me as the power swelled forth, eager to break free of the cage I'd confined it to since my dream with Lucifer.

"The more you use your abilities, the stronger they'll become," Kobal whispered against my forehead.

My eyes flew open as his became the color of gold. He was all I could see at first, but I sensed something more beyond his broad shoulders. Turning my attention from him, I gasped when I realized I now saw the sky through his eyes and that thousands upon thousands of creatures swarmed in a giant mass above us.

Their bodies were the color of tar as they zipped about overhead faster than a hummingbird. Some of them were still rising from the earth, moving sluggishly upward in waves before me. Their hollow mouths hung open to reveal the pits of nothingness their souls had become.

I'd have bet almost anything these eyeless creatures with their long, twisted gray faces were the foundation for the grim reaper. The ends of their blackened souls looked like robes flapping in the wind as they rose in a swaying rhythm. Once they hit the sky, they moved as rapidly as their brethren through the air.

These things were hideous and so cold they chilled me to the marrow of my bones. I wanted to pull Kobal closer so I could share his warmth, but I couldn't. He'd brought me here because he had to feed. I'd told him I could handle this, and I would. My teeth chattered, but I could do this. I could and would do anything for him.

"River?"

"I'm fine," I murmured, wondering if my voice sounded as raw as the rest of me felt.

His hands slid over my flesh, but it did little to warm me. "We're leaving."

"No."

"You're freezing to the touch."

"I told you I can do this, and I can. I'm not leaving until you've fed."

He flexed his hands, but he turned away from me and lifted a hand toward the sky. Some of the wraiths screamed, their awful cries unlike anything I'd ever heard before. It was the sound of death.

CHAPTER THIRTY

River

I didn't see anything come out of Kobal's hand, but I felt the power within his vibrating muscles. He separated one of the wraiths from the others, drawing it toward him as it writhed and thrashed within his pull. Its scream became a howl that made my stomach twist.

It was only three feet away when Kobal stepped forward and enclosed his hand around its throat. The wraith flailed about until it became nothing more than a black blur. Kobal's eyes closed as whatever he did to the wraith caused his bronzed skin to darken and his golden eyes to glow in a way I'd never seen before.

The wraith's jerking movements eased. Kobal released the wraith. It hung in the air before him, its face more twisted than before as its jaw had descended another inch and its eye sockets had expanded. I swore it stared straight into me and didn't like whatever it saw there. Malice and hatred radiated from it as it floated closer to me.

"Get away from her!" Kobal snarled at it.

Ignoring the lethal undercurrent of Kobal's tone, it crept closer to me. Kobal snagged hold of it, drawing it against his chest with a roar. I took a step back when the marks on his body vibrated and the wraith screamed so loudly I thought my eardrums would rupture. Unlike the ghosts who couldn't be touched, the demons could inflict severe damage on these creatures.

Kobal's marks deepened to a jet black. His skin became a darker brown color as his muscles swelled larger before me and the veins in his arms stood out starkly. With an abrupt thrust, he flung the creature away from him. It fell to the earth, flopping as it tried to take flight but only succeeded in dragging itself away.

He tilted his head back to the sky before he lifted his hand to draw another one down to him. I watched as he fed from three more, all of them wise enough to not bother me before returning to the sky.

When he was done, he turned to me, his eyes alight and his skin fairly glowing with whatever nourishment he'd taken from them. I didn't know what to say to him, but I recognized the hunger for my body in his gaze when he took hold of my waist and drew me against him. "We need to get you warm."

"The wraiths are so cold," I murmured.

Swinging me up, he held me against him. Feeding caused his body temperature to rise and it felt like I was wrapped up in a warm blanket. I pressed closer against him as his hands ran up and down my arms.

"I should have stopped feeding sooner," he said.

"I'm fine." I nuzzled his neck. "How do you feed from them?"

"I take in their essence," he said. "It's excruciating for them. It's the worst thing they can experience in Hell as it literally drains a piece of them. All demons feed from them in such a way."

"What about the angels, how do they feed in Hell?"

"Angels feed from souls too. Whether it's from their happiness and giving them bliss like the ones in Heaven do, or from inflicting suffering such as we do. The fallen angels adapted once they entered Hell."

"Probably another thing that separated them further from their bond with life," I murmured.

"Perhaps."

"But only the fallen angels know what really caused it to break and they're not going to tell me," I said.

"No, they're not."

Leaning forward, I kissed his lips. "What other pain do the wraiths experience?"

"There are many torments in Hell. I'd prefer not to share them with you."

He would if I asked him to, but it was a subject we'd both rather drop. He rubbed his hand over my back and down my spine when I released a contented sigh. "I feel better now."

"Good enough to show me what you've been teaching your-self?" he asked.

I didn't want to leave the warmth of his arms, but I'd waited long enough to show him what I was capable of now. "Yes. Stop here."

He set me on the ground and I took a reluctant step away from his embrace. Taking a deep breath, I knelt to rest my fingers against the earth. I closed my eyes and tried to rid myself of all other thoughts as I concentrated on the ground beneath my fingertips.

The life teeming within the earth flowed into me, further defrosting my bones. My eyes opened as sparks of golden-white light danced across my fingers. I kept my hand against the ground as I lifted my other palm before me and allowed the ball of energy to grow.

I flipped the ball over before me, circling it through my fingers. The golden-white glow of it illuminated Kobal's face, making him even more radiant as he watched me. The last time we'd worked together on this, I'd barely been able to form some-thing the size of an apple, and I hadn't revealed I could do much better than that when I'd worked with Corson and Bale.

The light pulsed further within my fingers, growing until it reached beyond my palm and became nearly twice the size of a basketball. "What I did to Azote earlier was the first time I'd ever done anything like that. The life burst out of me in a stream of energy with him, instead of a ball."

"I saw. Hit me with it," he commanded gruffly.

I did a double take as my eyes looked from the ball to him, then back again. "No!"

His eyes lifted to mine, and I could see the glimmer of pride within their depths but also his steely determination. "I'll be fine. I've fed and I need to know some of what you are capable of. Hit me with it."

"No."

He grabbed hold of my wrist, causing the ball to swell larger as his life flooded me. Before I could do anything to stop him, he spun my wrist around. The ball followed the abrupt movement. I tried to jerk it back as he thrust my hand forward, slamming it against his chest. An explosion lit the air around us, momentarily blinding me. His grip on my wrist was torn free.

"No!" I shouted as he shot five feet backward and into a tree. The impact of his body caused it to splinter down the middle. I launched to my feet and raced toward him. "Kobal!" I gasped, falling before him and clutching his cheeks between my palms. His head turned toward me; he blinked as he tried to focus on me. I tore his burnt shirt back to reveal the puckered and blistered skin beneath it. Tears filled my eyes as I gazed at the wound I had created. "Why did you do that?"

"You pack a punch, Mah Kush-la," he murmured and gripped my hands.

"Why did you do that?" I demanded again, my concern for him fading to exasperation when he smiled at me.

He pushed himself up against the tree. "Because now I understand more of what you're capable of, and your powers are still growing. More practice will only strengthen your abilities. I was prepared for the blow and still look at what happened."

"I hurt you."

"*I* hurt me." He pressed my hands against his chest on either side of his reddened skin. Already some of the blisters were fading. "And I heal fast. Far faster since you've become a part of my life."

My lower lip trembled. "Really?"

"Yes." He wiped away the tear spilling down my cheek before clasping the back of my head and drawing me down for a kiss. "Don't cry. I'm fine."

"You still shouldn't have done that."

"Believe me, I won't do it again."

I couldn't help but chuckle as he smiled against my lips. "You *know* you bring out the force of life in me more than anything else."

"And I thrive on that. I'll fuel you for the rest of our days."

I flinched at the reminder that my days were far more numbered than his were.

"Don't think of it," he breathed against my lips, guessing at the direction of my thoughts. "Focus on the here and now. On *me*."

That was so unbelievably easy to do when his teeth were nibbling on my lower lip. "You're injured." I tried to pull away, but he didn't release me as he kept brushing his mouth over mine.

"I could be near death and I'd still crave you."

I glanced at his chest. His shirt still had tendrils of smoke curling from the charred sides, but his skin wasn't as red anymore.

"Don't you know you can kiss it and make it better?" he teased.

His words made me laugh, but I resolutely pulled away from him and settled against his side. My hand fingered the still-warm edges of his shirt when he draped his arm around me.

"When you connected with me so you could see the wraiths, was that the first time you've connected with someone since your dream with Lucifer?"

"Yes," I admitted and stifled a yawn. "I couldn't take the

chance of connecting with him again in a dream so I worked to shut the ability down."

"I don't want you to fear any of your abilities, River."

"I don't fear them, not anymore. I actually enjoy them, most of the time, but I don't want to see him again."

"I understand," he murmured.

"I feel like it's inevitable that I will see him again though, no matter what I do."

Kobal didn't respond. He didn't have to; we both knew I was right.

CHAPTER THIRTY-ONE

KOBAL

I watched River as she nestled against my side, her black lashes sweeping her cheeks. Even with all of the bumps and ruts we went over as we drove, sleep held her captive. I brushed my knuckles across her cheek before focusing on the road again.

In the back of the truck, the others bounced around and muttered curses, but they had all insisted on riding with us again. River had filled me in on what had occurred while we'd been separated, and I realized she'd made some friends, or at least earned their loyalty and trust by trying to keep them safe from Azote.

Some of the humans had finally stopped being assholes and recognized she wasn't an object of their fear and was worth following to Hell itself.

My hand stilled on her face. She snuggled closer and pressed her lips against my throat. I glanced over at Hawk as he eased the truck over a series of potholes in the road. The angel on the dashboard clattered against the windshield, drawing my attention to it.

"I don't like that thing either," Hawk said.

I stared at the small blonde angel with the green eyes. "Why not?"

"One, the room where she found it was creepy. Two, that angel at the truck stop was a bigger dick than you demons."

My eyebrows shot up at his statement, but I couldn't stop the laughter that escaped me. Hawk's shoulders relaxed. River smiled in her sleep, and from the corner of my eye, I saw the heads of the others turn in our direction. "I'll agree with that statement," I told him.

He smiled at me, and I knew then that River had changed the dynamic between us all. I had somehow become more human in their eyes through my relationship with her. Two months ago, that would have infuriated me, but now I didn't mind it as much. I actually liked these humans, and as long as they kept treating her well, we wouldn't have a problem. If they turned against her, I'd kill them.

"Are all angels like Azote was?" Hawk asked.

"All the fallen ones are. They're the only ones I've ever met."

Corson poked his head through the window. "They have to go to the bathroom, again."

The more bumps we hit, the more the humans had to stop. I gestured for Hawk to pull over to the side of the road. He parked the truck before a stone church with a gold cross on the front of it. The church appeared entirely intact except for the gaping hole where its roof used to be.

River stirred, her eyelids fluttered open, and she rose from my lap. Her forehead furrowed and her mouth pursed when her gaze settled on the roofless church. She stared at it for a minute before looking at the angel on the dashboard. Something about her attention to the angel caused my skin to prick.

She rubbed at her eyes and stifled a yawn. "Why are we stopping?"

"The humans have to use the bathroom."

Her mouth quirked in a smile as she grabbed the door handle and pushed it open. I held the door for her while she climbed out of the truck. The other humans went toward the woods, but River headed for the church.

"Don't you have to go?" I asked.

"In a minute," she murmured.

I scanned the trees and surrounding area, drawing in deep breaths of air as I scented and searched for a threat. The only smells I detected were burnt earth and the fresh vegetation drooping beneath the July sun. I stayed close by her side as she approached the church and walked around to one of the windows.

Placing her hands against the side of her head at her temples, she rose on her toes to peer through the dirt-streaked, stained-glass window. My gaze went to the horizon as a flash of movement caught my attention. A doe with a fawn poked her head out from behind a house. Her ears perked up when she spotted us before she and her baby took off into the woods.

Stepping away from the window, River turned and I walked with her toward the back of the building. A beam from the crumpled ceiling had torn a hole into the side of the wall when it had fallen.

I grasped her arm when she went to climb the rocks spilling out of the hole. "What are you doing?"

"I'd like to look around."

"It's not safe in there."

"It is."

I could tell by the color of her eyes that she wasn't having a vision, but something about the look she gave me caused me to release my hold on her and let her do what she needed to do. "I'll go first," I told her.

She opened her mouth to protest but closed it again and stepped aside. I adjusted my feet as I walked across the pile of shifting stones. Standing on top of the thick layer of stone and wood, I surveyed the wreckage piled on the floor of the ruined church. The place reeked of mildew and rot, but I didn't see anything unusual or hazardous below.

Turning, I held my hand out to take hold of hers. I helped her to climb over the rocks and watched as her gaze roamed over the high walls before focusing on the couple feet of debris beneath our feet. She took a step forward, but I pulled her back and held her close as we climbed down to the floor of the church.

"What has drawn you in here, River?" I inquired, my voice reverberating within the cavernous building.

"I'm not sure if anything has." She removed her hand from mine as she picked her way carefully forward.

I followed her as she moved past the shattered remains of a couple of pews poking out from the rubble. She walked to the altar covered in wood and rotting shingling from the roof. Her frown deepened as she focused on the stained-glass window of an angel tucked behind and to the right of the altar. The angel's blonde head was tipped back to the sky, her hands clasped in prayer and her green eyes vibrant in the sunlight filtering through the window.

"It looks like the figurine you have in the truck," I remarked.

"It does," she murmured.

Her head tilted to the side as she seemed to be straining to hear or see something within the shadows and cobwebs hanging in what remained of the rafters. Rays of sunlight streamed through the stained-glass window, causing multiple colors to play over her tanned complexion and caressing her body in an almost loving manner.

In that moment it seemed the world was as deeply connected to River, as she was to it. She'd said the loss of her bond to the earth and all things living would break her, turn her into something evil like Lucifer, and I believed her. I couldn't feel her connection to life and the world around her, but I knew the bond I felt with the hounds, how intricate a piece of me it was, and what it would do to me if it was ever severed. I wouldn't risk doing anything to her that could possibly destroy her link to the earth.

Which meant there would be no turning her and no eternity for us.

The hounds within me stirred as my fangs lengthened from the impulse to turn her, to make it so there could only *be* eternity for us. However, she would no longer be River if I did that and somehow ruined her connection to life. She may grow to hate me for it and it could make her become like her father. I would rather die than have that happen. I was going to have to continue to deny every one of my instincts for the rest of her fragile life.

I watched her, mesmerized by her and the bliss she took in soaking in the warmth. I fed on death; she fed on life. That was the way it had to stay. A warm smile spread across her lips when she turned to focus on me.

"Is that what drew you here?" I asked and waved a hand at the stained-glass angel.

"Not everything is a vision or insight with me. Sometimes I'm simply curious. Despite its destruction, there is still something calming about this place."

She felt calm while all I wanted was to get out of this place. I had River now, because of that, I wouldn't change the past, but I still hated these winged bastards and their creator for the chaos they had caused by throwing Lucifer out of Heaven rather than dealing with him themselves.

Her hip bumped playfully against mine when she walked by me before she stepped up to move past the altar and toward a door at the back. She wiped away the cobwebs hanging from the door-jamb before taking hold of the knob. She pushed against the door, but it didn't budge.

"What an odd vine," she murmured.

Her fingers stretched out to brush over something I couldn't see from my angle, but her words caused my blood to run cold. "No! Don't touch it!" I shouted at her.

I leapt onto the altar, racing across the debris toward her. Her hand was still stretched out when she turned toward me with a confused expression on her face. Before her fingers, the vine twisted and a piece of it shot toward her.

She almost fell over when she took a step back and her heel caught on some debris. Arriving at her side, I grabbed her and spun her around as another vine lashed out at her. The vine hit me in the back. Its prickly red leaves sliced like shards of glass through my shirt and across my skin as it slid over my flesh.

"Shit!" I exploded at the same time the vine released an audible cry of pleasure.

Reaching behind me, my hand enclosed around a three-inch-thick vine as more of them shot out to try to ensnare us. River gasped in my arms when a vine sliced across her cheek. Another cry from the plant filled the air. My fangs extended as blood beaded across her skin and rolled down her face.

All of the red leaves stood up as one; they did an odd shimmying motion. I'd witnessed this kind of attack before when they'd been trapped deep within the bowels of Hell, feeding on whatever scraps were tossed their way. Now they had discovered a feast on Earth as the needle-like tendrils beneath the leaves rolled and vibrated eagerly.

I pulled River closer in an attempt to shield her from the vines shooting out to slice over my skin. I grabbed one as it dug into the flesh of my wrist, slicing to the bone. Flames shot up my arm and around my back, searing into the plant and causing its pain-filled scream to echo in my ears. I tore my burning shirt away and tossed it aside before it could sear River.

She threw her hands over her ears as flames tore across the vines, scorching the leaves and causing the screams to echo higher. I kept my flames away from her flesh, but she didn't shrink from them, and then I realized flames were spreading over her arms too, rising and falling with mine.

Her ability to release fire was fueled by her fear, but like her ability to control the flow of life, it appeared her fire also reacted to me. I didn't know if she realized her flames were rising up to join with mine as she remained bent over with her head down against the vines. Like my flames didn't hurt her, hers did not burn me.

Releasing her, I took a step back. My breath caught when I realized how much of an angel she looked like with her head bowed low, her back hunched forward, and the flames on her back protecting her like folded wings tucked against her spine. Yet there was something entirely demon about her with those flames encircling her as she rose up before me.

Unable to keep the fire away from her clothing this time, her shirt and bra fell away from her, baring her flesh to me. The shells on her necklace heated, but it didn't break as the flames didn't quite reach it.

She focused on the vines still dancing and slithering across the wall, unable to decide if they were willing to brave coming at us again or go without the blood. Lifting my hand, I took the choice from them as I set fire to the rest of them. River raised her hand beside mine, adding her flames to the inferno.

The vines withered and broke, screaming as they fell on the debris littering the floor. River's hand fell away as the flames died and she stepped forward. She didn't have to speak for me to know she intended to try to put the fire out; I grabbed hold of her arm before she could.

"We have to get out of here," I told her.

"It's going to catch on fire," she protested.

"We can't stop that." Smoke wafted up from the pile of debris beneath our feet as flames ate at the vines and crept toward what was left of the ceiling. "Come."

I lifted her so her chest was pressed to mine, keeping her as covered as I could with my body while I walked with her toward the hole we'd entered through. "Those things are dead, right?" she asked.

"The ones in here are," I answered.

Her face paled. "In here?"

"There will be more."

"Great."

I should have prepared her better, or I should have been better prepared, but I'd never expected for the seals to start falling at all, never mind so rapidly. The vines had been kept behind the sixth seal, which meant seals four and five had also fallen and their occupants were now free.

The hounds. Still alive, I reassured myself, but something was seriously wrong if three more seals had been opened. How many more had fallen that we didn't know about yet?

Corson jumped through the hole, landing on the debris with his talons extended. His eyes darted around as he searched for a threat before noticing the flames licking toward the roof and crackling up from beneath the floor. Behind him, Hawk and Vargas came through the hole with their guns at the ready.

"I heard screaming," Corson said as he retracted his claws and rose to his full height.

"Akalia vine," I told him.

His gaze slid past us to the growing fire. "Are you sure?"

I glanced down at the blood drying on my arms and body before looking pointedly at the still-trickling trail of blood on River's cheek. The flames danced in his orange eyes as his claws came out once more. Bale and Erin appeared at the top of the debris to stand beside Hawk and Vargas.

"Give me your shirt," I commanded Corson.

Without hesitating, he grabbed the bottom of his shirt and pulled it over his head. River glanced down at herself, her eyes widening as she realized the top half of her was naked against me. Her cheeks became redder than the fires around me as Corson handed over his shirt.

"Your fire went across your back," I told her as I turned her away and stood over her to keep her sheltered from the others. "It reacted to my fire."

"I see," she mumbled as she tugged the shirt on. It fell nearly to her knees, making her appear smaller. "It's only ever come from my palms before or up around my wrists toward my arms. The fire is growing stronger too."

"Yes, or at least around me it is."

"Is the akalia dead?" Corson demanded when I turned to face them again.

"I hope so. I'm not in the habit of burning down churches," River muttered as I helped her climb the rocks to join them.

"That would kind of be like burning down your own home," Corson said to her. The look she shot him would have made a human run away. Corson didn't run, but he did take a step back. "Or not."

"Not, definitely not," she said. Smoke floated like mist around us as we turned to watch the church burn.

CHAPTER THIRTY-TWO

KOBAL

"Lucifer won't stop until he's opened all of the seals, will he?" Corson asked.

I didn't want to think it was true, that he wouldn't be so stupid to open *all* of the seals, but I knew he wasn't going to stop.

"The seals?" Hawk asked.

"The seals holding back the worst of Hell. The creatures even demons don't want to deal with, but they have evolved over the years within the pits of Hell. Creatures that weren't allowed to roam freely in Hell because of what they could do. My ancestors began locking them away hundreds of thousands of years ago, and now Lucifer is setting them free. You humans believed there were only seven seals, but there are a couple hundred of them."

Hawk blanched, Vargas kissed his cross, and against my side River trembled. "And all of those things are coming here?" Vargas asked.

"With the akalia vine, we know at least the first six seals have been opened. I'm not sure how many more could have fallen. Some of the seals housed things that would never be able to survive up here as they thrive on shade and fire, but many of the others *can* survive here."

Erin planted her hands on her hips as she stared at me. "Why would Lucifer open the seals?"

"If he can open the seals, he won't have to come to Earth until it is completely overrun with the horrors of Hell and there is little opposition left to him here. Once he arrives, this world would be his for the taking. He knows the mess he will create; he simply doesn't care. Part of the plan with River had been to try to lure him out of Hell. He won't be lured out now. These creatures will wreak havoc on Earth and destroy as many humans and demons as possible before he rises," I said.

"Won't they destroy him too when he rises?" Hawk inquired.

"Not if he's the one setting them free," I replied. "They'll follow him."

"Son of a bitch," Hawk muttered and ran a hand over the stubble on his head.

"Couldn't have said it better myself," Corson said. "The gateway has to be closed."

River thrust out her chin when Bale and Corson looked toward her. Hawk and Vargas exchanged a glance with each other.

"You can close the gateway?" Hawk inquired of her.

"I don't know," she said. "They think I might be able to, but no one knows for sure."

"If she can't close the gateway and she can't enter Hell…" Bale's voice trailed off.

I clenched my teeth to rein in my temper when River glared at Bale. I didn't want River taking one step into the pit of Hell, but the alternatives weren't any better, perhaps worse.

I could take her from here now, return her to the wall, and we could make a stand there. However, I had to admit not even *I* could protect her from every abomination of Hell. Eventually, they would outnumber us and everything would be lost when they did.

I may not care much for most of the humans, but looking back at Verin and Morax as they ran toward us, I knew I couldn't sacrifice all of those who had depended on me just to keep River alive for a few more years, if we were lucky. Thousands upon thousands had died over the years to fight for me to take my place as the rightful king of Hell, and no matter how badly I wanted to keep River from what she was about to face, I could never turn my back on those who had been lost and the ones who still fought.

River had become the heart I'd never realized I could have, but the demons gathered around me had been my friends, followers, and fighters for centuries and some, such as Corson, for over a millennium. They would never turn their backs on me in such a way. They would all die to protect River for me, and I would fight to the death for any of them.

River wouldn't walk away from this either. I would have to drag her kicking and screaming back to the wall. I'd seen the love she had for her brothers; she would do everything possible to ensure they had a future.

She was growing stronger every day. Her fire ability was increasing. With her ability to draw on life, she'd tossed Azote onto his ass and heaved me into a tree, even though I'd been prepared for it. What would she be able to do with more time? But time was something we were running out of, and I had no way to get more of it for her if the seals continued to fall.

"We will stop him, no matter what it takes," I said.

"Should we turn back?" one of the humans asked, drawing my attention to the fact they'd all gathered around us as the church fire continued to grow and billow into the sky.

I could feel the eyes of the demons boring into me. They would agree to whatever I said, but I knew they had already weighed our options too. Continue onward and still have a small chance of success, or turn back and face a turbulent future and near certain death.

"There is no turning back," I grated through my teeth.

"We don't know what's out there!" I recognized the speaker as the same woman who had become hysterical over the gargoyles. "We've already lost half our numbers, and now you're saying some of the *worst* of what resided in Hell is here and more of it could be set free any day now."

"There's nothing worse than us," Bale said with a flick of her red hair over her shoulder. "There is simply more mindless, but as you can see, we beat the gargoyles, the akalia vine is burning, and we leveled the revenirs. Keep your eyes open, stay alert, and you will survive."

"*You* beat the gargoyles," the woman said. "*We* were decimated."

"Enough, Jackie," Hawk said brusquely.

"No, not enough! Don't think everyone hasn't noticed how you three have ingratiated yourself to them, earning extra protection and following *her* around."

The malicious glance she gave River caused the hair on my nape to rise and my lips to skim back.

"Who picked this girl?" Bale demanded, her gaze scathing as it raked over the young woman.

"I was picked because of my fighting skills," Jackie said. "Skills I have no chance of using against monsters such as you and your kind, and whatever *she* is."

Again, her eyes burned into River. Releasing her, I stepped toward the girl. "I'd suggest you stop looking at her like that; otherwise, you'll be making your way back to the wall. *On your own.*"

"That would be death," she whispered, her lower lip quivering.

"I'm a monster. I don't care."

"Kobal," River said from behind me. Her hand encircled my wrist as she stepped beside me. "We'll get through this," she said to Jackie. "We all knew there would be casualties when we left the wall, but this has to be done. It's the only hope any of us, or our loved ones, have of being able to survive. The wall isn't going to hold out forever. If we turn back now, all will be lost."

"Of course you're willing to keep going. You're one of them, or *whatever* you are, and you're sleeping with *him,* so he's going to protect you more!" Jackie retorted.

River's hand tightened on my wrist, but she couldn't stop me from advancing on the girl. "Not the head!" she gasped.

Jackie took a step away from me, then another. Shax moved forward to stand between us before I could reach her. He lifted his hands in a conciliatory gesture.

"I'm not going to kill her!" I snarled at him.

"Frightening her isn't helping," Shax replied calmly.

I focused my attention on Jackie again. "You can cry and carry on. You can think what you will of us, but you *ever* talk to her in such a way again, it won't be your head I tear from your body in order to silence you."

Jackie's jaw dropped open before she closed it again and slapped both of her hands over her mouth.

"Nice," Shax muttered. "Diplomacy is not your thing."

"Fuck diplomacy. We're the only thing standing between her and certain death. If she doesn't like it, then she can go back." My gaze shifted to the rest of the humans gathered behind Jackie. "You may have as many as another five years before it ends or as little as tomorrow, but Lucifer's followers will only gain in strength, and they *will* make it to the wall. Not only will most of you die when that happens, but so will most of the millions of other humans who have managed to survive for this long. The ones of you who are killed outright, will be the lucky ones. Those unfortunate enough to survive will be enslaved and tortured. There are more humans and demons making their way inland to help us. We *will* meet up with them at the gateway and find more protection."

At least, I hoped they were still coming. They most likely wouldn't encounter gargoyles, but there were other obstacles out there now that the seals were collapsing so quickly.

"Everything contained behind those seals won't be in this area either. They would have spread out to claim their own territory, something they've never been allowed to do before. If we're able to close Hell again, many of them will die," I continued.

"And those that don't?" another human asked.

"We'll kill them."

"How long have these seals been open?" another asked.

"Not long," Corson answered. "The revenirs move quickly as they can spread through the dead, and the gargoyles can fly. The akalia vine is slower than they are, but still faster than some others, and we're only a couple of days away from the gateway we seek. I'd say it's been a month at most since the first one fell, but most likely only a couple of weeks."

The other humans shuffled uncomfortably from foot to foot. Captain Tresden finally stepped forward; I eyed the man, not at all liking his unwillingness to take control of his people. Sweat beaded across his forehead and trickled down his cheeks as he stared at the people gathered around him. He was keeping his slowly unraveling composure hidden better than Jackie, but it was only a matter of time before he cracked.

We'd done our best to pick only those we believed would survive this journey with their minds still intact, but there had been no way to completely guard against picking someone who wouldn't do well out here.

My gaze slid to Erin, Hawk, and Vargas as they stood near Corson and Bale. All of their faces were composed of stone, their eyes unrelenting. One of them would be the best choice to take over for Tresden when it became necessary, maybe even before, but that discussion would be better to have someplace away from the burning building behind us.

"We have to go, now," I commanded brusquely as the fire snapped loudly in the air and a breeze pushed the smoke toward us. "The flames will only draw attention to this area."

Taking hold of River's hand, I kept it clutched in mine as I hurried back to the truck and opened the door for her to slide inside. The others climbed into the back of the truck and settled in. Turning away from the church, I slid behind the wheel, started the vehicle, and shifted into drive as the sun lowered in the sky. We wouldn't cover much distance before we had to stop again for the night, but we had to get as far from here as possible.

CHAPTER THIRTY-THREE

RIVER

My knuckles ached as I leaned forward over the wheel, but I didn't lessen my death grip as all around me screams echoed through the unnatural tunnel of akalia vine that had grown up to enshroud the road. A fresh burst of flame on my left didn't tear my attention away from the rutted road. We'd encountered the tunnel about a half an hour after we'd left the burning church behind.

I'd realized forty-five minutes ago why the vines hadn't blocked off the road. The minute the last vehicle crossed into the tunnel, pieces of the vine descended in search of fresh meat. I shuddered as more fire burst free and eerie, hissing screams emanated from the writhing vine surrounding us.

On the other side of the road, Corson sliced the bottoms of the vines with his talons and brushed them aside when they fell on him. Behind him Bale and Shax worked at slicing away the vines with machetes while on the other side of the road Morax and Verin did the same thing. The demons were covered in blood from the slices the hideous vines tore across their skin when it managed to get in a blow against them.

All of the humans remained within the vehicles. Erin was sprawled inelegantly across Vargas and Hawk, looking as disgruntled as the two of them did. With little air flowing through the tunnel, the truck had become stiflingly hot with the four of us crammed into the cab, and I was finding it increasingly difficult to breathe. However, that had little to do with the heat and more to do with my concern for Kobal.

The sun should still be in the sky, but the vines, smoke, and fire filling the air obscured any hint of remaining daylight. Kobal shot me a look over his shoulder when I cracked the window in an attempt to get some fresh air flowing through the cab. None of us smelled particularly great right now, but the air outside wasn't any better as the cloying scent of smoke and the rancid garbage stench of dying akalia vine filled my nose.

"Close the window," Kobal commanded before releasing another blast of fire at the seeking vines.

I ducked when one slapped against the glass, inches from the opening. "You should let me help you. It will go faster," I offered for the hundredth time.

"No. Close the window."

"Kobal, be reasonable about this."

The look he shot me left no room for reason as his eyes became their stunning, amber color. He'd been edgier ever since we'd left the church earlier. Now he was being completely obstinate. I knew he worried he wouldn't be able to keep me safe, that there was far more danger out here than he'd expected, but he couldn't keep me locked away either.

I stopped the truck, but before I could grasp the handle, he slammed his hand against the door. "Listen to me and stay in there," he said.

"Kobal—"

"I said *no*, River. If we need your help, I will tell you."

My eyes narrowed on him. "No, you won't."

He didn't deny it, but while he was holding the door shut, a vine slid down to slice across his bare chest. If I continued to sit here and argue with him, he would only allow the vines to keep doing that to him. I slid my fingers through the open window, seeking a connection with him no matter how brief. Sparks danced over my fingers when he touched them before pulling his hand away.

"Don't just stand there then, get back to work," I said and rolled the window up.

He glowered at me through the glass. I smiled sweetly in return, though I felt anything but sweet, and the smile was forced. I sighed in relief when he turned away from the door and focused on the vines whipping toward him once more.

Hawk snorted and Erin giggled while Vargas shook his head. I shifted back into drive and eased my foot off the brake. There had to be an end to this tunnel somewhere. Hopefully, it was somewhere soon, but the vines canopied the road for as far as I could see.

My gaze traveled over the hideous vines squirming over top of each other. Their palpable desire for blood made my stomach turn. Their screams and cries would haunt my nightmares for the rest of my days.

"Before you came into camp, no one would have dared to stand up to him," Erin said to me.

"Most still wouldn't," Hawk pointed out.

"True," Erin admitted, "but I have to say, I'm not quite as terrified of him as I used to be. The other demons were at least somewhat approachable, well, most of them anyway. Bale's about as friendly as a cactus, and I'm pretty sure Morax might want to eat us."

"I don't think they actually eat humans," I told her.

"So far, no, but who knows," Erin replied. "Kobal loves you."

Vargas and Hawk both scowled at her, obviously not in the mood to discuss anything in the least bit romantic. I bit on my lip to keep from laughing at the looks on their faces. They'd probably happily climb out of this cab right now and go play with the vines if it meant getting to avoid any talk of love.

"He does," I replied.

Her brows drew together and her mouth pursed. "When he ripped off Eileen's head, no one knew what to make of it."

"I did," Hawk muttered and shifted in his seat. "The guy was *pissed.*"

Erin rolled her eyes. "Obviously, but many didn't think it was because of love."

I glanced at her before resuming my hunched-over-the-wheel position that made my back scream in protest. "Then what did they think it was?" I inquired.

"I don't know," she admitted. "Some crazy, demon possessiveness thing that made him think he owned you. Others assumed he was nuts."

"Not owned," I murmured, "and not nuts."

"It's not something we'd ever seen before," Erin said. "He'd come across as distant and lethal the few times he'd been in camp before you arrived, but he's not. At least not with you, and I think he cares for the other demons too."

"He does," I said. "I don't know how to explain any of it."

"You don't have to," Erin replied.

"Thank God," Hawk muttered.

A small burst of laughter escaped me. It felt good, given the constant screaming and oppressive air surrounding us. I leaned further over the wheel, hoping to see some sign of a break in the tunnel, but all I saw was more darkness. A bead of sweat trickled down my temple and I hastily wiped it away. I glanced nervously at Kobal, hating the fact he was out there and bleeding and there was nothing he would let me do to help him.

"Where are you from, Erin?" I asked as a way to distract myself from our surroundings and my anxiety over Kobal.

"Me or my parents?" she inquired. "I know most have a hard time figuring out my heritage."

"Both."

"I was born and raised in Boston. My dad is first generation American from South Korea and my mom came over from Ireland when she was ten. She still has the faintest hint of an accent." A wistful smile played over her lips before she turned to look out the window. "I volunteered to go to the wall so I could help them take care of my six younger siblings."

Hawk released a low whistle. "Seven kids."

"Yeah, our family really struggled after the war."

"I bet."

"Where are you from?" Erin asked me.

"Bourne. I don't know what my father was, but my mother was a mix of Italian, German, English, and Native American."

"And you?" she asked Hawk.

"Falmouth," he replied. "I'm a melting pot too, but one of my dad's ancestors came over on the Mayflower. I volunteered so I could help support my family too."

Erin elbowed Vargas in the ribs. "What about you?"

He grunted and rubbed at his stomach. "I was born in Peru. We moved to the U.S. when I was seven and settled in Worcester."

"Why did you volunteer?"

Vargas shrugged. "This is my country and I'm going to fight for it."

"Good reason," Erin said.

I waited for them to ask me about what I was, but though they *had* to be wondering about it, they never issued the question. One of these days, they would get the answer, I would make sure of that, but for now, they were okay with what Kobal had told them. They were better than I was about such things.

After a few more minutes, Erin spoke again. "I have got to pee so freaking bad right now."

"Please don't," Vargas said.

"I won't." But they all winced when she shifted her weight again.

Another hour passed before I saw the faintest rays of light at the end of the tunnel. I exhaled loudly before leaning further over the wheel as I tried to ascertain if it was really a break in the vines or if I had yearned for it so badly I was imagining it.

"Is it really there?" I whispered.

"I think it is," Hawk said as he leaned forward beside me.

I glanced toward the angel on the dash before focusing on the road once more until we broke free of the vines. The breath exploded from my lungs. I was pretty sure my muscles were never going to unknot, and the stink coming off of me would kill a goat, but we were finally *free*. I cracked open my window, and when Kobal didn't tell me to close it again, I rolled it the rest of the way down. Erin did the same with the other side. I eagerly inhaled the fresh air flowing through the vehicle.

Kobal and Corson continued to walk next to the truck, unwilling to stop until Kobal called for a halt almost half an hour later. Erin nearly fell out of the truck when I pulled to the side of the road. She bolted for the woods before anyone could stop her.

"Wait!" Vargas called after her.

She vanished from sight.

"I'll get her," Corson said and loped away toward the woods.

My legs quaked when I slid from the truck and my foot was cramped, but I somehow managed to remain standing. Kobal clasped my elbow when I took a stumbling step on my protesting foot. "I stink," I murmured.

"You do."

That was my man, never one to pull punches. It made me want to kick him almost as much as kiss him.

"So do you!" I retorted.

His full lips curled into an endearing smile that had me rethinking the kicking aspect. "I do," he agreed.

Corson and Erin reemerged from the woods. Corson shook his head as he walked. "Just piss on them next time," Corson told her.

Vargas and Hawk blanched and exchanged a nervous look. Erin grinned at Corson before giving Hawk and Vargas a devious smile.

"Hopefully, we won't have to go through that again," Kobal said.

"Let's hope," Vargas said and rubbed at the cross on his neck before releasing it.

Tilting my head back, I stared at the darkening sky as the first star broke through. I turned to see tendrils of smoke rising over the land from where the vines had formed their tunnel. I didn't like the idea of being so close to them or the smoke.

"We're going to take fifteen minutes to rest, eat, and then move on," Kobal said, seeming to read my mind. He kissed the top of my head before releasing me and walking over to where Captain Tresden was directing everyone to start unpacking the trucks.

The man stopped when he saw Kobal approach. I didn't hear what was said, but few of them looked pleased when Kobal walked away.

"They're exhausted," I said when he returned.

"We all are," he replied absently. "But we can't stay here. We're too close to those vines and the fire."

Erin dug into the supplies in search of food and water while the rest of us took turns going into the woods. Fifteen minutes later, we were all munching on trail mix and stale bread when Kobal pulled onto the road again. I'd been hoping for something more substantial, but I wasn't going to complain, at least it was easing the rumbling in my belly.

With the windows down and the others in the back of the truck once more, my stench wasn't so overwhelming. Finishing off my trail mix, I crumpled the bag and shoved it into the glove box. I leaned back to watch the headlights bouncing across the pavement. Their dim glow did little to illuminate the way as the night pressed against us. I kept expecting the world to fall away and for us to plummet over the side into nothing.

Or into Hell.

CHAPTER THIRTY-FOUR

RIVER

"Cold?" Kobal asked when I rubbed my hands up and down my arms.

"No. It's all so creepy. It's like there's nothing out there anymore, only this endless road carved through our country leading nowhere."

"It leads somewhere."

I inhaled deeply and turned to stare at the scraggly, barren landscape I barely recognized anymore. Before there had been green vegetation and life growing in and around the bombed-out and burned-down homes. Now there was life still, but it was nowhere near as abundant and none of the homes around here remained standing. Some of the life I sensed out there wasn't life I was familiar with or could identify.

After another couple of hours, Kobal pulled to the side of the road and parked the truck. "We're far enough away from the akalia to stop for the night and I smell water," he said.

I leaned over to give him a peck on the cheek before opening the door and climbing out. I stood, inhaling the fresher air, but there was a strange cloying scent on the breeze that was neither pleasant nor unpleasant. It reminded me of honeysuckle at the same time it reminded me of fire. It was such an odd combination that I couldn't figure out if I should pinch my nose closed or inhale eagerly.

"What is that smell?" I inquired.

"Nuclear fallout." Erin smiled as she suggested it, but I could hear the anxiety in her tone.

"Is it?" I asked Kobal.

"No," he replied. "It's probably some plant life in the area."

Vargas leaned over the side of the truck to dig through the supplies in the back. He pulled out a yellow box with a metal handhold and turned it on before pulling out a black, handheld device.

"It's not radiation," Kobal said impatiently to him. "We checked this area before."

"Don't care," Vargas muttered as he walked around the area with the radiation detectors.

I watched him until he came back and put the devices away. "Everything is reading normal."

"Good," Erin said and turned back to the truck.

My thought exactly. "You said something about water," I said to Kobal.

"I did." He gathered my bag of supplies before tugging his own from the truck.

He slung his bag over his shoulder and kept hold of mine as he took my hand and led me across the small clearing, down an embankment, and through some small pines and oaks. I surveyed the woods as we walked, taking in all the details that were similar and different than the forests I was used to.

The oak leaves were green, but they didn't shine and were a more faded green than the vibrant ones I was used to. The pine tree's needles drooped as we walked by and like the oak leaves, these were also a faded green color. Maybe this area was experiencing a drought right now, but something felt more off about this place than that simple explanation allowed.

Stepping around a few of the trees, my concerns about the plant life vanished when I spotted the large lake. The moon shone on the water, lighting a pathway across its smooth surface. Lightning bugs zipped over it, their flashes of light reflecting in the water like shooting stars falling from the sky.

Crickets chirruped and I heard the distant hoot of an owl from one of the trees across the way. The crisp smell of the water called to me, and I was about to strip when Kobal tugged on my hand and gestured toward a section of small willow trees hanging over the shoreline of the lake. They'd grown tall enough that their limbs bent over and their leaves skimmed the surface of the water to provide a natural, private canopy.

I followed him around the edge of the lake toward the trees. Looking at the shoreline, I didn't see any signs of drought as the water lapped high against the banks the lake had carved into the land. Reaching the privacy of the willows, I released Kobal's hand to unbuckle the guns at my waist. I placed them on the bank before setting my katana beside them and eagerly pulling my soiled clothing off. Kobal remained silent as he stripped beside me and tossed his clothes aside. I grabbed my bar of lemon soap and small bottle of shampoo, before plunging into the warm water.

A blissful sigh escaped me as the lake lapped and flowed around my skin. The water rose up high enough to cover my breasts before I ducked my head under the surface and came back up again. I scrubbed myself as I listened to the sounds of others trudging down to the lake from different points in the woods.

Kobal stayed by my side, his naked body moving to block mine if anyone ventured too close. They wouldn't be able to see us beneath the willows anyway. My eyes skimmed over my body, my brow furrowing as I realized that the numerous bruises I'd received from Azote were already fading. I should have had them for at least a week, probably two, but they looked as if they would be gone tomorrow or the next day.

My hands fell into the lake as I turned toward Kobal. "My bruises are healing faster than normal."

He tore his attention away from making sure no one came near us to focus on me. His eyes skimmed over me before landing on the faded bruise running down my left side. It had been black yesterday. Today it already had a yellowish tinge to it and was more brown.

"Like me, you are healing faster," he murmured as he took a step toward me, rested his hands on my shoulders, and gently turned me before him to inspect the bruises on my back.

"How is that possible?"

He was silent as he studied me before turning me to face him again. "Our bond has made you stronger and you're drawing on the life around you more."

"But I'm not."

"You're doing it without realizing it. You always have. But now that you're using your ability more, it's growing and it's powering you more. It has helped to accelerate your rate of healing."

"Huh." I had no other response for that as I mulled over his words.

"It's a good thing," he said quietly.

Tilting my head back, I smiled up at him. "It is," I agreed. "It's just strange, but I'm okay with not being a walking bruise anymore, and maybe it will help heal broken bones faster too."

He kissed my forehead before releasing my shoulders and taking a step back. "I'm sure it will, but I don't intend for you to find out."

"Me either."

I returned to bathing while he kept an eye on the woods. It was while I was washing the shampoo from my hair that it hit me the feel of *everything* here was different. I stood up in the water and stared at the ripples radiating out from me. Lifting my head, I spotted some people across the lake bathing close to each other. There were a few more a hundred or so feet to the left of them.

Beyond them, I studied the sickly looking woods as my fingers skimmed over the surface of the warm water. I felt a pulse within the lake, but it was more sluggish than what I was used to. The smell here was different, the trees not as vibrant. We were getting closer to the gateway to Hell and the world was changing.

"It feels different here," I murmured.

Kobal stepped in front of me and rested his hands on my shoulders again. The brush of his chest against mine caused my nipples to pucker as I moved closer to him. Beads of water slid over his body in rivulets I longed to follow with my tongue. I watched one trickle all the way down to where it dripped into the water. I licked my lips as my fingers slid over the carved muscles of his abs.

"How does it feel different?" he asked, his voice husky as my hands dipped lower.

I bit my lip when the head of his thick shaft emerged above the water line, swelling before my eyes. Unable to resist, I slid my fingers over its silken tip, rubbing the beads of water over the sensitive flesh before stroking my hand over his length. His breath rushed in, and his body jerked in my grasp. I smiled when I lifted my head to take in the rapt expression on his face as he watched my hand working over him.

"How is it different, River?" he prodded.

His hand caressing the underside of one of my breasts made it difficult to recall what we'd been talking about. "The flow of life here, it's not the same," I said. "Before, the world felt fluent and malleable. Now it feels *stuck,* almost like in sap or... I don't know how to explain it."

The look on his face made me realize he was contemplating throwing me over his shoulder and dragging me out of here. I'd seen that same look a few times since we left the church. His hand stilled on me.

"We can't leave," I said before he could speak.

"I know," he grated from between his teeth.

"We're close to the gateway to Hell now. The earth isn't the same here. It makes sense that it wouldn't be. I just hadn't considered the possibility until now. We'll get through this."

"*Mortal.*" The word was said in such a ragged, desperate tone of voice that it tore at my heart and my hand stopped moving on him. His eyes had turned amber at the word; they blazed with life and the wildness of the hounds within him.

"I always have been."

He dragged his hand through his wet hair. His anguish and uncertainty beat against me as I used my body and hand to maneuver him back toward the bank.

"River," he growled when I bent to run my lips over his chest and my tongue slid out to lick away the water on his flesh. The taste of the lake water on his fire-scented skin filled my senses and kicked my desire into hyperdrive. "We must talk about this."

"Later," I murmured as I slid my tongue over one of the hard ridges of his abs before lowering my head to lick over the deep line carved down the center. Sparks danced across my fingers as I traced his rigid muscles with my fingers. They lit his silken, damp flesh in a golden glow.

I couldn't get enough of his taste, of his scent, and the feel of him straining within my hand. Bending lower, I ran my tongue around his belly button, but it was the enticing head straining out of the water toward me that beckoned to me the most. I'd yet to touch him or taste him in such a way, not because I didn't want to, but simply because it hadn't happened yet. Now, nothing would stop me from knowing him in this way.

His hands gripped my shoulders, and he stopped breathing when my lips hovered over him. Ever so slowly, I ran my tongue across the head of his shaft. Within my hand, his erection swelled and strained toward me. A smile curved my mouth before I licked over him again.

∾

KOBAL

"*Shit*," I hissed when River's mouth slid over the top of my dick.

Her tongue trailed over the sensitized flesh as she moved, tasting me with an eagerness I'd never experienced before. There was something we should be discussing, but for the life of me, I couldn't recall what, nor did I care to, as I watched her.

Bracing my elbows against the bank, I lifted my hips out of the water. Her smile deepened before she slid further over me, her tongue lapping away the water dripping down me as she worked her mouth and hand over my cock. Pleasure spiraled out through me as my fingers dug into the mossy riverbank.

I almost shouted aloud when her other hand slid down to cup my heavy balls and she rolled them within her grasp. When a strand of her hair fell forward to shield her features, I pulled it back to expose her face to me once more. Her eyes fluttered open, their violet depths met and held mine as I slid my hand over her cheek and down to cup her full breasts. A small moan escaped her and her eyes closed again.

I couldn't stop my exploration of her body as my hand dipped over her side and back up to rub her hardened nipple. She moved forward, her breasts brushing over my thighs as she pulled me deeper within her, sucking and licking me in a hungry way that had me on the verge of exploding.

I gritted my teeth against the urge to come. *Not yet.* The hotness of her wet mouth on my flesh was almost more than I could bear. Her other hand fell away from me to trace over my side before her nails dug into my ass and she pulled me deeper into her.

My free hand shot out and seized a root of the willow tree exposed by the water. I watched her head bow and dip and lost myself to her tongue and lips. My fingers threaded through her hair, holding her closer as my hips rose and fell with her movements, and I resisted thrusting harder into her mouth.

The pressure built steadily within me until I neared my breaking point. "River, I'm going to come. Must... stop."

Her eyes flew open when I tried to draw her away. Their amethyst depths burned into mine, but she didn't pull away as she watched me. "River…"

Releasing my ass, her hand came forward to cup my balls once more. Unable to take anymore, a guttural shout escaped me as I came in a rush. Her tongue slid over the head of my pulsing cock, taking all of me into her, before she pulled away from me.

My eyes latched onto her as she licked her lips and rose from the water. Beads of liquid trailed over her delicate flesh and into the lake. I'd just found my release, yet I grew hard again as I watched the water sliding enticingly over her lithe body.

Rising out of the water, my hands fell on her waist before I lifted her against me. "Did you like that?" I demanded hoarsely as my tongue ran over her ear.

"Very much so," she whispered. "You taste delicious, like fire and salt. Addicting."

Unable to stop myself from claiming her, my fangs sank into her shoulder. Her legs wrapped around my waist as she opened herself to me and I felt the heated wetness of her sex against my cock.

∼

River

The piercing pain of his bite rapidly faded to be replaced with the euphoria it always caused to wash over my body. My arms encircled his neck, drawing him closer as his tongue licked my shoulder with his fangs still within me. His lingering taste on my tongue and lips was like an aphrodisiac. I hadn't been lying when I said he tasted of fire and salt and I wanted more.

I *needed* him inside of me with a desperation that had me clawing at the slick, taut skin of his back. The strength of his reaction to what had just transpired between us, and the thrill of power that reaction gave me had me aching for him.

The heady evidence of his arousal rubbed against my wet

center before he thrust upward and into me. He drove in so deeply, I swore he touched a piece of my soul. I nearly keened in ecstasy, but managed to keep it suppressed as my teeth sank into his shoulder. Sparks arched from my fingers to play across his flesh. The water rippled and flowed around us as he braced his legs apart and I began to ride him.

CHAPTER THIRTY-FIVE

RIVER

"We have to see how your power is working," Kobal told me as soon as he finished buttoning his pants.

I pushed back a strand of my damp hair and shoved it behind my ear before bending to tug on my boots. The katana shifted on my back with the movement and my guns bounced against my side. Glancing up at him, I tied my boot as I watched him shove our things into our bags. Normally, he relaxed at least a little after sex, but not this time.

"I'm sure it's fine," I said. "I still feel the connection."

"But not as strongly."

"No, it's... different here, but look at how quickly I'm healing. It can't be that different."

"The fact you're healing faster could be from the life you drew from the earth before reaching here. It could also be from the life you harvest from me and the strength of our Chosen bond." He turned toward me, nearly spilling the contents from my still-open bag. "Your ability to harvest life is because of the life around you. If you're not able to feed from it in the same way, it will affect your power."

"You mean it will affect *me*." The realization made my fingers slip away from my shoelaces and my heart sink as a fear blazed to life within me. "Like Lucifer."

"I didn't say that."

"But it's what you're thinking." I now realized where all of this pent-up tension was coming from as a hollow feeling spread through my body. I accepted I could die. I would die if it was necessary to save my brothers and so many others, but I was not willing to accept that I could become anything like that bastard ancestor of mine.

"No, River, that's not what I'm thinking. You still feel the connection. We have to make sure you can still use it in the same way."

He wouldn't lie to me. If that was what he was worried about, he would say it, but now the idea was embedded in my head.

Deep breaths. One day at a time, one minute at a time; that's the only way you'll get through this.

"Well, you just had my power sparking pretty good," I reminded him, hoping to coax a smile from him and ease the mood. It didn't work as he stared resolutely back at me.

"I haven't changed, but you're feeling the world around you differently. We have to know how that will affect you."

"Okay, we'll find out."

"Now."

Now all I wanted was sleep, but I could tell from the look on his face, he wouldn't get any rest until he knew. If I was somehow defunct in this land of strange smells and stranger life pulses, he'd never sleep again, I was certain of it.

I took a deep breath and rested my hand on the ground. Beneath my fingers, the pulse of life within the earth swirled up to meet me. A small smile played across my lips as the intricate bond worked its way over me. It may not feel the same in this area, but it was still there and the life force was like a familiar, comforting blanket as it slipped over me.

"It's sluggish," I muttered. Lines formed around his mouth when his lips compressed. "But I can still feel it and draw on it."

That reassurance didn't have the anticipated effect as he remained unmoving before me. Closing my eyes, I dug deeper, pulling at the slower pulse beneath my fingers and drawing it upward. It slithered through my hand and up into my arm. I looked down, half-expecting to see black running through my skin, or over it as it almost felt like tar, but all I saw were golden-blue sparks shooting from my hands instead of golden-white ones.

They were a darker color than normal, but they still danced across my fingers like little bolts of lightning. I couldn't help but smile as the sparks twined around my wrist and traveled toward my elbow.

"Form the ball," he commanded.

Turning my other hand over, I let the sparks grow and coalesce together there. The pull of the earth started to flow more easily through me as I became better accustomed to it, and the energy fed into the ball. Grinning, I flipped the ball within my fingers, turning it over and making it spin so fast that sparks shot out the sides of it. Like the sparks on my fingers, the energy forming the ball was darker in color, but I could feel the power thrumming through it.

"Now throw it at me," he said.

My head jerked up at his words. Before I could respond, he came at me. Knowing what he planned, I turned my hand over and smashed the ball back into the ground. Smoke drifted upward from the charred mark I left upon the earth.

"*No,* that is not going to happen again," I grated through my teeth.

He ran a hand through his disordered hair. "You have to test your powers, River."

"I just did. It scorched the earth the same as it always has. There is no difference, except that it's a little more difficult for me to dip into at first, but it's already becoming easier as I adjust to it.

However, hurting you is the equivalent to how you would feel if you hurt me."

"I'd never harm you."

"I know that! But if you did, how would you feel about it?"

"It would destroy me."

"That's how I felt the other night when you used my power against you, and I'm not doing it again!" I couldn't stop my foot from stomping on the ground, but I didn't care if the act was childish. He *had* to understand.

Closing his eyes, he gave a brisk nod before turning to gather our things again.

"Kobal." He glanced at me over the set of his rigid shoulder. "I *can* do this."

"I know you can."

"Then relax a little."

I walked over to stand before him. My fingers trailed across his taut skin and across the markings and flames on his arms. Those marks undulated beneath my touch when sparks flickered from the tips of my fingers. His skin warmed and his breath froze when I caressed the fresh bite mark I'd left on his shoulder. I rose on my toes to kiss his lips when motion to my right caught my attention. Frowning, I dropped down to stare at the spectral vision in the tree line.

"Angela," I whispered.

Kobal spun away from me, throwing his arm out to push me back from the nonexistent threat. I grasped his forearm, pushing it down as I stared at the girl. Through her body, I could see the young saplings of the forest and the underbrush lining the floor. She remained unmoving, her blonde hair falling about her shoulders and her green eyes somberly watching us. Kobal's head moved as he searched the forest for her.

"You don't see her either," I murmured.

"Who?" he demanded, his fangs extended and his eyes a molten gold.

"The little girl. She's standing right in front of us, watching us. At first, I'd assumed she was a figment of my imagination when I saw her from the house. Then, I assumed she was maybe some kind of ghost, but she's also more colorful than any ghost, and if you can't see her..." My voice trailed off as I tried to puzzle that part out.

"Why didn't you tell me about her?"

"She's not a bad thing."

"You can't know that."

My fingers dug into his arm until he turned to look at me. "*I* can."

His muscles relaxed a little, but I could still feel the hostility thrumming through his body when he turned to look at where I'd indicated. "Do you still see her?" he inquired.

"Yes."

As I watched, Angela lifted her arm and pointed toward where we had left the others. My heart plummeted into my shoes. "We have to get back to the others!" I blurted. He bent to retrieve our bags, but I snatched hold of his hand. "Now, we have to get back *now*."

Releasing his hand, I spun away and ran toward the camp. I ignored the underbrush and trees tearing at my pants and shirt as I leapt over fallen debris and dodged obstacles in my way. Kobal stayed beside me, but he was far faster and could get to them before me.

"Leave me!" I cried as his hand shot out to stop a tree branch from slapping me in the face.

"Never."

"Kobal, you must. Something's wrong."

"Did you have a vision?"

Maybe that was what little Angela was. Maybe my visions had chosen a new way to manifest themselves in her. "I just *know*!"

The second the words left my mouth, gunfire tore through the air and screams shattered the still night. My lungs burned and my legs felt like rubber, but I kept pushing myself forward. "Go!" I shouted at him.

Instead of leaving me, he spun around, seized my waist, and lifted me. My legs instinctively locked around his waist, and my chest molded against his as his long legs ate away at the ground between us and the camp. I kept my head buried in his shoulder to avoid the branches slapping and tearing at me.

Despite the extra burden of carrying me, he'd barely broken a sweat by the time we burst free of the trees, and his breath was no faster than normal. I lifted my head to take in the unfamiliar figures darting in and out of the trees as the humans fired at them and the demons clashed against the ones they could catch. The features and figures of the attackers were obscured by the blood-red cloaks covering them from head to toe.

Kobal pounded across the earth as more gunfire erupted. I spotted Hawk lunging at one of the figures who had their arms around someone else. He bared his teeth as he leapt again, but the figure swung out an arm, knocking him aside.

Vargas jumped into the fight to try to help, but before he could get more than two feet, he was slammed into the ground by another figure. A spate of gunfire filled the air. The creature on Vargas howled and jumped away before fleeing into the trees.

"Hold on!" Kobal grated in my ear before throwing out his arm.

Fire shot from his fingertips, blazing across the earth and blasting into one of the hooded creatures. It howled in agony, its body going up like tinder. I gawked at where it had been standing less than a second before, but didn't get much time to stare as Kobal came to an abrupt halt and released another wall of flame at the fleeing creatures.

I didn't know what drove me, but I unwrapped one arm from his neck and gripped his forearm. Fire erupted from my palm, swelling his flames to higher levels and causing them to illuminate the clearing around us as if it were the fourth of July.

So much power in him. It licked over my skin, burning

through my body and making me shiver. His other arm tightened on my waist as he held me to him and the fire continued to flow around the clearing.

The Chosen bond makes demons stronger. Kobal had told me this, had told me it was part of the reason Lucifer was looking to separate us, but for the first time, I truly understood it as the flames danced over our hands and around our wrists. Working together, the power grew and coalesced around us in a bond that electrified my skin.

The cloaked figures screamed as they fled into the woods, moving with the easy grace of ghosts or wraiths, but our fire wouldn't have destroyed either of those things in the way it had destroyed these things.

Like a bucket of water had been thrown on him, the flames stopped flowing from Kobal as they drew back into him. With his flames harnessed once more, mine sputtered out.

I could barely think as my mind spun over what had happened. "The Chosen bond makes us stronger," I managed to choke out.

"Yes."

"Is that why your flames don't burn me?"

"Part of it. The other is I can control my power more than you can. If I don't want to burn something, I don't."

"Amazing."

I slid my legs from around his waist and stepped back as I surveyed the damage to the clearing. Grass that had been green was now black, and fresh saplings were burnt toothpicks. There were scorched marks on the earth from the creatures Kobal had set on fire. Some people huddled near the vehicles, some were crying, others tended to the injured, and more looked about ready to start shooting at the first thing that moved.

"What were those things?" I asked.

"I have an idea, but without seeing the face of one, I'm not positive."

I shuddered at the sounds of sobbing and whimpers of pain

filling the air. I took a step toward where Vargas lay on the ground with Bale at his side, but Kobal pulled me back against him.

"She's taking care of him," Kobal said.

I searched for Hawk and Erin, but I couldn't see where Hawk had fallen through all the smoke drifting around us. Kobal kept me close to his side as he approached Corson. The demon was wearing two red earrings that hadn't been there the last time I'd seen him.

"Canagh demons," he said before Kobal could ask.

"What are those?" I asked.

"You would know them better as incubi and succubae," Kobal replied.

"Are you serious?" I blurted before I realized it was a stupid question. With everything we'd seen, it shouldn't surprise me they were real too.

I didn't get a stupid response from them at least. They both simply stared at me before turning away.

"We need to assess the damage. Gather the others as you go," Kobal said to Corson.

Kobal kept me near his side as Corson split off to patrol the camp and we moved in the other direction. I continued to search for Hawk and Erin but didn't see them anywhere. An uneasy feeling was growing in the pit of my stomach when we stopped at the truck we'd arrived here in.

Vargas stood by the truck, leaning against it with his hand on his head and a disposable ice pack against his temple. His right eye was swollen nearly shut, and blood trickled from the corner of his lips.

"Three vehicles have been destroyed from bullets in the engine or gas tank," Morax said, his tail thumping against the ground as he walked over to join us.

"Did they kill anyone?" Kobal inquired.

"No, but they did take five of the humans," Bale said.

"We have to find them!" I blurted.

"We cannot delay the mission for five humans," Kobal

replied. "There is far too much at stake. Every second that passes could mean another seal is being opened."

"Two of them were Hawk and Erin," Bale said.

"No," I whispered as my heart twisted in my chest.

A muscle in Kobal's jaw jumped. His hands clenched before he shook his head. "We cannot stop to look for them."

My teeth scraped back and forth as I glowered at him. He was right, I knew it. The lives of five people were nothing compared to millions, but I wouldn't leave here without trying to find them first.

"They are two of our best fighters," I pointed out, knowing reason instead of emotion was the best way to go with this. "They always keep their head in a bad situation, and they are *leaders*. Many here aren't."

I bit back the words that they were also my friends, the only friends I'd made since coming here. That point wouldn't sway him. He understood loyalty and friendship. He would die for Corson and Bale, but I knew he would also leave them behind if one of them had been taken. They would expect him to in order to complete what had to be done. Maybe Erin and Hawk would expect the same thing, but I couldn't do it.

Vargas moved closer to us. I could sense his disapproval of the decision by the set of his shoulders and the lines around his mouth and eyes, but his lips remained clamped shut. He would do whatever was deemed best. He was a solider; I wasn't.

"Vargas is still here. He is a leader," Kobal said. "And we have others. Corson—"

"Humans," I inserted. "We need more *humans* who can lead. Captain Tresden is as petrified as the rest of them."

"Vargas," he replied.

Thrusting back my shoulders, I stared relentlessly at him. "I'm not leaving without at least trying to find them. We'll be here until the morning anyway. We have to try."

"It is too dangerous to be out there at night. Every soldier knew this possibility could happen to them. They were prepared for the fact they would be left behind if it was best for the mission."

"You're forgetting that I never signed up to be a soldier. Fate brought me here, and maybe the lives of five humans means little compared to the bigger picture, but I'm not giving up on them. They wouldn't give up on me."

"You *are* the mission. Of course they wouldn't give up on you."

I gawked at him, feeling as if he'd slapped me in the face.

"Fuck you!" the words burst from my mouth before I'd realized I intended to say them.

Apparently, Kobal's tactful diplomacy had rubbed off on me somewhere along the way as I forgot all about trying to keep emotion out of this in favor of reason. Reason wasn't working and that statement had *pissed me off.* The demons and Vargas all took a step back from us. The humans who had been seeking protection by gathering closer, moved further away.

Kobal's nostrils flared, and his eyes narrowed on me. "Fuck me?"

"Yes, *fuck* you!" *Shut up you idiot. This will get you nowhere with him.* "And fuck the mission too!" So much for shutting up.

The cool, collected way he maintained himself unnerved me more than if he'd been shouting swears at me too. "And fuck your brothers too, I suppose?"

My breath rushed out of me like someone punched me in the stomach. I would do anything for Gage and Bailey, but as much as I loved them, I would forever hate myself for walking away from my friends right now.

"That's low," I told him.

"That's the truth," he replied. "I am not risking you by going after them."

He rocked back on his heels as he surveyed me almost casually, but I knew he was coiled tighter than a rattlesnake ready to strike. He'd throw me over his shoulder and forcefully carry me from here, I was certain of it. And I may just blast him with a ball of life if he tried.

"No, the truth is, we are not turning our back on those in need. We can't. I won't leave them to whatever fate lies in store for them, and given what little I know about incubi and succubae, it will be *horrible*."

The heads of those around us bounced between us so rapidly it may have almost been comical, if I didn't feel as if I'd already lost this battle. I was unraveling and only a thin thread was keeping me tethered to control.

"You're getting in that truck," he said.

"No, I'm not."

He came at me, swooping down to lift me against his side.

"Stop it!" I cried, unwilling to kick and scream at him like I wanted to. I was going to try to retain what little dignity I still had and go about this in an entirely different way. "Kobal, put me down."

Ignoring me, he pulled the truck door open. Without a word, he thrust me inside. I went to leap back out, but he lowered his face so it was mere inches in front of mine. His eyes became molten gold; the ruthless expression on his face robbed me of my breath.

"I will tie you into this vehicle if I have to!" he snapped.

"If you do this, I will *never* forgive you. This isn't tearing someone's head off who tried to kill me. This isn't defending me—"

"Yes, it is!" he barked.

"No, it's not." I took a deep breath to calm myself before continuing on. "This is completely ignoring my feelings, completely going against what I feel must be done. You're saying you don't care about how I feel if you do this."

"I care too much for you, that's the problem. Get out of this truck and it will be the last time you move about freely." With those last words, he slammed the door shut.

Resentment and misery warred within me as I watched him

268 BRENDA K DAVIES

walk toward the others in the side mirror. I knew why he was doing this, knew how much the possibility of my death troubled him and how much he loved me, but it was taking everything I had not to blast the door from the truck before zapping him so hard in the ass he wouldn't be able to sit for a week.

Though it was an *extremely* tempting proposition, I couldn't do it. There was a better way; there had to be. I faced forward, my teeth grinding together as I studied the night still alight from the dying flames. Trying to talk to him would do nothing. He wouldn't budge and he would tie me to the truck. If I pushed him and he tied me up like livestock, our relationship would be irrevocably changed, and not for the better.

I hated what he'd just done. He would never live this moment down for the rest of my life, but I could understand and forgive this if I was still able to find a way get to Hawk and Erin.

CHAPTER THIRTY-SIX

KOBAL

I kept watch of River's rigid back as she remained sitting in the truck, seething. It didn't matter that she was mad or that I disliked making her mad. All that mattered was keeping her alive. Going after those five humans was a risk I refused to let her take, even if I had come to respect Hawk and Erin.

The canagh demons were not a species she should mess with, not if this group of them were kidnapping humans. The canaghs fed on sexual energy, but it was rare they took those who were unwilling to their bed, and humans wouldn't survive them long enough to be satisfying. I had a feeling I knew whose group had taken her friends, and if I was right, I especially didn't want River around that hideous bitch.

There was only so much I could take when it came to the dangers to her life.

River would forgive me one day; she would have to. Turning away, I helped to gather some more of the scattered supplies and right the overturned trucks. Corson shot me a disgruntled look as he tossed a case of water into the back of a truck.

"What would you have done?" I demanded of him.

"Not that," Bale said. "If some guy did that to me, I'd have his balls hanging from my neck."

Corson winced and instinctively shielded himself. "Shit, Bale."

She flung back a piece of her fiery hair. "It's true, and from what I've seen of your Chosen, Kobal, she doesn't back down and she has no fear. She's plotting, trust me on this."

I glanced at where River remained in the truck. She hadn't moved in the past half hour. An hour ago, she'd been melting in my arms, now she may try and fry me if I went near her. "I won't have her near the canaghs and you know as well as I that the mission is more valuable than five human lives."

"Not to her," Bale said quietly. "You're rehashing past mistakes by forgetting she's human and she's not a soldier like the others here. Most of these humans have been at the wall and fighting this war for at least five years, many longer. They're more hardened than she is. They obeyed the rules she's refused to follow from the beginning, and she's only been with us for a few months."

I continued to stare at the back of River's head before turning away. Bale was right, but so was I. "I've made my decision and it will not be swayed."

"I can't wait to see how that works out for you," Bale replied with a smile.

"Tact, Kobal, you really should learn how to start using it once in a while," Corson said.

I snatched a backpack off the ground and tossed it into the back of the truck. "I left our bags by the lake," I recalled.

"I'll get them," Corson offered.

He jogged across the clearing to the tree line. Glancing at the truck again, a bolt of panic shot through me when I realized River wasn't there. I ran across the ground to the truck. I grabbed for the door handle when I spotted her curled up on the bench seat, her head resting on her hands.

Her gaze flickered toward me and her chin jutted up before she looked away. "You'll forgive me."

I knew she'd heard me, but she didn't so much as glance in my direction again. Slapping my hands on top of the pickup, I turned away and stalked back toward Bale who smirked at me. "Oh yeah, I definitely can't wait to see how this goes," she said and turned away.

Apparently, being a woman sympathetic to another woman's plight was enough for someone to toss aside centuries of friendship. I scowled at her back before returning to gathering the salvageable supplies.

Corson reemerged from the woods and jogged over to throw our bags into the back of the truck River sat in. "What is she doing?" I demanded when he walked over to me.

"Looks like she's sleeping."

"Good." I turned as the humans gathered closer to us. In the light of the moon, I could see the haggardness of their features and the dusky circles under their eyes. No matter how I wanted to push on, they were nearing a breaking point.

Tact, Corson had said. It may not be the wisest choice to stay here with the smoke still rising into the air around us, but the humans didn't look capable of moving on right now.

"We'll rest until daybreak. Then we're leaving." Some of them nodded at my words, but most of them glanced nervously around the clearing. "The canaghs won't dare to come back here tonight," I assured them.

Their shoulders slumped, their relief was nearly palpable as more of them nodded their agreement. Walking away, I returned to the truck and peered inside at River's slumbering form. *Safe, alive.* That was all that mattered, I told myself, but I ached to hold her right now, something I knew she wouldn't let me do again for a while.

I glanced at the moon hanging above the trees as it made its descent. *What if I go after them?*

I would be able to bring them back if I found them, but I would be leaving River alone here, vulnerable to an attack. I didn't dare risk sending any of the others and having them not return. We couldn't hand over more lives for those who had been taken. I'd make her understand that tomorrow, after she'd had a chance to get some sleep.

The truck shifted beneath my weight when I climbed into it and settled with my back to the cab. I didn't look at Erin and Hawk's bags tucked into the supplies. They may have been humans, but they had been loyal to River and the mission. They deserved better than they were getting.

I rested my head against the truck as Corson and Bale climbed into the back with me. I watched as they settled in to sleep. Closing my eyes, I tilted my head back, but there would be no sleep for me, not tonight.

My eyes cracked open as the sun broke over the horizon two hours later. I hadn't fallen asleep, but I'd dozed off for a few minutes before the sun came up. Rising to my feet, I jumped out of the back of the pickup and walked over to the passenger side door. My hand froze on the handle when I saw the empty bench seat inside.

Impossible!

Blood roared in my ears. I grasped the handle so fiercely it broke off beneath my hand. Wrapping my fingers around the edge of the door, I clawed it open with a loud wrenching of metal that woke Corson and Bale. They blinked dazedly at me when I tore the door from the truck and threw it aside.

I froze, my mouth going dry and my body vibrating with the impulse to rip the vehicle to pieces with my bare hands. My eyes latched onto the hole in the passenger side floor. She had *burned* her way out of the truck. The control of her power it had taken, the patience...

But that couldn't be possible. I would have smelled the metal and plastic burning away; I'd smelled nothing.

Then I realized her demon ability hadn't done this. No, this was the devious angel side of her through and through. The use of that power was the only explanation for the lack of smoke and odor.

Bale and Corson hovered at my shoulders. They must have seen the hole in the floor at the same time as they both released an explosive breath and stepped away from me.

A piece of paper on the dashboard grabbed my attention. I snatched it and looked down at the scrawled words...

The mission is taking a detour.

RIVER

Once I managed to escape the truck undetected, I fled for the woods line, determined to get as far from the camp as possible before Kobal realized I was gone. I'd only have an hour at most to gain ground on him, and I didn't know if that would be enough. He'd be coming for me, and he would destroy anything in his path to get to me.

What I hadn't expected was to find Vargas hiding in the woods, waiting for me. "What are you doing here?" I demanded.

"I've learned you don't take orders well. I knew it was only a matter of time before you figured some way to get out of that truck and go after them."

"I'm not going back."

"I'm not asking you to."

"You were okay with leaving them behind before."

His mouth quirked in a smile. "I know we must stay focused on the mission, but as Kobal pointed out, *you* are the mission, and we have to keep you protected." Oh, wouldn't Kobal love to hear his words thrown back at him in such a way. "I'm going to keep you safe. Besides, they're my friends too. However, if we survive this, could you please keep Kobal from killing me?"

I grinned at him. "I will, but we have to go."

He nodded his agreement and followed me into the woods. I ran so fast I barely saw the branches and underbrush snatching

and tearing at me as I plummeted down the side of an embankment. Beside me, Vargas cursed and almost lost his balance when
we slid through the wet leaves coating the side of the hill. His
breath sounded loudly beside me, but neither of us slowed. We
had no time to lose.

After a quarter of a mile, I realized how lucky I was he'd
anticipated my actions and joined me. I'd planned on running in
the direction those creatures had fled in the hopes of somehow
stumbling across them, or maybe having my visions or Angela
help guide the way.

Instead, Vargas tracked the black blood falling from the
injured creatures as they ran through the woods. Blood I never
would have noticed or even seen with the small flashlight he held
clasped between his teeth as he moved. The sun broke over the
horizon as we stumbled across a road with large splatters of blood
leading to the right.

The weight of the katana bouncing against my back was
reassuring as we followed the trail. My hands brushed over the
guns at my side, but they would be my back-up weapons. As we
ran, I kept myself attuned to the pulse of life around me. Somehow, I'd managed to pull power from the earth while inside the
truck. I don't know if it was because I was panicked or furious,
but there was no denying my power was growing, and I'd crisp
fry every demon who stood in the way of getting our
friends back.

My legs and lungs burned but even though it was different
here, the earth beneath my feet revitalized me. After a mile,
Vargas gestured for the two of us to go back into the woods. Slipping behind some boulders, he pulled off his pack and handed me
a bottle of water. I almost wrenched the cap off to gulp down the
warm water. When I was done, I poured some into my hands and
scrubbed at the dust from the road sticking to my face and
eyelashes.

It was so tempting to lean against the boulders and sit for a
minute, but there was no time for rest, not now. I could almost

feel Kobal breathing down my neck. He would have noticed I was gone by now. He was faster than us, and he would be *infuriated.*

I took another swig of water and capped it. "I don't think it will be much farther," Vargas said.

"Why not?" I inquired.

"They probably hunt close to where they live."

I glanced at the road again. "Let's go."

We broke away from the boulders and ran up the small hill to the dirt road. My feet thudded against the dirt as we ran. Dust kicked up around us, coating my clothes and hair and sticking to the sweat trickling down my face, but I didn't dare slow down.

Not until we reached the edge of the darkness.

Vargas and I stopped abruptly at the edge of the black circle created by the branches and vines growing up to create a canopy around the massive structure before us. The vines pressed against the sides of the building, making it impossible to move around to the back of it. There was only one way to get inside this place.

Looking more closely at the tangled branches and vines, I realized it wasn't akalia vine mixed in with everything. These vines were thick and black with thorns the length of my fingers growing from them. I never would have been able to close my hand all the way around one, if I dared to touch it.

My head tilted back to take in the structure in the center of the vines. Holes and cracks marred the graying boards; they were all crooked in one way or another and some were nailed haphazardly to the building. Maroon streaks smeared at least half of them.

Is that blood?

Tearing my attention away from the boards and the disconcerting possibility, I strained to see past the gauzy red material covering all of the windows. The candlelight dancing behind the material was the only source of illumination within the thick shadows surrounding the building.

Bordello. I didn't know where I'd ever heard the word before, but it fit this place perfectly. *Bordello of the damned.*

I rested my hand on the guns strapped to my waist. Beneath

my feet, I felt the sluggish pulse of life. I had to keep focused on that life; it was our best option for making it out of this place alive.

This is a bad idea! I didn't know if death waited for us in there or something far worse, but it was too late to turn back now; we were here. I had an irate demon closing in on me and Hawk and Erin were inside this place.

"They're going to know we're coming," Vargas said.

"Maybe this doesn't have to be a fight." My voice sounded nowhere near as casual as I'd intended.

"I'll go alone," Vargas volunteered.

"No one is going in there alone."

His chocolate eyes surveyed me as he seemed to be debating what to say next. "Keeping you safe is the mission."

I was unable to stop myself from wincing. This whole being referred to as the mission thing was really starting to grate on my nerves. "Don't. I'm not a mission. I'm me, and I'm going in there."

I sounded far braver than I felt as sweat trickled down my back and my hands trembled. I hadn't come this far to back down now.

"I doubt you would listen anyway," Vargas said.

"I wouldn't," I confirmed.

A smile tugged at the corners of his full mouth before he focused on the building before us again. Taking a deep breath, I turned my attention back to the monstrosity once more and stepped forward. I could feel the cool hand of death creeping over my flesh to encircle my neck when we left the warmth of the sun behind for the shade of the vines. I held my breath as I waited for the vines to come alive and attack us, but they remained where they were as I took another step.

I decided as we approached the sagging porch that Kobal had every right to kill me when he caught up to us. I had no doubt he would find me; I only hoped we were free of this place with our friends in tow when it happened.

We were almost to the porch when the shimmering image of Angela materialized at the top of the stairs. I didn't need her incessantly pointing behind us and bouncing on the balls of her feet to tell me the best idea would be to turn around and go back, but I climbed onto the first step and continued onward. Her arms started to wave as she pointed behind us again; her mouth opened and closed in words I couldn't hear.

She threw her arms out before her as if she could push me back when I stepped from the top stair and onto the porch. Unlike the ghosts, I didn't feel cold, or really anything at all when I passed through her. She stopped waving her arms. Her eyes filled with apprehension, and if I hadn't known better, I thought tears glistened within them as she turned to watch us stop before the door.

The doorknob didn't move beneath my hand when I took hold of it. I could blast the door open with a ball of energy, or maybe we could shoot the handle out with our guns, but there was the possibility our friends were close to the door.

Bordello of the damned. And I was going to knock on the door as if it were any other place.

I grabbed the metal piece of the heavy knocker attached to the door. I didn't know what the creature with the fangs and pointed snout attached to the knocker was, but I prayed it didn't reside inside.

The metal clanged loudly upon the door and echoed in the air around us. Goose bumps covered my flesh as the door swung open.

CHAPTER THIRTY-SEVEN

KOBAL

I detected River's fresh-rain scent on the air as I pursued her, along with a spicier and more masculine odor. *Vargas.*

The three of them had shown they were more loyal to River now, but I hadn't expected this kind of mutiny. I'd kill the man for going with her instead of stopping her.

Easy. Killing him would be the way to guarantee River forever shut me out, but since I couldn't choke her, I'd happily choke him for a little while.

Judging by her scent, they weren't far ahead of me, but still too far for my liking. Splotches of black blood amongst the leaves caught my eye as I ran. The sickly sweet scent of that blood wasn't enough to throw me off of River's trail, but I despised the cloying odor. They were definitely following the canagh demons.

What they'd do to her, especially if it is Lilitu...

I shut the possibility down; I'd lose my mind if I dwelled on it too much. Racing up a small embankment, I burst out onto a road where I spotted more blood splatters trailing over the dirt and booted footprints. Turning, I followed the blood trail and the increasing allure of River's scent.

Behind me, other footsteps slapped onto the dirt road, but I didn't look back at Corson and Bale as they followed. The delay of even a second could cost me her.

~

RIVER

Vargas and I stepped into the cavernous building. I was studying the shadows playing over the large single room we'd entered when the heavy door closed behind us. I spun, but instead of someone standing behind us there were only more light and dark shadows coalescing in a way that made my vision blur before coming back into focus.

What did I do by coming here? Just find the others and go!

Turning, I focused on the building once more as I searched for anyone I knew within the large, barn-like building. The eaves of the building sagged above us. Bits of the vine overhead could be seen through the cracks in the ceiling. Wails of decadence and woe rose and fell in volume as the cries bounced off the walls.

All around us, figures crept forward from behind the sheer red material hanging throughout the room from the rafters to the floor. The building was almost entirely wide open inside, except for the material dividing this lower level into smaller room-like sections and a set of stairs leading to a loft across the way. More candle-light danced across the gauzy material blocking off the loft above.

The staircase to the loft wound down to a stage at the other end of the building. My heart leapt when I spotted Hawk and Erin lying on the stage with two of the others who had been taken. They appeared to be sleeping or unconscious. I refused to believe they were dead, but then if they were dead, they probably had little value to these creatures surrounding us. I didn't know what had happened to the fifth person, but I had a pretty good guess as the moans grew louder within the room.

Pale, delicate fingers curled around the edge of the red material beside me. My breath froze in my chest at the sight of the pink claws that stood out starkly against the red. A head appeared next to reveal a gorgeous blonde woman peering out at me.

From behind her, more men and women emerged from the shadows, moving with surreal grace and all possessing a mesmerizing beauty. What little clothing they wore was so sheer there was nothing left to the imagination.

Beside me, Vargas's eyebrows were in his hairline. His hands clenched around his gun as the canagh demons closed in around us. The demons' heads tilted to the side. Their gazes were curious as they licked their lips and eyed us with a hunger that had my flight reflex screaming at me to listen to it.

I remained where I was, mostly because my feet felt frozen to the floor, but also because I wanted my friends back. Movement from above caused all the ones closing in on us to take a step away. My gaze went to the staircase as a woman, dressed in a sheer, blood-red dress that did nothing to hide any aspect of her body, descended the stairs. The skirt swirled about her calves as she moved with the grace of a ballerina.

I couldn't tear my gaze away from her when she stopped at the bottom of the stairs with one elegant hand resting upon the newel. Her blood-red, talon fingernails matched the color of her hair spilling about her shoulders and waving against the breasts exposed by her diaphanous dress. Sex oozed from every one of her pores, and she knew it as her tongue slid out to lick across her ruby-red lips. The woman's emerald eyes surveyed us as if she were inspecting some bug and considering stomping it.

Beside me, as if under some spell, Vargas's body swayed toward her. I grabbed his arm to hold him in place. Seeming to come back to himself, he shook his head and thrust back his shoulders. I held him for a minute longer before releasing him again. I had to have my hands free.

What could this woman do? Could she make him go to her against his will? I'd heard the legends of incubi and succubae, that they fed on humans during sex, but I had no idea what they were truly capable of.

It had been a *big* mistake to bring Vargas here. I hadn't known what I'd expected from these demons, but I had mistakenly believed if we avoided their beds, we would be able to get away from them.

I'd never expected to come up against the pull these things possessed. I would 100 percent deserve Kobal's *I told you so,* if we made it out of here, but first I had to make sure we made it out. Vargas had followed me into this place of the damned, and he would leave it again if I had to torch everything in here to ensure it.

Widening my stance, I focused on the dim pulse of life beneath my feet once more. It wasn't much, but if I dug deeper, beneath the boards, I could feel the cool dirt of the earth as if it were slipping through my toes.

I could possibly feed off the life force of these things, but I'd prefer not to get close enough to them to try, and I had a feeling the pulse they radiated would be sickening. However, if push came to shove, I'd feast on these things if I had to.

The life of the earth seeped into me, but my fingers remained spark free as the woman took a step toward us. I preferred not to let any of these things know what I might be capable of unless it became absolutely necessary.

"This is a first, our prey coming to us," the woman said in a husky voice that slid over my skin like silk.

She was a pit of iniquity and it radiated against us now. Beside me, Vargas swayed again and a dazed look filled his eyes as he lowered his head to stare at his feet.

I have to get him out of here!

Raising my chin, I held her gaze as I spoke. "You took some of our friends."

She tossed a strand of hair behind her shoulder. "If we did, then they are ours now, as are you."

"No, they aren't and neither are we."

"No?" She laughed as she practically glided across the floor toward us. "You have no idea what you walked into, dearie, but you'll learn."

Her fingers skimmed over Vargas's arm, causing him to moan when she walked around him. The lascivious smile she gave me revealed two small fangs in the top of her mouth. "I could take him upstairs now, and he wouldn't argue. He'd trip over himself to get there. And you," she said to me. "The things I will do to you, the sounds I will cause you to emit, the pleas you will issue for me to stop even as you're begging me to continue."

My eyes narrowed on the woman as she stepped toward me. Then, her gaze latched onto my neck. With a ruthless shove, she pushed Vargas out of the way and came at me. He stumbled forward before regaining his balance and shaking his head as if trying to clear it from a fog.

Her hands clasped my shirt. She went to pull me forward, but I dug my feet in and grabbed hold of her wrists.

"You've been marked!" Her disbelief and fury beat against me.

"Let go of me!" I hissed, my hands constricting on her wrists.

One of her nails tore through my shirt. It scraped against my skin to leave small beads of blood on my flesh. She leaned closer to me, inhaling deeply. My heart thundered in my chest as she peered at me from under her thick fringe of red lashes. I would torch this bitch before I ever let her feed on me or my friends, but I didn't want to start a fight when we were so outnumbered. Not if there was some small chance we could walk out of here without incident.

"Smell so sweet, so ripe for the picking," she murmured. "I smell demon on you though." Her gaze went to the marks on my neck again. "Couldn't be."

My eyes held hers when she leaned away from me. Malice flashed within those emerald depths as her lips skimmed back to reveal those small fangs once more. "Couldn't be!" she spat. "Not a human, he wouldn't choose a *human*."

Kobal had said demons would know I belonged to him, and

apparently he'd been right, but the knowledge of who my Chosen was only seemed to infuriate this woman more. I somehow managed to keep it together as I gestured to the stage. "We came for our friends."

"He may have marked you, but you walked into *my* nest. That means you are mine now as are your friends. I will have you wasted and wanting so badly you won't remember your name or his."

"Try it and I'll have you screaming in agony. We don't have to fight, just let us leave here with our friends."

She laughed before releasing my shirt and sliding her hand suggestively over her breasts until her nipples puckered. "Silly human, there is no leaving a canagh demon."

"If you know who has marked me, then you'll know he's on his way."

"He's not here now, which leads me to believe he's realized his foolishness in marking a human. A male demon rarely allows his Chosen out of sight for long, and he would *never* allow her to come to me."

I couldn't explain to this woman what I'd done and I didn't intend to try. The cloying scent of her engulfed me, threatening to gag me when she leaned toward me. Done with trying to play nice, I threw up my arms, knocking her back a step. She fairly spit with anger before she recovered. I thought she was going to fly at me and slice me apart with those talons, but she remained where she was, her eyes burning into mine as she ran her hand down the front of her gown.

Murmurs rippled through the crowd, and excitement pulsed from the other canagh demons as they moved closer to us.

CHAPTER THIRTY-EIGHT

RIVER

The woman's countenance never changed when she lashed out at me, her talons whistling as they sliced through the air. I jumped back, barely managing to avoid their deadly arc at my throat. This wasn't Kobal and training. This woman was out for blood, *my* blood. She swung at me again, this time an upper cut that would have broken my jaw and sliced my jugular open.

My leap to the side brought me up against Vargas, jarring him out of whatever strange stupor he'd been in. He blinked before pulling his gun free and pointing it at the woman. One of the other demons leapt forward. The demon smashed his arm down on Vargas's, causing him to lose his grip on his gun. It clattered against the wood floor when it hit the ground. Vargas swung at him, but the demon had already stepped away to watch the woman as she circled me like a shark on the hunt for its prey.

She came at me again, swinging wildly in her growing frustration. Before she reached me, the world fell away to allow the battle to unfold in my head. It was only her and me now, and I saw every move she would make seconds before she made them.

A strange sense of calm descended over me as I swung my fore-arms up, blocking each of her blows.

When she drew her arm back, I leaned against the beam behind me, lifted my leg, and drove it into her chest. Stunned gasps filled the room when the woman reeled backward and crashed into another beam.

Silence descended over the other demons. The pounding of my heart resonated in my ears when her eyes lifted to mine. Hatred burned within their clear, green depths, but I also saw curiosity and disbelief there. Vargas looked between the two of us as the woman pulled herself away from the beam.

"*What* are you?" the woman hissed.

"We only came for our friends, let us take them and we'll go," I told her.

Her eyes traveled over me and for the briefest of seconds I almost believed she would agree to my terms. Then, she came at me so fast my mind barely had a chance to process her intentions until she was almost on top of me.

Before I had a chance to react to her new attack, the front door crashed open with so much force it flew off its hinges and across the room to smash against the stairs. The shattered wood of the doorframe rained down on the occupants of the room. The other canagh demons leapt back and threw their hands over their heads to protect themselves from the debris. They scattered out of the pathway of the seething demon who stepped inside.

Vargas threw himself to the floor and rolled across it to retrieve his gun. He bounced back up close to the ruined door. The wreckage and noise didn't deter the woman as she swung at me again. I dodged the claws arcing toward my chest by ducking out of the way. They sliced into the beam behind me, tearing splinters from the wood and rending a bellow from Kobal that rattled the windows.

Shoving my hands into the woman's chest, I pushed her away from me and scrambled low to avoid the lethal talons of her other arm descending on me. I hadn't completely risen to my full height when an arm slid around my waist, pinning me against a much-loved chest. I would have breathed a sigh of relief if I hadn't felt the fury vibrating the muscles beneath my touch.

Kobal thrust me behind him, bracing his feet apart as he faced the woman across from us. Vargas stood behind me, paler than normal but his eyes were clear once more, as whatever hold she'd had over him was broken.

Hatred no longer twisted the woman's exquisite features. Her expression was now composed into the beautiful face that would make the angels weep once more. "Kobal," she purred with a swish of her hip.

"Lilitu," he grated.

She smiled as she fluffed back her blood-colored hair. "You know I would have welcomed you to join in the fun. There was no reason to destroy my door."

"Not here for fun," he replied, nudging me back another step.

I shot him a disgruntled look, but my protest died at the burning intensity and the harshness of his amber gaze sweeping over me. If I pushed him now, I had no idea what he would do. His lips skimmed back when he spotted the blood beading on my skin. His wrath blasted over me in a wave I swore blew the hair back from my face.

Lilitu's eyes flickered between the two of us, and then she sneered at me. Before me, the marks on Kobal's arms shifted in response to Lilitu's hostility. I half expected the beasts to burst free of him, but they remained caged in preparation for a fight.

"You couldn't have marked her on purpose," Lilitu said in disbelief.

"I mark what is mine," Kobal said flatly.

Around Lilitu, the other canagh demons murmured again. They shifted and moved back to allow more space down the center of the cavernous building. Shadows fell across the busted doorway, briefly blocking the little bit of light that had spilled in from outside. Turning, I watched as Corson and Bale slipped inside.

"Yours?" Lilitu scoffed. "Come now, Kobal, we both know you could never be satisfied with taking only one woman for the rest of your days." Her talons trailed down the front of her dress. They slipped over her breasts before stroking over the flesh of her belly exposed by the cutouts in the sides of the gauzy material. "I can clearly recall what that taking was like, as I'm sure you can too."

The blood drained from my face so fast I was amazed I didn't pass out. I kept my face impassive as I tried not to let my distress show. Lilitu made beautiful look like the understatement of the year. She oozed sex, and I was certain she knew exactly what to do to please a man. I'd known Kobal was the exact opposite of a saint long before I'd started sleeping with him, but she was something I never could have imagined.

"Give us the others and we'll leave," Kobal replied, ignoring her words completely.

Lilitu's hand stilled on its way back up her body in the valley between her breasts. "You could always share," she suggested in a husky voice. "She must taste delicious."

"No one else will *ever* touch her. If you try, Lilitu, it will be the last thing you do."

"She's so young, so inexperienced. I have more than a few here who would be eager to teach her how to make a man beg for more. I'm sure you recall the way I had you begging for more."

This time I was unable to suppress a shudder at the hurt her words caused. I hated this place and these *things*.

"I don't recall," he replied.

I thought it might have been actual distress flitting over her perfect features before a smile curved her lips once more. "You'd appreciate her so much more after my men are done teaching her. I can guarantee it."

Some of the eerily beautiful men stepped forward, their perfectly chiseled features looking almost fake. A few of them raked their eyes over me before licking their lips. One, with platinum blond hair took hold of his erect shaft and fondled himself as he stared at me.

With a swift step to the side, Kobal seized him by his neck and snapped his head to the side with a sharp thrust of his thumb to the man's jaw. I could only stand and gawk as fire burst from Kobal's hand to encompass the face of the screaming demon. The man's eyes burned from his head as flames burst out of his eye sockets and rolled up to consume his blond hair.

Kobal tossed his flaming body aside, letting it fall to the floor as if it were no more than a mosquito he'd swatted from the air. "Look at her again, and I'll burn you all to the ground," he snarled at the others. Their mouths gaped open as their eyes remained locked on the burning body of their fallen companion.

Whatever interest any of the men had been showing toward me vanished in a heartbeat. They all glanced at me before focusing on Lilitu once more. The amusement and lust had vanished from Lilitu's gaze. Now the pupils of her eyes had become pinpricks as they focused on Kobal with murderous intent.

CHAPTER THIRTY-NINE

KOBAL

"That was *my* servant!" Lilitu spat.

"You have others," I replied calmly, though I was tempted to engulf this place in flames, grab River, and drag her from here. I wanted to kiss her as badly as I wanted to throttle her. She'd walked herself straight into the hands of our enemies.

Lilitu had broken off from some of the other canagh demons over a thousand years ago. She'd enslaved some of them with her powerful, ancient blood before aligning herself with Lucifer after I'd climbed from her bed, never to return. Now all I could hope was to get River out of here without Lilitu poisoning her with her words and actions, but I knew she wouldn't leave her friends without a fight.

"I'll have you begging at my feet!" Lilitu yelled.

"Let's not become delusional about this. Simply give us the men and woman you took earlier and no one else has to die."

"I'll tear her to pieces," Lilitu vowed.

I bared my fangs at her as beneath my flesh the hounds surged toward my fingers. They also recognized River as theirs, and any threat toward her was one they'd gladly take down. Lilitu's eyes darted toward my arms as the marks pulsed with life and fire danced over my fingers. As soon as we were out of this building, I would destroy everything within it.

I gave a pointed look at the hounds before focusing on her again. "*Who* will tear whom to pieces?"

Lilitu smiled seductively as she pushed aside her fury to fall back on who she innately was, a seductress.

"Come now, Kobal, we had a lot of fun before. We can have it again." She moved forward, gliding across the floor so smoothly it seemed her feet didn't touch the boards. River stiffened behind me. "You would like to watch *me* with the girl, no?"

"No. Bring our people to us or I am going to start torching *every* one of your servants. I'm out of patience, Lilitu."

"You harm another one of my servants, and I will feast on her until she's nothing but a shriveled husk."

"Lilitu," I growled.

She stopped five feet away from me and thrust out her hip. "We were good once—"

"Once!" I barked. "And I never returned. Your lure is not as powerful as you believe it to be."

Shocked murmurs from the canaghs followed my statement. To this group, she was their queen, their most powerful, and the words I'd uttered were the ultimate insult to her. *All* returned once they were satisfied by a canagh demon; once was never enough. It was believed their drugging kiss would forever ensnare someone, making them out of their mind with lust and unable to think of anything else as their bodies fed the canaghs need for sexual energy while they wasted away to nothing.

I'd made sure not to kiss Lilitu the night we were together. It had been playing with fire to risk lying with her, but after all the talk of the canagh, and especially Lilitu herself, I'd been determined to try my hand at her. I'd been younger and dumber then, fresh off a lost battle to Lucifer and determined to conquer something. It had been a rash decision and a forgettable experience.

"Bring them to me, especially *her*," Lilitu commanded the other canaghs as she pointed a finger at River. "*Now!*"

Around me, the canaghs shifted and shuffled their feet as they glanced between me and Lilitu. They were lovers not fighters, but this group of canaghs were also caught up by their need for her blood and the power she held over them. Lilitu was exceptionally strong due to the sexual energy she'd drained from countless demons and humans over her many years, but she was no match for me. If she came at me, she would die. Her followers knew this, but they would do as she commanded and their numbers far outweighed ours.

"This does not have to be a battle," Corson said from the doorway.

"You are trying to take our prizes from us," Lilitu replied. "I will not allow it." Then her gaze latched onto River, blazing with animosity as she poked the tip of a fang with her tongue. "She will also not be leaving. They both came to us. They are *ours* now."

"You have no chance against me," I told her.

"We outnumber you."

"*You* are the first one I'm coming for." No fear showed in her eyes, but her hands slid back to her side and the seductive pose she'd taken vanished. "Your servants may outnumber us, but they will have no queen to follow by the time I'm done with you."

Her fangs sliced one of her ruby lips. The trickle of blood flowing forth caused all the other canagh demons to undulate as their hands trailed lasciviously over their bodies. They all fed like she did on one's sexuality, but each of her servants also received a single drop of her blood a year. A drop that imbued them with the same amount of energy as feasting on the sexuality of five demons. A drop that kept them hooked on her for another year and eager to do her every bidding.

Behind her, I saw Hawk begin to stir. He lifted his head to look around before grabbing Erin and shaking her arm. She blinked up at him, and he rested his finger against his lips in a shushing gesture. He pointed to the two other men with them. Erin nodded and turned to wake one of the men as Hawk pulled his gun free and aimed it at Lilitu. He met my eyes over Lilitu's shoulder and I gave a small nod.

"Can you stop my servants?" Lilitu murmured. "When they're so hungry."

"River, stay behind me," I commanded her.

Reaching my hand behind me, I seized River's forearm and jerked her to the side as Hawk fired his weapon. Lilitu screamed when the bullet pierced her back and tore through her chest. I felt the breeze of the bullet against my cheek but didn't move as it embedded in the beam beside me. The canaghs cried out in ecstasy at the scent of her blood before leaping forward to defend their queen.

I dodged slicing talons before hitting three in the chest with a ball of fire that sent them spiraling away into the gauzy material covering the room. Sparks and flames shot up around the humans and demons sprawled out on the pillows beyond. They were so ensnared by the canagh's spell that they barely moved as the flames spread around them.

I took a step to the side and pinned River to the beam behind me when she tried to move around me. "You disobeyed me once; you'll do as I say now! Stay behind me!" I snapped at her.

Her eyes widened, the violet of them shimmered and danced in the flames. Turning away, flames wrapped around my wrists as I threw my arm out and set the hounds free. River's hands landed on my shoulders. Her touch sent tingles of power over my skin, causing it to become electrified as the hounds barreled across the floor. Between her touch and the swell of her power mingling with mine, my flames leapt higher over my arms.

The hounds trampled half a dozen canaghs under their massive paws as they raced around the room. Screams resonated from the canaghs as bones and cartilage gave way beneath the jaws clamping down on them. By the doorway, Corson and Bale worked on carving their way through those closest to them. Hawk and Erin had risen from the stage with the other soldiers and were firing their weapons as they approached us. Vargas stood near my side, shooting at any of the canaghs who tried to come at us.

All of Lilitu's composure vanished as her murderous gaze landed on River. I couldn't let her live. It wouldn't matter to her if Lucifer wanted to keep River alive; Lilitu would do everything she could to see River's life ended.

I kept River pinned against the beam when Lilitu leapt at me, her claws whistling through the air. I grabbed her wrist, snapping it back before driving my fist into her nose. Blood exploded from her once perfect face, causing the canaghs to cry out again as the flames continued to eat at the wood.

Lilitu's free hand sliced across my arm, digging into the bone. I felt the crackle of River's power against my shoulder before her other hand shot out from behind my back and a burst of golden-white light erupted from her. Like I'd seen her do with Azote, this blast of energy and life streamed from her hand. It slammed into the center of Lilitu's chest, sending her spiraling head over heels into Hawk. The coppery scent of Hawk's blood filled the air when Lilitu's claws carved down his side before she fell on top of him.

Lilitu's motionless body lay sprawled across Hawk's immobile form. Through the smoking hole in her chest, I could see Hawk's abdomen and the blood seeping across his shirt. The other canaghs froze as Lilitu's heart stopped and the last of her powerful blood spilled around her. The wail the canaghs released drowned out the roaring sounds of the growing fire. They fell around their queen; her blood slicked their faces and hands as they eagerly lapped up the last of her lifeblood.

"Hawk!" River cried.

Vargas and Erin pushed at the demons kneeling around their dead queen, trying to clear a path to their friend, but the canaghs wouldn't move away from her. River squirmed against my back as the hounds prowled through the remains, consuming their dinner. Corson and Bale killed the few straggling canaghs who had yet to fall upon their queen and came to stand beside us.

I grasped River's wrist on my shoulder and stepped aside to pull her away from the beam. "Keep hold of her," I commanded Corson and thrust River's hand at him.

His fingers enclosed her wrist; his eyes were wary as he held her hand before him and surveyed River's fingertips with unease. The hounds bounded to my side, shoving through the canaghs as I pushed them ruthlessly out of my way to get to Hawk. The canaghs snapped at and swiped their claws at me when I grasped Lilitu's shoulder and thrust her way.

The gaping wound River had torn into Lilitu's chest drew the canagh's attention away from me and they fell on their dead queen once more. Hawk blinked up at me before his eyes closed and his head lulled to the side. Unable to take the time to assess the damage done to him, I grabbed his arm, hauled him up from the floor and flung him over my shoulder.

Stalking back through the flames and cloying smoke filling the building, I held out my hand for River's wrist. Corson shoved it eagerly into my grasp. River stumbled beside me when I pulled her forward, but I quickly righted her as I hurried her through the growing inferno.

"Is he alive?" she breathed.

"Yes."

She's human. Her humanity and love for others is one of her greatest strengths, I reminded myself as I tried to rein in my remaining rage and fear. That strength had caused her to destroy Lilitu with a single blast because she'd hurt me.

Her humanity was also one of her greatest weaknesses. A weakness that had driven her to rescue her friends and nearly gotten her killed.

"Wait!" River cried. "There are more people and demons in the shadows! We have to get them out of the fire!"

My hand squeezed her wrist when she tried to dig her feet in. "It's too late for them," I told her and pulled her forward.

"You can't know that!"

Turning, I wrapped my arm around her waist and lifted her

from the ground. Whatever she saw on my face caused her to lean away from me. "I *can* know that," I snarled. "There is no saving anyone else in this building. They are too wasted and too far gone to the canagh demons to try."

Her struggles ceased as I carried her out to the porch and down the steps. I didn't dare release her until we were free of the carrou vines surrounding and shading the burning canagh nest. I set her on her feet but kept hold of her wrist as I bent to set Hawk on the dirt road. I didn't trust her for a second not to try to rescue some of the others still inside.

Kneeling, I examined Hawk's wounds. Blood continue to spill form his body to pool on the dirt road beneath him. His side had been sliced open deep enough to reveal the gleam of his ribs and some of the muscle of his abdomen. His breathing came in shallow gasps and his skin was white, but I was fairly certain he would survive.

The heat of the growing fire beat against my back as I glanced over my shoulder at the engulfed building. The flames shot all the way up to the thick carrou vines, causing them to spark and wither. The stench of the vines, burning wood, and flesh filled my nose. None of the canaghs attempted to escape; they were all too consumed by the bliss of their queen's blood.

Taking a deep breath, I finally felt steady enough to look at River again without saying or doing something I might regret. The shadows lining her amethyst eyes made them stand out starkly against her tanned complexion. I didn't get a chance to decide what I would do with her before she threw her arms around my shoulders and buried her head against my neck.

"I'm sorry," she whispered. "I know it was stupid. I know I put us all in danger, but I couldn't leave them, not to that." She trembled so hard, her body vibrated mine. "Not to *that*."

Some of my anger faded as I pulled her closer. "You can't do this again, River," I told her as I kissed her temple. "You have no idea what these demons are capable of. One kiss, and you could have been trapped by them. You would have willingly let yourself burn like the other humans and demons in there because they were too far gone to think to save themselves. They're not even screaming."

Her teeth rattled, and her spine quaked beneath my fingers. Rising, I stepped away from Hawk's body as Erin and Corson knelt beside him. The other two humans rescued from the building moved away from us as I walked River a few feet away.

"Shh, Mah Kush-la, it's over now." I stroked her raven hair back from her face before grasping her chin and tilting her head up. "Your friends are alive."

She nodded before dropping her head to my neck once more. I embraced her as the hounds rubbed against her legs, seeking to give her comfort. Lowering my head, I rested my lips against her temple. If I had my way, I'd never release her again.

Taking a deep breath, she straightened her shoulders. "I'm okay."

Reluctantly, I lowered her to her feet and slid my arms away from her. One of her hands absently fell to Crux's head before she focused on Hawk. "Is he going to make it?" she asked Corson.

"There's a lot of blood." He pulled back the ruined remains of Hawk's shirt to survey more of the blood seeping from the claw marks slicing through his skin. "A lot of his and a lot of Lilitu's too." He shot me a look at this realization. I shook my head at him and he returned to exploring the edges of Hawk's injuries. "Some stitches will close it. He may require blood though."

Vargas tugged his shirt over his head. Kneeling at Corson's side, he tore the shirt into strips before binding it around Hawk's chest. "We have to get him back to the supplies. We can stitch him there," Vargas said.

Corson grabbed Hawk's arm and swung him easily over his shoulder. Bale and Corson glanced at River before looking to me. "Did she just do what I think she did?" Bale inquired.

"Take down Lilitu? Yes, she did," I replied as I slid my arm around River's waist and pulled her close. Her eyes remained steady and unwavering as they all stared curiously at her.

"Were those all of the canagh demons in there?" Erin asked.

"No," I replied. "There are more out there, but not all of them are like Lilitu and her followers. Some are on our side, others refuse to choose a side, and still others follow Lucifer. It is the same amongst all of the demons."

River turned her head toward the fire. The flames reflected in her eyes as they danced across her face. Turning her away, I led her down the road back toward where we'd left the others.

CHAPTER FORTY

RIVER

I remained unmoving in the seat beside Kobal, my head bent as I watched the asphalt flash by through the hole beneath my feet. Air rushed in from the missing door, a door I'd learned Kobal had wrenched from its hinges the minute he'd discovered I was gone.

My hand fell on his thickly muscled thigh. His eyes slid to me; the lines of his face were severe and unyielding. I sensed his lingering displeasure with me, but I still wasn't entirely thrilled with him either.

"You wouldn't listen to me," I said quietly.

"There was a reason for that."

"They're alive because of us."

His teeth scraped together as his hands tightened on the wheel. "I can't talk about this. You disobeyed me—"

"I'm not yours to command!" I cut in. "I am your Chosen. I have allowed you to mark me, to share my bed, to be a part of my life, the *biggest* part of it, but I have not allowed you to become my dictator. You are in command of the demons and the humans, but not of me. I never agreed to that."

"As my Chosen you *are* mine."

"And you are mine, but I would never order you about, throw you over my shoulder and command you to stay like a dog."

His mouth quirked in amusement. "I don't think you could throw me over your shoulder."

Sparks danced across my fingers when they dug into his thigh. I glowered at him as I tried to control my temper. It never worked out well when we bashed heads with each other, but still I was tempted to smack his head off the driver's side window.

I took a minute to steady myself before I spoke again. "I understand we're from different worlds. You are a leader, a fighter, and used to being obeyed, but you have to talk to me. No matter what this is between us, it will never work out if you continue to order me around like that instead of talking with me."

His body became as still as stone when I uttered the words "it will never work out." Those words tore at my heart and shredded my insides too, but they were true.

"I know you love me," I whispered.

"Too much," he grated.

"And I love you, but you cannot treat me like that."

His hand fell to mine. "I won't let anything ruin what you are."

I opened my mouth to respond but closed it again. I had no words for that. "Please don't do that to me again," I finally said.

"I will try and speak with you. It will be difficult, but I will try." I smiled and kissed his cheek. That was more than I'd expected from him. "But you must listen to me. I know this world and these creatures. I never wanted you exposed to those things."

"Because of what passed between you and Lilitu?"

His upper lip curled in disgust. "She never should have said those things in front of you, but not because of that, though I wish you hadn't heard it. I can't keep you from all of it, but I want to shelter you from as much of the hideousness of my world as I can. You've already seen far more than most humans, been expected to deal with far worse, and have a heavy burden on your shoulders. I will do everything I can to make it at least a little easier on you."

"Kobal," I breathed, my heart melting at his words. I couldn't possibly stay upset with him when he said things like that.

"But you have to promise me, if I am commanding you and you don't like what I'm saying, you will not take off again. You can hit me with a ball of fire—"

"My fire has no effect on you."

"You can knock me on my ass with one of your energy balls—"

"I just killed someone with it. I would never use it on you."

"Lilitu didn't see it coming and she had no idea what you are capable of. Next time, hit me with *some*thing, I will be prepared for you, but don't ever take off like that again." Squeezing my hand, he lifted it and rested it over his heart. "When I discovered you gone,"—his eyes were black pools of emotion when they met mine—"I'd never been more terrified in my life."

My breath caught in the face of his vulnerability. Kobal was many things, but vulnerable and open were not among them.

"Do not do it again, Mah Kush-la."

"I'll never do it again and I'll zap you first," I vowed.

"Good."

"You know, before I met you, I was always rational and didn't have a temper, or at least not one that I showed very often."

His eyebrow quirked. "I doubt that."

"It's true," I replied. "I had to take care of my brothers. I had to make sure they were fed and protect them the best I could from our mother. The few times I got mad enough that I fought with my mother, she threw me out of the house."

A vein in his forehead throbbed to life. "Where did you go when she did such a thing?"

"I would stay with my friend, Lisa, and her parents."

"Did you like living with them?"

"I did," I admitted. "Lisa's mom would cook us breakfast every morning. Her dad always played games with us, and there were family dinners every night. I would catch fish for them, not because I had to, but because I wanted to. They considered me a part of their family and treated me like it."

"Then why did you leave their home?"

"Gage would be a big enough pain in the ass that my mother would finally agree to allow me back home, and I would return for my brothers. I think Lisa's parents would have taken Gage and Bailey in too if they could have, but my mother never would have allowed such a thing."

"Why not?"

I stared at the road whizzing by beneath my feet again as I thought over his question. "Because she would have had no one to feed her and do her bidding without us. She would have had no one to abuse, and she so enjoyed her abuse. It was the only thing she ever found any real pleasure in. The only reason I agreed to leave my brothers behind when Mac came for me was because I knew they would be going to live with Lisa. I would have fought Mac to the death otherwise."

His hands twisted on the steering wheel as his knuckles turned white. His head turned slowly away from me, but I could feel the tension thrumming through his body. "Did your mother hit you?"

"Her words were her biggest weapon."

"*Did she hit you?*" he bit out.

I didn't shy away from the golden embers burning in his eyes when he looked at me again. If my mother had been standing before him now, he would have gutted her without blinking an eye.

"I couldn't react to her," I said instead of answering his question. I'd prefer not to recall those few times when I'd been certain she would finally do what I felt she'd always wanted to do, and kill me. "I had to remain as calm as possible around her. She took my brothers from me when I did react to her, but with you, I can't control my emotions sometimes. You make me react before thinking."

"I make you lose all control."

I nestled against his side. "Yes."

He rested his fingers against my face and brushed back strands of my hair. "Why do you think that is?"

"I'm not sure. I'm comfortable around you, I know that no matter what I do…" My voice trailed off, I sat up as I tried to puzzle the rest out. "You get angry with me, you try to order me around, but you'd never purposely hurt me. No matter what I say or do, you won't turn from me; you won't try to punish and inflict pain on me. I pushed you away and you still gave me my brothers."

"I'd give you the world, Mah Kush-la, if I could. And if I ever meet your mother, she'll know pain."

My breath hitched in at his words. "Kobal—"

"There is nothing you could do to stop me from loving you, that is why you fight me and disobey me."

"Or maybe I disobey because I'm not meant to obey," I replied.

A small smile curved his mouth. "No, you most certainly aren't."

I settled against him again, taking comfort in the warmth of his body. "No matter how much you infuriate me, there's nothing you could do to stop me from loving you either," I whispered.

He rested his hand on my shoulder and drew me closer against him. I glanced at the closed window separating us from those sitting in the bed of the truck. "Do you think it would be better if we told all the humans what I am?" I asked. "It may help to calm them if they had an idea of what and who they are fighting for."

His smile faded away. "No. There is no way to know how they would react to the knowledge and we can't take the risk they'd do something foolish. If it was only the ones with us now, perhaps it would be best, but there will be other humans joining us at the gateway and rumors will spread."

"Being kept in the dark is often more frightening than being informed."

"And sometimes ignorance is bliss. Many might not like that they are fighting with and for Lucifer's daughter—"

"Descendent."

"You don't even like it. Are you willing to take the chance at least one of them won't try something reckless with the knowledge?"

"I don't know, maybe," I murmured.

"It won't be today, so let's discuss this at another time."

There were some battles I was more than willing to let go, for now. I tried not to drift off but the sound of the tires on the road and the warmth of him enfolded me in a warm cocoon. Eventually, exhaustion drug me into its unrelenting depths.

The sun was in the middle of the sky when the truck pulled to the side of the road. I stirred, pressing closer to Kobal when his arm slid around my waist and he kissed my temple. "It's time for a food break," he murmured.

I reluctantly pulled away from him, but the pressure in my bladder and the rumble in my stomach had me sliding out the missing door. I made my way to the woods before returning to wash my hands with water and accepting my ration of beef jerky and a can of beans.

"How much further is it?" I asked Kobal when we walked over to sit by the truck.

"A day at the most, maybe less," he replied.

I gulped down my cold spoonful of beans. "Almost there," I muttered.

His hand rested against my arm. It seemed he simply needed to touch me as his fingers caressed my skin before he stepped away. I climbed into the back of the truck to join the others and sat on the metal siding.

Across the way from me, Hawk was propped up against the side. His skin was still ashen, and the white bandage covering his chest had a maroon stain on it, but at least he was awake again. Thankfully, he hadn't required a blood transfusion. Erin handed him a can of beans and a package of jerky.

"How are you feeling?" I asked him.

"Like claws raked my ribcage and half a pint low, but I'm alive, thanks to all of you."

"Don't thank me," Kobal replied. "I'd planned to leave you."

Erin lifted an eyebrow at his statement but didn't comment. Hawk gave a brief nod. "I would have done the same."

Kobal shot me a pointed look I chose to ignore. "That wasn't an option," I replied.

Hawk surveyed me as he ate his beans. Erin gave me a grateful smile and a small thumb's up Kobal didn't see.

"I don't like that you went with her," Kobal growled at Vargas.

"Leave him be," I said, lowering my can of beans in case I had to leap forward to defend Vargas.

Vargas blanched under Kobal's unrelenting stare, but he stood his ground. "You told us she was the mission. I stayed with her."

Kobal scowled at him, but he didn't say anything more. I scraped the bottom of my can with my spoon, savoring every last bit of it before shoving it into the trash bag.

"It's time to move on," Kobal said and stepped away from the truck.

My shoulders slumped. I would have given anything to have one day to sit beneath the sun and soak up its rays. To savor the simple joys of life before possibly having it taken away from me.

That wasn't to be though. I took hold of Kobal's hand and allowed him to help me from the truck.

RIVER

It was night when we stopped again. The stars were beginning to brighten the endless sky as the red moon hung on the horizon. "Blood moon," I murmured.

Kobal remained mute beside me, sitting rigidly in his seat. The tension in him had been growing steadily throughout the day as we drove closer and closer to our destination. When he turned to me, his hand snaked out to wrap around my neck. His thumb brushing over his marks caused me to shiver.

His head bent as his lips slanted over mine in a kiss that made my muscles go weak and my pulse quicken. Opening my mouth to his, I melted against him when his tongue swept in to taste the recesses of my mouth. He thrust deeply within me, demanding and voracious as my tongue eagerly entwined with his.

Pulling away, he broke the kiss and rested his forehead against mine. "I'd give anything to take you from here," he rasped.

"I know."

He didn't release me but pulled me with him when he climbed out of the truck. He placed me down once we were free and gathered our supplies from the back of the truck. I waited nearby, my body desperately seeking to connect with his.

I had no idea what tomorrow held for us, but I suspected we would be arriving at the gate.

CHAPTER FORTY-ONE

River

Waking the next morning, I stretched leisurely and reached for Kobal. I rolled over when my hand fell upon the empty spot where he'd been lying only hours before. Lifting my eyes, I spotted him standing at the front of the tree line. I stared at his broad back, admiring the curve of the carved muscle lining it and the intricate markings on his skin.

Gorgeous wasn't enough of a word for him, I decided as I propped my head on my palm and drank in the sight of him. Sensing my attention, his head turned. The early morning sun brought out the deep brown strands in his nearly black hair as it filtered over him. I could see the clear bite mark I'd left upon his bronzed skin last night.

Something visceral inside of me reacted to that mark as my fingers twisted into the blanket beneath me. Sitting up, I brushed the hair back from my shoulder, my nipples hardening and my heart beating faster when his eyes settled upon the fresh bite mark my shirt sleeve had fallen from my shoulder to reveal.

"You think we'll make it today?" I inquired.

"I do."

I tried to look past the trees, but from where I sat, I couldn't see the others. "Will I be able to go into Hell if I have to?"

"We're going to find out, but if there is a way for you to close the gateway from the outside, you won't have to go in."

I had no idea how I was going to be able to pull that off. I drew on the life from the earth, and I could throw fire, but closing the unnatural gate to Hell, something not even Kobal had been able to do, well, that sounded completely insane.

"And Lucifer? What about him?" I inquired.

"If you succeed in closing the gate, we will worry about him after."

"And if I fail?"

Walking over, he knelt before me and took hold of my chin. His thumb rubbed over my lips as he studied me. "It will *not* be failing."

"Since Bale had her vision, and before we ever met, everyone has expected me to be the one to stop this. The last hope. If I can't close the gate, then maybe I could take on Lucifer himself. But if I can't do those things, it *is* failing. It's failing everyone I love and care for. It's failing all of humanity."

He leaned forward to kiss me. "Yet you didn't run from this," he murmured against my lips.

"I was never given the chance."

"You were. You just didn't take it. After the gargoyle attack you could have fled. When you slipped free of the truck yesterday, you could have fled and never looked back, but you didn't."

"You would have found me."

"I would track you to the ends of the earth and back, but I would not force you into this, River. Not anymore. I would find another way to fight him, and if you told me to turn back now, I would, for you. You've made this choice. No matter what happens, you will *never* be a failure, not in this."

Leaning forward, I let myself drift into the comfort of the arms he slid around me as I tried to convince myself his words were true. "What will you do if this doesn't work?" I asked.

"I will continue to fight."

What a brutal life, but it would also be mine. "Fight no matter what," I whispered. My fingers slid through his thick, silken hair. "My Chosen."

His arms constricted to the point of bruising, but I didn't complain. I needed him more than I needed air right now.

"If we defeat Lucifer, you will become the leader of Hell. You'll have to go back," I said.

"No, I won't. I can allow demons to come and go between Hell and Earth in order to maintain their immortality, and I could return myself when it became necessary for me to do so. However, I will always come back for you, River. *Nothing* will keep me from you."

Except death, but I didn't say the words. My mortality was already a fact we were both aware of. He may be one of the most powerful creatures on Earth and in Hell, but he could also die. It was only tougher for him to do so than me. My hands ran over his back, feeling the flex and bunch of his muscles beneath my palm.

"You'd be willing to do that for me?" I asked.

"I would do anything for you, and we have become accustomed to this world. We enjoy many things about being here instead of Hell. We may not care so much for humans, but we would be willing to share Earth with them."

I laughed at the teasing gleam in his eyes when he pulled back to look at me. "And what if the humans don't want to share it?"

He shrugged and ran his finger down the bridge of my nose. "They will have about as much say in it as we had about their tearing our world apart."

I couldn't argue with that. Humans had created this mess; if Kobal's followers decided they were going to stick around after all of this was settled, they should have the right to do so. They were the only reason the human race was still here right now.

"We should go." His voice was hoarse with desire when he pulled away. "If we continue to stay, I won't leave." I gave him a flirtatious smile as I ran my fingers over his arm. "Temptress."

"You love it," I teased.

"I do."

He kissed my forehead and reluctantly pulled away from me. Rising to his feet, he walked back over to the tree line. I studied his back for a minute more before tossing aside the blankets and getting up. I'd pulled my pants and shirt back on before falling asleep last night, but I had left my weapons lying nearby. I strapped my guns to my side before sliding my katana over my back again.

I brushed my hair and teeth, using my water bottle to rinse and spit before joining him. The others were already moving about, preparing to leave when we emerged from the woods and walked out to join them. Resting my hands on the side of the pickup, I pulled myself over it to join Hawk, Erin, and Vargas in the bed while Kobal went to speak with Tresden and some of the other humans.

Erin was pulling away the bandages around Hawk's chest as he munched on a piece of stale bread. "Does it hurt?" I inquired.

"Surprisingly, no," Hawk replied and picked up a crumb from his shirt to eat.

"Good pain meds," Vargas said.

"Haven't taken any in a while."

Erin pulled the last of the bandages away. I understood the saying jaw hitting the floor, and I was pretty sure mine did when his torso was revealed. The jagged slices of Lilitu's talons raked across his tanned, muscular torso were puckered as they stood a good inch off of his chest. The gashes were pink against his skin with black stitches crisscrossing his flesh.

No blood swelled up from the slices anymore, but that wasn't what had me gawking like an idiot.

I wasn't any kind of medical expert, but I was fairly certain those wounds looked at least two weeks old, not barely a day. Either Hawk was some kind of miracle healer or—

A piece of jerky and some trail mix being thrust under my nose distracted me from Hawk's chest when Kobal held them out.

As my mouth watered, I snatched the food away from him and bit into the jerky. It tasted better than steak to me, and I barely suppressed a groan.

"Well, I'll be," Hawk said, drawing my attention away from my rabid eating as he gazed down at his chest.

"Amazing," Erin murmured and fingered the edge of one stitch.

Beside me, Kobal stiffened and his eyes narrowed on Hawk's bared torso. Corson had been walking toward us, but he froze in midstride when he saw Hawk's chest. His gaze flew to Kobal, whose jaw clenched.

"Wrap him back up," Kobal commanded.

My appetite abated at the gruffness of his tone and the disbelieving, almost resigned look on Corson's face. "Is everything okay?" I asked

"Fine, that should remain covered to prevent infection though," Kobal briskly replied.

He turned away from me before I could read his expression. Erin gathered some fresh gauze, tape, and bandages. Ever so carefully, she recovered the wound. Hawk didn't even flinch as she worked.

I finished off my meal, but I couldn't take the same enjoyment in it as I had in the beginning. An unsettling sensation churned through my belly while I watched her. I tried to keep it from happening, but there was a tremor in my hands when I slid the elastic band from my wrist and pulled my hair into a knot at my nape.

Climbing from the truck, I walked over to where Kobal stood by the driver's door, and rested my hand on his arm. "Is Hawk going to be okay?" I asked in a low murmur.

He barely glanced at me when he responded, "He'll be fine."

"You're not telling me something."

"You saw him. He's healing well."

"He is, almost too well."

"Kobal!" Bale called, drawing his attention to her as she

jogged over. "Morax spotted lanavours not a mile away from here. We have to go."

Kobal pulled open the driver's side door. "Get in," he commanded brusquely.

My hackles rose at the command, but the look on his face silenced any protest over his high-handed manner. Every time someone spotted the lanavours, the demons sought to get away from them. I didn't ever want to encounter one of them. Bale jogged around and slid into the passenger seat next to me.

Kobal started the truck and pulled out of the clearing with a squeal of tires. I didn't look back as the other vehicles followed behind us. The truck fishtailed on the road before gaining traction on the broken asphalt. Bale's hand shot up, bracing herself against the roof to keep from spilling onto the roadway.

I gripped the dashboard to keep from getting a concussion as we raced over the broken roads. Before me, the angel figurine rattled on the dash as she stared toward Heaven.

CHAPTER FORTY-TWO

KOBAL

"Why is Hawk healing so quickly?"

I nearly groan aloud, but I had known River wouldn't let it go so easily.

"People heal differently," Bale said.

River's lips pursed at Bale's words. She didn't look at all appeased by Bale's innocent countenance. I glanced in the rearview at the closed window behind us and the group sprawled out in the back of the truck.

"Not that differently," River replied. "He was half dead yesterday."

"He's fine," I assured her.

I refused to tell her what I suspected was going on within his body and that he may have to be destroyed, not after what she'd gone through to get him back. Hawk had been dying when Lilitu had fallen on top of him. When her blood had mixed with his... *Shit!*

I should have suspected it when Corson said it was his blood and hers, but Hawk hadn't appeared to be dying when Corson said it. Lilitu's blood must have already worked its way into him while he'd been lying in the building.

Only time would tell if he would complete this change without dying or having to be destroyed. If he did survive it, it would become impossible to keep what had happened to him from River, and she would learn immortality could be possible for her, which was something I did *not* want.

I craved an eternity with her, but I couldn't be the one who destroyed her if she didn't survive the change, or if it broke her bond with the life around her and destroyed her. It was a choice I didn't want her to have to make, not with everything else she had to deal with.

River turned to focus on me. "You keep saying he's fine, but don't you think he's a little *too* fine already for having been sliced to the bone just yesterday?"

Beside her, I could feel Bale's inquisitive and pitying gaze on me. I had no idea how to avoid this questioning and Bale knew it. "I do," I admitted.

"What is going on with him?"

"Lilitu's blood has helped him heal," I replied.

Her hand flew to her mouth. "That can happen?"

"Yes, sometimes."

"Will he be okay?"

"Time will tell."

It may not have been the entire truth, but I hadn't lied to her either. The idea of possibly having to lie to my Chosen made my fangs prick. The discontent of the hounds, the most loyal creatures in the world, could be felt as they stirred beneath my skin. They would not take the chance of losing her, but they couldn't understand the tenuous position I now found myself in with her.

If I killed Hawk before he completed the transformation, she'd hate me forever. If I told her the truth, she may choose to accept eternal life and possible damnation with me, or she could reject it and embrace her inevitable death. I didn't know which was worse.

I could make Hawk's death look like an accident, a result of his injuries. I glanced at the young soldier in the mirror. He had no idea what awaited him. It may be a mercy to end his life before he realized what had happened to him. But could I look River in the face again after if I killed him? Could I sleep beside her, be within her, knowing what I had done and how much she would hate me if she knew the truth?

The simple and only answer was no. I'd only grow to hate myself over time and it would never be the same between us again.

The realization made me take hold of her hand. She stared at me, her fingers winding around mine as she rested her head on my shoulder. "Should we tell him?" she inquired.

"Maybe later. For now, let him heal some more first."

KOBAL

The setting sun lit the building in the center of the clearing in hues of red and orange that made it almost impossible to read the sign hanging over the gothic, double front door. I shook my head at the building, one that hadn't been there the last time I'd come through this area. The skelleins had been busy since I'd last seen them and I'd be willing to bet money that the group of skelleins on the other side of the gateway, the one in Europe, had erected something on their side too.

The last time I'd been here, nearly five years ago, the area had still been littered with rubble from the explosion the humans had caused when they tore through the veil separating their world from ours. The remains of those humans who had been killed in the original explosion, and those slaughtered by the first wave of confused and infuriated demons who had spilled forth, had still been here. I saw no sign of their remains now as green grass had grown forth to overtake the charred patch of broken and bloody land that had been here not so long ago.

At one time, the remains of the winding government laboratory that had once sat here had still been rising into the day. Now, any sign of it was gone and there were actually patches of flowers in the beds in front of the building. Not only had they been busy building, but the skelleins had also been planting fucking flowers.

If I had one guess, I would bet this wasn't a home either, but something far more in line with the drink-loving, unpredictable, inquisitive natures of the skelleins.

"What is that?" River asked when she lifted her head from my shoulder.

"This is it," I told her.

She glanced at me, her eyes wide. "*This* is the gateway to Hell?"

"The building is new, but the gateway is in there."

Waiting for River.

Taking a deep breath, I shoved the door open so forcefully the metal hinges screeched as the door bent backward.

"Kobal..."

Her words trailed off when I turned toward her and thrust out my hand. The sensation of her skin sliding over mine eased some of the pressure building within me, but I was volatile enough to set fire to the world right now.

"Don't let go of my hand," I commanded gruffly.

"I won't," she vowed.

The promise did nothing to pacify me or the hounds. They disliked her being here as much as I did. I pulled her flush against my side, snarling at one of the humans when they approached. "Get back!"

The young man held his hands in the air and hastily took a few steps away. River wrapped her free hand around my arm. "Kobal, don't. You knew this was coming. It will be okay."

I had known it was coming, but I hadn't expected for it to be this difficult to walk her in there myself. "There will be some creatures inside who will seem shocking to you, but they won't harm you. They are the other guardians of the gates, besides myself and the hounds."

"If they're guardians, won't they be eager to defend it?" she asked.

"Not against me."

"What exactly is in there?"

"I'm not entirely sure how to describe them. They're more something you have to see to believe."

She pulled her lower lip between her teeth and bit into it. "Sounds intriguing."

"That's one way to describe it." I turned to face the others as they cautiously approached us. "Corson and Bale will come inside with us along with Erin and Vargas. The rest of you are to stay here with Verin, Morax, and Shax watching over you. We'll be back out shortly."

"I'd like to go," Hawk said and took a step forward.

"Your injury—" River started.

"It will be fine," he replied briskly. He focused his gaze on me. "I want to go. I can be of use."

River tightened her grasp on my arm. "You said it wouldn't be dangerous inside."

I didn't know if he should be in there, but if he was changing…

Then he might have more right to be in there than any of the other humans, and he could be of more use than the rest of them. Or he could be a bigger threat. If that was so, there were beings in there who would happily take him down and also take the problem off my hands.

"Fine," I relented.

"What about the other demons and soldiers, the ones you said would be meeting us here?" River asked as we walked toward the building.

My gaze flickered down to her. Her face had paled, her full mouth was compressed into a thin line, and a sheen of sweat beaded her forehead, but her step didn't falter as she continued toward the building. "They should be here soon, if they were able to make it this far," I told her.

"Good. I want to get this over with."

And I wanted to keep her from this for as long as possible. "I know."

I tore my gaze away from her as we reached the front of the wooden steps.

CHAPTER FORTY-THREE

RIVER

I stared at the large, wooden building before us. Weathered, gray shingles made up the siding. My head tilted back to take in the white sign hanging from the chains above us as we climbed the steps to the porch. In need of oiling, the chains creaked in the slight breeze drifting over us as the sign swayed back and forth.

The Last Stop, had been sprawled across the sign in black paint.

How fitting, I thought and squeezed Kobal's hand.

I could feel the power vibrating beneath his skin, feel his discontent as the markings on his arm rippled. The hounds were seeking to get free to protect me, perhaps take me from here, but he kept them leashed. I couldn't imagine the strain he endured to make his own body obey his will.

We'll get through this.

Kobal pushed open one of the large wooden doors to reveal the shadowed hall within. The smell of alcohol and mildew drifted out to greet us. I lifted my hand to my nose to block the stale scents but stopped myself when the loud ting of piano music resounded through the air. The upbeat melody brought to mind the movies of dance halls in the twenties I'd seen as a child. Beneath the music, I detected a steady stream of chatter and laughter.

"Is this a bar?" Vargas blurted.

"The last stop of the night," Hawk said and slapped his forehead.

"The skelleins built a bar around the gateway to Hell," Bale snorted.

"Are you really surprised by that?" Corson inquired.

"No," Kobal said.

"Not at all," Bale replied.

"What is a skellein?" Erin asked.

"You're about to find out," Corson answered. "But they are one of the two sub-guardians of the gates."

"What are the guardians of the gates?"

"I am the main guardian, but we were all created to make sure only those who are granted permission are allowed to enter and exit Hell. I control the gateways, the skelleins decide who is worthy of going, and the hounds guard them against anyone who would try to attack me or who breaks the rules. Then Lucifer found his own way into Hell and changed it all, and humans further changed it," Kobal explained. "Before Lucifer arrived, some demons were actually allowed to pass back and forth through the gates. The guardians all worked together to make sure all the laws were obeyed when a demon was in the human realm."

"Amazing," Erin murmured.

"How did the skelleins decide who was worthy of going?" Hawk asked.

"They have tests that must be passed. Anyone brave enough to approach the skelleins in the first place, already passed the first step. Most demons avoid them," Kobal continued.

"That's encouraging," Vargas muttered and glanced toward the inside of the bar.

"It will be fine," Corson replied. "Kobal is the king, after all."

"As fellow gatekeepers, the skelleins have almost always been on their own," Kobal replied. He glanced down at me. "They may not have been born of the Fires of Creation like myself and the hounds, but they share a bond with us. It's not as close, but it is there. They're also not fond of orders."

I smiled at him even though I had no idea what to make of this. Kobal kept the door open for me to step inside. Flickering torches hung in the bronzed sconces lining the walls of the stairs leading up before me. The maroon carpet on the steps was threadbare in some spots and in desperate need of a cleaning, but I could still make out blue and gold swirls running through it. Another set of stairs led down to a lower floor, but no torches lit the way and I couldn't see much through the shadows darkening the bottom of the steps.

Kobal locked his arm securely around my waist before resting his hand on the wooden rail. The piano music died away for a few seconds as we climbed the staircase before someone began to pound enthusiastically on the keys again.

Arriving at the top of the stairs, I froze with my foot in midair. My heart slammed against my ribs as my stunned brain tried to process what it was seeing.

It *couldn't* be, but it *was*.

My foot hit the floor as the others stepped off the stairs behind us. Before me, a horseshoe shaped bar took up almost the entire floor. At least a dozen tables were scattered around in what I could only call the restaurant area. However, I didn't think these creatures did much eating, at least not of food. Pieces of wood, jigsaw puzzles, boxes, and other assorted things were scattered across the tables and the surface of the bar. I was pretty sure I saw a Rubik's Cube in the back.

All of the tables were occupied, but most of the patrons were gathered around the bar with mugs full of beer sitting before them. They all turned, as one, toward us the second the piano stopped playing. Silence descended over the bar, and my breathing sounded labored in my ears while I struggled to process what I was seeing.

I jumped and nearly screamed when a cuckoo clock in the

corner went off. My eyes were drawn to it as the bird slid out and yelled cuckoo seven times before disappearing. Silence once more descended, but this time I could make out the tick of the seconds on the clock.

"Holy shit," Vargas muttered.

In the dim glow of the torches surrounding the bar, over a hundred or so skulls stared at us, shining like a mirror reflecting a flash. There were no eyes in their empty sockets, yet I felt as if every one of their gazes burned into us.

Some of them wore hats, some wore ties, and others had flowers or necklaces draped around their necks, but they didn't wear pants or shirts or dresses. Going by the different accessories they sported, I could guess at which ones were male and which were female, but there was no other way to tell the difference.

Their teeth clacked together as chatter rose up between them. There was no skin or lips to pull into a smile, but their jaws tilted in such a way they appeared to be grinning at us. Their skeletal frames resembled a human's or perhaps a demon's, as Kobal and many of the others didn't look all that much different than us body-wise. Most of them were about four and a half feet tall. Some were smaller, some were taller, but they were all around the same height.

"Kobal! It's Kobal!" some of them cried eagerly.

"He's returned," others murmured.

"We thought he'd given up."

"Humans, he's brought *humans*!"

"Why would he bring humans?"

"What can it mean?"

"Do you think one of them could be who they were looking for?"

My head bounced around as I tried to follow the rapid-fire conversations from the skeletons filling the bar. My gaze latched onto the bony feet of the ones sitting on the stools before me as I realized almost all of them had their toes hooked around the bottom of the stools.

"Which one would it be?" one asked eagerly.

"He's holding *her* hand."

All of them fixated on our hands at once before those empty eye sockets rose to me. I tried to step back, but Bale was behind me, blocking the way.

"She's easy on the eyes," someone approved.

I almost pinched myself to see if I'd fallen asleep, but I knew this was completely real.

"I've never been more disturbed in my life," Erin murmured.

I had to agree with her. I had no idea what to make of this. The bar was so normal, so a part of our world, yet entirely a part of *theirs*. One of the skelleins, wearing a tie and top hat, lifted his full mug of beer and downed the contents in one gulp. My head tilted to the side as I breathlessly waited for the liquid to start pouring out from between the bones of the skeleton-like figure, but not a single ounce slid free. Nor did I see the liquid making its way through his body, though I could clearly see the female skeleton sitting on the other side of him.

"Ay dios mio," Vargas muttered and kissed the cross on his necklace when the skeleton placed his empty mug on the bar.

Another skeleton, wearing a wide-brimmed hat with a big daisy in the center of it and a ruby ring on her right hand, made her way down the inside of the horseshoe bar. What I assumed was a female skellein, lifted the empty mug from the bar, filled it at the tap and returned it.

"What are they?" I murmured.

"Skelleins," Kobal replied.

"Yes, but are they magic or something?"

"They're not skeletons as you know them. It's simply the way they evolved in Hell."

It was a *freaky* way, and I couldn't get over it as they continued to watch us. "We've come for the gateway," Kobal said to them.

"You know what must be done," another said as it rubbed its bony hands together eagerly.

As I processed his words, I swallowed heavily picturing the "what must be done" as something horrific.

Kobal's muscles bunched, and he threw his shoulders back. "As your king, I don't obey those rules."

"You don't," another replied. Again, all of those black eye sockets focused on me and I could feel the weight of their empty stares. "The humans will have to though."

I could hear Kobal's teeth grinding together before he spoke. "You will allow us entrance to the gateway."

"We will allow the demons in your presence entrance, as they have all passed the tests and gone through the gateway before. However, you know any newcomer must pass the test in order to be granted entrance. It is the law. Only those who are meant to pass through the gates shall. The hounds can turn them away after if they choose."

I glanced at the markings on Kobal's body. The hounds could turn us away? I'd never been more confused in my life.

"The hounds have already accepted them and granted them entrance. You'll let them pass or I'll unleash the hounds," Kobal warned.

As one, all of the skelleins rose around the room. Whatever smiles there had been vanished in an instant and a wave of menace washed from them. They may look as flimsy as a skeleton, but I sensed the power emanating from them. If those bones decided to charge us, I had a feeling their sharp little fingers could tear the flesh from our body in seconds.

Kobal braced his legs further apart when he stepped protectively in front of me. His lips pulled back in a sneer to reveal all four of his fangs as they lengthened in preparation for a fight.

"Easy, Kobal," Corson counseled. "They're on our side in this."

"What must be done to enter?" I blurted. "I can do it!"

"No," Kobal said.

"She's willing," one of them said eagerly.

"I will do it for her," Kobal said.

"Not allowed!" a bunch of them chorused.

"You already have entry. They must pass the test on their own!" others cried.

I felt like a bouncing ball as I tried to follow the voices erupting from everywhere at once.

"Wait!" I yelled to be heard over the growing cacophony filling the room. "Tell me what I have to do first!"

"You're not doing it," Kobal stated.

"What is it?"

"You must answer a simple riddle," a skellein with a cane replied as he twirled it in the air before bouncing its tip off the ground.

"Yes, yes a riddle," others said eagerly and finished off their drinks. The empty mugs were quickly refilled by the skellein with the daisy hat.

"Just a simple riddle or four if the others care to join you," the one who had been speaking with Kobal said with a smile.

I had an extremely bad feeling about this. "I'm not very good at riddles," I admitted.

"Oh no!" some of them yelled.

"You must be!"

"Would be a pity to fail."

"It's the only way you'll pass."

I could barely keep up with the lively conversations, so I kept my gaze focused on the skellein with the cane who stood before me. "What happens if I get it wrong?"

"We take a pound of your flesh."

My stomach churned sickeningly. "I'd never survive that!"

"That's the point, for a human," another one said. "For a demon, we take the pound and when they've regenerated, we ask another riddle. If they get it right, they pass. If they get it wrong, we take another pound. *No* one leaves until they get a riddle right once they have agreed to it. Some have stayed for years and others have been denied passage by the hounds after."

Erin's hand flew to her mouth, Vargas kissed his cross again, and I'm pretty sure I probably looked about as green as Hawk did following that statement. *Years* of torture at the hand of the beer-swilling, piano-playing skeletons would be Hell on Earth.

"She's *never* going to do it," Kobal declared.

"Then she won't pass. If you attack, we will fight and some-one's flesh will be taken," the skellein replied. "But we are allies, Kobal. We do not wish to fight with our king and fellow guardian. We have no choice in this matter. These laws were established hundreds of thousands of years ago by *your* ancestors and you are the one who left us here to protect this gate. Anyone looking to pass through must complete the steps and this is one of them."

"*She* is your queen," Kobal said. "She will rule beside me."

The voices in the bar ramped up. "A queen, a queen!"

"We must celebrate!"

"A *human* queen, how strange!"

"But even the queen must pass the test the first time if she is to travel through the gate!"

"Oh, yes, she must!"

"All non-guardians must complete the steps to gain entrance. It has always been the way. It will *always* be the way."

I gave up on trying to follow their excited chatter and waited for it to die down again. The one with the cane thumped it against the floor, quieting everyone in the bar. "Congratulations, my king on finding your queen, but it is true, you know she must pass too in order to enter. Like the hounds and demons who follow you, we will accept her as our queen, human or not, but you know we are bound by laws…"

His voice trailed off. His fathomless eyes focused on Kobal as he seemed to be waiting for him to pounce. I held my breath while I waited to see if Kobal was going to jump on him and rip him apart. He was rigid and unmoving against my side. The barely leashed hostility within him yearned to break free and rain down destruction on these creatures and anyone else who got in his way or threatened me.

"The laws of the gates were changed when the humans broke into Hell," Kobal said. "The laws are different now."

"Not *our* laws!" someone from the bar shouted.

"I *am* good at riddles," Erin said from behind me. "Could I do it for all of us?"

Excited murmurs raced through the crowd once more. "Never had that happen before."

"Could be interesting."

"But each person is supposed to be worthy."

"Finally something to stir things up."

"Do you get many humans trying to cross through?" I inquired, yelling to be heard over them.

"Oh, aye," the one with the cane replied. "You humans are such a strange lot. Some of you come for curiosity, and some come because you believe you can actually be of help to us."

Titters of laughter escaped from some of them and they elbowed each other in a jovial, conspiring way.

"And still others believe Lucifer is simply misunderstood, that they will be able to help fix him or make a difference. Morons. Some believe he is a God and worship him. And, of course, there are still demons looking to exit and enter. After the humans first tore open the gateway, we were unable to stop the flow of those escaping Hell, but over the years, we have gotten a better grip on it," the one with the cane continued.

"What about the things escaping the seals?" Vargas inquired. "Are you stopping them?"

They all turned toward him and I felt the hostility in the room ratcheting up again. "Take it back," Hawk hissed at Vargas from under his breath.

"I don't think I can," Vargas whispered back.

"What is behind the seals are abominations that should never be set free. They obey no rules," one of the ones at the bar said. "There is no stopping their outpouring, not until the gate is closed and the seals are stopped from falling."

"We might be able to help with that," I said, and Kobal's arm tightened around my waist.

The one before me planted his cane into the ground and leaned closer. His head canted to the side as he studied me. "You've definitely marked her, my king," he murmured. "But how would any of you be able to help with closing the gate? You are humans."

"Some of our kind figured out how to open it. Perhaps we can figure out how to close it," I fibbed.

"Does not matter. You must pass the test!" another shouted from the bar.

"How many have been allowed to pass through?" I asked the skellein peering at me.

He waved his bony hand through the air. "A few, but if they thought to survive Hell, they were sadly mistaken."

Wonderful.

"Let the other girl do it. Take a pound from her for every riddle she gets wrong," another of them said.

"No!" Concern for Erin made my voice shriller than I'd anticipated.

"What will it be then?" the one peering at me asked.

"I'll be the only one answering," I said. "The others will stay here."

Kobal's fingers dug into my waist as his chest vibrated with the low growl he emitted. He may not choose to fight these things, but if I messed this up, he would tear this entire bar apart even if they were his allies. He'd never allow them to take a pound of my flesh. I had to get this right, otherwise I'd cause a rift in Kobal's forces, but I really was bad at riddles. I couldn't recall one I'd ever gotten right.

"I'm going with you, no matter what," Erin said. "I came this far; I *will* see it through."

"So will I," Vargas said.

"Me too," Hawk said.

I turned toward them. "You don't have to do this. You can stay here where it's safe and your skin remains where it should."

"So will it be all of you answering, or only one?" someone from the bar inquired, completely ignoring my words.

"Only one," Erin said. "Me."

"Erin, no," I protested.

"We'll each be answering our own question," Vargas insisted.

The skellein before me raised his bony fingers and rubbed his chin. I found myself staring into the empty place where his nose should have been and at the back of his skull. "I'll make it more interesting. If only one of you answers *three* riddles correctly, all *four* of you can pass. If they get one wrong, then all four of you will lose a pound."

CHAPTER FORTY-FOUR

River

My flesh had never felt so cold before. I couldn't resist rubbing my hands over my arms as I struggled not to lose my meager lunch.

"Is that allowable?" one of the skelleins called out. "Aren't they all supposed to prove their merit?"

"What of the laws?" others called out.

The skellein with the cane peered at us before turning to face the occupants of the bar. "I think it will be proving their merit if they all stick together on this. The laws state that we decide if someone is worthy or not to pass through our tests. However, we've never come across something like this before, so we shall put it to a vote. Those who are willing to allow one to answer three questions for all of them, raise your hands."

They exchanged looks before every hand in the bar shot up. "It seems we all agree it shall be fun to try something new!" the skellein with the cane declared before turning back to us.

"I will not allow this to happen," Kobal grated through his teeth.

"I can do this," Erin insisted. Her ocean blue eyes burned

intensely when she turned to face us. "I really am good at riddles. I *can* do this."

"You can walk away," I said.

"You said you sucked at this, and I can do it, so let me."

"You owe me *nothing* for what happened with the canaghs."

"I know that. I'm doing this for my friend and because I've never backed away from a challenge. I'm also very curious as to what this gate looks like."

"We all are," Hawk said, and Vargas nodded beside him.

A lump formed in my throat. More objections swelled within me, but I held them back. I would stand by their decision even if I didn't like it. Kobal's eyes had become a piercing amber when I focused on him again.

I rested my hand on his arm, drawing his attention away from the skelleins to me. "We have no other choice. Erin can do this."

"Thank you," Erin said.

"None of the riddles can be anything about Hell or demons," Bale declared loudly. "The humans know nothing of our world and the laws have always been meant to be fair."

The skellein before me rubbed his chin while some chattered their displeasure over those terms and others their acceptance. "The riddles will involve things only dealing with the human realm," the one with the cane declared. There were happy thuds on the bar following this and disgruntled sounds, but no one argued with his declaration. "Are you all in agreement of the terms then?"

"Yes," the four of us replied.

Kobal didn't speak as he watched the walking, talking set of bones across from us. The skellein stared at him before bowing his head. "It is what must be done, my king," he murmured. "If she were not your Chosen you wouldn't argue against this. If it were not our laws, we would not disagree with you on it, as you well know."

A muscle twitched in Kobal's jaw. "I know, but if this goes wrong, we will fight," he vowed.

"I hope that does not happen. Truly, all of us wish to only stand with you."

A chorus of agreement ran through the bar. "For our king," one of them said and raised its mug of beer.

"For our king!" they cheered, their glasses clinking together before they downed their contents.

"Weirdest fucking demons yet," Hawk muttered and I nodded my agreement.

The skellein with the cane focused on Erin once more. "Brave girl." Turning away, he threw his hands into the air and twirled his cane around. "Who will ask the first question?"

"'Tis my turn!" one yelled happily from the restaurant area.

The black bandanna he wore around his head was askew and sliding to the right. Across his left eye was an eyepatch with a pearl in the middle of it. Grabbing his mug from the scarred wooden table, he shoved back his rickety chair and rose to his feet. Pale liquid sloshed over the sides of his glass as he walked.

"Unbelievable," Hawk muttered. "It's fucking One-eyed Willy."

I didn't know who One-eyed Willy was, but despite the horribleness of this situation, I bit back a hysterical laugh as the skellein approached us. It was all so surreal that I couldn't quite believe we were actually standing here, preparing to answer riddles from walking skeletons. The first of which believed he was a pirate.

The pirate stopped a few feet away from Erin. He finished off his beer and placed it on the bar. By now, I knew it didn't happen, but I kept waiting for liquid to trickle out of him like it used to with the one baby doll I'd had as a child.

"I know!" Pirate clapped his hands together beside his right earhole.

The clacking of the bones made me wince. With baited breath, I waited for his fingers to break off and fly in different directions. His fingers remained intact and his jaw pulled back into a grin. Stepping closer to us, his empty eye sockets peered intently at Erin who didn't break the skellein's unwavering stare.

"There's a land where there's mummies and daddies but no babies. Books but no libraries. Mirrors but no reflections. Kittens but no cats. Cattle but no cows. Lollipops but no candy, and trees but no forests. It's the land of what?" the pirate inquired.

My stomach sank. I was pretty sure the pirate had spoken in a foreign language. I didn't know what to make of the jumble of garbage that had spilled from his mouth. I didn't dare look at Erin; I didn't want to add unnecessary pressure to her, but I was dying to know if she'd understood anything of what he'd said.

I was still trying to puzzle out what language the skellein might have been speaking, when Erin replied, "It's the land of double letters."

The entire bar became silent before a cheer went through the crowd. The skelleins clanked their mugs together; beer spilled over the dark wood surface of the bar in sloshing puddles.

"I guess that was the right answer," Vargas said slowly.

"Yes," Kobal said.

Hawk rested his hands on Erin's shoulders and massaged them enthusiastically. "You got this!"

The one who had asked the question waved his fingers and gave Erin an elegant bow. Turning away, he made his way back to the table and settled in as another one made his way forward. This one wore a baseball cap turned backward and a pair of cowboy boots. It took everything I had not to laugh at the spectacle of those bony legs disappearing into the oversized boots.

The skellein stopped before us and tapped his finger against his chin as he stared at Erin. The click of his finger hitting against his bone sounded like a tree branch scraping across glass.

Finally, he spoke. "I have four wings, but cannot fly, I never laugh and never cry; on the same spot I'm always found, toiling away with little sound. What am I?"

I didn't have a chance to speculate what that could possibly mean before Erin answered. "A windmill."

Now, when everyone in the bar cheered, so did Hawk, Vargas, and I along with Corson and Bale. Only Kobal and Erin remained mute and watchful. The skellein gave her a brief salute before returning to his stool to cheer with the others.

"Why are they having so much fun with this if she's getting them right?" I asked.

"They will take the flesh because it's the law, but the complexities and cleverness of the mind are what they enjoy most," Corson replied. "These demons love their puzzles and riddles."

That was for sure, as I now realized all the things scattered across the bar and tables were some form of a puzzle waiting to be solved. The skelleins were grinning as happily at us as leprechauns did at their pots of gold. If they weren't planning to tear the skin from our bodies if Erin got a riddle wrong, I may have actually gotten a kick out of these creatures.

Another one lifted his mug and swung off of his stool. His toes clicked on the wooden floor as he did an odd little two-step toward us and pulled off the black felt hat sitting on his head.

"You're fine competition, miss, but now I've got one for you," he said happily. "The measurement of time that can't be found on a clock, but can be looked upon on a map.

Who am I?"

Erin's mouth pursed as she contemplated his words. The skelleins settled down once more. I held my breath, my lungs burning as the seconds ticked into minutes on the cuckoo clock. I couldn't bring myself to look at Erin as a bead of sweat slid down my temple and curved around to my chin. Convinced wiping it away would distract Erin, I didn't touch it.

I kept expecting her to blurt out the answer with the same ease she had before, but I found myself drawing air into my deprived lungs as another minute went by. The jovial atmosphere of the bar vanished, and a menacing air intensified within it.

More sweat slid down my back, adhering my shirt to my skin. "You must answer," the one who had asked the question said.

I finally dared to look at Erin. Her finger tapped against her mouth, and her eyes were half closed as she muttered something. At first, I didn't realize she was repeating the riddle to herself, but then I heard the word "time."

You can do this, those words remained lodged in my throat so as not to add more pressure to her. Kobal was unmoving, his eyes focused on the bar. Behind Erin, Vargas and Hawk had paled. Erin's lips moved as she ran through the riddle one more time.

"You have to answer now, or it is a forfeit," the questioner said.

Erin's lips moved as she finished saying the riddle to herself one more time. "I am Missi*ssippi*?"

The rise of her voice at the end made it come out as more of a question than a statement. I turned to the skellein, my heart hammering as I tried to figure out if she was right. It made sense now that she'd said it, but she'd hadn't had the same confidence with this response as she had with the first two.

Across from her, the skellein put his hat back on, took a sip of his drink, and lifted his mug high into the air with a loud cry. I didn't know if his shout had meant *tonight we feast on flesh*, or if it had been another celebration of a puzzle well solved. Around the bar, all the skelleins cheered and stomped their clattering feet on the ground.

Someone had to let us know if she'd been right before I screamed.

The skellein bowed to Erin before doing his odd little two-step away. He was almost to his stool when he threw up his feet and clicked his heels together at waist level.

"Are they going to skin us or not?" Hawk demanded.

"Bring her again, Kobal!" one of them cheered.

"The gateway is at the end of the hall!" another cried.

I guess that was our answer. Grabbing hold of Erin, I gave her a hug. Vargas embraced her next. Then Hawk lifted her up and spun her around as he whooped loudly. Erin almost fell over when he set her back on her feet, but Corson grasped her arm to steady her.

"Nice job," Corson said.

"Thanks," she said and straightened her hair.

I glanced at Kobal as he took hold of my elbow and led me down the hall toward a set of glass doors. As we walked, the skelleins leaned back on their stools and held out their palms to Erin when she strolled by. Her brow furrowed, but then she lifted her palm and began to high-five them as they continued to cheer loudly.

"Smart and pretty," one of them said eagerly. "My kind of lady."

Erin blushed but continued to slap the palms facing her, some of them turned to slap five behind their backs too. They were an odd group, a little disconcerting to look at, but their enthusiasm was contagious. By the time we arrived at the door leading to the hall, they were all chattering happily again. The one at the piano burst into a fast-paced song that had many of them tapping their feet to the music.

My smile over their happiness vanished when Kobal pushed open the door to reveal the hall beyond. He kept me close against his side as we made our way down the hall. The dull wood of the wall emphasized the deep-red carpet beneath my feet.

"Were those things demons too?" Vargas asked. "Or something else entirely."

"They're a breed of upper-level demon," Kobal replied. "After what the humans did, I left the skelleins here to protect the unnatural gateway the best they could, and the hounds are protecting the seals."

"But something is happening to the hounds," Erin said.

"Yes."

"Interesting," Vargas murmured as he rubbed at his cross.

My fingers went to my necklace; they ran reassuringly over the shells as we stopped at the end of the hall and stood before another wooden door. Kobal rested his hand against the knob as he watched me.

"This is it," he said.

I thrust my shoulders back, bracing myself for the Hell beyond that door. Glancing behind me, I dimly heard the enthusiastic play of the piano as the skelleins continued their celebration. There would be no music beyond this point, of that I was certain.

Turning the knob, Kobal shoved open the door.

CHAPTER FORTY-FIVE

RIVER

I could only stand and stare at what lay before us. The entire drive had been nothing but burnt-out and bombed homes, towns in ruins, cities crumpling, broken bridges and roads, and bones dotting the landscape, but life had been steadily rebuilding in those areas. Plants, animals, and humans had been reclaiming their land. Green grass had begun to flourish. Birds had sung and chirped. Insects had returned, and somehow, life had continued.

But here, here there was nothing but death and melancholy encompassed within four walls that looked as if they were going to fall over at any moment. The walls had been slapped haphazardly up around the hole. There was no door, no way out other than the one I stood in. There also wasn't much of a roof. I tilted my head back to let the rays of the sun filter over my face, giving me some warmth when all I felt was chilled to the bone.

Staring at the broken boards above me, I knew there had once been a solid roof but it had been shredded and destroyed by something. *Gargoyles,* I realized when my eyes landed on a distinct, gargoyle shaped hole above me. They'd torn the ceiling apart when they'd been freed from their seal and flown out of the gateway.

My gaze slid back to the haphazard walls, and I wondered how many times the creatures fleeing their seals had torn them apart. How many seals had fallen?

There was no way to know without going into Hell, and the only way to stop them from escaping was to close the gate.

Would Lucifer come here if he discovered I was here?

I realized the answer to that question as it flitted through my mind. He wouldn't come here. He had no faith in me being able to close this hideous hole and was counting on me having to go to him. I knew what he sought from me too: Kobal.

Kill two birds with one stone.

I'd been trying not to look, but my eyes were drawn to the pit before me. The top of the hole was at least ten feet by ten feet wide and was a gaping maw of blackness. I'd expected flames or something to be shooting out the top of the hole but it remained free of any spurting fire. From where I stood, I could see something that looked like a trail leading down the inside of the hole, one that had been carved into the rock walls winding away into nothing. Though nothing threatening loomed from the pit, the longer I stared at it, the more I felt as if all of the air was being sucked from the room.

"I pictured bigger," Erin murmured.

"It was, at one point. I was able to close it more than halfway, but I'm unable to close it any further," Kobal replied.

"I don't understand how the skelleins can keep anything from going in or coming out of that," Hawk said.

"They're a lot more vicious than they look. They may not be able to contain what is coming out of the seals or the fallen angels, but they'll massacre a fair amount of the lower-level demons and any higher-level who dare to try to escape," Bale said. "They'll also stop most of them from trying to get back in."

I couldn't tear my gaze away from the gateway. The blackness of it, the *nothingness* of this hole made me feel as if my heart pumped ice through my veins with every lumbering beat. My hand pressed against my mouth as despair welled up to the point of tears.

Bleak and brutal, everything vile and wrong with the world sprawled out before us. I could feel the weight of the souls that had been entrapped there, feel their wretchedness as if it were my own. I bit back a wail as my heart swelled within my chest and my shoulders hunched in on themselves.

"River?" Kobal asked softly.

Kobal seized my cheeks and tilted my head up. His face swam before my eyes as I briefly saw two of him. "Easy," he murmured, his thumbs brushing over my cheeks. "Focus on me. Breathe."

I realized he was blurring before me because tears were pouring down my face and I couldn't get them to stop. Choking sobs tore at my heart and twisted my stomach into a knot. He pulled me against his chest and enveloped me in a hug. My fingers dug into his back as I gasped for air and tried to ease the anguish rattling my body.

Lifting me, he carried me toward the door and flung it open. He walked with me back into the hall. His hands ran over my hair, soothing me as he knelt and settled me into his lap.

"Hush, Mah Kush-la, you'll never see it again," he whispered.

"What's wrong with her?" Erin asked.

Kobal didn't answer; I didn't think he knew. *I* didn't know, but my tears were finally easing and the sorrow in my chest was lessening. I inhaled a tremulous breath. My teeth settled against the mark I'd left on his neck last night. Acting on instinct, I bit down on it, opening it once more. A sigh of pleasure escaped me when I felt the renewal of the connection between us.

Drops of his blood fell upon my tongue. The fiery, coppery taste of it was comforting and familiar. His hands entangled in my hair, and my eyes closed as he turned me toward the wall, sheltering me from the others. I pulled him closer as the last of my tears fell on his shirt.

Reluctantly, I released my bite on his flesh and leaned away from him. His hands smoothed my hair away from my face as his gaze searched mine. "What happened?" he demanded.

"I could feel them, *all* of them. The souls. The misery. The pain." I shuddered and rested my hand over my heart. "It was all right here, within me, so close and real."

"She feeds on the pulse of life," Bale said.

"I know that," Kobal replied brusquely.

"She'll draw on the energy and emotions coming from Hell too."

"Oh," I breathed in realization.

A muscle in Kobal's jaw twitched. "We're leaving," he declared.

He kissed my nose and went to rise, but I grabbed hold of him, pulling him back. "No, we can't."

"You can't go back in there."

"I can. I wasn't expecting the raw emotions before. I'll be better prepared for it now."

"No—"

"We can't turn back, not when we've come so far. I won't allow it."

"*I* won't allow you to suffer."

"We all must suffer in life. We all must know grief and loss. The only alternative is death."

As his hands tightened on my cheeks, the agonized look on his face tore me apart, but we couldn't turn back now. "Not this much, not for you," he said.

"It has to be me."

"*No.*"

"Don't make me blast your ass," I said with a small smile. He didn't look at all amused as his face remained remorseless and his eyes unyielding. "I can do this."

He kept hold of my arms as he helped me to my feet. "If it happens again, I'm dragging you out of here whether you like it or not."

I couldn't argue with him. My bones felt like they'd shatter when my feet hit the floor. Taking deep breaths, I braced myself for the emotional barrage about to hit me once again. Hawk, Erin, and Vargas all watched me with mixed expressions of concern and uncertainty.

I kept hold of Kobal's hand as I walked forward, drawing on his strength. Bale stood by the door, her green eyes uncertain. On the other side of her, Corson looked as if he were tempted to drag me away from here too. I subtly shook my head at him, knowing he would only flare Kobal's desire to pull me away if he spoke up against me returning to the gateway too.

Corson rested his hand on the door handle; I nodded for him to open it. A muscle twitched in his cheek, but he shoved the door open. My legs quivered when I walked through the door again and down the steps. My body felt like spun glass, but I managed to keep it from breaking apart.

"*Staying!*" I grated through my teeth.

Kobal's hand squeezed mine, his energy flow calming me further. I couldn't rely on him to hold my hand all the way through this though. Unfolding my fingers from his, I released him and tried to take another step forward. I found I couldn't move.

Okay, fine, simply stand here and don't turn into a sobbing mess. It's still an improvement.

Closing my eyes, I took another deep breath before opening them once more. From here, I realized there were caves or at least tunnels within the pit too. They branched off to somewhere within the gloomy bowels before us. I'd seen pictures of the Grand Canyon, and though this pit was nowhere near as large, there was something about it that reminded me of the world wonder minus all the beauty and wonder. I tried again to move forward, but my feet remained locked to the scorched earth beneath me.

"You really don't think Lucifer will come for us?" Erin inquired.

"No, he'll continue to try to bring down the seals," Kobal replied.

"Won't he try to stop River in case she can close the gateway?" Hawk asked.

"He... he doesn't believe I can," I said from between my chattering teeth.

Kobal rested his hand on my hip. "Why do you say that?"

"Because it's... what he believes. He'd be here now if he believed otherwise." It was true and we both knew it.

"They'd be on our turf up here," Bale said. "Where you humans can also help to fight them."

"Plus the skelleins. They're an easygoing, fun-loving sort most of them time. Just don't piss them off. They'll tear the flesh from your bones then," Corson said.

"Yeah, kind of got that," Hawk muttered.

I focused on the conversation as a way to drown out the sorrow from the pit pounding against me.

"Lucifer will wait for us to go to him. It's been years since we've been inside so even if we have more demons with us, and River, they'll still have the advantage of whatever nasty surprises they have in store for us," Bale said. "You humans will be able to avoid going inside. None of you would survive in there for long."

"Will I?" I croaked out.

Kobal's fingers dug into my waist as he stepped closer to me. The feel of his flesh against mine helped to further ease the emotions battering against me. I sought out his life force, allowing it to envelope me.

"We're hoping so," Corson said.

"What if I'm not?"

"We'll worry about you entering only if you're unable to close the gate," Kobal replied. "And if not, we will figure it out then."

CHAPTER FORTY-SIX

KOBAL

It took me another half an hour, but I finally convinced River to concede to leaving the gateway for the day. Black shadows encircled her eyes, making them shine brightly. The way her shoulders hunched and her hand remained limp in mine reminded me of an eighty-year-old woman, not a vibrant, powerful, twenty-two-year-old.

The music died the minute we stepped into the bar again. All laughter faded away as the skelleins turned toward us. The fact the drink and party-loving gatekeepers had built a bar didn't surprise me. That they had distinguished themselves from each other was something I never would have expected to see. I'd known the skelleins for over a millennium, and not once had they tried to differentiate their sexes or personalities from each other. Thirteen years on Earth had changed that.

Their eyeless gazes latched onto River. "It *is* her," they said as one.

The one who had first approached us descended from his barstool. His cane clicked across the floor as he walked. I may have worked closely with the skelleins for over a thousand years, but I'd never learned any of their names. They'd never attempted to change that.

The skellein tilted his head to peer up at River. "Do not fret, World Walker." River's head lifted, her hand clenched on mine at his words. "It will get easier for you."

"Why did you call me that?" she whispered.

"Because it's what you are. You can walk the three worlds like no other living creature can, but the worlds are not balanced the same as the mortal realm. For you to become accustomed to another plane takes time, but you will grow to handle it."

"We don't have time."

"We will have to find it for you somehow, my queen," the skellein replied.

The skellein turned toward me and though his face held no expression, I felt sorrow from the creature, something else I never would have expected from a skellein. I'd only ever known them to experience two things, fun and mayhem.

"It must have been difficult for you to bring her here," he murmured to me. I remained silent as I studied the man before me. There was far more to the skelleins than I'd ever realized. The skellein rested his hand on River's arm. "We have faith in you, World Walker."

"Back off of her," I growled at him. "We have no idea what is going to happen. Don't pin all of your hopes on her."

A flicker in River's eyes was the only indication she gave to her uneasiness over his words. She glanced at me. "No pressure," I told her.

The small smile she gave me caused some of my tension to ease. Wrapping my hand around her head, I pulled her against my chest and kissed the top of her head.

"Three worlds?" Hawk inquired.

I didn't bother to try to prevent the skellein's answer. These three were as loyal to River as she was to them. It was time they knew what they were protecting.

"The demon part of her will eventually allow her to enter Hell, but as part angel, she could walk into Heaven as well," the skellein answered.

Erin inhaled sharply behind me. Hawk and Vargas shot River assessing looks.

"The only time the gates to Heaven have opened to allow something that wasn't a soul through, was when they threw Lucifer and the other fallen angels out. Those gates will likely never open again," I told the three of them.

They still looked as if they had no idea what to make of any of this, but Erin and Vargas managed to nod while Hawk had an *aha* expression on his face. "That's why the ghosts were so adamant about you talking to the angels for them," Hawk said.

"Ugh, ghosts," the skelleins groaned as one, and River actually chuckled.

"But if the gates to Heaven did open, she would be able to venture in. It would also be an adjustment period for her." The skellein with the cane squeezed River's arm. "Of course, she would have to figure out a way to get there and I don't see any wings." He leaned forward to peer around her back.

"No wings," River croaked. "How long will it take me to adjust to being so close to Hell?"

"That remains to be seen."

"There are too many relying on me. It has to be soon."

"And you must be alive to be relied on," I grated.

"You are strong, vibrant. When you come back tomorrow, it will not be as bad, and the next day it will be even better. Before you know it, you will grow accustomed to it and you'll be able to withstand it with ease," the skellein replied with authority.

River didn't look convinced when she glanced up at me.

"We're leaving," I said.

The skellein stepped aside, allowing us to pass by him and down the stairs. The sun still hung in the sky when I pushed open the door and ushered River into its light. She tilted her chin up, closing her eyes as she absorbed the warmth of its rays. The shadows under her eyes lessened as she absorbed the life flowing around her.

Turning to Vargas, Hawk, and Erin, I held out my arm to stop them before they could walk down the steps. "You tell *no* one else what you learned about her in there, or what I will do to you will make losing a pound of flesh feel like fun."

"Not a word," Hawk vowed.

"If I hear one murmur about what she is, I'll kill all three of you."

"Kobal!" River protested.

"I'm still not sure what she is or how it's possible," Erin replied, "but no one will ever know what I learned. What about the skelleins, will they tell someone?"

"They're the keepers of riddles and secrets. Nothing they know or see is ever revealed. Plus, they are Hell-born demons that have been helping to keep Lucifer imprisoned for six thousand years. They see Lucifer's entrance into Hell as a failure on their part, one they've been trying to put to rights ever since," Corson replied. "They'll never reveal what they know about her."

"I see," Hawk murmured and rubbed at the stubble lining his chin and cheeks.

I kept my arm around River as I hurried her down the steps and away from the curious stares of the humans who had remained in the clearing. Shax jogged over to us and jerked his head to a small copse of trees. "I set your things up over here." He ran an assessing gaze over River. "Are you okay?"

"Yes," she replied.

She settled onto the grass near the blankets Shax led us to and pressed her palms against the grass poking up through the burnt-out earth. The others gathered around us, watching as the earth beneath her hands revitalized her. A rosy hue crept into her face once more. My heart swelled with love when a beautiful smile curved her full mouth.

"I never realized how *much* it nourished me," she murmured.

"You wouldn't. You've never been apart from it," I replied. "I knew some of your powers were fueled by the force of life, but I didn't realize it nourished you too. Like the trees around us, the earth feeds you."

Her fingers slid through the grass. "I will learn to absorb nourishment from Hell also."

Already part demon, she could throw fire and mark her Chosen as I marked her. But as part angel, she had the most beautiful violet eyes I'd ever seen and fed from the flow of her surroundings. As part human, she had one of the most protective and passionate natures I'd ever encountered.

What would the absorption of Hell do to her? Would it bend her, break her? Could that be what had also helped to twist Lucifer into the creature he was now? On Earth, I could keep her connected to this world. I could not protect her if she absorbed Hell into herself upon entering it and it changed her.

"That was never supposed to be part of this," I told her.

"Make a deal with the Devil," River said with a laugh.

"Kobal—"

"I do *not* like this," I interrupted Corson. "What will absorbing Hell do to you?" I demanded of River.

"There is only one way to know," River said and turned to the others. "Could you please leave us for a bit?"

"Of course," Corson said.

They slipped away into the shadows of the woods or headed back toward where the humans were gathered. Rising to her feet, River came toward me. Her hips swayed and her hair fell about her shoulders in tumbling waves as she walked. Stopping before me, she slid her hands up the front of my shirt and flattened them against my chest.

Her mouth parted as golden-white sparks danced across my flesh beneath the material of my shirt. Those sparks were the same color they'd been before we'd entered this more deadened area of the country and she'd started having a more difficult time drawing on the life force of the earth.

"You are my greatest source," she whispered. "The one who

keeps me grounded and makes me feel the most alive. Nothing else can make me feel the way you do. With you by my side, I can face anything."

"I'm worried about what being around Hell and feeding from it will do to you."

"I'll withstand it." Her hands slid down my stomach to the waistband of my pants. She believed it. I longed too, but the idea of losing even a small piece of her was more than I could stand. "Together we can get through anything."

My arms swept around her, pulling her firmly against my chest before crushing my mouth to hers. She moaned when I slid my tongue over her lips. Her mouth parted and her tongue brushed against mine as I delved in to taste the sweet recesses of her mouth. More sparks shot across my flesh as I pressed her against the trunk of a tree.

Pulling away from me, she impatiently tugged my shirt over my head and tossed it aside. Her eyes lit up when they landed on my chest and her tongue slid out to lick her lips. The hunger in her gaze caused my cock to swell against the front of my pants. I'd never grow tired of this woman, never be able to get enough of her.

Her hands rested on my chest as her fingers trailed over my markings there. Beneath her touch, my flesh rippled and power surged toward her, causing the sparks on her fingers to grow until they danced within her spectacular eyes.

"Chosen couples are stronger together," she whispered. "Always yours."

"Yes." My hand entangled in her hair to pull her head back before claiming her mouth again.

CHAPTER FORTY-SEVEN

RIVER

Over the next week, the six of us traveled back inside the bar and to the gateway every day. Each day, I was able to withstand the harrowing effect it had on me a little more. I was even able to get closer to it, though I had yet to reach its side. Kobal remained taciturn and watchful, but he didn't drag me away from the gateway like I'd dreaded he would on that first day.

After we left, he would take me away from the others and allow me to take energy from him. I felt like a battery in need of recharging every time, but the recharge time was steadily decreasing.

The one good thing about not being able to charge straight up to the gateway and try to figure out a way to close it was that five other demon and human groups from different sections of the wall joined with us over the week. Some arrived with only a handful of survivors, but some arrived with more survivors than we'd had. At the end of the week, there were over eighty new humans and twenty-eight demons added to our numbers.

"What will the humans do if we have to go into Hell?" I asked

Kobal when we made our way back out of the bar after a new record of five hours near the gate.

"They'll stay here and hold the ground as best they can. The other humans are here to protect you, and that's all that matters."

"You make them sound expendable."

"We are." My head shot toward Hawk as he uttered those words. "We all knew it when we left the wall. Your life was always the most important, but none of us knew why. Most still don't."

"*No* one's life is more important than another," I bit out.

"But in this case, it is."

I refused to argue with him further as we stepped outside. It was like entering a warm house after being trapped out in the cold for hours. My fingertips tingled, heat traveled through my extremities, and life flowed through my veins. I was becoming better attuned to the gateway, feeling less malnourished every time we left there, but I still craved this. I burrowed closer to Kobal when he lifted me up and carried me away from the others.

Later, we reemerged from the woods to rejoin everyone. I settled in beside the small fire Hawk and Erin had started near the edge of the woods while Kobal went to speak with the group of demons gathered near the stairs of the bar. Vargas sat across from me, turning a spit with a rabbit on it over the fire. Behind Hawk, a group of some new female arrivals had gathered. They whispered and giggled behind their hands as they watched him.

Since we'd settled in, a fair amount of the new women in the camp had been drawn toward Hawk. They flirted as they batted their lashes and tossed their hair over their shoulders. Hawk was handsome, there was no denying it, but it was almost as if these women had never seen a man before with the way they acted.

"They are so hard up," Erin muttered and tossed a stick into the fire.

Hawk glanced over his shoulder at the women. "Annoying is more like it," he replied.

"You're simply irresistible," I teased, but the stiffness didn't leave his shoulders and he continued to scowl at the flames.

"Go get some," Vargas said. "I would."

Hawk draped his arm over his bent knee. "Already have, or at least one of them, and she needs to move on now."

"You're a pig," Erin told him.

"Maybe, but I never made any promises."

"Which one is she and what's her name?" Erin asked.

"The skinny blonde over my right shoulder. Her name's Sarah, or clingy pain in my ass, but I guess once you have the best, you forget about the rest."

"Ugh!" Erin and I groaned.

"You're gross." Erin threw a handful of grass at him before resting her chin on her knee.

Over Hawk's shoulder, I noticed Sarah glaring at Erin. An uneasy feeling twisted in my gut, but I had no idea why I would feel that way. I tore my attention away from the girl and back to Hawk. "I have to agree with Erin," I said to him.

He smiled at us, but his eyes were distant and troubled.

"How are your wounds?" Vargas inquired of Hawk as he rotated the rabbit. The delicious scent of roasted meat made my mouth water.

"Healed," Hawk replied.

"Completely?" I asked, unable to keep the shock from my voice.

His eyes lifted to mine before darting away. "Completely. There's only the scars now and they're fading."

"Amazing," and odd, but I kept that to myself. Hawk was troubled enough about his rate of healing. He didn't need the fire throwing, energy-harvesting girl using the word odd about him.

Kobal had said Lilitu's blood had closed Hawk's gashes faster, but it was still an amazing rate of healing. My gaze drifted past Hawk to where Sarah and the other women stood. My hand ran over the grass as I watched them. Had Lilitu's blood done something more to him?

"Impressive," Vargas murmured. He pulled me out of my reverie when he touched my arm.

"Huh?" I asked.

"That's impressive," he said and gestured toward my hands.

I'd been so lost in thought that I hadn't realized golden-blue sparks were dancing across the tips of each one of my fingers. I pulled my hands away from the earth and flexed my fingers. They may know more about me, but I still felt exposed when my powers sparked to life around them.

"What percentage of everything are you?" Erin asked.

"Human mostly, or at least that's the way I feel, but that's also what I spent most of my life believing I was. I always knew I was different, but I still felt entirely human."

"And now?"

"Now, I don't know. Part demon, part angel, and none of it makes any sense to me still."

"How is it possible you're any combination of angel and demon?" Vargas inquired.

I'd been waiting for that question and was fairly surprised that it hadn't come sooner. Maybe they'd been trying to figure it out on their own, or maybe they'd been afraid to ask and curiosity had finally won. They deserved to know, but I still hated the whole Lucifer as an ancestor thing so much I found myself reluctant to tell anyone.

They wouldn't think less of me for it, I knew, but acknowledging it made it all the more real. Settling back, I kept my fingers curled into the ground as I explained Lucifer being cast from Heaven to die on Earth, but somehow finding a way into Hell where he survived.

I also explained how he'd managed to leave offspring behind during his time in our realm and that I was the last of his descendants. I didn't say he was my father, like the demons and fallen angels insisted on calling him. I simply couldn't bring myself to do that, but I did admit he was my ancestor.

They looked as baffled by it all as I still felt, but they didn't call me a liar and none of them got up to walk away and leave me behind.

Vargas kissed his cross and turned the rabbit once more. "It's a miracle to be able to do and see such things as you."

Those words took me back for a second. "I guess."

Unable to look at them any longer, my gaze traveled to the bar and the demons still gathered by the stairs. With his height and size, Kobal stood out from the rest of the group, but then I knew I'd be able to find him anywhere.

With the doors of the bar closed, I could barely hear the strains of the piano playing. It was a sound that never ceased as I'd come to learn the skelleins rarely slept.

I blinked when Angela suddenly materialized on the porch of the bar. Her hands folded before her as she watched those gathered in the clearing. Every night around sunset, she would materialize there to watch. I didn't know what to make of her presence. All the other times she'd appeared to me, something bad had happened or it had been in warning, but I'd had no visions of anything coming and nothing had happened on the other nights she'd shown up here. She seemed merely curious as she watched everyone gathered around the bar.

Still, the sight of her made me uneasy, and I couldn't help but worry it was a harbinger of something bad coming.

Kobal stepped away from the crowd of demons, blocking my view of Angela as he walked toward us until he settled at my side. When I could see the porch again, she was gone. My gaze returned to the clearing, but all I saw were the other humans gathered around their small fires, cooking their dinners. The girls behind Hawk finally gave up and walked away. Sarah remained for a few minutes, staring at Hawk with such yearning that it made my skin crawl. Finally, she walked away too.

Corson, Bale, Verin, Shax, and Morax left the other demons behind to join us at the fire. Kobal slid his arm around my waist, drawing me into his lap. Sitting here, feeling the heat of the flames on my skin and his warmth enveloping me, I could almost believe everything would be okay.

We'd made it this far, farther than so many others who had set out on this journey with us. I'd gained friends along the way too, more friends than I'd ever believed I'd have after being torn away from my home and thrust into this unknown world.

A world that had given me the gift of Kobal. My hand encircled his and I drew it into my lap, holding it there. We'd reached our destination, attained part of our goal, but there was still so much further to go. I had to figure out a way to try to close the gateway. What that was going to be, I had no idea, but I'd figure it out once I could get close enough to stand at the edge of the gateway.

And if I couldn't figure out how to close the gateway, that left only one other option: entering Hell and confronting Lucifer himself. That prospect wasn't as terrifying as it should be, not with everything else we'd been through so far. Lucifer might just be puppies and kittens after gargoyles, Azote, killer vines, and canagh demons. I seriously doubted he would be, but I was much better prepared to face him now than I had been when we'd first left the wall behind to come here.

Until the day came where I closed the gateway or came face to face with my ancestor, I planned to enjoy what time I had left here with Kobal and my new friends. I kissed Kobal's smooth cheek before resting my head on his shoulder and snuggling closer to him. It didn't matter what lay ahead of us, I knew we could get through it together.

The End.

The Road, Book 3 in the series, is now available.
The Road on Amazon: http://bit.ly/TheRdAmz
Read on for an exclusive excerpt from The Road.

Stay in touch on updates and other new releases from the author, by joining the mailing list.
Mailing list for Brenda K. Davies and Erica Stevens Updates:
http://bit.ly/ESBKDNews

THE ROAD

River,

Standing at the edge of the gateway, I understand two things… One, I have no idea what I'm doing and two, the gateway to Hell is not closing. Now, there may be only one option left to me, to all of us. I may have to enter the one place I'd hoped to avoid throughout this journey. I may have to enter Hell.

Unfortunately, a change in events takes the choice away from me.

Kobal,

I always knew the idea of River entering into Hell could become a reality, but I expected her to be by my side when, or if, it happened. I expected to be there to protect her, but she's gone in alone. Now, not only am I trying to catch up with her, but I know Lucifer will soon learn of her entrance into my world, and he will be after her too.

I just don't know which one of us will reach her first.

Sneak Peak
Kobal

Everything flashed by me in a blur as I raced deeper and deeper into Hell. *The longer she's in here...*

I broke the thought off. She couldn't be that far ahead of me and she was strong enough to give anything in here a run for its money, including Lucifer. The heat of my home enfolded me, brushing over my skin as the familiar scents of fire and brimstone assailed me. They were scents I never could have forgotten, I bore them on my skin and in my genetic makeup.

Turning a corner, I leapt over the charred and mangled remains of a lanavour lying at the edge of the pathway. *River*. She was still out of their grasp, still moving deeper, or at least she had been ten minutes ago judging by the smoke curling off the remains.

I didn't look back at Corson, Shax, and Bale as we traveled further into the pit. Hell had been my home for over a millennium, the place I'd been created to protect and rule over, yet all I wanted was to find River and drag her from here as fast as I could. This was not my home, not anymore. *She* was my home and she was in danger.

I was moving so fast, I nearly crashed into Erin when I turned another corner. Her blue eyes were bloodshot, her face looked sunburned, but she remained standing when many of the other humans were leaning against the wall or each other.

"Where is she?" I demanded.

Erin adjusted her grip on the woman she and Vargas carried before pointing down the hill. "Leading them away," she croaked out. "Hawk's with her."

So she could withstand Hell well enough to keep moving through it, and Hawk could too. Bale and Corson exchanged a pointed look, Shax leapt forward and clutched Erin's arm when she swayed on her feet.

"We couldn't keep going," she rasped out, sounding as if she'd eaten a pound of dirt.

"Shax, get them out of here," I commanded.

"What of you?" he inquired as he kept hold of Erin's arm.

"We'll be fine, but they won't make it out of here on their own. When you get above, have Morax contact me."

Shax lifted an eyebrow at this, they all knew I didn't tolerate anyone else in my mind, but there would be no help for it now. Morax's ability to communicate telepathically was something I kept resolutely shut off in my mind, and something he knew better than to do without approval or necessity if he didn't want to eat his tail. This situation definitely qualified as necessary.

Turning away, Shax nudged Erin aside to take hold of the shoulders of the woman I now saw was the one who had become attached to Hawk. A purplish bruise marred her temple. I didn't have time to ask what had happened to her as the earth beneath our feet began to quake. Startled cries came from the humans, they clustered closer to the walls when the earth gave a mighty heave and the ground shifted three inches before falling back into place.

Screams rent the air as some of the humans were knocked off their feet and others flung themselves against the walls.

"Silence!" I barked and took a step closer to the edge of the path. I only heard a couple more whimpers before all sound stopped.

Bale, Shax and Corson stepped closer to the edge with me. Below us, a pinpoint of light emerged where none had been before. My fangs lengthened as the light at the bottom of the pit spread.

River

"What was that?" I gasped as I pressed my back and palms flat against the wall behind me. My chest heaved with every one of my breaths as my heart beat wildly in my chest. The ground surged again before settling back into place.

"I don't know," Hawk muttered from beside me.

Glancing at him, I noticed he was paler than he had been up

until now, but he took a step away from the wall and crept toward the edge of the roadway. "Hawk!" I hissed when he stopped at the edge.

The earth had literally moved under our feet and he was leaning over a pit with no railing and no bottom. "It might have been an earthquake," he said.

"Probably not the best idea to stand so close to the edge then," I replied.

He didn't pay me any attention as he stared into the bottomless pit. "There's light down there."

"What?"

I peeled myself off the wall and took a cautious step forward. Earthquake or not, I didn't like the idea of the earth moving beneath my feet one little bit and I was terrified it was going to do so again, but this time it would fling us both over the edge. Despite common sense, I was still drawn irresistibly forward by my curiosity and the perplexed look on Hawk's face.

Reaching the edge of the road, I leaned forward to peer into the abyss below. What had only been darkness before now had a growing wave of light emanating from it. Knowing I should move away from the edge, I still found myself gawking as the illumination spread over the walls and rose steadily toward us.

"What is that?" Hawk muttered.

"I don't know, but I don't think it's anything good."

Glancing behind me, my heart leapt into my throat when I spotted the lanavours rounding the corner and coming toward us. "We have to go!"

I grabbed Hawk's wrist, drawing him away from the edge as one of the lanavours bore down on us at the same time the world exploded in a wash of light from beneath us. The ground lurched out from beneath my feet once more as I was thrown backwards.

~

Kobal

"Get back!" I shouted when light shot up toward us.

Turning, I spread my arms wide to protect as many as I could when the glow increased. I felt no heat against my back but the world around me was brighter than I'd ever seen it in here. The humans ducked and covered their heads. Dropping the girl, Shax threw himself over Erin, using his body to shield her as Vargas draped himself over a couple of others.

Air rushed up around me, tearing at my clothes and beating against my skin as it battered my body. Screams rang in my ears; it took me a minute to realize they weren't coming from the humans but from the radiance illuminating the jagged walls around us. Within the light, faces rushed past me, heading toward the gateway. The flapping wings blew my hair back as they propelled the creatures ever higher and faster toward the surface.

Most of the faces going past us were weathered and wrinkled. Their heads were tilted back to look at the world above, but one lowered her head to glare at me while another released a scream, folded her wings against her side, and dove at me. The air around her tapered body whistled as she came at me like a missile.

I braced my legs apart and held my hands up in preparation for the attack. At the last second, I took a step to the side and backhanded the creature in her head. She screamed again when her body smacked into the pathway with enough force to crack the rock beneath her. Humans scrambled to get out of the way as Bale leapt forward and drove her foot into the woman's side.

The woman's body rose three feet off the ground from Bale's kick before thumping down again. She remained lying prone on the rock. Corson's talons extended as he walked over and sliced through the woman's neck. Her head rolled until it stopped a few feet away from Bale.

My shoulders heaved, my teeth grated together as I spun to watch more of them flying passed us and toward freedom.

River

I rested a hand against my ribs as I pushed myself up until I could prop myself on my elbows. I watched the rush of winged, old women flying by us within the upward flow of light. Screams from the women filled my ears, air rushed over me as the women's wings propelled them higher.

The lanavours, also thrown back by the explosion that had rocked the pit, were regaining their feet. Their heads tilted to the side as they watched the women soaring higher into the air. Rolling to the side, I pushed myself up and stumbled toward where Hawk lay against the wall he'd been thrown into.

I fell at his side and pulled his arm to roll him over. Blood trickled from a gash on his forehead and a bruise marred his right cheek but his chest rose and fell steadily and I could feel his pulse in the wrist I held.

"Hawk," I said and dragged him back a few feet when a couple of the lanavours turned to look at us. "Hawk, get up, we have to go."

He groaned and cracked one eye to look at me. "What happened?"

"I think another one of the seals gave way," I muttered and pulled on his arm again, dragging him toward me when a lanavour stepped in our direction. "We have to go, now. The lanavours are coming again."

He shoved himself over. His head hung down as he knelt on his hands and feet. Resting my fingers on the rocks beneath me, I drew on the flow of life within this place as I warily watched the lanavours. The flap of wings drew my attention to the women as one of them hovered at the edge of the roadway, her head tilted to the side while she inspected us.

My stomach twisted sickeningly as the snakes she had for hair slithered upward, their tongues flickering out to taste the air. Normally snakes didn't bother me. Seeing them attached to someone's head though was more than a little unsettling, as was the dog snout on the woman's face. Her wings made me think of angels as they were covered with white feathers. Some of the others who flew past her had wings like those of a bat.

"What are they?" Hawk inquired.

"I don't know and right now I don't care. We have to get out of here," I said and stumbled back to my feet.

The woman continued to watch us before she started to smile. "Someone is looking for you."

With those words, she nosedived at us.

The Road is now available.
The Road on Amazon: http://bit.ly/TheRdAmz

FIND THE AUTHOR

Erica Stevens/Brenda K. Davies Mailing List:
http://bit.ly/ESBKDNews

Facebook page: http://bit.ly/ESFBpage
Facebook friend: http://bit.ly/EASFrd

Erica Stevens/Brenda K. Davies Book Club:
http://bit.ly/ESBDbc

Instagram: http://bit.ly/ErStInsta
Twitter: http://bit.ly/ErStTw
Website: http://bit.ly/ESWbst
Blog: http://bit.ly/ErStBl

ABOUT THE AUTHOR

Brenda K. Davies is the USA Today Bestselling author of the Vampire Awakening Series, Alliance Series, Road to Hell Series, Hell on Earth Series, and historical romantic fiction. She also writes under the pen name, Erica Stevens. When not out with friends and family, she can be found at home with her husband, dog, and horse.

39635431R00214

Made in the USA
Lexington, KY
21 May 2019